Pride Publishing books by Angel Martinez

Wild Rose, Silent Snow
Boots

Offbeat Crimes
Lime Gelatin and Other Monsters
The Pill Bugs of Time
Skim Blood and Savage Verse
Feral Dust Bunnies
Jackalopes and Woofen-Poofs
All the World's an Undead Stage

Anthologies
50's Mixed Tape: The Line

I0607634

Lijun

FIREWORKS & STOLEN KISSES

ANGEL MARTINEZ & FREDDY MacKAY

Fireworks & Stolen Kisses
ISBN # 978-1-78686-364-5
©Copyright Angel Martinez and Freddy MacKay 2018
Cover Art by Emmy @ studioenp ©Copyright June 2018
Interior text design by Claire Siemaszkiewicz
Pride Publishing

FIREWORKS & STOLEN KISSES

Dedication

For anyone who has never felt like they quite fit into the boxes, live life outside and out loud.
— Freddy Mackay

For Mom, who bought me all the folklore she could find.
— Angel Martinez

Authors' Note

Because Haru is agender, the pronouns used by the character are they/them/their. This is an historically older use of the singular pronoun that has resurged in everyday use in the non-binary (enby) community. While the agender identity is not discussed in this book, there is a natural progression and storyline throughout the trilogy in which Haru's preferred pronouns are revealed to other characters.

Chapter One

The Dessert Siege

Back straight, back straight. Is this person my social equal? Tally offered a *futsurei* to be safe while the evening's host introduced him as the new Urusar from Wisconsin. He wished Dad had come with him. As hard as he tried to think of this as just another business conference, the names and places had started to run together. Back home, he might have reached for the worry stone in his pocket. Here, that might be rude.

The ballroom was gorgeous, with the doors to the terrace rolled back to reveal the view of Mt. Fuji. Tables groaning with food lined the walls. Arrangements of blood-red flowers decorated every table. Everyone seemed to know everyone else, though that might have been an illusion created by nerves.

"Wisconsin?" the middle-aged woman inquired with reserved decorum. "That is the state of cheese, yes?"

"Very true." Damn it, he'd forgotten her name. She was the Uruma, the village mother, to one of the larger cities to the south. "Though thankfully the state is more than just cheese."

She laughed politely, turned to greet another conference-goer, and Tally hoped it had been a dismissal. He shouldn't have felt out of his element. Employees depended on his decisions all day, every day. Meetings were his lifeblood, or at least took up most of his life. Not to mention these were *his* people. The perfectly draped Global Lijun Alliance banner dominated the front of the room—there for anyone, human or lijun to see. For the humans, it was simply a trade organization. For the lijun, it was survival, a shared bond of secrecy and a way for lijun communities to thrive.

Except Tally would always stand outside, which simply made diplomacy that much more important. When his father had gleefully announced his retirement as Urusar, village father of their community in Wadiswan, Tally knew his duty. He'd been groomed for it all his life. He'd taken up the leadership mantle with the sobriety and respect it deserved, even though some of their lijun neighbors had whispered about another deadly serpent leading them.

Uktena.

Tally couldn't escape his heritage or his lijun type, but he was here at this conference to continue his father's work—to ensure his community thrived, that the lijun under his care were safe, and to fight against the ancient prejudices that branded him as *dangerous*.

He retreated to one of the buffets to nibble on sectioned oranges with his back to the wall so he could observe. Not everyone at the welcome dinner was as bound by formalities. The younger attendees had dressed in a variety of styles and more or less appropriately. Nearer the terrace, a young woman in a leather miniskirt tapped her boot heel to music only she could hear. On the other side of the room, a handsome young man in a strange mix of business formal and rebel-casual lounged against the bar. The suit jacket and expensive jeans fit in well enough. The faded T-shirt and rainbow suspenders? Not so much.

Tally thought he would introduce himself to this interesting person, but an older gentleman beat him there and spoke urgently to the young man, who made an impatient gesture and stalked off.

Too bad. He'd been an…otter? Tally surreptitiously flicked his tongue out to taste the air. Difficult to tell in such a large gathering, but he was sure he was right. Something beyond the rainbow suspenders drew him to the otter, a yearning that he didn't want to deny. He was about to follow when someone touched his arm.

"Herr Bastille, is it not?" A man with flame-red hair, an educated European accent and a calculating smile stood at his elbow. "I am Gerhard Klug. I understand you are a hotelier?"

Tally offered his hand rather than a bow and smiled in return. "Good to meet you. Tal-tsu'tsa Bastille. Everyone calls me Tally. Yes, I run the family business back home. Several properties."

"Good. Good." Herr Klug put an arm on his shoulder and steered him toward the bar. "I'm hoping we could discuss a possible business arrangement."

"I'm always interested in discussion, Herr Klug." Tally signaled the bartender. "What are you drinking?"

"Gerhard, please." The fox lijun laughed. "You'll make me feel old. And they have a pear brandy here that is good."

Tally ordered the brandy and a whiskey sour for himself. Yes, Gerhard was obviously here to woo him, but Tally didn't like being put at a disadvantage right from the start, even with something as small as who paid for drinks. "What is it you do?"

"I have glassworks," Gerhard said as he hopped onto the stool next to Tally's. "My family has been in glass for several centuries. While we have commercial lines, we have sites dedicated to custom work, as well."

Tally had the oddest image pop up at the phrase *in glass* of littles foxes running about under cheese domes. Of course he knew what Gerhard meant and the more focused part of his brain perked up at the mention of custom work. "Oh? What sort of custom work?"

Gerhard pulled a small tablet from inside his suit jacket. "For restaurants. For hotels. *Erholungsort*…what is the word? Resorts."

Tally answered the fox's calculating look with a soft laugh. "I have the feeling you've brought a portfolio. Please, let's have a look."

"Thank you. It's very kind of you to give me a hearing." Gerhard opened the tablet between them as their drinks arrived. "We have contracts across Europe. This first set is work we recently added for a winter resort in Sweden."

They leaned in together to inspect the photos, Tally nodding and asking questions here and there. The images showed wine glasses, water goblets, tumblers and beer glasses in beautiful shapes and colors, with the property name and logo etched discreetly into each piece. Tally particularly admired the champagne flutes with the snowflake-shaped feet. Lovely, though he gave no outward indication that he reacted to any one set more than another.

When they reached the end of the photo samples, Tally sat back, sipping at his whiskey and making Gerhard wait. "It's a very interesting thought. Though I imagine a certain percentage of that pretty glassware vanishes from the properties as souvenirs."

"Ha. I'm sure some of it does. Though not offering the prettiest glasses in the guest rooms most likely reduces that number."

Gerhard's eyes twinkled as he laughed and if Tally had been someone who craved casual sex, Gerhard might have been a candidate, but his heart would only be half in it. The other half had already left the room with the handsome otter. The suspenders were a beacon, a flare sent up, and Tally was going to speak with the otter of definitely-not-straight orientation that evening if it killed him.

"I'd like you to work up some samples with the resort manager at Sapphire Lake." Tally didn't mention immediately that the manager was one of his sisters. "We'd need to see physical pieces, of course. Then we can discuss the possibility of starting a small contract there first. I do have properties in Europe, but allow me to begin closer to home."

"Very good. A pleasure, Tally, surely." Gerhard extended a hand and they shook—a gentlemen's agreement to further negotiations.

When Gerhard Klug finally let him go with an exchange of business cards, the otter was nowhere in sight. Uncharacteristically disgruntled, Tally left the main ballroom to check some of the smaller venues where different sorts of food were on offer. The first meeting room had been set up as a sushi bar, which seemed a good place to find an otter. He wasn't there. The second was a room dedicated to international cuisine, offerings from host countries of previous years. No otter.

The third was a paradise of desserts which had drawn the children since the beginning of the evening with its siren song. Tally hurried his steps when he picked up shouting from that direction and he skidded to a stop in front of the door.

* * * *

"Attack!" Haru bellowed, holding up their — *broom?* They squinted. Well, close enough for a katana. It served their purpose — as they weaved through the tables. Several staff members took a step back, losing any placid expressions. "Never retreat! Death or chocolate!"

One server glanced toward the open door of the banquet hall. *That's the one that'll break first.*

Several high-pitched giggles rounded out the mighty roars the kids gave as they charged the dessert tables. Fast at first, then everyone skidded to a stop, making sure all attention was on them as they slowly pushed forward again. How could the council consider it okay to withhold all those treats from the children? It was cruel and unusual punishment, making the kiddies wait for the adults. By the time all the different welcome activities were done, most of the little ones would be in bed passed out. Stupid, selfish adults. Know-it-alls. Always sticking their noses where they didn't belong.

Well, Haru didn't want to adult anymore tonight. Thus, dessert warfare. They tried to remember why pilfering the fine desserts would make things better, but couldn't. A cloud of fuzz made everything less focused. Oh well, it made sense to Haru anyway. They hiccupped as their regiment of underlings rounded the beautiful ice sculpture in the middle of the room.

When they'd first suggested raiding the dessert room, the littlest ones had jumped on the bandwagon immediately, though the older kids had tugged on friends' and siblings' hands. Haru could tell the older boys and girls wanted to as well. The kids just needed a reason. One little reason that would push even the reluctant ones over the edge. Then everyone could all have fun and eat the cake too. That was when Haru had suggested a re-enactment of the Siege of Inabayama Castle. The children were here to learn about lijun history after all. What epic two-week battle campaign wouldn't hold a feast to enjoy the spoils of war?

The older kids had taken the bait.

Next thing they knew, the kids were looting—no, *gathering*—supplies from the cleaning staff and making makeshift armor from cushions. Though Haru wanted to make sure there wasn't any lasting damage to any of the potted plants once the campaign was over. But Kaho's idea was genius, and who was Haru to deny good battle tactics?

The tricky part had been getting down the hall from where the kids had hidden by the pool to the dessert room. Haru had been convinced Urusar Akaike would stomp out in front of them and demand a return to the welcome dinner so they could 'mingle' like a respectable clan member. No way. No one was dumb enough to spend any more time with those stuffy shirts than necessary. The old fussbucket was up to his tricks and Haru was having none of it. Urusar or no Urusar. Akaike-san had gone too far this time. Pretending he needed Haru along for the help.

A bark escaped from one of the wolf lijun, setting the whole regiment into a fit of laughter. Haru felt the corners of their mouth twitch. Oh yes, this was much more fun than any plans Akaike-san had for the dinner. A current of excitement ran through the regiment as the kids broke out into smaller groups of twos and threes, the sweat of their prey enticing them further, harder.

It cut. Not only that Urusar Akaike was trying to pawn them off—again—or that their parents went along with it—again—but how everyone lied to them about why Akaike-san needed them at the conference. It hurt. Haru was more than a piece of meat to offer up to the best match. They wanted more. They deserved more. They wanted love. Not a *match*.

Hence the running away…to the pool. Where they'd found all the kids. Bored and sad. Haru couldn't have that. No. Sad was not fun. The kids would grow up all too soon anyway. Like them. Then they'd have to follow all the rules, like Haru. Be stuck, like Haru. Drinking alone at a party where they didn't want to be.

Haru wanted none of that for the kids.

A tug on their jeans had Haru looking down. They misstepped to the side, but straightened quickly. Little Kaho had taken hold on their leg, one dirty thumb still in her mouth and her eyes locked on the centerpiece on the main banquet table. A five-tier chocolate cake with fresh fruit adorning each layer.

Mmm-hmm. That cake definitely had to be good eats. Haru smiled down at the little girl before ruffling her short hair.

As soon as they got to the conference they'd sought out Kaho and her parents, happy to see a friendly face, even if she was four years old. At the last Biannual Japanese Lijun Conference they'd struck up a friendship, and her parents had been happy to get a free babysitter again. Being their clan's Urusar and Uruma meant her parents couldn't keep track of her like the little one needed. So Haru hadn't been surprised when they'd found her in the pool with everyone else instead of bed. Kaho had been the first to want to raid the dessert room, too. Her light brown eyes gleamed with unholy joy.

Not surprising from a tanuki lijun like herself. She was made for mischief. Like the mischief their little band was getting into.

The servers had taken a defensive position in front of the tables. *Lot of good that would do them.*

Stubborn fools. The staff were outfoxed. Literally. Several of the fox lijun had already circled round the back of the hall while Haru and the rest of the children drew attention to themselves. The foxes were just getting into position as Haru and their regiment broke from the tables. It was hard to pretend their regiment wasn't about to wreak havoc. The staff didn't have a chance. One of the foxes snuck behind the weak link of the servers then let out an eerie, high-pitched laugh.

The server jumped a good ten centimeters in the air. The moment his feet touched ground again he was off, wheeling toward the door at full-speed. His fellow staffers shifted uneasily, the bitter, salty taste of their nervousness mingling with the sweet aroma of cake and chocolate and all things nice.

Several hands shot out from under the table. More servers yelped and jumped. Two more broke away from the formation, one using language Haru preferred Kaho didn't hear. They growled and flicked one of their pilfered stones at the man. Not hard. It only hit his ass. The guy hollered and held his bottom like he'd been shot.

"Ready?" Haru shouted, smiling when several sets of panicked gazes flicked toward them. They lifted their 'katana' like any good samurai. "Aim!"

Laughter bubbled up from the children. Hands rose, mud sliding down their skinny arms. Grins, wide and filled with glee, were worn on every single one of their faces. The servers no longer had blank expressions, and one of the staffers broke loose from the line, bolting as he swore at Haru and the kids.

"Fire!"

Before the server got even three steps from the tables, a volley of mud-balls flew through the air, several hitting them squarely in the back. The rest were aimed at the remaining staff, but the nervous server certainly got more than a few.

"Coward!" Kaho yelled then stuck her thumb back in her mouth. Haru decided it really was best to ignore the dirt on it.

They loped forward, swords at the ready. More of the line broke, servers knocking into each other as they tried to flee the carnage. Mud-balls struck with dangerous accuracy. A stick that looked a little too much like a spear nailed the table with a loud thunk and stuck. Haru would have to have a talk with one of the children about sharp, pointy things. The server closest to the projectile tripped over his own feet trying to escape, landing in a rather large mud-puddle. At least, Haru hoped it was a mud-puddle. The consistency looked a little off, though. Smelt wrong too.

Poor bastard.

"Oh well, all's fair in war and chocolate, isn't it, Kaho-chan?"

A smile turned the corner of her lips and she gave one sharp nod.

The regiment advanced toward the table. Shouts and exclamations tapered off as the staff escaped the banquet hall. A large water bubble broke over one of the more insistent servers, finally breaking her from her vigil at the table. Haru hoped she thought it had been a water balloon. As she ran by, Haru stole an appreciative glance at the pretty bra she wore under her white shirt. Maybe they should find her later, offer her a towel and an apology. A proper and sincere apology.

But a tug at their leg drew Haru's attention to the matter at hand. Pillaging the desserts.

Kaho bounced over to the table, eyeing the five-tier chocolate cake.

"You really think you can carry that out of here?" Haru asked.

The determined look in her eyes said she did. The others were already busy loading up plates and serving carts. Maybe if they got one of the bigger kids to help shuffle it over to the cart, then everyone could share in the large victory prize.

By the time Haru wrangled one of the carts over to the table, Kaho had climbed up and was teetering on tiptoe as she plunged her chubby little fingers into the top tier. Eh, she was allowed. No one else had thought to go after the big prize. Haru admired a woman who set high goals for herself. No way they wanted to share any cake after where her hands had been, though.

"All right. Not sure how we're going to do this, Kaho-chan."

A chocolate-covered face turned toward him, her cheeks puffed out. "Cake!"

"Oh, I know. Best prize of them all. It's just so big." Plus the table seemed to be tilted. Or maybe that was just them. Maybe the fourth bottle of sake had been a bad idea. Or maybe the fifth. Had there been six? Haru sighed. However many it had been, they'd consumed at least one bottle too many.

Haru wasn't sure they could move the large cake even if they had been sober.

Kaho's puffy cheeks filled their view. "Cake! Yummy cake!"

Several of the older children were already herding part of the regiment with its ill-gotten goods back to their base. The groups of fours and fives were to meet in twenty minutes once they'd made their escape.

A loud bang had the regiment ransacking the table turning toward the back of the banquet room.

Humongous.

The man was definitely big. In a 'wow, how'd you grow like that?' kinda big. Had its merits, but he wasn't someone familiar.

Haru put themself between the oncoming intruder and the children.

"Hurry!" The man waved his hands in front of him in a shooing motion. "The manager is coming."

Were they being shooed? Haru and the kids all cocked their heads in unison as everyone blinked at the stranger. Long, flowing black hair billowed around him with each step he took toward them.

"Ah, oh. Okay. Um, any of you speak English?"

"I do," Haru replied. So that was what the words were. They shook their head, trying to clear the alcoholic haze. Ooh, that was not a good motion. Their head and stomach protested it.

"I'll get the cake, you get the kids. You need to leave. Now."

"Okay." Haru paused, looked up, took a step back so they could get a clear look at the man's face and said, "Thank you."

Haru pulled Kaho out of the cake—her dress was never going to be wearable again—and tucked her against them. They ignored her loud protests as they waved the children toward the escape route on the other side of the room.

"Go! Go! Go!"

"That's a window!" the large man hissed. *Hissed?*

"It opens!" *One hopes.*

One of the young teens in front pressed on the side of the glass and it popped open, swinging outside.

The mystery man laughed. Deep and rich, the sound did something funny to Haru's stomach. Though the sake might be at fault. Hard to tell. Humongous-san huffed out a "Thank the Gods for patio doors," as the group all dashed outside.

Haru nodded. Hot stuff wasn't wrong. They leaned and took a hard right, following the kids. The procession ran quietly, efficiently along the wall. The only noise came from the clank of the food carts they'd, um, *borrowed* temporarily. Even Kaho had stopped her protests.

Smart girl. She pressed hard against Haru, only her neck stretched out with her head turned on their shoulder so she could watch behind them. Her little chubby fingers dug into the front of Haru's chest, most likely covering their shirt with chocolate. Haru chuckled and rubbed their chin over her head as the group snaked its way around the hotel perimeter. The regiment twisted and turned, following the small footpath toward their destination.

When the group swung into an outcove, a door had been propped open. The kids slinked through, Haru and Humongous-san bringing up the rear. The regiment shuffled the last few meters into another open door leading to the indoor swim area.

"What happened to the pool?"

Haru glanced back at Humongous-san, trying to gauge whether he was going to have a coronary or laugh. His lips were set in a tight line. It could have gone either way. In the end, he snort-chuckled.

"You don't know how glad I am that this isn't my hotel this evening."

"I am pretty sure it is only dirt. Do you think the filters will get it out?" Haru grimaced.

Humongous-san cleared his throat, his face still struggling against one expression or another. Had he been staring at Haru? Maybe. "After a fashion. The filters will need to be replaced. The, ah...they'll probably have to drain it."

Oh dear. Guilt gnawed at Haru's gut, but the shouts of laughter and triumph didn't give them time to stew. Kaho squealed, kicking out. They almost dropped her, but managed to keep hold. By the ankles, yes, but her head did not meet concrete. It counted as a save. Haru juggled Kaho until she was right side up and put her down. Their little tanuki went straight for Humongous-san.

"Cake!"

"Don't you think you've had enough cake?" Humongous-san's dark eyes sparkled as he took her tiny hand in his.

"Cake!"

He laughed and nudged the cake cart over to a chair where she could reach it. "Fine. But don't make yourself sick."

"Ha!" Haru barked out then cleared their throat. "One can never have too much cake."

Kaho's eyes met theirs before she nodded once. Her little fingers went right back into the top tier. *Ooohs* and *aaahs* echoed in the room as the kids popped a squat and dug into the ill-gotten gains. Warm fuzzies filled Haru's chest as they watched the children stuff their faces. The kids talked with each other as much as they ate.

"Thank you," they said, turning to Humongous-san.

Their spy? Savior? Turncoat? Had one hand on Kaho's back, steadying her as she chowed down. He flashed a smile before his gaze moved to something behind Haru. A few *Koropokkuru* had toddled out from behind the plants and were making their way along the wall toward Haru and their accomplices. These tiny, human-like beings stuck to the shadows more often than not, and were a real treat to be seen, but the *Koropokkuru* were a wary race. Their new companions were desperate not to be seen and failing miserably.

"Pretend you do not see them. The *Koropokkuru*, the little people, are painfully shy."

"Oh, yes, um." Humongous-san focused back on steadying Kaho.

When Haru began pulling plates, their new friend got the hint and served up some cake. The tap at Haru's leg came shortly, followed by a few soft words, barely audible, asking for a slice.

"We are happy to share," Haru replied then passed plates, dipping down and back to give their guests as much privacy as possible. "Here you go."

"*Arigatou.*"

"*Dōitashimashite.*"

The *Koropokkuru* hurried away, ill-gotten cake in hand, a couple stopping to add the treats the children put on the floor for them. Haru really had bumped into a good group of kids today, and thanks to Humongous-san, the kids and Haru were able to enjoy their escapades.

"You helped make their night." Haru gestured over their shoulder to, well, everyone. *And mine.* "Getting caught would have put a damper on…the *celebration.*"

"So, uh, why were you attacking the desserts?"

"Re-enactment of the Siege of Inabayama Castle. A"—Haru burped. *Ew.* That did not feel good. Or taste good—"major battle between the Oda clan and the Saitō clan." Haru made a waving motion and sat down next to Kaho. She planted a chocolate kiss on their cheek and handed them some cake. They tore off a piece and popped it in. Humongous-san made a choking sound. *What were we talking about? Oh, right.* "Family feud really. Oda was supposed to inherit anyway. But Oda won, became a major *daimyō* and initiated the unification of Japan. Sorry, must be boring to you — Mister?"

Humongous-san tilted. Or maybe that was Haru. The fuzz in their head made it hard to concentrate properly, and everything moved in weird ways. The sweet yumminess of the cake made their stomach flip. The room needed to stop trying to turn. Haru's stomach protested the motion.

"Bastille." Humongous-san offered a brief courtesy bow. "Tally Bastille. History teacher?"

"No, physics, but I love history."

"I don't mean to offend you, but you don't look well."

"Not feeling the best." The confrontation with Akaike-san hadn't helped.

"Who?"

"What?"

Tally's? Yes, Tally. His nostrils flared. Was that a tongue flick?

"Who is Akaike-san?"

"Oh. My Urusar." *Asshole.*

Tally put his free hand on Haru's shoulder. Why was he doing that? And what did that look mean? "Is there anything I can help with?"

Haru laughed. "Ha! No. I, um, doubt it. Unless you can love me? I deserve it, to be loved. I am not some kind of meat, just to be handed off to whomever. I want to love...and be loved. Is that so wrong?"

"No," Tally whispered, then swallowed hard. "It's not wrong."

"See? Why is that so hard—oh!" A burp, a long and hard one, interrupted Haru's indignation. Then again. And again.

Tally crouched in front of Haru, all his hair billowing around him like some kind of cloud. It really was pretty. Especially with how it set off his russet skin, almost like he glowed copper and golden.

Another burp came up, but it was all wrong. Tally's dark eyes widened to saucer size, at least it looked that way to Haru—afraid they might fall in. A hand tightened on Haru's arm as Tally whispered, "Oh, crap."

A deep, thunderous gurgle came up. Wet and bitter. Tasting all kinds of nasty. And all of it spewing right into Humongous-san's lap.

Chapter Two

Muddy Waters & Hangover Blues

Not quite how I'd imagined it. Tally couldn't help a little smile as he washed the worst of the sick off in the pool's restroom. It wasn't like the stories where two people stared at each other across the room and made their way into each other's arms in a chorus of shining stars and unicorns. Fine. The stories about *Em'halafi*, that one destined match of a lifetime, weren't quite that bad, but they could get sappy.

He'd never heard of one involving drunken dessert sieges and throwing up on shoes.

Though now he couldn't find the stories far-fetched at all. Em'halafi were quite real. He'd seen it with his own parents, but he'd always thought falling so hard, so immediately like that was for other people. Until that evening when a rainbow-suspender-wearing otter had drawn his gaze in a superconducting magnet sort of way. Tally had felt compelled to find him, frantic until he did, then their eyes had met and Tally had fallen into a deep, lightning-lit well.

Nothing had ever struck him with such clarity before. He always questioned himself, always backed up and took stock, re-evaluated, weighed things carefully. Not with this. He *knew* and he didn't even know the otter's name.

He turned to the teenager at the next sink who was in the process of washing icing off a smaller child's hands and face — some sort of bird lijun from the scent, both of them. Tally gathered up the few Japanese words he had. "The...cake samurai. Name?"

"I speak English, Mr. Bastille." The youngster said it respectfully, but there was a grin trying to fight its way out. "The cake samurai is Tanaka Haru. They are an otter clan, mostly."

"Oh. Thank you. I should try to return him to his family after we make sure all the kids are accounted for."

The teenager — crane, Tally thought after a discreet air taste with his tongue — frowned up at him. "Maybe it would be better to let them find him."

"Why would you say that?"

The crane boy shrugged, though, and returned to cleaning up his younger counterpart. Maybe the clan's Urusar was intimidating, or maybe the boy's clan didn't get along with them. Feuding clans were rare these days, but active dislike certainly still existed. That didn't concern Tally too much. He was an outsider without connections here, and he did need to speak to Haru's clan to feel them out regarding how they felt about a match with a foreigner of a different lijun type.

Maybe they're progressive and don't care as long as Haru's happy.

Overly optimistic, maybe, but the stars seemed to be aligning for Tally that evening. All things were possible. With the older children's help, Tally made certain all the little ones found their families first, including a certain tanuki who was mostly chocolate icing by that point. When he returned to the now-abandoned pool area, Haru was still passed out on the chaise.

Tally crouched beside him, smoothing the hair back from his forehead. "Haru? Time to get you to your room."

No response. He didn't expect one, really. Someone had really overdone it. Tally allowed himself a few more seconds lost in admiration. So perfect, even drunk off his gourd. Watching Haru sleep was a little creepy, though, so Tally slid his arms underneath and lifted Haru with a little huff. He wasn't *small*, exactly, but he was lean enough that Tally could manage.

Haru snuffled in his sleep, nuzzling against Tally's shoulder and fastening his fingers onto Tally's shirt in a death grip.

"I have you," Tally murmured as he headed out of the pool area. "Don't worry."

"Hmmm." Haru wriggled to get his head more comfortably supported and settled in Tally's arms with a soft sigh.

Perfect. Tally felt as if his heart were thawing after a long frost, one he hadn't even been aware of. This was what he'd been missing, the second half of his heart to hold in his arms. He carried Haru back toward the convention rooms, though he stopped at the information table instead of dragging Haru through hallways of too-interested eyes.

"Excuse me? Do you know where I can find the Akaike clan? I need to return someone to them."

The two rabbit lijun behind the table twitched, glanced at each other wide-eyed then turned back to Tally. Finally, one of them managed in softly accented English, "Sir, maybe it would be best to leave him on a chair and we will let them know where he is."

"I... No, I can't do that. Not a problem at all for me to take him where he belongs." Tally gave them his most gracious smile. "And I do need to speak with them."

"Yes. Of course." The smaller of the two gave him a little seated bow. "They have a suite of rooms on the tenth floor, right beside the elevators. Sir...if it is not too presumptuous? They are very traditional."

That stopped Tally. He wasn't certain if that meant something different here. *Traditional* back home meant conservative, lijun who sometimes clung to old ways and weren't always happy about the modern need to mix in human society in ways that meant the lijun community prospered along with the humans around them. There were good things in the old traditions. The *lijun first* attitude wasn't one of them.

Tally thanked the staff members and hitched Haru up higher as he made his way to the elevator lobby. The other guests waiting gave them a wide berth and let them take the first available car alone. Not that Tally blamed them. Collectively, he and Haru smelled terrible.

A set of double doors stood beside the elevator bank, recognizable as a suite by the scrollwork around the frame and the doorbell. One of Tally's older hotels had doorbells on the suites, too. Always seemed like a little touch of class to him. He juggled Haru so he could ring the bell, while Haru muttered something and clung tighter.

The older woman who opened the door appeared surprised at first, but then she caught sight of Haru and her expression darkened. She snapped something at Tally in Japanese.

"I'm sorry. My Japanese is terrible," Tally managed, hoping his accent and nervousness didn't make the words incoherent.

She glowered at him, then turned her head and called into the suite. An answering call came from somewhere on the left, though Tally had no idea where since she barred the door. Soon an even older gentleman joined her. He seemed familiar but his stern, forbidding expression threw Tally. He swallowed hard.

"Good evening, sir. I—"

"How dare you bring him back like this?" The man kept his voice low but it was sharp enough to cut glass. "What is the meaning of this?"

"He, ah." Tally took a breath, startled by the venom in his eyes. "Haru appears to have had a bit too much sake. I found him and made inquiries..." Yes. True. Maybe with some things omitted in between but that wasn't for him to tell. Now Tally recalled where he'd seen this otter lijun before, arguing with Haru at the reception. "I brought him to you because I need to speak to you... You are Akaike-san?"

Akaike drew himself up to his full height, just about at the top of Tally's shoulder. "I am."

"My name is Tal-tsu'tsa Bastille, sir. I'm the new Urusar of Bastille clan in Wisconsin. I know this might sound unusual, but I met Haru this evening and knew."

"*What* did you know?" None of the slicing cold left Akaike's voice but his eyes had narrowed speculatively.

"That Haru is my Em'halafi. My one." Tally tried to take a step forward so they weren't talking in the hallway but neither otter moved. "I'd like to discuss marriage—"

Akaike finally moved aside and pointed. "You will put Haru down this instant! This is most unseemly. He is not some houseless boy, but a Satislit of exquisite training."

Tally hurried to place Haru down on the indicated sofa, then ended up going down on one knee when Haru refused to release his death grip on Tally's shirt. "Haru? You have to let go now," Tally whispered. Haru rooted closer and placed a kiss on Tally's jaw, all with his eyes still shut.

"Outrageous!" Urusar Akaike roared. "You will remove yourself this instant, young Urusar! If you wish for a match, you will do this properly through your parents instead of pawing at a Satislit to whom you have not been formally introduced!"

"Yes, sir. I'm very sorry. Really." Tally fought desperately to loosen Haru's grip, though it was difficult to do it and remain gentle. Finally he was free to stand, though Haru's whimper as he broke contact nearly ruined his heart. He offered the Urusar a bow. "Thank you for your patience. My parents will be in touch."

The Urusar's expression was still thunderous as he closed the door firmly behind Tally. The Uruma's steady gaze had been more thoughtful. That gave him hope. Tally took a long, shuddering breath and made his way back to the elevators.

Could've gone worse, right?

He'd call Mom and Dad in the morning and convince them if he had to beg and plead. A proper match.

Traditional. *That* kind of traditional. Dad didn't need Tally to tell him how to negotiate, of course, but whatever it took, Tally was prepared to throw it in the pot.

Back at his own room, he put the chocolate icing and throw-up-stained clothes out for the valet and put himself in the shower long enough for the bathroom to fill with steam. He toweled off in cursory fashion, opened the door and let himself relax into his snake form. It had been a long day and he needed to let go for a bit.

The soft carpet felt good against his scales, easy to glide over. Tally stopped at the full-length mirror on the closet door and reared up to inspect his scales. He did hope Haru didn't find this part of him frightening. So many lijun did, the rumors about uktena never quite dying out. Uktena were too scarce, the prejudices too old for the myths to die. Yes, he was a *big* snake. There was that. As large around as a ten-year-old oak. But the silver-white scale shining on his forehead and the horns marked him as not a regular snake. Maybe Haru would find him handsome as a snake? Maybe he knew better than to be afraid?

Well, it would come out all right. They'd figure it out. That's what Em'halafi did.

* * * *

"No, Dad, listen." Tally juggled the phone from hand to hand as he shrugged into his suit jacket, the everyday navy Armani rather than his best Hugo Boss, which he'd sent out to be cleaned. The likelihood of it being a total loss was in the high percentiles. "I'm sure. He's the *one*. I didn't know from across the room, but when I looked in his eyes…yeah. I knew."

"And he barfed all over you? That's something to tell the grandkids, I guess." Dad was still snickering. Mom laughed in the background.

"Please, I need you both to take this seriously." Tally felt five years old again, trying to explain something he felt was terribly important to parents who thought his sincerity was just too cute. "Haru is my Em'halafi. The one person in this whole wide world who's my actual match. But his clan's really old school. All about tradition. I might be Urusar now, but you're still my parents. I can't be the one to start this process."

"Hmm. This is an otter clan?" Dad turned from the phone to talk to Mom, their voices muffled and urgent. "Your mom says clever boy for having an otter as your fated love."

Tally huffed as he checked his tie in the mirror. "This isn't part of the *we need to do something about the declining otter population* thing. I mean, yes, it's a plus, but I didn't plan it this way."

More muffled conversation and laughing from their end. "Your mom's teasing. She knows you don't have a clandestine bone in your body."

"I have to get to the security meeting, Dad. Tell me you'll contact the Awi Tamgradat."

"Won't do to be late." All the laughter had fled from Dad's voice. "Go, go. Oh wait. What was the family name so I have something concrete for the matchmaker?"

"Tanaka. One of the kids gave it to me, but it's Tanaka Haru. The Urusar's name is Akaike."

"Perfect. Should be enough to start with. I'll email you anything I find out. This time difference is a pain."

Tally said goodbye to his parents and hurried to the elevators. He'd been too excited to sleep and his stomach was too jumbled for breakfast. Not the way he preferred to start a day of meetings, but he'd manage. Somehow. Tally's mind wandered to Em'halafi and to last night, running through it again and again.

If a person had to be sick, the pool area was probably one of the better places to do it. Tile floors cleaned up easily and there were plenty of towels. Tally had cleaned up the worst of it and stripped off his jacket and dress shirt while he'd marshalled the older children to get the younger ones cleaned up in the restrooms adjacent to the pool area.

Miraculously, Haru hadn't gotten any of the sick on himself. Only Tally. Now that was a talent. Impressive and gross all at the same time. The little tanuki, Kaho, had been a lost cause, of course. Tally's second to last act of the evening had been to return her to her parents, chocolate dress and all. They hadn't been pleased, but tanuki parents usually understood their children's overarching need for mischief. But returning Haru to his Urusar—that had been hard. The way Haru had clung to Tally, whimpering. Tally still found it hard to believe he had to go halfway around the world to find his destined match, but the GLA conference was no longer on his list of dreaded things to do as Urusar.

Mate...oh, Gods, thank you. He was going to be useless all day, reliving the feel of Haru in his arms, the scent of his hair, the sight of that gorgeous, animated face. Before he'd passed out, of course.

In between meetings, he would do some hard praying for negotiations to work, though his parents were shrewd. It had to work. Then Tally would marry his one true mate and everything would be perfect. Not that his life was horrible. But...

Tally took a huge breath so he wouldn't sigh. The pair of human women in the elevator with him had already edged away as far as they could. Even the humans saw him as intimidating, though that was solely due to his size. Had they been rabbit lijun, they probably would have refused to get in the elevator car with the big scary death serpent in the first place.

No matter how peaceful, how law-abiding an uktena was, they couldn't shake those automatic reactions from other lijun or dispel the weird myths that still circulated. No one was going to die if Tally breathed on them in his human form, for Gods' sakes. The opposite of revulsion was true, too. Naturally. There were people attracted to him because he was supposed to be so deadly or some who had a Native American fetish. Some of his lovers had wanted him because he was so *exotic* and *dangerous*. Such a thrill.

It was maddening and tiresome. And lonely. When Haru had looked at him with those soulful brimming eyes and said he just wanted to be loved, Tally's heart had cracked a little. He understood that so well. Someone who would see him and not the legends. Someone who could look past the what and love who he was.

He accepted the folder from the cat lijun attendant at the entrance to the meeting room and sat through the meeting on autopilot. Oh, he took notes. He'd review them later. He heard what was said, but didn't really absorb any of it, and since he didn't have any security breaches to report, he didn't have to actively participate. Cyber-security was the latest quibble. Tally had his own thoughts, but it wouldn't do for a young upstart like himself to give advice or suggestions to the older Urusars and Urumas, either. Tally understood his place here.

The family chat buzzed toward the end of the meeting, messages filling up his phone at an alarming pace.

Meli: you met your Em'halafi? OMG!
Nan: what is he/she/they like?
Hal: Dad said he threw up on you
Lahi: Oh, Gods, that's horrible :(
Che: You scare him, Tal?
Mom: Of course not. The young man was a wee bit intoxicated.
Addy and Nan: Did you get him drunk? O_O
*Meli: *gasps**
Tal: NO! NO! I rescued him from a dessert raid. He was already drunk
Mom: He's a nice, young Satislit from an otter clan. He's an otter 2, right, Tal?
Hal: Did he really trash the pool?
Nan: Dessert raid?
Tal: More like a siege. Yes on the otter.
Addy: Is that why I got this bill — huge, painful bill — across my desk? What kind of otter is he?
Meli, Hal, Nan, Lahi and Che: Ooooooh, Tally's in trouble!

How? Just how did they always manage to answer at the same time?

Dad: Haru was just entertaining the lijun, kids, like you guys haven't done worse.
Hal: Late as always, Pop
Dad: Hal...
Addy: Srsly, this bill, Tally

*Mom: We've got the Akaike clan on the phone. Your dad
needs to concentrate.*
Lahi: What? Tally can't talk for himself?
Che: Lame, bro
Mom: Children!

Tally closed down the app, needing to focus on the
new policies update and escape from his family's nosy
questions. But he didn't close it fast enough to miss
Marnie's cat icon pinging with *You found your destined?!
What is she/he/they like?* Except Tally knew hardly
anything. It was hard to answer when all he wanted
was to get to know his Em'halafi better. But soon. It
would be soon.

After the meeting, the interminable, endless meeting,
Tally wandered the hotel's main floor trying to decide
on a restaurant for lunch. Most of the conference-goers
broke off into well-established groups at lunchtime and
Tally found himself on his own—not comfortable
enough to ingratiate himself into any group and
certainly not sought out by anyone except for business
conversations.

He finally decided to go back up to one of the
restaurants on the top floor, the bistro with more
Western-style seating so he wouldn't feel so odd eating
alone. The view of Mt. Fuji was breathtaking and a
huge part of Tally yearned to be out on the mountain
instead of stuffed into a suit in a civilized venue. The
menu was impressive but fussier than his stomach
wanted that day, so he settled on the chef's salad and a
glass of wine.

One glass. That wasn't irresponsible, was it?

When the food arrived, he finally felt relaxed enough
to take in his surroundings. He appreciated all the

leather and wood. Gave the room a cozy, intimate feeling, though the space was quite large. Low ceilings and soft coverings for floor and walls kept the noise level down. Someone had understood restaurant design beyond the purely visual when they'd built this space.

Even with the sound baffling, Tally picked up a familiar voice and his heart sped. There. Across the room away from the window, there was Haru. Overjoyed, Tally gathered his courage and all his best manners to go say hello, but the expression on Haru's face stopped him.

He sat with an older gentleman who shared some of Haru's features. Except for that one phrase Tally had heard across the room, they kept their voices low, but they were obviously arguing.

Okay. Now would definitely not be a good time. Tally bit his lip and eased back into his chair, studiously *not* trying to eavesdrop.

* * * *

"The hotel has to drain the pool."

Haru winced and pressed their palms against their temples. "Not so loud, *Otōusan.*"

"What were you thinking?"

Not much, apparently. Totally worth it, though. Vague images of the siege flitted through their memory. Laughter from excited children was the most prominent, and it warmed their chest. They'd made the kids happy. Kaho had squealed with joy. They remembered that much. Nothing else really mattered.

A loud sigh escaped *Otōusan.* "What are we going to do with you?"

"Can the hotel definitively say it was me?" The words weren't easy to put together. The loud, continuous thump against their skull made it hard to concentrate on much of anything.

"No. Not precisely."

"Then how can you assume it was me?"

"Know anyone else with rainbow suspenders?"

Well, those wouldn't be coming out again during the conference. Haru sighed and closed their eyes. A groan escaped them. Something for the pain would help. Maybe. The lights were too bright. People were all fuzzy when they looked around. Words felt sharp and pointy, especially the ones Father used when talking *at* Haru. Because that was what he was doing. Not listening. But talking at Haru. Ever since their Urusar had dragged them out of bed this morning, people had talked over them.

Shoving Haru in the shower hadn't helped their mood. They hadn't been that drunk. Haru dipped their head and sniffed their shirt. It smelled of sake. Or maybe that was them? Wow. Had they really gone through so many bottles that alcohol still sweated out of their pores? The shower hadn't helped the smell even a fraction. Okay, maybe they'd been that drunk. It hadn't been their goal. They'd just been so angry about having another match shoved at them during the welcome dinner.

Haru opened their eyes as they leaned forward. They cradled their head between their hands as they stared at Father. Words were leaving *Otōsan's* mouth, but bounced right off Haru. None of them made any sense. They needed something to clear their mind and settle their stomach.

"Noodles," they said.

"What?"

"Does this place serve udon?"

Once again *Otōusan* gave Haru one of those looks. The ones that made them shrink back and feel guilty about being a disappointment. Again.

"You haven't heard a word I've said."

"No." *Might as well not lie.*

A raspy sigh left Father. Both of them were doing a lot of that. Sighing. Not that it was unusual.

"I think we can manage to scrounge you up a bowl. You're going to need it."

"Yes."

Maybe they'd be able to find little Kaho. Her smile and chubby hands were all Haru needed as a pick-me-up. Kaho's intense gaze held a mutual understanding of how boring and monotonous the meetings were, and it spoke to Haru on an instinctual level. Maybe she needed looking after, or they could look after each other. Any time with their little raccoon-dog was worth the ire of Urusar and *Otōusan*.

A large bowl filled with noodles was placed in front of Haru. "Ooh, yes."

"Sirs." The waiter bowed and quickly left.

The smell alone rejuvenated Haru. Their mouth watered as they spied the tempura. *Prawns. Lotus root. Sweet potatoes. Gobo.* If Father was ordering them treats, then he couldn't be too upset with them.

"Wait, isn't this restaurant the one that serves Western food?"

"I asked a favor. There are other restaurants in the hotel."

"Gods, thank you."

Otōusan grunted, but didn't say anything else. He sat back, resting his hands over his flat stomach. There was a look in his eye Haru wasn't too sure about. They'd woken up too tired, not up to adulting yet. They'd figure it out once they had more than two brain cells to rub together.

Haru picked up their chopsticks, inhaled the heady aroma of the soup again and said, "*Itadakimasu.*"

Oooh yes. They slurped up the weighty noodles, the food hitting the right spot. Their stomach. After a few mouthfuls they picked up one of the prawns and devoured it in two bites. They groaned. This was what they needed. Not to be dumped in a cold shower, or to have people push and prod them, or to be yelled at, or worse...or to have that disappointed stare of Father's pinned on them.

Noodles fixed everything, especially after a night of drinking.

Every slurp helped Haru feel more like themself instead of a comatose slug. If Father had ordered them some udon to start with, there wouldn't have been an argument—oh, dear Gods. Haru stopped mid-slurp and looked up at *Otōusan*. They gulped, forcing down their mouthful. The noodles sat heavy in their stomach.

Otōusan grinned, clucking his tongue. "So, are you with the world again?"

"What are you doing here?"

"Are you going to have that prawn?"

"Yes." Haru automatically protected their treat with the chopsticks.

Alarm skittered through Haru like a thousand needle pricks. They checked the time on their Seiko Prospex. One-thirty. How long ago had Urusar Akaike contacted Father?

"You were in Ishikawa this morning," Haru said, picking up the prawn. Their heart clenched before they asked the next question. "How'd you get to Tokyo? Why?"

"I flew."

Haru dropped the prawn. *Otōusan* immediately poached it, popping the savory treat into his mouth and chewing. But flying would cost so much money, especially if it was a last-minute ticket. There was no good reason for Akaike-san to fly Father to Tokyo. None. A distinct ringing began in Haru's ears.

"You flew?"

Otōusan nodded.

"Why?"

"Why do you think after all the destruction you caused last night you are still here?"

"Because they don't know it was me? *Otōusan, why* are you here?"

"You have a match."

"Excuse you," Haru replied as a hum ran through their body. Fight or flight. Their mind hadn't decided which yet.

"I'm serious, Haru. The Imsi Tamgradat is already set for three nights from now. It'll give your mother time to get here, and the groom's parents."

"No. I cannot have a match." Doom welled up inside Haru. Things were getting serious. Very serious. And way too fast. The formal attitude spooked them. "I don't *want* a match. It's so, so...*last* century."

"Yes, you do." A grin, something Haru rarely ever saw, cracked Father's serious expression. "In fact, from what Akaike-san told me, it's a destined match. Apparently, you met your Em'halafi last night."

The declaration stunned Haru. Any rebuttal they had planned dried up. Their tongue stuck to the roof of their mouth. No words would come. Could come.

"His connections are the only reason the Akaike clan has not been tossed from this hotel." Father's harsh words bit into Haru.

"Someone claims to be my mate?"

A glint entered *Otōusan's* normally calm brown eyes. "Your destined match."

"Some idiot still believes in Em'halafi — destined matches — in this century?"

"Yes."

"What kind of psycho still believes in mates?" Haru protested. This couldn't be happening. Not to them. Haru wanted to meet someone, fall in love, build a family. Not be *matched*. Didn't matter how they'd been raised by the clan. Just because they had been trained as a Satislit, a *bride-son*, didn't mean the clan should sell them off. Their chest filled with a burning hot spark, flaring up bright and ugly.

Otōusan raised a hand and leaned forward, stealing another prawn from Haru's udon. "The kind that doesn't mind getting thrown up on and still wants to marry you. The kind that has already kept you from getting into trouble with the hotel, other clans. He must have some sway if he can keep the hotel off our backs."

Which meant money. Haru bared their teeth at Father. The family was selling them out.

"The terms of the proposal are more than generous. This Tally will do good things for the clan."

"But — Wait, did you say I threw up on him?" Haru's brain would catch on the most embarrassing detail out of all this ridiculousness. They had no recollection of any spewing. They didn't smell like puke. Just alcohol. What kind of idiot would set up an Imsi Tamgradat after that kind of humiliation?

"You did."

"And he still wants to marry me?"

"He does." *Otōusan* nodded. "This clan, they have *kawauso*, Haru. Otters, like us."

Another declaration striking Haru dumb. It hurt, mainly because they knew what it meant. Their Urusar had probably already signed on the dotted line. Part of Haru wanted to be furious. Rage at Father. The ball of flame swirled inside their chest, ready to break out in a turbulent eruption. It wasn't fair.

"Don't screw this up, Haru. Not this one."

Otōusan slid a picture in front of Haru. *Humongous.* A sense of déjà vu hit them as they eyed the man, but they couldn't place it. Black flowing hair. Expensive suit. Tailor-made. Had to be for a guy that big. Dark, brooding eyes. Next to the picture was all the pertinent information.

Job: Hotelier/Property Management.
Annual Salary/Investments/Holdings —

Wow.

Age: Thirty-four.

Only eight years older than Haru. Not horrid.

Blood Type: O positive.
Status: Urusar.

Gods help them now. Haru would never survive under one of their thumbs.

Species: Uktena.

What? "You're kidding?" Haru lifted their gaze to Father's. He must've seen something on Haru's face because the refusal came fast.

"No."

"This, this...a snake?" How could Father do that to them?

"What better match could I give you than an Urusar? I never thought— He's your destined, Haru."

Haru huffed. Maybe they couldn't sabotage the dinner outright. Didn't mean they wouldn't fight it, because the fight response had definitely kicked in. There were ways to make their feelings known on the subject.

"Haru." The warning was clear in *Otōusan's* voice.

"When is it again? The dinner?"

"You have three days to prepare. It's scheduled for Friday night, after the big fundraising banquet."

Plenty of time then. Haru already had a plan forming. Hopefully they could steal away for a bit to set it in motion.

"Haru, I am asking as your father, don't screw this one up. Please."

Chapter Three

Snake Eyes & an Indecent Proposal

When Dad had sent the time for the Imsi Tamgradat, the betrothal feast, Tally had snaked out. Overjoyed and panicked was not a good combination for him. He'd needed to lock his hotel room door, take his serpent form and curl up in a sunbeam for a good hour to calm down.

When he reached half-dozing in his puddle of sunlight, his brain kicked in and he managed to human again. He couldn't do this on his own. He needed reinforcements. Ten in the morning. It wasn't late back home, right? Even if it was, neither Gunther nor Marnie went to bed early. *Laptop. Skype.* He called Gun's number, knowing he'd be picking up in Colorado and Marnie back home. Two of his oldest friends from school, he tried them since at least one of them was likely to answer. They both did.

"Hey, Tal!" they said over each other in that awkward way video chats often began.

"Hi, I hope it's not a bad time. I'm losing my mind."

"Are you?" Marnie purred, her bobcat showing plainly. "Little birdie told me someone found his Em'halafi in Japan."

"No. Get *out*." Gun's dark eyes went wide, then focused on Tally with his sharpest hawk glare. "And when were you gonna tell me?"

"I did. I'm sorry. I would've told me soon. It's just everything's moving so fast and I… I might be freaking out a little."

Marnie's expression went from smug to concerned. "What, Tal? What's freaking you out?"

Tally scrubbed at his face with both hands. "Gods. It's very traditional, the whole thing. Haru's clan. There's an Awi involved and they won't let me see him. You don't know how frustrating that is, to see him across a restaurant and have to pretend I don't."

"That's kinda sucky, but not freak-out level sucky," Gun said at his driest. "Tal, it's us. Spill."

"There's a betrothal dinner, a formal one, on *Friday*. I don't know what to wear. I don't know what's expected of me. I don't know how to greet his parents or if something's supposed to happen or if I'm supposed to bring something." Tally rested his forehead on the desk. "I'm dying here."

"Poor Tally." Marnie's fingers flew silently over her keys while Gun's heavy clackety-clack typing filled the silence. "Okay, if we look at the ILCD, there's some info on formal matches in Japan. You do need a present for your intended. Something nice."

"Nice?" Now he knew he was panicking, since he hadn't thought to check the International Lijun Customs Database.

"You know if your guy is a Satislit, Tal?" Gun frowned at his screen.

"I…think so. Pretty sure his Urusar said so."

"You need to do the bride-son thing, then. Jewelry's traditional."

He could do that. "All right."

Marnie spoke up again. "You greet parents first. Then your betrothed and you exchange gifts. Tal, you need to check this stuff with someone local. The database sometimes has weird stuff in it that's all jacked up."

"Yes. Of course. I need… I don't think I can go in a suit and tie."

"Probably not. Here, Tal, look at this site." Gun sent him a link with descriptions of formal Japanese clothing for men, complete with labeled diagrams.

"Oh, that helps. A lot. I can manage these things. And I think I know someone who can help confirm the details."

"That sounds more like our Tally." Marnie flashed a blinding smile. "You can do this."

"We wanna hear all about it after," Gun said with a thumbs-up. "We love you, Tal. Go get 'im."

Before Tally went shopping, he decided to call Mrs. Arakawa, the Uruma for that year's host family, for advice. She was pleased to help with a betrothal and accompanied him when he went shopping, tutting and herding him through the proper clothes purchases. She answered all his questions patiently, though she was a bit amused at his frantic fussing. She even came to his room Friday evening to approve and make sure everything was as it should be. He needed to send her something special as a thank you.

Most of the traditional formal wear Tally had managed to get into with minimal fuss was more comfortable than a Western suit and tie. Especially the tie. The loose *hakama* were definitely better than tight, fitted pants. The shoes, though... He frowned at his feet, hoping he didn't look like he was shuffling. The *geta* would take practice and he didn't have the time.

Now in the elevator with its mirrored sides, Tally hardly recognized himself. No one would mistake him for Japanese, but he felt oddly dislocated in time. Musing about tradition helped to stop him worrying over the details quite so much until he reached the meeting room, converted to an intimate banquet hall for the evening. A long, low table dominated the back wall, cushions set carefully along its sides. Elegant flower arrangements in blue and red sat in strategic locations on the table and around the room.

Tally's parents were there already and he greeted them first, then his hosts — the more imposing version of Haru — his father, attired in similar fashion to what Tally wore — and the considerably smaller, feminine version of Haru — his mother, in a kimono patterned with delicate, stylized koi and waves. He bowed to them, deepest courtesy, and offered the little box of candied tamarind that Mrs. Arakawa said was traditional for lijun grooms to bring to the bride-parents.

Next, the clan Urusar, Akaike, and again, Tally offered a deep bow of respect. The Urusar's eyes glittered watching him and the weight of his appraisal was a physical thing pressing on Tally's shoulders. At least he wasn't yelling this time. Their Awi Tamgradat, the matchmaker, stood beside him, beaming, and her regard managed to buoy him enough to continue. She took him by the elbow and led him to the center of the room.

Everything was so beautiful, so perfect, Tally was afraid to breathe too hard. He felt like a giant constrictor in too small a space as he towered over everyone and everything in this delicately balanced room.

Haru. He was supposed to greet Haru. Formally, of course. With a minimal exchange of words. He searched the room. Surely he was here? Wasn't the groom supposed to be the last to arrive? *Oh...wait...*

Near the right-hand wall stood a figure in a gorgeous blue and pink kimono, cherry blossoms against a stream, with long, black hair piled high and formal makeup painstakingly done. Haru.

Don't stare. Don't stare. Don't be rude. It was one of the hardest things Tally had ever done, though. The Haru of the rainbow suspenders had been gorgeous. This Haru was additionally breathtaking, in all his formal poise and dignity.

"May I speak to the *Satislit?*" he asked Mr. Tanaka, enunciating carefully. Satislit, the bride-son. Dad had confirmed that Haru had been raised in that tradition.

Mr. Tanaka inclined his head to give permission. The Awi patted Tally's arm and led him forward. Good thing. Tally wasn't sure he would've made it on his own. His legs shook. He hoped it didn't telegraph through the fabric of his *hakama*.

He offered another *futsurei*, since he was the petitioner here, and held his engagement gift out to Haru with both hands. The lacquer box contained a man's bracelet, gold with blue diamond chips. He hoped it wasn't too much.

"I'm pleased to see you here." Tally offered the formal phrasing that implied the Satislit's presence meant he had been accepted. *He's perfect. So lovely. So full of life.*

Instead of replying in the traditional manner, Haru took the gift silently. Was that also an option? No one said anything, so it must be. Haru glanced at the box without any kind of reaction before he set it aside. He picked up a tall, rectangular package wrapped in a patterned cloth finished off with an ornate bow — silver and blue with feathers sticking out of it. Haru surprised Tally with a *saikeirei* as he offered up the gift, holding it above his head.

Tally accepted it gravely, silently, since that seemed to be what Haru wanted. With a few shaky tugs, he undid the bow and folded back the cloth to find two black, glassy eyes staring back at him. He choked and nearly dropped the bottle. There was a *snake* in the bottle. A. Dead. Snake.

"I hope it is to your pleasing," Haru said quietly, straightening up slowly, his hands clasped together.

Dead snake, dead snake, dead snake. Tally's brain couldn't function beyond that and he risked a quick glance at the Awi for help. Her eyes were wide, her mouth in a little 'O' of surprise, but she recovered swiftly.

"Snake wine, Bastille-san. It is considered medicinal. A restorative." The words were soft but she'd narrowed her eyes at Haru.

Tally put on his best placid diplomatic face and held the horrid thing in both hands while he offered Haru an *eshaku*. This was not the time to make a scene, ask questions about intent or drop the bottle and look hysterical.

"Thank you," he said to Haru, in what he hoped was the same tone of voice as his initial greeting. Exchange concluded, he managed to put the bottle of horror on the table with only a little tremble. This had to be some sort of cultural misunderstanding. Yes. Had to be.

"*Habushu* has a positive effect on the male libido," Haru said as he plucked up his gift with one perfect manicured hand. His nails had been painted a dark purple. It was a lovely color on him, accenting the kimono in a way that spoke of meticulous attention to detail. But there had been a tremor in his voice. Was Haru as nervous as Tally?

"Oh?"

"Yes. And, besides, who does not want to display vanquished predators?"

Tally gulped, eyeing the bottle again. Something wasn't right here. Haru regarded him with cold, flat eyes. There should have been some spark of recognition, some acknowledgment of the camaraderie of the Great Dessert Siege. What had happened to cause this change in Haru? "Many snakes are beneficial predators. Good to keep in the garden."

Haru's expression tightened. "Even garden snakes will bite you."

A loud cough from behind them had Haru looking behind Tally at their families.

A nearly imperceptible sigh escaped Haru. His fingers swept over the lid of the lacquer box almost reverently before he opened his betrothal gift. There was a pause as Haru stared inside. Tally waited for any kind of reaction with jangled nerves.

Haru sniffed loudly and lifted the bracelet out of the box. The Awi gasped, one hand going to her chest. She nodded in approval, waving her hand in some kind of encouragement. Haru opened his mouth only to close it when the Awi hissed something at him. Haru tilted his head, much like he did when Tally had intervened at the dessert raid. Tally was beginning to suspect it was Haru's thinking face. His rosy lips thinned momentarily before he broke out a smile that felt *polite* and slid the bracelet onto his wrist.

The Awi clapped, beaming, then quietly, insistently ushered Tally and Haru toward the low table where his parents, his future in-laws and the clan Urusar now sat. Mr. Akaike wore a frown until he noticed Tally looking at him and it quickly disappeared. Had Tally done something wrong? He was sure he was supposed to offer his betrothal gift first.

Once they sat down, the niggle that something was off disappeared. Haru's mother fawned over the bracelet, and some of the pressure hanging over Tally released. Conversation was polite, all the expected things. Questions about Tally's business and the family from Haru's parents. A few polite questions about Haru's education and favorite pastimes from Tally's parents. At the center of the table, Tally and Haru sat side by side, not close enough to touch, though Haru took up the mantle of bride-son perfectly. He made certain Tally always had something on his plate, that his sake cup was always filled, but he'd fallen back into complete silence, eyes down, expression closed.

Tally did his best not to look, not to ask, telling himself that this was probably expected behavior. The feelings of *mate* and *want* were still as strong as before, but Tally couldn't help feeling that something was terribly wrong.

The food was mostly small bites of this and that. A little sushi, which Tally ate politely though fish was not his favorite thing, some noodle dishes, one of them redolent with ginger, which Tally adored. He made all the appreciative noises, made sure to have something of everything Haru placed on his plate and hoped he wouldn't have to eat so much that he couldn't get up from his cushion.

After perhaps twenty minutes of everyone being painfully polite and Haru being disturbingly quiet, Tally's intended finally turned to him with a sweet smile. "I ordered something special from the kitchen just for you."

Relief washed over Tally. Good. All the chilly distance was part of protocol then. He returned the smile and glanced over as the doors to the banquet room swung open, to reveal one of the chefs in white bearing a platter atop which sat a beautiful lacquer dish. The scents coming from the tray were…interesting, though Tally had trouble parsing through them.

Haru sat up expectantly, a happy smile on his face and his eyes bright. He even wriggled on his cushion. His fingers reached out as if eager to get ahold of the dish.

"Thank you," Tally said gently, pleased to see Haru so excited. "May I ask what it is?"

Haru turned to him, warm and open. "Unagi no Kabayaki."

Several gasps erupted around them.

"One of my favorite dishes." Haru's tongue snaked out and wet his lips. "I am honored to share it with you."

"Haru!" his Urusar barked out.

"Will you have some with me?" Haru turned toward Tally.

Tally stopped short of putting his hand on Haru's arm. He hadn't been given any leave to touch and maybe it wasn't proper. In an echo of Haru's words, he said, "I would be honored to."

A warm glow filled his chest. Everything was going to be fine. Haru *was* excited to be with him. This was… *Oh dear Gods.*

The chef set the lacquer box directly in front of Tally and he couldn't help jerking back, taking his cushion with him. In the beautiful black and red box lay a filleted and butterflied… It couldn't also be a snake, could it?

"I…it's…" He swallowed hard, looking frantically toward the Awi for help, but her face had reddened, her expression horrified. Nausea climbed up Tally's throat. "I don't think…"

"Hmm?" Haru pilfered a pair of chopsticks, clacking them together. "This will help boost our stamina and replenish our strength." Haru winked and held up a piece of the fluffy rice and meat. "To a long and fruitful marriage?"

Oh dear Gods.

"Haru!" A fist slammed on the table, causing Haru to jump and lose the piece of meat.

Relief swept through Tally. Whatever it was, he had a feeling he didn't want to eat it. *Please don't let that be snake.*

Haru turned wide-eyed toward his father. "What?"

"Now is not the time!"

"It is only eel."

Close enough. Nausea threatened Tally and he nearly lost some of his stomach contents.

"With as many Kwebabiads as we are exchanging, I thought showing our interest in the continued lines of our people was appropriate."

The Urusar and Haru's father were red-faced and nearly bent over the table. His mother had one hand covering her mouth and the Awi had placed her forehead on the table. None of them would meet Tally's or his parents' eyes.

"I'm sure it's lovely," Tally blurted out, scrambling to try to save the situation. Whatever Haru's motives, and while he wasn't sure he believed the 'continued lines' bit after being ambushed with dead snake wine surprise, it wasn't the time to try to call him out on it. "I…ah, I'm afraid I can't eat eel. I'm very sorry."

"Oh." Haru deflated, settling back into *seiza*. "I did not realize. I was just so eager to show you all the foods my people, us otters, enjoy. And with us being young males, though you are a little older, are you not—?"

"Haru, *please*," his father choked out.

"I thought food to help our stamina would be a good choice?" Haru plucked his pillow and tossed it to the side, immediately falling into a perfect *dogeza*. Butt high in the air. "I apologize for my ignorance and offense. If you do not want this match, I understand."

The Urusar yelled something sharply in Japanese. Haru jolted, though he stayed in *dogeza*. When Tally looked closer he saw a tremor running through his mate. He became more rigid and, as if he could meld with the floor, he pressed lower.

A throaty, "I apologize," came out.

No one spoke, all eyes on Tally. Haru's parents were pressed close to each other, and his Urusar was standing, one fist clenched. The Awi was glancing between Tally's parents, who looked as confused as he felt, and Haru's clan. She finally turned to Tally, offering a *keirei*.

"Haru will stay in *dogeza* until you decide."

No, no, no, he didn't want Haru bowing and scraping to him. It was a simple misunderstanding. Tally cleared his throat so his deep voice would be soft instead of growly with the shock still running through him. "You had no way of knowing. Please. I'm not offended." *A little freaked out, yes, but not offended.* "It's not something anyone would have thought of."

The Urusar's fist unclenched and he returned to his seat like a man waiting for Tally to change his mind and erupt in anger. Yeah. That was what people expected from uktena. Dad had always told him to keep his anger close, never show it. Normal anger from anyone else would never be met with the fear a little annoyance from an uktena was.

Haru's parents relaxed marginally, again like people tensed for something bad, while Haru sat up slowly, his beautiful eyes red-rimmed and his mouth set. Tally couldn't have him upset like this. It was his own fault for being overly sensitive. Of course they ate eel in Japan. He knew that, and they were otters for Gods' sakes. Stupid, stupid, stupid.

"May I help you back to your cushion?" Tally offered a hand, shocked when Haru accepted it, sliding his slender fingers into Tally's. Better. Oh, so much better. Haru had touched him.

While he slipped the cushion back to its proper place and helped Haru settle again, the Awi Tamgradat gestured to both sets of parents. Dad pulled a beautiful stationery envelope out of his breast pocket and Mr. Tanaka produced an equally elegant one. The envelopes passed through several hands along the table as the fathers exchanged contracts, and though they knew, the moms knew, and Tally knew exactly what they said, they still went through the ceremony of getting out reading glasses and perusing the documents.

The Awi produced equally elegant pens, black and gold, which she handed to the fathers who both signed and relinquished the documents to the mothers, who repeated the steps, with perhaps a little less serious bravado. Next, they went to the Akaike Urusar, who also gave them a thorough perusal even though he had written most of the language. Tally would sign as both groom and Urusar for his clan, unusual but necessary in this case. When all the parents and Haru's Urusar had signed, the Awi brought documents and pen to place in front of Tally.

He glanced at Haru, still tight-lipped and obviously unhappy, so he set the documents between them so they could both read. Tally knew every word. Negotiations had gone smoothly, but he'd been careful not to let anything fall through the cracks. Still, he read for formality's sake and signed where it indicated for both himself as groom and himself as head of village.

Haru had edged closer through this process, nearly leaning against Tally's shoulder. He finally asked so quietly Tally wasn't sure anyone else heard, "Where do I sign?"

Tally's stomach dropped. There was no place for Haru to sign, of course. The bride-son never did. They were being bartered away. But he didn't want Haru to think of himself as property. Yes, the deals were necessary, but this wasn't about the deal for Tally.

His jaw felt like it might crack he had his teeth clenched so tightly at his little act of rebellion, but he wrote Haru's name under his own and drew a careful line beside it on both documents.

He pointed to his unorthodox solution and offered Haru the pen. "You sign right there."

* * * *

The garden *was* lovely. It made the evening more bearable, looking at the carefully curated plants rather than their Xatiba, their fiancé. A burn hit Haru's mouth but they swallowed it back. They would behave. They would. Haru understood their place in all this farce.

Whether they liked it or not.

Like a good Satislit, Haru looped their arm under Tally's and placed their hand lightly on their fiancé's offered arm. They had hoped the feminine manner in which they had dressed themself for the dinner would be a turnoff for their betrothed, but somehow it wasn't. Seemed like Tally didn't care what Haru looked like. Masculine or feminine. Normally Haru would be thrilled about someone not caring. Too bad it had to be a match. But then the humongous uktena had barely balked at the engagement gift, forging ahead with the dinner and the contract, cementing them in a match. All because Tally *felt* it was fated.

Now didn't that cut? Haru taking a walk with a *match*, their Awi Tamgradat a respectful distance behind them, supervising so there wasn't any impropriety. It stung. The whole event was Haru's worst nightmare rolled into a perfect package of respectability and decorum.

Rage and humiliation clouded Haru's mind in a heavy fog. A tremor still shook their body from the confrontation at the dinner.

Banishment.

Akaike-san hadn't needed to threaten *banishment*. It had been wholly unnecessary. One step too far. Overkill. Unlike the harsh words Akaike-san threw at them accused, Haru knew their duty. Had been raised reciting their duty to the clan since they had been old enough to practice serving everyone tea. How their Urusar could even consider ripping Haru away from their fellow lijun, they didn't know. Mostly.

It was a good proposal. Really good. Highly beneficial to the clan, without a doubt. Haru had been shocked by how much the Bastilles were willing to pay and concede for them. But otters were sociable creatures, needed companionship. Ostracizing Haru for rejecting the match would've been cruel. But they hadn't turned the match down. Not really. Just voiced their...*displeasure* about being sold off. And hoped. They had hoped Tally had enough intelligence to realize he was wrong about the destined match idea being Em'halafi and call it off.

If Haru was honest with themself, they'd known since before the Imsi Tamgradat, they'd known they would fulfill their duty since *Otōusan* told them about the dinner. Haru had seen the determination in Father's eyes when he'd told them not to screw it up. Not only did the clan's honor rest on this match, but the family's. Anger kept Haru in denial about how much choice they really had.

Even after Tally had surprised them by drawing a line for them to sign on the contract, Haru knew they would sign regardless of how they felt. The gesture their fiancé made was a token display, nothing more. There was no legality to Haru's signature. His parents had taken it seriously enough, though. Haru had never seen *Otōusan* move so fast.

The way Father placed his heavy hand on Haru's shoulder, leaning over them to make sure they signed. They had—using a highly stylized Western script of their name and their stamp.

The unexpected smile from Tally when Haru signed, the flush of their fiancé's cheeks, had disturbed them. What exactly was wrong with the uktena? No sane person would want a marriage that started with subtle threats of death. Well, mostly subtle.

Haru stole a glance.

The cough from behind Haru reminded them the Awi was watching closely. Listening. Haru bit back a scream. They had already been sold, the life they'd built for themself ripped from underneath them just because Tally *felt* an Em'halafi connection. No more students. No more potato cannons and egg drops from the school roof.

Someone needed to learn hormones were stupid.

Beside them, the extra-large, how did he get that big, uktena cleared his throat. "So, ah. My house backs up to a lake. It's a little cold most of the year, but do you like kayaking?" An all too obvious cringe followed the question.

Haru paused, halting their walk. "Excuse me?"

"Kayak? Canoes? Boats of any sort?" Tally's hard swallow was probably audible several feet away. "I'd be happy to supply whatever sort you like best?"

So Tally planned to buy Haru's affection like their body? They frowned. "I have my own kayak. It is a little old, but I am used to it."

"Oh, that's perfect!" Tally's smile blossomed, then died just as quickly. "We'll have it shipped over. I've had mine since high school. Good to have familiar things." He flushed and shook his head. "I'm babbling.

Sorry. This is probably a little... You can ask me anything? Anything at all."

The Awi coughed.

Haru held in a more sharply worded question. Banishment. They had to remember they could still be banished by their Urusar until the marriage, or after, if they got sent back.

"What is your favorite color?" There, they could be polite, falling back on the proper etiquette questions.

Tally's shoulders slumped. "I, um, blue, I suppose. I've always thought picking a color was an odd thing to do, though. Colors are great. Why pick one? And...babbling again."

"Nervous about the wedding?" *Maybe he'll get cold feet.* Though Haru agreed on the ridiculousness of picking one color, not that they'd admit it to Tally. "Then—"

The Awi coughed again.

"Then should I pick out a rainbow kimono? Or blue? Which would please you?"

"Either would be great." Tally's smile was softer now, less of a nervous rictus. "But you wear whatever you want for the wedding. I'm happy with formal, with not, barefoot. However you'd like." He leaned closer and lowered his voice. "She really needs to do something about that cough."

"She does." Haru looked over their shoulder. Sorely tempted to stick out their tongue, they covered it up with a smile, turning its wattage on Tally. Weird Americans. Why did they like smiling? "So you plan on making no decisions for our wedding? I have free rein?"

One black eyebrow arched at them. "We'll do this together, don't you think? But I'm not running roughshod over anything you've set your heart on."

Damn asshole was trying so hard to be a gentleman. *Jerk.*

"As far as free rein, I would like to stipulate, yes, within reason. I'd rather not ride a horse into the ceremony or skydive to it."

"I see. So we are the traditional type then," Haru responded coolly and got them moving again. They shouldn't have been surprised. Tally had checked off every box for traditions this evening thus far.

"Ha. I'm not sure tradition applies to an uktena Urusar."

"Fair enough. I always imagined I would have a Japanese lijun wedding, though I am marrying into an American one?"

"If you'd like a Japanese lijun wedding, that's what we'll do. I'll need your guidance."

So damn polite. Haru hated him for it. For being so accepting of this farce. For wanting someone, Haru, because of fate. No one was that nice to a stranger without wanting something in return. Haru just hoped it wasn't too late for them when they figured out what it was.

"No, at least, there should be some of both, since the clans are creating an alliance."

"Yes, we can help each other figure out the details."

"I want Kaho-chan as a flower girl." Haru didn't know they wanted it so badly until the words popped out. Might as well see how far they could push their Xabita before reprisal.

"The little tanuki girl?" The corners of Tally's eyes crinkled as his smile grew. "Of course. I like her."

Angel Martinez & Freddy MacKay

"You know Kaho-chan?"

"Yes. One of my best shirts shared chocolate icing with her dress."

So Tally had been at the raid at some point. *Wait.* Haru stopped short. "What happened to her dress?"

"From what I gather, she climbed Mt. Cake during the Great Dessert Siege. She was more icing than little girl when I took her back to her parents."

They named the dessert raid? Who named it? Oh no. Not good. Haru had heard whispers over the past few days, but they hadn't connected it with their playful prank opening night. The pool was one thing, but the cake? That had been for the GLA. When Haru spoke, their voice sounded farther away — *higher.*

"Are you saying Kaho-chan swam in the large, very expensive, specially made chocolate cake for the lijun delegation?"

"Pretty much. And you told me it was a re-enactment of the Siege of Inabayama Castle. I'm sorry. I'm upsetting you…"

"They will never let her come. No wonder her mother would not let me say hello the last few days." The idea of not seeing their little tanuki again broke off another piece of Haru's battered heart. "I — " Haru breathed in deeply. Their voice cracked, and they hated that Tally was seeing them like this. They had to get themself under control. But Haru had loved the little mischief-maker since they'd hidden together under a staircase at the Biannual Japanese Lijun Conference last spring, pranking passersby. Kaho made a rather impressive ghost. "If you could persuade them to let her come, I would be in your debt. Or at least, talk them into letting me say goodbye."

Tally's soft smile had vanished, replaced by a hard expression, his jaw turned to stone. "It was just a cake. And tanuki parents should know better. There, you've given me a crusade. Kaho will come to the wedding."

The Awi Tamgradat didn't quite manage to stifle her groan, and Haru knew they'd be eating crow for months, but it'd be worth it. There were few people Haru would genuinely miss besides their students. Kaho was one of them. Her unfettered joy and exploration of the world weren't meant to be squashed. If they had to say goodbye to their life here in Japan, then at least they wanted the chance to do it with someone who loved them back.

Haru dropped to their knees, moving with practiced ease into *saikeriei*. They really did get into trouble too often, didn't they? "*Suminasen*, Urusar Bastille."

Above him, Tally hissed. "Please don't do that. Please. I'm just a businessman with a fancy title. Haru, please…"

Haru refused to look up. They knew if they did Tally would see their anger. Instead they pressed their head against the ground harder. If they had to marry, they'd be damned if their clan could call them out on inappropriate behavior again. Haru would be the perfect Satislit, then the perfect Uruma if it killed them, but it didn't mean they had to give their heart to Tally.

"*Doumo arigatou gozaimasu*, Urusar Bastille."

"Haru." Tally's whisper cracked and wavered as he leaned down to offer a hand. "It's all right. You're welcome. Whatever I'm expected to say here. Just please get up."

The Awi's feet came into view out of the corner of Haru's vision. They didn't move. She wouldn't be able to fault them for their behavior. The Awi couldn't report to their former Urusar about any breeches in etiquette. The traditional betrothal walk had been a success. Their new Urusar had offered to provide for Haru's wishes. They'd get a Japanese wedding, and Haru suspected Tally would succeed in getting Kaho's parents to attend too. The Akaike clan would be able to celebrate in its new fortune.

A few hurried sentences were hissed over Haru's head.

A gasp from Tally nearly made Haru break *saikeirei* to see what had been so surprising. Only their training had kicked in and kept them from committing the faux pas. Curiosity burbled up, leaving Haru to wonder why their Xatiba sounded so scandalized. If Tally wanted a Satislit for his match, then Haru would make sure he got exactly what he paid for.

"He's a person," Tally hissed, the first sign of any strong emotion from him. "Not...not chattel!"

"You must tell him," the Awi insisted, louder than her whispered explanation moments before. "Do not shame him further. This is what a Satislit is!"

"Gods' sakes." Obvious frustration colored the growl. "Not in my country, it's not."

Haru very much doubted Tally's claim. They'd read the contract. Money. Kwebabiad—multiple birth carriers for both clans no less. Housing. A return fee. And many more stipulations and exchanges that made Haru nauseous. Their clan might be traditional, but only one just as steeped in tradition would agree to such a deal. It was hard not to shout at their Urusar. Either of them. To call Tally on his bullshit. All Tally offered were pretty words. What he'd taken was Haru, in a contract, a match, all because he thought it was his right. Haru shook with the effort to keep all their fury in.

An explosive word came from Tally. It might have been a curse, but it wasn't in any language Haru recognized. Finally, in a voice rimmed with frost, Tally said, "Your gratitude pleases me. Up. Now."

Haru offered their hand, keeping their head down, eyes cast on the ground. Tally's large hand wrapped theirs, then moved to their elbow as he lifted Haru with ease. Their bodies were close enough to feel the coolness Tally radiated.

"It is my hope to please you, Urusar Bastille. Thank you for your praise."

Chapter Four

Guess Who's Coming to Dinner?

"Mom!" Tally gripped the edges of his dresser with both hands.

"Don't bellow, sweetie." Mom hurried into his bedroom, heels tapping on the hardwood. "Unless you're bleeding or dying."

"Maybe I'm dying? I can't get this tie straight."

Mom's mouth twisted as if she was trying far too hard to hold in a laugh. "Here. Stand up straight. Okay, not that straight, now I can't reach. I haven't done your tie for you since high school."

"I just want everything to be perfect. It wasn't. Perfect. In Tokyo. I don't know. I did *something*. I had to have." Tally heaved a long breath, trying to steady himself. "It was like Haru had never met me before the Imsi Tamgradat."

"Tal-tsu'tsa." Mom knotted his tie with practiced efficiency. "He was probably nervous and surrounded by eyes who were waiting for him to step wrong. I felt like any second someone was going to pounce on him. It made *me* nervous."

I want to love…and be loved. Haru had looked straight into his eyes with such longing, such need and said those words, and that's exactly what Tally intended, no matter what ideas Haru's family had put in his head. Not that he had any clear understanding of what those ideas were.

He'd managed not to stalk off after the scene in the garden, though he'd been furious. It had been a close thing. Anger had roiled in his stomach over Haru feeling an obligation to bow and scrape to him. That the Awi *encouraged* it. He'd wanted to flatten her, and wouldn't that have looked great? A six-foot-nine American decking a tiny Japanese woman.

Instead, he'd finished the appropriate social functions as expected that night, said his soft farewells to Haru and traveled back home the next day to prepare for his Satislit's arrival. Which would be perfect. Everything would be perfect. Mom and Dad had moved to the garden cottage on the other side of the property to complete their retirement. Tally had pulled in a decorator friend to redo their suite in the main house with bolder colors and more Asian-inspired furniture. He wasn't trying to recreate Tokyo, but a lower bed, more floor cushions, that sort of thing. He'd thought about remodeling the bath, too, but a week just wasn't enough time.

Little presents dotted the suite, chocolates and ginger candies, small electronics and clothes in some of the drawers. Wisconsin cold would be a new kind of cold for Haru, so some of the presents were necessities.

Dad drove to the airport. Tally would've crashed the car, he was certain. Then only standing in the international arrivals area remained, stalking the flight on his phone, shifting from foot to foot so he wouldn't pace. Mom finally made him give her the phone.

Passengers from what he believed to be Haru's flight started to trickle through and, even though Tally's view was better than anyone else in the room, he still craned his head this way and that for that first look.

There. Oh, there he is. Haru came through from customs, his face drawn and serious, his coat over his arm. Tally barely registered his mother and father with him, or the young woman, Misaki, who would be Tally's kwebabiad, his birth-carrier. All he could see was Haru, that beautiful face, those fathoms-deep eyes. The soft *yukata* he wore was blue, Tally hoped that wasn't because he'd said he liked blue, and Haru's hair was caught up in a ponytail. Tally appreciated that. Nothing worse than getting long hair yanked by luggage straps when one traveled.

He raised a hand to wave, then thought better of it. That would probably seem too...something. Overeager. Puppyish. American. It wasn't as if he was tough to spot in a crowd. Haru raised his head, met his gaze and the spark of welcome recognition Tally had hoped for didn't register. Obviously exhausted, Haru simply looked resigned.

Wait...wait... Okay, now they'd cleared the partition. Tally strode forward with a smile that didn't show all his teeth. Nope. No ugly Americans here.

"Mr. Tanaka, good to see you again. Mrs. Tanaka." He returned the brief courtesy bows, though he didn't miss Haru's mom elbowing him forward. Swallowing his heart back down since it insisted on leaping into his throat, he took that last step forward and all words of greeting decided to go find a coffee shop. "Haru."

"Urusar Bastille." Haru bowed in a *futsurei* then straightened. One of his finely manicured hands rose, shaking slightly, as if offered in expectation. Tally took it. Haru turned his head to one side and volunteered his cheek. "I hope my appearance pleases."

Tally leaned in, Haru's hand still clasped in his, and placed a soft, chaste kiss on Haru's cheek. He firmly ignored the stab of pain that formal greeting delivered, keeping his mother's words firmly in mind. *His parents are here. We're in formal mode still.* "Of course it does. It's good to see you. Was it a good flight?"

"A little long, but yes. Thank you for the first-class seats. I have never been so comfortable."

"Trans-Pacific flights in coach are tough. I didn't want you to go through that." *Um. What now? Right.* "Dad and I will get the luggage. You go ahead with Mom to the car. You must all be tired."

He reached for Haru's carry-on, the little drawstring pouch he should recall the name of but didn't, and was pleased when he was allowed to take it and the handle of Haru's rolling suitcase. Haru's lips twitched — making Tally notice there was a glossy red sheen to them — and his eyebrows drew together. Instead of following Mom, he fell into step behind Tally. The positioning felt odd, making the spot between his shoulders itch. Tally shuffled next to Haru and offered his elbow. He hoped the gesture was appropriate. Relief and a spark of triumph lit in his chest when Haru immediately took hold of it.

Dad, always thinking ahead, had already found a luggage cart for the rest and was loading up the suitcases with Mr. Tanaka's help. They had jengafied the baggage, the end result a tower of imposing height. Mom would have a fit when she saw it. Seriously. It was like they had to prove all of it could fit on one cart instead of getting a second one.

Good thing she'd gone ahead with Misaki and Mrs. Tanaka.

"Nothing planned for today." Tally split his attention between Haru and Mr. Tanaka. "The time change isn't easy, so just resting on the agenda. We'll have a proper welcome dinner tomorrow."

"Oh, thank you. Is there something I can help prepare for the dinner?"

Tally hoped he hid the wince as visions of snake wine and eels danced in his head. "Ah. Well. You might want to check with Addy when we get there? The kitchen gets a little chaotic when all my sisters are here, but I'm sure she'd appreciate an extra set of hands."

Haru was quiet for a moment, then said, "I can do flower arrangements? If it would please you."

"That sounds perfect." Not something he'd thought of. *Damn it. Flowers.* He could order some. He'd have to remember to call over to Petals and Thyme later.

"Good." Tension in Haru's shoulders bled out, and he no longer stood so stiffly as they walked side by side.

Maybe giving him something to do helps? Tally had to keep that in mind. Except for small murmurings here and there, most of the remaining walk to the car was in silence. They really must have been exhausted.

Back at the house, Tally went into full host mode, showing everyone to their rooms and carrying bags to the appropriate places. He'd hoped to have a minute or two alone with Haru, but no, Mr. and Mrs. Tanaka followed them to Haru's suite where they proceeded to poke about and chatter about this and that too fast for Tally to follow any of it. He hadn't realized previously how truly terrible his Japanese was.

He just hoped his in-laws weren't being too critical of his preparations.

Haru pulled open a few drawers, exploring the dresser, when he exclaimed in surprise. He pulled out the warm green corduroy pants Tally had hidden and turned to face him. The warm, open, excited expression he wore reminded Tally of the Haru he remembered from the Great Dessert Siege.

"I can wear trousers?"

For a moment, Tally was certain he'd swallowed his tongue and was about to die choking on it. "Yes. Especially in the winter. It just gets too cold here. Everyone wears pants when winter really hits. Whatever you're comfortable in, but we're pretty casual here normally."

"As you wish." Haru hugged the cords close. His mother looked them over with a critical eye, whispering something Tally couldn't pick up. Haru sighed and put the pants back in the dresser. "I *do* enjoy my *yukata*. The trousers will be for outside. Thank you."

But you were wearing pants when I met you. With rainbow suspenders. Tally wanted to yank Haru away and actually talk to him. But that wouldn't be proper. He was drowning in proper.

"Would it be all right to get refreshed?" Haru asked. "Yes?"

Haru's parents both cocked their heads, eyeing their son. Tally wanted to ask what they were so suspicious of, but figured if he was able to get them out of Haru's suite that he could count it as a win.

"We were going to serve some drinks and offer a light meal before everyone settled in for the night." Tally offered his arm to Mrs. Tanaka, who cooed over the attention. "Shall we?"

"Yes, please," she answered.

As they left, both Mr. Tanaka and Mrs. Tanaka shot a glance toward Haru, but they allowed Tally to lead them into the family room. His sisters and mom were already setting up a drink tray and snacks. He made sure both sets of parents were engrossed in conversation about current wedding trends before he stole away.

The shower wasn't running when Tally snuck back into the suite. It felt silly — *sneaking*. They were grown adults, but Tally supposed it was the only way since the Akaike clan was so mired in tradition. He settled onto the chair by the bed to wait, and silently sent up a prayer to the Gods he'd be able to show Haru things were different in Wadiswan, Wisconsin. There was no reason to stand on formality unless it was clan business. Though he supposed it might take some time.

Tally wanted the free-spirit otter who took children on a raid, terrorizing hotel staff. Maybe not *his* staff, but Tally knew there was more to his Em'halafi than what Haru had presented to him since the betrothal dinner. Unadulterated energy had oozed from every pore when Haru had led his little regiment on their raid. Protectiveness when he'd placed himself between the kids and Tally. When Haru had watched Kaho drown herself in cake, pure affection had filled his eyes and his smile.

What did Tally need to do to get that Haru back?

A loud splash had Tally up and moving toward the bathroom. He moved his hair behind his ear, wishing he had taken the time to braid it, then pressed against the door. Several more loud thunks made concern win over propriety. Last thing he wanted was a drowned Satislit.

"Haru?"

Another thunk.

Tally checked the knob, relieved when it turned, and opened the door. "Haru? Are you—oh my Gods. You are adorable!"

"*Chep!*"

An otter stood on his hind legs at the edge of the tub. In his paws he held a large stone. His tail stuck out behind him, Haru using it to help steady himself upright. Those deep, dark eyes Tally had fallen in love with stared back at him. Haru's nose twitched. His tiny chest rose and fell rapidly. Chances were Haru's otter sensed Tally's serpent.

This hadn't been what Tally expected when Haru asked to get refreshed.

"I mean, hi." Tally scooted inside the bathroom and closed the door. Wrong move.

Haru slowly went down to all fours then chucked the stone. Tally winced as the rock clattered against the tiles. Hopefully nothing was damaged. Or at least, couldn't be fixed. It didn't look like anything was chipped.

When he stepped closer, hands open, Tally noticed the bottom of the tub was covered with stones. All shapes and sizes. A little armada of rocks. "Oh, so, yeah. It's okay. Go ahead."

Instead, Haru's back hunched and he backed away from the bath.

Tally sat on the edge, hoping if he looked smaller it would make him appear less threatening, and picked up the stone. He juggled it between his hands. It was smooth and cool to the touch. So Haru had carried stones from Japan to Wisconsin with him? For a bath? Did Haru think he was in trouble for using them without permission? Tally wanted to ask why they were so important—he had a lot of questions, but he didn't think he would get an answer right now, especially since Haru wasn't changing back to his human half. Just then a warm heat pressed against his side, Tally's own worry-stone heavy in his jacket pocket.

Maybe he could find some common ground?

With slow, careful movements, Tally put Haru's stone into the bath. A prickle of awareness flickered through him. He knew Haru was watching, watching closely. His little paws flexed and retracted, scratching the bath mat. *Replaceable.* All of it, except for Haru. Tally only got one destined match.

"I like stones," Tally offered. "Maybe I can get my architect to draw up some designs? With the stones? I wanted to get the bathroom redone, but didn't have the time. But I guess you might have something specific you want?"

The otter sneezed.

"*Gesundheit.*"

Haru backed against the sink cabinet.

"I have a stone."

The otter's ears flicked. The only acknowledgment Tally got.

"My mom gave it to me."

Tally searched his suit pocket, his fingers hitting the surface and his hand wrapping around the stone out of habit. He opened his palm to Haru. The stone glistened under the lights, he'd turned it over so many times.

"It's a worry stone. Our Shafa made it for me when I was in high school." When Tally's hormones sometimes got the better of him. When he worried over making the wrong choice, making mistakes, always so anxious about mistakes. "The Shafa still cleanses it for me, even after all these years. Just had it spelled right after I came back from the conference."

Haru had crept closer, his nose level with Tally's fingertips. His dark eyes zeroed in on the stone. A paw came up, lightning quick, but it froze just as quickly.

"It's okay."

In fact, if Haru wanted it, he could have it.

"You can touch it."

The paw snatched the stone away and Haru scurried back to the sink cabinet. The otter sniffed the stone, then bit it, sniffed it again, then tumbled it between his paws. As the stone moved from one paw to another, the rigid stance Haru carried relaxed. Tally breathed a sigh of relief. He didn't want his destined match to be scared of his uktena. The dual spirits within him couldn't be separated.

A *churr* brought Tally's attention back to Haru. His otter scooted back toward the bath, the stone captured in his mouth, between his front teeth. Two shining black eyes were locked on Tally. He tried to sit easy, show he wasn't a threat.

Haru sneezed again, edging to the side opposite Tally.

"*Gesundheit.*"

The otter lifted up, standing on his hind legs, one paw on the tub. His claws flexed out then relaxed. Haru grabbed the edge and hauled himself into the tub, slipping into the water almost soundlessly. His lithe body twisted and turned in the small confines of the bath. The top of his head surfaced and he shot toward Tally, a V forming in the waves. At the last second he turned, flipping, and splashing Tally. Not a lot, but enough to get him a little wet.

Tally laughed, then noticed Haru had dived to the bottom where his rocks were. He had placed Tally's worry stone between a couple of his more colorful rocks. His paws patted the spot a few times, then used a claw to pop it out, before Haru packed it back carefully.

It was picture perfect. Haru was perfect. They could make this work. Tally felt it in his bones. In the way his heart squeezed when he saw how carefully Haru treated the gift from Mom.

* * * *

"The flowers are—" Tally looked at his sisters. "Are beautiful. Quite dramatic, don't you think?"

Addy laughed. "Dramatic works. I'm amazed Haru could work with flowers that big. Seriously. Those dahlias are monsters. And that fern has to be at least two and a half feet tall."

"Too much?"

Three identical blasé expressions stared back at him. *So that's a yes.*

"Is that a snake?" Nan asked, her arms crossed. She leaned in to examine the largest arrangement at the center of the table.

"Yeah."

"Don't they know we're serpents?"

"It's been explained."

There was a slight difference, nothing big enough that it hurt biological relations between species.

"Is that an otter?" Lahi asked, frowning. She pushed in as well, her earrings jangling as she tussled with Nan.

"Yeah, I think so." Tally loved his sisters. He did. When he'd decided to make sure Haru had stones for his flower arrangements, this wasn't what he'd had in mind. He'd been hoping no one would notice. However, the displays were bigger than life.

"What is the snake *doing* to the otter?" Lahi asked in a startled hush.

"Hugging it!"

They all jumped, surprised by Haru's sudden presence and announcement.

Lahi's eyebrow shot up. "Hugging?"

More like squeezing to death.

Haru nodded, smiling, and Tally lost himself as his Satislit began to explain the flower arrangements with an eager tone evident in his voice. The same tone he used when he'd explained it to Tally earlier, making it impossible to tell him it looked like the snake was killing the otter. Slowly. Painfully.

Oh, that mouth. That beautiful mouth had been done up. Tally found seeing Haru dressed up for him did things he couldn't quite parse out, but he liked it. He could acknowledge that much. A deep purple lipstick offset the rest of Haru's makeup perfectly. The pale violet on his eyelids complemented the silver he used for eyeliner. Several gemstones were placed around his eyes. Did he have matching stones on his nail? Oh, Gods, Haru did. Tally gulped. His otter wore a deep purple kimono, accented with bright pink cherry petals as a design element, and a turquoise obi. His black hair was half up and half down. The white jade hairpiece Tally had left on the bathroom sink finished the do. Tally was so fascinated by the whole display he almost missed what his Satislit said next.

"To show happiness between the two clans. For our marriage."

"Happiness?" Addy echoed, gesturing to the stone display.

"Yes."

Tally glared over Haru's head at his three sisters. They could not screw this up for him. He wouldn't allow it. Not when the in-laws were due to show up any minute with the Kwebabiads. He did not want Haru to freeze and go all proper on him. Not when Tally hadn't gotten a chance to see him — alone — since slipping out of the bathroom before they'd had dinner yesterday. Luckily his sisters spoke in desperation, words tumbling over one another.

"It is gorgeous."

"Definitely something special."

"A true display of unique artistry."

Haru offered an eshaku, beaming, before whispering, "Thank you."

He turned to the table, not catching the wide-eyed expressions Tally's sisters cast to him before crowding around Haru, talking excitedly over the table arrangements. Hopefully his brothers would catch on quickly when they finally arrived.

Nan elbowed him on her way back to the kitchen. Addy patted his arm in that way she had that was half sympathy, half *you did this to yourself.* Lahi opened her mouth to say something, but was interrupted by loud voices from the front hall. Their brothers had arrived.

They were tussling, still half in their coats, when they burst into the dining room. Though Nan and Lahi were the youngest in the family, no one ever guessed that by the way their two knucklehead brothers acted. Both unmarried, both unsettled despite their careers, they still lived like they were in college. They finally stopped mock wrestling long enough to notice other people were in the room.

"Hey, Tal! Hey, Lahi!" Che beamed at them, not the least bit aware of possible impropriety in front of a guest. "And that's Haru, right? Hey, Haru!"

"Dude," Hal drew out the word as he approached the table. "Why's there a snake killing a weasel?"

Tally managed not to bury his face in his hands, no matter how hard he wanted to. "Otter. Snake is hugging. Go see if Addy and Nan need help with something heavy in the kitchen."

Che rolled his eyes. "The great and powerful Urusar has spoken. Come on, Hal, before we get assigned something worse to do."

"Do that." Gods, he hoped Addy found something to keep them out of trouble. Nan was the chef in the family—had landed a sous chef position at the highest-end restaurant in the family resorts because of skill rather than nepotism—but Addy, who managed the hotel side, was the organizational queen.

Tally risked a quick glance over at Haru, who appeared to have turned into an ice sculpture, frozen solid, eyes wide, fingers trying to bury into the back of one of the oak dining room chairs. *I will kill my brothers. No. Killing would be too quick.*

"They, ah..." Tally cleared his throat once his brothers had cleared the room. "They're a bit young for their age still."

Haru turned to Tally and dipped his head. Those purple lips were pressed together hard.

"Lahi, maybe Haru would like to see your guitar. You did bring one, didn't you?" Tally's voice sounded desperate inside his head. He hoped it didn't translate that way on the outside.

"What kind of question is that?" Lahi tossed her head, earrings chiming. "Of course I'm not coming over without one of my babies. Come on, Haru. This one's a Taylor. Spruce and rosewood. Even if you're not into guitars, it's a very pretty one."

If Haru had been in otter shape, his ears probably would've swiveled in interest. He offered Tally a bow and followed Lahi out to the front room. *Good. Good.* Tally let out a long breath, hoping his family wouldn't scandalize Haru too much more that day.

Yeah. Sure. Who was he kidding?

The doorbell rang and it took Tally several anxious seconds before he remembered this was his house now and he'd better go see who it was. Haru's parents couldn't be back with Misaki yet. Mom had promised to rest and come over closer to dinner. A delivery he'd forgotten? Entirely possible the way his brain was short-circuiting these days...

Tally opened the door and had to lower his gaze a considerable distance before he spotted his visitor. "Sam. Hey."

"Hi, Tally." She squeezed past him into the house, since Tally had forgotten to step back and clear the doorway. "I *am* supposed to be here for dinner, right? Kwebabiad meet and greet? Or was I supposed to come later?"

"No, no. Dinner. Yes." Tally scrubbed both hands over his face. "I'm sorry. Just a little distracted today."

"Things not going according to plan?"

"Not...well, mostly. Sort of." Tally jerked his head toward the interior of the house. "Come on, you should meet Haru while things are more or less calm."

"You and your sibs have scared the poor Tokyo otter, haven't you?" Blue eyes narrowed at him. "Lead on, Mr. Distracted Urusar. I'll try to fix whatever you've broken."

* * * *

The guitar was beautiful, just as Lahi had said. It wasn't Haru's instrument, but she let them try a few plucks and chords. Lovely tone. It had a calm sound they appreciated. Lahi — and Haru had studied the family tree thoroughly, so they knew it was short for Galilahi — was just as maddeningly American as the rest of Tally's family. Too physically intrusive, too familiar. Weirdo, just like the others, but not as weird as Tally. At least she wasn't as loud as some of the other siblings. The boys... Haru shook their head. They tumbled together like rocks beating against the shore.

But none of them were the problem. Haru's problem was their Xabita. The humongous psychopath. Haru strummed the strings again, smiling at the luminous sound. Too bad their fiancé wasn't as easy to handle as the guitar.

The man infuriated Haru. Any attempt to insult him slid off as if he'd mentally greased himself. Haru needed to know where the danger points were, how far they could push, and how were they supposed to figure that out if Tally never reacted? Though he had reacted the once to Haru's painfully proper show of submission. Haru wasn't certain what part of that had made him angry.

Maybe this last attempt, showing themself being squeezed to death in imitation of how this match made them feel...maybe the image pleased Tally. That wasn't a happy thought at all. Their friends back home had been horrified, even afraid for them.

Don't ever look at him when he's sleeping, it's certain death.

If he Sahnkes to serpent and breathes anywhere near you, you're going to die.

Uktena eat any mates who aren't also uktena. Everyone knows that.

Old fisherwife tales. Stories to scare kids with. Haru didn't believe any of that. *Mostly.* There were a couple times Tally's tone had sent unwelcome fear riveting through Haru's belly. They checked their finger positioning and played a minor chord, amused by how they could imitate how they felt with the guitar. Should they take lessons? If their mother found out Tally liked listening to guitars, she'd insist on it before the wedding. Haru cringed. That would be a short learning curve.

Haru did not want to ignite their mother's fury, or get on the Bastille clan's bad side. Not really. They'd have to live with these people—if they couldn't get the wedding called off. They still clung to a small piece of hope that Tally would forget the idea of destined matches, though it did not seem likely. The slip in the bathroom yesterday, getting caught off guard in their otter form, had only served to make Tally more determined.

The infamous uktena anger hadn't surfaced yet. Haru kept poking and it was nowhere to be seen. Tally might have been a wealthy, entitled jerk, but he wasn't a killer. *Probably.* He didn't seem to have any stomach for violence, if the reaction to the snake wine was an indicator. That *had* been an epic moment. His face…

Best thing Haru had seen in years. The struggle had been real for Tally. For one glorious moment, Haru had thought he would call off the wedding agreement.

Of course it hadn't been. Now they would live in Wisconsin. The cheese state. That snowed. Lots of snow. Beer seemed to be in abundance as well. Not Haru's preferred drink. Sake really was their true love. Hopefully they would be allowed to have it.

Haru blinked, then checked their hands. Lahi had been talking, adjusting their fingers, but they'd missed several sentences. An apology was on their lips when the object of their frustration strode in with a bright smile — interrupting with the most startling news of the evening.

"Sam, this is Haru Tanaka." Tally indicated them with a flourish. Sure. Show off the prize. "Haru, this is Samantha Weber, your Kwebabiad."

The moment her scent hit them, all their species instincts kicked in, and Haru had to quell the urge to wriggle in their seat. *Otter, otter, otter*, their senses screamed, poking at them to shift, to run and engage in new otter greetings, to find water and play. They pushed the urges down because Satislit etiquette said to greet her with due respect. She would mother their children, carry their pups for nine months then hand them over. They offered her a *futsurei*.

Sam gave them a wink and a proper *eshaku*. "Good to meet the man I'll be making babies with."

Haru nearly dropped Lahi's guitar — saving it by inches. Were all Americans so gauche?

"Sorry, maybe that was rude." Sam dropped into a nearby chair, her smile saying she wasn't sorry in any remote way. "We've just met. Tally, be a dear and run along now. Haru and I should talk."

The mountain of Haru's fiancé gaped, glancing between them. Then, to Haru's absolute astonishment, Tally left. Lahi carefully gathered up her guitar, made some excuse about needing to help in the kitchen and followed him with a less wounded expression.

Haru moved about the front room in a nervous fit. Their hands wouldn't keep still, and they didn't have one of their stones. Tally's worry stone popped in their head, buried in the bath with their others. It had made them feel better. Maybe it shouldn't stay in the tub. The idea of Tally catching them with it made Haru toss the thought aside. They had no intention of giving off any more mixed signals after last night. Their otter had been too in control.

Out of the corner of their eye, they observed Sam as they fidgeted with the framed photos and other knick-knacks. Yes, they needed to size her up. They couldn't help it, just like they couldn't help repositioning the trinkets on the shelves as they pretended to clean up. Their lives would be intertwined by blood. Haru knew how their clan treated Kwebabiads, and while it wasn't cruel, it was not something Haru wished upon any woman.

Sam didn't act like a Kwebabiad. Not with how she sprawled herself out on the chair. She wore her hair in a bob, blonde highlights glittering under the lights, the whole cut accentuating her clear blue eyes. She wore a nice pair of dress slacks with a sleek modern top. She completed the look with chunky jewelry, amber set in silver. If they had met under different circumstances, Haru would've asked her out. Except they couldn't. They'd been sold. Haru held back a sigh and turned back to the pictures. No need to show her, or any of the Bastille clan, that kind of weakness.

All the pictures of Tally had him smiling happily with his crazy family. Christmas. Thanksgiving. Swimming. What were they doing in that one? Haru turned the photo. Nope, still didn't make sense. Sam's heavy gaze followed Haru around the room. Her legs swung, thumping against the bottom of the chair. Despite her easy dismissal of their Urusar, she hadn't given any more orders, forced a conversation. What did she want? Haru picked up another picture, all by itself on a large shelf, and nearly choked. It was of Tally and Sam, arms locked in a friendly manner.

When they turned to ask with the picture in hand, because how could an otter be so at ease with a lijun who was their natural predator, she was smiling.

"It's from when I signed on to be your Kwebabiad. Tally will probably have one of you and Misaki soon, and the four of us. He has this idea of starting his family shelf now that we're all here."

"Does he?"

"Yes."

"How did you two meet?"

"Tally and I met in middle school," Sam said. "Some boys thought it'd be fun to flip my skirt."

"And he rescued you?"

"No, he had to pull me off the pipsqueak who called me a bitch. Only one strong enough."

"Huh."

"Little rat bastard deserved the beating I gave him, no doubt, but I would've gotten in more trouble if Tally hadn't broken up the fight."

Haru didn't know what to say to her declaration. It was almost like Sam was bragging, but not? Instead, they decided to put the picture back on the shelf. Haru wanted to hate her on principle — that she was another custom forced onto them because of tradition. But…she was their Kwebabiad. They felt attracted to the style she presented, along the unusual mix of her personality. A bit alarming, for sure, but she also sounded like fun. The sparkle of mischief in her eyes said she knew how to play. Haru loathed the idea of not being good to her. Sam wasn't in any better position than they had been with this deal.

"Kicked Tally in the nuts in the process, too. Poor guy spent lunch in the nurse's office."

"You what?"

"I nailed him *good*. Poor baby thought he'd never have kids."

How could she be so…so matter-of-fact about attacking her future Urusar?

"Anyway, later Tally said it was his fault and he didn't want me to feel bad about the near-nut-crushing incident."

Crazy snake. That had to be it. Tally was certifiably insane. Had to be. The man *liked* to be hurt and humiliated. Haru was going about their subterfuge all wrong. Then again, Sam seemed odd as well. As were the siblings. Maybe it was just all Americans.

"Haru?"

"Yes, Kwebabiad Weber?"

"Please don't."

"I am sorry?" they replied. "I do not mean to offend."

Sam stood and crossed the front room. She got right in Haru's personal space, pushing in. They stepped back but all they got was wall. Sam trapped them. Her blue gaze searched theirs as one of her hands went to their biceps. Sam nosed right in, not giving a millimeter. Her woodsy smell filled their lungs. She smelled *good*. Like *outside* and *water*. *Earth*. Sam spent time as her otter, much more than Haru got to. Would they be allowed to play?

Their noses touched, sending a shiver through Haru. They couldn't stop returning the rub if they tried. They nosed, moving to their cheeks. She sniffed their ear and they returned the favor. They bumped foreheads as their hands went to each other's arms, creating a dance as they moved.

"Better, much better," Sam breathed.

Haru wanted to agree, but couldn't say as much. Instead they rubbed their noses together again. For the first time since they'd stepped in the serpent's den, they felt relaxed, safe, in pleasant company that wasn't going to eat them.

"It's Sam. No titles. No last names. You and me…" Sam pointed between them. "We have obligations, but it doesn't mean we have to be cold and distant about it. We'll have kids, Haru. *Otter* kids. And as much as Tally loves all the clan's kids, otter kids need otter grownups."

"They do." Haru had always wanted kids. To love them. Feel their warmth. Give love in return. They had just thought they'd get to do it with someone they cared about. Not a match. "But, do you even want to be my Kwebabiad? Are you—" *Doing this because you have to*? It'd kill them. "I do not want my pups to think they are not wanted."

"I get it." She linked arms with them and drew them back to the sofa, though she gave them space again when they sat so she could face them. "The clan asks for volunteers when we need Kwebabiads. When I heard Tally's Satislit would be an otter, when they showed me pictures, heck, yes, I volunteered. I want kids. I'm not really enthused about a marriage thing, relationships in general aren't something I do, but I want kids. And these would be my kids, your kids, Bastille kids, so they'd have more love than they know what to do with."

"He will not eat them?" *Well, fuck.* Did that just come out of their mouth?

Sam pressed her lips together hard and her face turned bright red. When she expelled a sputtering breath, Haru realized she was trying not to laugh. "I'm sorry. It's not funny. Um, someone's been telling you things, I'm guessing. No. Tally would never eat kids, any kids. He doesn't even eat a lot of meat."

"Good. That is good. Ah." Haru was going to burn into a cinder from embarrassment.

"Lots of people are still scared of uktena. So they spew lots of misinformation. But you're here with Tally, so I'm guessing you're not all bound up in all the old superstitions," she said with a pat to their leg and a bright smile.

No, just bound and sold by tradition. But at least one of Haru's fears had been assuaged. Their children would be loved. Haru leaned in, nosing Sam's ear. She'd take getting used to, but having Sam around would make Haru feel less alone. Someone else would understand otterisms.

"Thank you."

A throat cleared from the doorway. Tally stood, hands behind him, with his brows bunched together. Haru pulled away from Sam and put a respectable distance between them. A glow lit Tally's eyes, and Haru began to slip to the floor to apologize, but a firm hand took hold of their elbow. Sam gave them a frightening smile as she pulled them up, and escorted

Haru out of the front room, walking right past their Urusar.

"I like this one, Tally. And yes, I'm favoring him because otter."

"Good." Tally followed them out, walking *behind* them. "I was hoping."

That made no sense. None.

As they stepped into the formal dining room, the noise died. The sudden focus on them and Sam caused their chest to seize. Sam winked and gave their cheek a kiss before abandoning them over to Tally.

Traitor.

Tally stuck his arm out expectantly. Once again Haru was forced to bite back a sigh and made themself smile. They took the offered gesture and allowed themself to be led to the head of the table with their Xatiba.

Okaasan's eyes narrowed when Haru sat down before Tally, but she beamed when Tally kissed Haru's cheek before seating himself. The touch had been soft, hesitant almost. Haru swallowed hard.

The siblings were rushing the last dishes out to the table, a complicated dance during which Haru expected collisions, but got none. Chairs clattered as the last of the Bastilles sat down and began reaching for dishes. There was no decorum to the process, no serving of husbands, no younger siblings serving older. They just grabbed the nearest dish, plopped something on their plates and passed the serving dishes along to the next person. Haru sat in frozen horror and found that Tally had served them several dishes before they recovered.

Haru glanced over to their parents and Misaki, also in a state of shock. None of them had put a single serving of food on their plates. An expertly placed elbow to Tally's side made him glance down at Haru in confusion. Haru turned their gaze to their parents.

Tally cringed then cleared his throat. "Guys."

The siblings didn't stop, though, everyone chattering, moving food down the line. The look on *Otōusan's* face did not bode for good things.

A loud whistle broke the chaos, hurting Haru's ears, but it got everyone's attention. Tally's mother stood at the other end of the table, one hand down on the top, the other on her hip. She wasn't smiling. In fact, her not-smile was downright terrifying.

"We have guests," she said as she sat back down. "Let's pretend we have some manners, shall we?"

All the heads whipped in Tally's and Haru's direction.

Right then, more than anything else that had happened since the betrothal dinner, Haru saw their future. Fear struck deep within their core.

A haze settled over them as Haru said *itadakimasu* then began to serve Tally, Mother in turn serving Father. The Bastille clan watched for a few minutes in silence, then slowly began serving each other. Not in the proper way, but the table had settled.

"Your clan is rather enthusiastic, Haru," *Otōusan* said, the words numbing Haru further.

My clan.

Okaasan agreed. "Lots of energy. I imagine as Uruma you will be kept quite busy with your clan duties."

My clan.

Bastille-*okaasan* chuckled. "It will be nice to have some help. It wasn't fair Achak got to retire before me."

"Haru is lucky to have gotten such a wonderful match with your son," his mother answered. "We hope he will live up to your example."

"I think Tal got a good deal out of the match, too. They make such a handsome pair."

The world narrowed down into echoes. Haru knew they had replied, started giving the correct responses because their parents had relaxed, as much as they would, and were even cracking a smile here and there. Mother and Father had said, "Haru's clan." Their parents were already thinking of Haru in terms of a Bastille, not Akaike, cutting them off from home and family. Haru had known it was coming, it was expected, but it still blossomed into an ache. Tally protested loudly at more of his mother's teasing, but he also talked about how Haru would be filling in a missing part of the clan now that he was here. Bastard even took Haru's hand in his and smiled down at them, stealing a kiss — causing a squeal of excitement at the table.

All Haru could do was smile as their lips broke apart.

As they looked over the people gathered, talking, serving each other food in awkward fits and spurts — their *clan*. Haru's. Yes, they could've done much worse. At least Tally was close in age, seemingly jovial, and even they could admit that the uktena was handsome, but Haru wasn't *ready*. Not yet. Hadn't wanted a match. Love, they had wanted love. Not to be responsible for others. Or to be an Uruma. Not to have a clan, their *clan*. Theirs to take care of. Their heart seized momentarily, the ache making them rub at it until their heart started beating in a tachy rhythm again.

The only place that was home was here. There was no going back. Haru's duty was to Tally and the Bastille clan. Because, despite what Akaike-san thought, or their parents, Haru did understand their duty, and they would never, ever walk away from it.

Damn if that realization didn't cut worse.

Chapter Five

Explosive Desserts

"Oh, it's lovely." Addy held the champagne flute up to the light. The foot was a brilliant blue, one might even say sapphire, and the Sapphire Lake logo with its sinuous, intertwined S and L was etched in the same blue high on the bowl near the lip. The effect was both elegant and charming.

Tiny *oooohs* came from the edge of the desk, several dark little heads peeking over the top. The office brownies crept closer and sat in a circle to gaze up at the champagne flute. Spindly limbed and no taller than an average coffee mug, they'd moved in shortly after the resort had been completed. Years later, they were less skittish of Tally and the lijun staff, but still cautious.

"You may touch," Tally said to them in his softest voice. "But no carrying off the crystal."

"Never, Mr. Tally!" the oldest squeaked with indignation. "Just looking. Sparkly."

They had an understanding, one the brownies mostly adhered to. They chased away any mice or insects they found trying to get a foothold and the staff left out plates for them in the kitchen at night. Once in a while, they would take something — a sock, a hand towel, a spoon — but never enough that Tally begrudged them.

"It *is* sparkly," Addy agreed. "Really beautiful work."

"Don't let Herr Klug hear you say that or he'll double the price," Tally said with a smile. "He does good work, I won't deny that, but we can't let him think we're pushovers here."

Addy laughed and smacked his arm, something she could do in the privacy of her office but that she'd never stoop to in front of staff. "I see your wheels spinning. You want him contracted for our European properties."

"People would appreciate it for what it is there. Not that people can't here, but it would be more often overlooked." Tally tapped the shipping box with its samples. "But we'll start here and see how well they deliver internationally. How professional their estimates and staff are. How well they keep deadlines. If they impress me and, more importantly, you, we'll talk about expanding the contract. It's all yours. Lowball it but not so far that he'll be insulted. He's cagey, but Gerhard Klug is an artist, too."

"Thanks for trusting me with this, Tal." Addy replaced the glass carefully in its case.

"You above all others. He thought he could flirt with me." Tally kissed the top of her head. "You'll be much more ferocious than I would."

"You're just still trying to get on my good side because of that bill from Japan."

"True."

Addy laughed as he left the offices and headed toward the front of the resort for an important meeting, though not with business clients.

Tally strode into The Partridge Room, the adorable little restaurant tucked in a corner of the resort that only served brunch and high tea, where his mom was having tea with Misaki. Nervous? Yes. Enough to want his worry stone back from Haru's tub, but they needed this meeting to understand expectations, especially since Misaki hadn't even looked at him yet.

"There you are." Mom got up and poured a cup of tea for him, too. "Tally, I think Misaki has some things she needs to say to you."

Tally sat with the distinct feeling of ambush creeping over him. "Of course. Anything I can help with."

Misaki lifted her head, turned to face him, her cheeks flushing as she said in clear, perfect English, "I won't be your concubine."

What? Oh. Oh, dear Gods. Tally cleared his throat and shifted uncomfortably, staring into the depths of his tea. "Good. That's...good. You're quite beautiful, and under different circumstances— That is, if I hadn't already found my destined match..." This was not a conversation he wanted to have in front of his mother. Damn the desire for chaperones. "I will never touch you in any way if you don't want me to. In fact, I'd rather hoped we could be more modern about this part."

She gave him a sharp nod when he glanced up again. "*Hai*, Bastille-san. I hoped that also."

"We didn't go into specifics for the Kwebabiads in the contracts since I wanted to give all of you young people the space to work things out for yourselves." Mom folded both hands together atop the table. "I see that was a mistake. Since we are old-fashioned in some ways, with belief in destined matches, and since you did go through a traditional Satislit negotiation, there were some unhappy misunderstandings that you'd want *everything* the old way, Tally."

Misaki reached behind her for her messenger bag and pulled out a folder, which she turned toward him. "I have gathered data on how uktena and nure-onna genetics might work most fortunately together. You have banked gametes already, yes?"

Banked…? Right. Tally's face heated. Again, this in front of Mom, and she looked like she was trying not to laugh. *Thanks, Mom.* "I, um, have, yes."

Misaki nodded again. "Thank you, Bastille-san. I know these are delicate matters. I do not wish to cause you distress. But this is the nature of my position with you."

Here he'd thought he would be comforting and reassuring his Kwebabiad. Silly of him.

"I will do my best to provide three healthy children." Misaki turned to a page that looked suspiciously like another contract.

Why, yes, it was.

"I took the liberty of preparing an additional contract since our situation is unusual. If you would look it over? This is the agreement specifically between you and me, outlining the details of our roles in regard to the children, if there are any. While the doctors assure me that I am able to, we may not be compatible for any number of reasons."

"I understand. The genetics…"

"Quite. We will try for the number of months specified in the contract. If we are unsuccessful, a new Kwebabiad will be found for you. Is this acceptable?"

"It…" Well, he *had* wanted to go with the more modern method of in vitro fertilization and implantation rather than sleeping together, as she did.

He just hadn't thought it would be quite so clinical. He glanced over the document, noting a schedule for her return to Japan if the IVF didn't take. "It is. I want it clear that our clan recognizes Kwebabiads as legal mothers, though. You are more than welcome to stay and make a home with us and the children, or to have shared custody, if that's what you prefer."

She stared at him, something warring in her dark eyes as they bored into him. Finally, she gave him a hint of a smile. "Bastille-san, you are very kind for one of reptilian nature. I was led to believe... No. That would not be appropriate to say. I thank you. But I am perhaps more used to my independence than you might have anticipated in a Kwebabiad. I have begun the process of seeking employment here and appropriate living quarters."

Tally took the pen his mother handed him. "We'll make every effort to see to your comfort while you're looking." He was pleased to see that she had stipulated visitation rights for herself with the children, at least, so he signed with a flourish and managed a shaky smile. "Thank you for being so candid. And so prepared. Might I ask your profession?"

Her spare smile grew just a hair. "I am an attorney, Bastille-san. Who better than a serpent with sharp teeth to help shore up the legal battlements of the clan?"

"Truer words." He saluted with his teacup and turned the folder her way so she could sign as well. All things considered, Haru's clan couldn't possibly have made a better choice. "What type of law do you practice, if it's not prying?"

"Contract law." Misaki's eyes crinkled at the corners.

"International?"

When she gave him a nod, Tally tapped the pen on the table. "I may have a position to offer you."

"Send the offer to me, Bastille-san. I will consider it."

"Good. I told you he was reasonable and modern," Mom said to Misaki as if Tally weren't sitting right there, until she turned to him. "Now scoot. You need to catch up to Haru and Sammy on their grand tour of the bakeries and florists of Wadiswan."

Misaki's eyebrows rose when Mom turned back to her.

"I'm still Uruma and he's still my son." Mom sipped primly at her tea. "I still get to boss him around, Urusar or not."

* * * *

"Oh, this is…is?" Haru looked to Sam for some help. How could they describe this kind of atrocity to human and lijun kind alike? Why pumpkin spice? What was wrong with Americans? She shook her head with an emphatic 'no' so no help there. "Different."

"Oh! I'm so glad you think so," replied Jones-san. The deer lijun's hovering was making the tasting excruciatingly painful. "Why don't you try the almond-vanilla cake?"

It was just as dry as the pumpkin spice one. No, actually, it was like eating sand. Haru and Sam reached for their glasses of milk at the same time and took a big swallow. It wasn't enough. Haru drained the glass.

"Too much vanilla?" Jones-san asked, wringing his hands together. His nervous tics were about to set Sam off if the twitch in her eye was any indication.

"No, no, just so many cakes," Haru answered.

"Of course. Are you excited for the wedding?"

"Yes." Not even a bit, but picking out the cakes had been fun until they'd gotten to Best Bakery.

"It'll be nice to get some more otters in town. We need some more of us little guys," Jones-san replied. "We were happy to hear Sam agreed to be your Kwebabiad. Are you going the traditional or modern route with the pups?"

How was that even appropriate to ask? Maybe Americans thought it was okay?

"Traditional," Haru replied as Sam said, "Modern."

Oh, that was... Being the future Uruma, Haru supposed the town would be in their business more than others since they had come in as a foreigner. They had wanted the clan to know they felt vested in clan matters, as was right. But the last thing they wanted was Sam unhappy with anything in the arrangement.

"We are still deciding," Haru offered weakly, and Sam squeezed their hand.

"Well, it's nice to hear you're thinking about doing it the right way. How about we celebrate?" Jones-san trotted away, letting them know he was going to get some dessert wines to try with the cakes.

"Sorry," Haru said, but Sam was already shaking her head.

She nosed in, breathing against Haru's neck. They relaxed until she said, "Hey, it's where you're from. We'll figure it out later."

Haru let the assumption go, because it wasn't a conversation for now. "Unfortunately we still have cake."

"If we leave now, do you think we can get away before he catches us?" Sam raised one perfect blonde eyebrow at them.

"I am afraid he might follow us. How does he stay in business?"

"Tourist town with resorts. And his wife makes the cookies."

That would explain it.

"Though we should try the cakes at Tally's hotels," Sam suggested, fidgeting with the napkin. "I mean, isn't the wedding going to be at Sapphire Lake Resort?"

"Yes." Despite Haru's need for neutral ground, it was the best location for the clan to celebrate. "But it would be rude not to try the other bakeries in town. Too many of them are clan."

Sam nodded, sighing. "What's left?"

"The chocolate."

"That's hard to screw up."

Haru and Sam glanced over at the slices of cake. They both winced.

"It looks...crumbly," she said finally.

"Yes."

"How many more tastings do we have?"

Haru checked the calendar on his new phone, another present from Tally. "Four."

"We're never going to make it," Sam groaned.

"I need something besides sugar," Haru agreed.

"Can we say we need to get to another appointment?"

Sam squeezed Haru's hand as the two of them shared a look.

"We wouldn't want to be late, would we?"

Haru hated to think what their mother would've said if she were here. Luckily, she wasn't. She had decided to stay home with Bastille-*okaasan*, deeming Sam a suitable escort for their outings, but not before she scrutinized Haru's appearance. They'd been lucky to leave the house wearing a form-fitting brown cashmere sweater and the green corduroy pants Tally had given them. They'd finished their hair off with the white jade hairpiece decorating their bun.

Wearing Tally's presents pleased his mom enough she didn't check their bags before they left. Sam had helped smuggle out boots while Haru had their bipride belt. Being able to wander around town in something they liked, without their former family breathing down their neck, allowed Haru to relax a fraction. Sam made the mind-numbing process of preparing for the wedding easier too. Her light touches and friendly affection eased the ache in their heart. Though they knew any spectacle would get back to Mother and the Bastilles if they screwed up today's tastings, so they fell back on their training when dealing with clan.

Just as Jones-san came back into the tasting room, the bell from over Best Bakery's door chimed, letting a cool breeze in with it — and Tally. Big and imposing as ever. The expertly cut brown suit he wore fit him perfectly. The braid was an unexpected touch. It softened his demeanor.

An earth-shattering explosion of a bottle breaking split the air.

"Jones-san, are you well?" Haru jumped out of their chair and ran over to the deer, who was shaking so hard Haru worried he was having some kind of episode. "Jones-san?"

Tally stood three steps inside the shop and came no further. His voice was soft, gentle, as he greeted them. "Haru. Sam." A slight hesitation and a formal nod. "Alan."

"Urusar Bastille." Jones-san wouldn't look at Tally, instead he focused on the floor. "Excuse me while I get something to clean this up."

Haru watched Jones-san's backside as he disappeared into the back of the shop. "What was that?"

Tally cleared his throat. "Ah. Well. Alan may not be terribly pleased to see me, since we recently canceled his contract with the resorts."

"Oh no." Haru glanced toward the back. "This is, is…so inappropriate."

Awkward too. Incredibly awkward.

Jones-san came back out with a bucket, mop, and a bunch of rags.

"Can I help?" Haru said, concerned about the excessive shaking.

"No, please, Satislit Tanaka. Thank you."

"Should we come back? I am afraid we have another appointment."

"Yes, any time. Just call my wife to set it up."

At the dismissal, Haru grabbed their afghan and pulled it on. "Thank you."

The three of them hurried out of the door, Tally falling into step beside Haru. A kiss fell on their cheek right before Tally hooked their arms together. Every time Haru was left in his Xabita's company, his touches became bolder, more assured. Every time, Haru's fear and worry made their abdomen clench tighter, their panic simmering just beneath the surface.

"I'm so sorry about that. But it didn't occur to me until Mom mentioned you wanted to check out *all* the bakeries… I'm sorry about the awkwardness. And that you were subjected to those excuses for baked goods."

"Where to next?" Sam asked. "I'd like to get the taste of that pumpkin spice cake out of my mouth."

"Yes, please. Though I said I would reschedule." Manners sucked sometimes.

"Hmm. You're certainly welcome to, but it might be more uncomfortable for him at this point."

"Quite." Haru would find an acceptable excuse. Somehow. "I think the Kits and Cupcakes bakery was next."

They cut over a block, then went east for two more before they ended back on Main Street. The shops here were definitely designed to appeal to tourists. They were well taken care of and had similar motifs, but the owners had taken the time to individualize them where they could. Fun signs and even more memorable names were at nearly every shop.

The Kits and Cupcakes bakery had baby raccoons climbing up the sign, the one at the top reaching out for a cupcake. Bright colors adorned the shopfront, a white face with bright reds and pinks, making the raccoons pop against them.

"Aw, how cute," Haru said. The boldness of the design surprised them, especially since the owners were lijun. The Bastilles hadn't been worried about this kind of blatant display?

"They make excellent chocolate croissants," Sam whispered as they entered and several chimes sang out. "You need to try them before we leave."

"Count on it."

Humans and lijun filled the bakery, unlike at the Best Bakery where only a couple of people had stopped by during the tasting. Warm, buttery smells mixed with fruity and chocolate ones, causing Haru's mouth to water. Tally led them over to a doorway and through it, leading them to a room filled with cakes and pies. All different kinds lined the cases, and Haru was having trouble keeping it together. So many goodies.

Was that a chocolate cake with buttercream frosting and pecans? Haru pressed against the glass. Oh, it was.

Warmth covered their back, followed by deep chuckle. "Should've known you'd go for the chocolate."

"Chocolate is life."

"It is," Sam agreed.

It was only when Haru realized Sam was to their right that they connected the dots as to who was pressed over them. *Tally*. Haru jumped back on instinct, but that only brought them closer together. Their back molded to Tally's front. An arm wrapped around their stomach. A deep hum vibrated against Haru's back and Tally's breath ghosted over their ear as he kissed the base of Haru's jaw. Just that and nothing more before Tally backed away.

A cheery woman's voice broke Haru's surprise. "Oh, Mr. Bastille, welcome. This must be our—your fiancé? Welcome."

A beautiful, stout woman with a bit of plump to her face beamed at him, though her smile faltered when she looked at Tally. Maybe the clan wasn't as comfortable with the uktena as Sam had said. The raccoon lijun recovered nicely when she turned back to Haru, her eyes bright.

"I hear you're in need of a cake?"

"I am. Thank you for seeing us, Timms-san." Haru eyed the chocolate. "How many different kinds of samples do you have?"

"I'd suggest going heavy on the chocolate ones, Sarah," Tally offered from behind Haru.

The raccoon baker twitched at his voice but didn't let her smile slip as she led them to a table at the back of the room and began to bring out lovely little rectangles of cake. Chocolate icing with chocolate. Yellow cake with chocolate. Chocolate with cherry filling. With almonds. With raspberry. And, the most celestial wonder of them all, the chocolate pecan.

All the yummies created an excessive amount of excitement between Haru and Sam, their eagerness feeding into one another in an endless loop. They could almost forget that they'd be banished if they screwed this match up. Almost. Cake definitely helped push the morose thoughts away for a while.

"Mmmm," Haru groaned when the crunch of the pecan filled their mouth with the chocolate.

"I've found heaven," Sam agreed.

Tally tasted with them, though he remained silent and smiling as he let Haru and Sam debate and discuss the merits of each offering. It was hard to decide with so much delectable chocolate at their fingertips. Sarah darted little glances at Tally from time to time, though she was professional and friendly throughout.

They thanked her as they rose, Sam debating the merits of the raspberry filling. Haru tended to agree with her, their tastes similar.

"I am told I must try your chocolate croissants," Haru said as they headed toward the door.

"Oh, yes, please do," Sarah replied, then ordered her daughter to fetch a few. "On the house."

"Thank you, Sarah," Tally merely said. "Excellent choices. We'll be in touch."

Haru had to wonder if all his fiancé's business dealings were so abrupt. Not brusque, precisely, and not rude, but as if time were a finite thing that Tally felt forever slipping through his hands.

* * * *

Tally was flagging by the time the cake testing had finished and he had to stifle a groan when Sam informed him that florists were next. He didn't have to tag along, of course. He could've made excuses about an important meeting or some emergency at work. The time in Haru's company was worth it, though, especially since he got to bask in glimpses of *his* Haru, the one who engaged in dessert raids. The one who had been painfully absent in the presence of his parents.

So, florists it was. He made certain to voice polite opinions here and there, to nudge in one direction or another when he *had* an opinion. That question from Haru about Tally relegating all the decisions to him still stung, but he didn't interfere too much. Sam and Haru were having too much fun with this.

The first stop was Petals and Thyme, whose sign announced that they were florists and herbalists, though Tally knew most of the business came from the floral side of things. Before the doors even stopped chiming, Fred bustled out from the back wiping his hands on a towel, beaming.

"Tally! I didn't know they'd be dragging you along."

He accepted the firm, perfunctory handshake with a return smile. "It's not dragging if you do it willingly. Fred, this is Haru Tanaka. Haru, Fred Voronoy. We used to play lacrosse in high school."

Fred held a hand out to Haru as well, and Tally was pleased Fred didn't do anything more than shake, no overenthused arm pumping, no macho *who can squeeze tighter* nonsense. "It's good to meet you. The clan's been abuzz. I'm just so happy someone finally landed this giant snake. We were starting to wonder if he'd be the only Urusar in living memory with his own mom acting as Uruma his entire life."

Haru's expression had shuttered again, but he managed a polite, "Thank you, Voronoy-san. It is a…an attractive town."

"It is a cute place." Fred chuckled, sounding momentarily like his raven half. Then he clapped his hands together. "Books! Let me get the books and you can tell me what sorts of things you're looking for."

Tally sat next to Haru with Sam on the other side so they could lean over the sample books. He wanted to be as close as he could without making his otter uncomfortable. Seeing Haru relax and open up as he and Sam talked over the cakes and flowers helped that nugget of worry recede. The more time Haru spent away from his overbearing parents, the better. They murmured about this and that, but Haru's expression of polite interest slowly became one of concern, his forehead crinkling as they paged through wedding bouquets.

"These are all…" Haru waved a hand at the page, obviously struggling for a word that wouldn't offend. "Very Western."

Fred took the seat opposite, nodding. "They are. It's what I have most call for. But if there's something different you'd like, just point me to a picture, a website, describe it for me. I'm happy to do custom work, and I might not even charge a wing and a leg since it's Tally."

He handed over a pad and pen to Haru, who stared at the blank page for a moment before he began to draw. Everyone drew closer, so Tally sat back. He didn't want Haru to feel crowded. Besides, he could peer over Haru's shoulder easily enough to watch him draw what appeared to be a globe of flower shapes with a handle.

"Something simple and traditional." Haru finally glanced up from his careful drawing.

"Oh sure. I've seen the globe-shaped ones. Those are beautiful. Chrysanthemums? Roses?"

Haru squirmed, gaze back on the page. "I would like to think about specific flowers and their meanings. We *are* trying to combine our rituals."

"Of course. I'm acting like I have the contract already." Fred leaned back and laughed. "Even if you go with another florist, I'm happy for you both. Congratulations."

The rest of the florist visits started to blur for Tally — some human, some lijun. He would try to nudge them toward lijun-owned businesses whenever possible, of course, but an Urusar had to be fair.

By the last florist appointment, Tally had progressed from flagging to wilting. He offered Sam and Haru a huge smile and hoped he didn't sound desperate when he said, "Lunch?"

"I think we're wearing the big guy out." Sam gave him a critical up and down look and Haru's lips twitched in a quickly hidden smile.

"Lunch would be pleasant," Haru said. "After all the sugar."

"Excellent. My car's two streets over." Tally turned and started walking that way. "We'll go up to Sapphire Lake so you can see the venue. And have food."

A golden globe of light warmed Tally's chest when Haru took his arm again. He felt so...right. As if he should always have been there, and he would be there, always. Tally silently thanked the GLA for holding the conference in Tokyo, thanked the makers of rainbow suspenders and thanked a little tanuki in a mostly chocolate dress for bringing them together.

The drive out to Sapphire Lake wound through dense coniferous forest, dark and lovely, with no sign of civilization until they rounded that final bend. It was always as if the resort had sprung up from the ground at that moment, gleaming and welcoming, with its sprawling hotel and conference center and its attached casino tucked into the left side. A sideways glance at Haru in the front seat gave him the satisfaction of seeing his otter wide-eyed and fascinated for a single moment before he got his expression back under control.

A liveried valet in burgundy hurried down the steps to take charge of Tally's Bentley, fumbling the keys when Tally tossed them over.

"Mr....Mr. Bastille." The poor kid was shaking.

"Be gentle with my baby." Tally winked and gathered his party in front of him. His attempt at reassuring didn't seem to do much good if the quavery *yes, sir* behind him was any indication.

He swept through the lobby, careful to acknowledge every employee he saw along the way, by name if they were close enough, a wave and a smile for the ones manning reception. He strode onward to The Den, the café at the far right of the hotel, cozier and less fussy than some of the other offerings. And they had prawns for Haru.

"Diane." He lifted a hand in greeting as they approached the hostess stand. "Have anything open for three?"

"For you, Mr. Bastille? Always." Diane's smile was genuine, if a little too bright, but she gathered up menus and led them off with graceful efficiency, as always.

Haru was going to get whiplash if he didn't start paying attention to where they were walking. If he'd been in his otter half, Tally felt sure his nose would be twitching, ears swiveling. As it were, all the stones and waterworks had Haru taking small steps away from their conga line before righting himself again.

Until Haru saw the tanks.

An excited hiccup escaped him as he sped up and went directly to them, abandoning Tally and Sam. This was the Haru he'd been missing. The excitable happy one from the Great Dessert Siege. Haru's nose flattened against the aquarium glass, his dark brown eyes growing large and glistening with excitement.

"Ooh. Mmmm. Yummy treats."

Tally chuckled. "As many as you like. They have a wonderful selection of river fish here, too. Don't know if either of you would be interested."

Haru groaned a "yes, please," but his gaze was fixed on the prawns. The moan was music to Tally's ears. He yearned to hear one of those for himself. Under different circumstances and someplace not so public.

When their meals arrived, a selection of fish and shellfish for the otters, a salad for Tally, he enjoyed the sight of both his guests tucking in with abandon more than he had anything in quite some time. He didn't enjoy the taste of prawns himself, but he had the feeling that he wouldn't mind licking that bit off the corner of Haru's mouth.

After lunch, Tally led them on a leisurely stroll through the conference center so Haru could see the choice of rooms and he could explain how they could be configured.

"There's planning staff, of course, to help with all of that. All they need is an approximate guest number."

Tally stopped in the center of the grand ballroom. "Unless you want the wedding outside. We do that a lot around here and the weather's usually good still for Harvest Moon."

"That would be lovely," Haru said, balancing his stolen plate of treats. "Outside is nice. It would feel good to be by the lake."

"Excellent." Tally grinned and pulled the phone from inside his suit jacket. Three texts had staff hurrying into the ballroom within moments. "Linda, Harry, change of venue…"

He sketched out needs and possible wants as his event coordinators took frantic notes. From pergola to removable dance floor, they had the means and the equipment. They'd certainly done it for other wedding parties. Too late, he realized he'd completely taken over and he cringed.

"Haru, I'm sorry. I get a little overly tactical sometimes. Was all that all right? Something…any part of it you need changed?"

"It sounds as though you have it well in hand? I get the fun part of decorating it all."

Tally's relief blossomed into a grateful smile, that warm spot in his chest expanding farther. "Perfect. Division of labor is a wonderful thing."

"Urusar and Uruma are supposed to complement each other." Haru nodded in agreement, holding his pilfered plate of prawns close. He popped another one in his mouth. The moans he made chewing on his 'treat' wound Tally tighter than when his serpent coiled up and sunbathed on a rock.

The stolen touches and kisses had to get him by for now, but he fervently wished for some alone time to get to know his mate better. The in-laws were making that damn near impossible, though. Their *propriety* would be the death of Tally. He just wanted his Em'halafi and for the house to fill up with their love. When another of Haru's satisfied groans spliced the air, Tally's cock pulsed in response and nearly broke his resolve to adhere to Haru's need for custom. Tally wanted to steal his otter away from the ballroom and hole up somewhere until the wedding, away from this ridiculousness. Except Sam was right there, watching, judging. But those moans…

I need to have prawns on hand…at all times.

One last stop with the catering staff to get menu negotiations started, where Tally stepped back again to let Haru make his wishes known. Tally spoke one word during the process, one word that caused Haru to give him one of those twitch almost-smiles.

"Prawns."

Tally felt as if he'd been tumbled down a rock-filled streambed by the time the day was over, though it had been a lot accomplished in a short stretch of time. He was tired, but it was a satisfied tired.

Some of the reactions to him accompanying Haru that day had him suppressing sighs, though. There were even humans who feared him in a primal way. Only the lijun knew what he was and feared his heritage specifically. More likely the humans simply reacted to his size. Even townspeople and clan who had known him all his life.

Old prejudices died hard.

None of that mattered. Everything was falling into place and the wedding at the Harvest Moon would be perfect. Life would be perfect with his mate at his side.

* * * *

Tally had spent far too much time picking out clothes the afternoon of the engagement party. This would be the official celebration with family and friends, with the entire clan invited, even if they wouldn't all necessarily come. Haru took such time, such care with his appearance, and Tally was starting to get something of an inferiority complex about it.

Sure. Suits were easy. He had beautiful ones on hand. This didn't feel like a suit kind of party, though. He wore his suits like armor, almost as if he could keep the world at bay that way. Tonight, he needed to appear more open, more accessible. Softer. Yes.

A good pair of dress slacks, black, and a forest green chamois shirt was what he finally decided on, with the black ankle boots. He braided his hair carefully and fastened off the end with the tie from his grandmother, the one with the silver serpent with jade eyes.

There. That wasn't bad, was it? Less intimidating? More potential family man?

He hoped so at least, as he loped down the stairs to see how preparations were coming and to be sure he would be on hand to answer the door. He didn't even make it to the bottom of the steps before the doorbell rang.

"Gunther!" Tally cried out as he flung the door open. "I didn't know you were coming today. It's been too long since you've actually been here."

"Six-seven years? Definitely too long."

"Who dragged you out of Denver?"

"Addy called. She said I could either get my butt here for the party and the wedding or she'd come out to Denver and haul me back." Gunther winced. "Didn't need that happening in front of Urusar Pike."

"He still giving your mom grief?"

"Pike would have the whole family tossed if he could. But having a bird lijun representative on the council has always been a requirement."

Tally frowned. "Why does it feel like things have gotten worse since we last talked, not better?"

"Later, Tally. Now isn't the time." Gunther's golden eagle showed through his ruffled expression. One he hadn't shown since the Pike's former Urusar had been shot down by a hunter. "I'm not going to say I missed you or anything sappy…"

"Come here, damn it." Tally pulled him into a crushing hug, complete with competitive backslapping. It *had* been too long since he'd seen his childhood shadow. "I missed you too."

"Gun!" Two set of footsteps pounded up the front walk and Pete and Lily Dignan, the prairie dog twins, flung themselves at Gunther from either side, making him stumble and laugh.

"We didn't know you'd be here," Pete said in a tone that managed both pleased and accusatory.

"Good Gods. I hope I don't have to repeat this all night," Gunther muttered. "I was coming for the wedding. Addy insisted I get here earlier."

"Gunther Curley, as I live and breathe," a soft, sardonic voice said from behind Gunther's shoulder. "Or is it a hologram?"

Lily snickered. "Pretty sure h-h-hologram h-h-hugging isn't a thing yet, Marnie."

Tally reached around the group hug and pulled Marnie in while clamping his lips on the words *I didn't hear you come up*. No one ever heard a bobcat lijun coming and Marnie didn't need to hear it for the three million and first time.

"I'm so glad you're all here," Tally said instead. "Nan and Addy are browbeating, ah, directing the caterers still, but Mom and Dad are in the den having drinks with some of the old folks if you want to pop in and say hi."

"Where's this mysterious Satislit of yours, Tal?" Marnie peered around as she padded into the house. "I've heard rumors from gorgeous to just a teensy bit weird."

"Haru's upstairs. He'll be down soon, and he's not weird." Tally tried to keep his expression neutral but he must still have been venturing toward sulky glower territory because Lily snickered.

"Tal, sh-she's razzing you."

He kissed the top of Lily's head and finally cleared the doorway to let his friends inside. *His friends.* The four of them had been the only ones who treated him like a person when they were kids and not like a deadly monster to be feared or like the Sardu, the Urusar's heir, to be sucked up to in a lijun-heavy school.

Lily's stutter had been the catalyst. Much worse when she was little, she'd had days where she hadn't spoken at all. When she'd tried, the crueler children had imitated her to taunt her, and called the twins Pete and Re-Pete. Tally had put a stop to it, or had tried to. Gunther had waded in because the fight hadn't been fair. Marnie had bitten one of the tormenting boys because, as she'd put it later in the principal's office, he was a creep.

They'd become inseparable afterward. Tally had done his best to keep them out of trouble and they'd kept Tally from feeling like the untouchable freak no one liked but no one wanted to offend.

"Tally?" Mom called from the den. "Is that Gunther? Send him in here so he can explain why he never calls."

Marnie chuckled and gave Gunther a shove in that direction. "Guess we never really grow up in their eyes."

"Someone come with me." Gunther hung up his jacket on one of the pegs by the door, his gaze darting from one to the other. "Come on. You can't send me in there to be eaten alive."

"Tally's parents haven't eaten anyone all year," Pete reassured him with an innocent smile.

"I'll g-go with you, Gun." Lily took his arm. "They h-have to be nice to me. I plow their street."

"We'll see what's left of you in a bit," Tally called after him, their laughter washing over him like warm sunshine.

The sound of soft footsteps on the second-level landing had Tally looking over his shoulder, wondering which of the Tanaka party was joining him. A golden glow filled his vision momentarily before his eyes focused on Haru gliding down the stairs. All the air in his lungs escaped in a whoosh, leaving Tally breathless. As usual, Haru's appearance was meticulously put together. Between the lavender lips and darker eyeshadow with diamond stones accenting the makeup—

It should be illegal for someone to be so beautiful.

It wasn't surprising to see Haru in another kimono — no, the long-sleeved ones were called *furisode*. Tally still worried he was wearing them because of the in-laws, but after the wedding they'd see what changes would happen. As long as Haru was happy.

The sleeves of *furisode* billowed around Haru as he descended, giving him an ethereal image. One sleeve had a black and silver design woven into it, branches of cherry trees with blossoms popping out from it. A similar design was on the bottom of the *furisode*. Different shades of cherry blossoms swept over the front and onto the shoulders. The *obi* was a bright lavender with a turquoise *obijime*. Haru's hair was up in a bun, loose curls around it. The white jade hairpiece Tally had given him was on prominent display. The updo allowed Tally to see the burnt orange *nagajuban* underneath.

"Oh, wow, Tally," Marnie whispered. "They said he was pretty, but *not* like this."

"Gods, Tally." Pete shook his head.

Tally swallowed, holding out a hand as Haru met him at the base of the stairs. This was why he was developing a complex about his looks, but he couldn't help puffing up a bit at the awed comments from his friends. A smile, bright and warm, flashed in his direction and Haru allowed Tally to pull him close before his gaze moved to Marnie and Pete. Curious and open.

"Welcome," Haru said, offering an *eshaku*.

"Haru, these are my friends." Tally winced inwardly. He hoped Haru didn't assume Pete and Marnie were his only friends. He had at least two more. "Marnie Whittaker and Pete Dignan. Guys, this is Haru Tanaka."

"The famous Haru Tanaka," Marnie purred. "All the lijun shopkeepers in town are talking about you, you know."

Haru stiffened slightly, his smile straining. "Good things, I hope?"

"Oh, honey, the best things." Marnie's soft laugh sounded like an extended purr. "You'd think you were a God descended from the clouds. I love your outfit tonight. Absolutely gorgeous."

"Thank you." Haru's cheeks darkened, but his body relaxed next to Tally's. "I do not think I am worth all that praise, but it is nice to hear."

"It's true what they say about otters, though. You guys do know how to dress," Peter replied.

"Side-effect from our spirit half. We tend to preen quite a bit."

"Ha! Too bad that's never affected Gunther's ability to dress himself," Marnie said with a choked snicker.

"He can't help being a little colorblind, Marnie. Be nice." Tally gave her a warning frown.

Still chuckling, she patted his shoulder on the way past. "Fine, fine. I'm going to go say hi to your sisters. Promise. I'll behave."

Tally lifted Haru's hand to kiss his fingers. "You do look like you descended from the clouds this evening, though. Absolutely stunning."

"I am happy my appearance pleases."

Pete was staring at Haru in an odd way that Tally couldn't quite parse. "Huh. Well. Different manners. Tal, I'm gonna go see what's left of Gunther. I'll catch up in a bit."

What was that supposed to mean?

But where Lily struggled to communicate sometimes, Pete often didn't try, keeping his thoughts to himself. Haru surprised Tally by staying beside him to greet guests. He probably believed it was the polite thing to do, but Tally felt like he'd grown three extra inches with Haru on his arm. Beside him. *Gods.* He might explode if he felt any happier.

A fluttering buzz of tiny wings distracted Tally and he whipped toward the sound to find one of their resident garden pixies tugging at Haru's perfectly coiffed hair.

"Jasper, no!" Tally made shooing motions, careful not to clip the pixie's wings.

Tiny blue face pinched in an expression of extreme annoyance, Jasper turned to Tally and stomped his foot in the air.

"I know Haru has beautiful hair, believe me." Tally tried to ignore the half-puzzled, half-judging look Haru was giving him as he reached back and tugged three strands loose from his own hair. "Here. For your nest. Now outside please, before someone accidentally shuts you in the house."

Jasper snagged the hair Tally offered with a pleased squeak and zipped back out the door.

"Sorry. He's a bit of a pain sometimes, but mostly harmless."

Haru nodded slowly, regarding Tally with a raised eyebrow and an expression Tally couldn't quite read.

Once the majority of the guests had arrived, they left the front hall to mingle and snack on the food set out between the dining room and the family room. Tally perused the tables looking for a special one he'd requested...ah. There. In the far corner of the dining room.

"Haru?" Tally pointed to the separate table of shellfish and various smoked and pickled fishes. He felt suddenly awkward, as if maybe he shouldn't mention it. But... "That table's especially for you."

A glint appeared in Haru's eyes. "Oh, this is lovely."

Haru went from composed and elegant to practically vibrating as he scrutinized the offerings.

"He thought of me."

It was barely audible, but Tally heard the surprised whisper and he thought a bit of his heart had chipped off to hear it. That apparently it wasn't normal for someone to think especially of him. That would change. Tally was going to move sun and stars for that to change.

More than happy to stand in that corner and watch Haru pick carefully over the offerings with happy little murmurs and sub-audible moans, Tally let the guests come to him. Congratulations, small talk, requests for meetings, minor grievances, they all reached him through a soft-glowing blanket of happy.

"Tally! Oh, there you are." Mom waved from the doorway to the kitchen. "Help me get everyone outside. It's about that time."

Time? Right. They were supposed to go out to the lake. Champagne. Toasts. Presents. Then they'd be allowed to bow out of the party, Haru and him. Tally wasn't certain what he hoped for after that, but any alone time with Haru, without people watching their every move and word, would be wonderful. The guests would be distracted by the upcoming fireworks and no one would bother them.

He snagged Gunther, still in one piece and gnawing on a drumstick, to help herd guests and let Haru wrangle his family. With a lot of last minute snatches at goodies on the buffet tables, everyone was good-natured enough about being shooed outside where another long table had been set up near the lake. Champagne glasses, in the process of being filled, lined one half of the table in regimented rows. On the other half sat presents in various shapes and sizes, gifts for the Argaze and Satislit to be.

Dad picked up one of the empty champagne glasses and tapped on it with a spoon, the gentle chime enough to get the guests' attention.

"Honored guests, my beloved family, esteemed clan members." Dad paused a moment as one of the servers put a full glass in his hand and others began to circulate with full trays of glasses for the guests. "I've always known that our Tal-tsu'tsa would succeed me as Urusar. It was almost as if he knew from birth himself, our always responsible Tally. But we had begun to fear that he would do so alone, without a partner at his side as is right and proper. And we feared that he would never find the other half of his heart, his Em'halafi, forced to take up the mantle as a solitary Urusar someday."

He lifted his glass toward Haru. "It is with great joy that we prepare to welcome Haru as his Uruma, his partner in all things, his heart's delight to stand beside him and ensure he doesn't worry himself to pieces over the welfare of the clan."

Dad turned and lifted his glass toward Sam and Misaki, standing arm in arm nearby. "And to increase this joy, we are honored beyond measure to have Kwebabiads for both Tally and Haru." Addy and Nan came forward with a basket each, piled high with little presents and symbols of fertility such as eggs and pomegranates. "We thank you for accepting this sacred and honored role for the clan and we wish you many children and all the wonder and love in watching them grow."

Misaki accepted her basket with a polite bow, Sam with a huge grin and a kiss to Addy's cheek.

Again, Dad raised his glass in a sweeping gesture to include all the guests. Canny devil had managed to time it perfectly so everyone had champagne now. He waited until glasses were raised in answer. "To Tally and Haru! May they have many years of joy and plenty!"

"Tally and Haru!" came the answering roar from the gathered clan and Tally felt his throat closing up, his eyes prickling.

He took a quick gulp of champagne so he wouldn't embarrass himself and laughed when Gunther started the inevitable chiming on his glass.

Haru turned to him with a puzzled frown.

"They want us to kiss," Tally whispered as the chiming grew louder and louder, more guests joining in. "They won't stop until we do."

A huff escaped Haru, but he put his perfectly manicured hands on Tally's forearms and angled his head back, presenting those perfect lips for the taking. He wanted to crush Haru to him, desperately, but didn't want to muss him in front of everyone. Instead he put his hands on Haru's shoulders and met him halfway, his entire body igniting when their lips met firmly, for more than a fleeting touch.

The guests broke into whoops and wild applause as Haru pulled back, his face flushed. Dad was bellowing above the noise for everyone to stay by the lake for cake and the fireworks to come.

Tally leaned in to whisper in Haru's ear, "Now's when we're supposed to make our escape."

He waited for Haru's nod before he took Haru by the hand and hurried them inside, past the caterers in the kitchen, past a stray teenage couple canoodling on the sofa and up the steps in the main hall. At the door to Haru's suite, Tally wrapped an arm around Haru's waist and pulled him in to try for a more thorough kiss, but he met definite resistance.

"Haru?" Tally stopped and loosened his hold. "What's wrong?"

"I—I am not sure this is proper."

"We're going to be married in a few days. It's not as if…" Tally bit back a sigh. If he listened to his body right that moment, the heated hum of his blood, he was going to do something he regretted later. Gods, he wanted. So badly it was like a knife to the gut. But no. Not unless Haru was ready and enthusiastically willing, and if Haru's upbringing told him no, it was no. "Of course. I'm… I'm sorry. You're so beautiful tonight. I got a little carried away."

Haru dipped his head, though Tally thought he felt a tremor run through his otter. "It honors me that I please you. Thank you for waiting."

"Thank you for telling me. Always tell me. Please. Haru…" *You don't need to be so formal when it's just us. I'm practically a puddle standing here with you and it's so, so hard.* Tally kissed the top of Haru's head, careful not to interfere with the coiffure. "Good night, Haru, love."

"Good night, my…Argaze."

* * * *

Slipping out of their *furisode*, Haru breathed a sigh of relief. *That was close. Too close.*

Tally wasn't ugly. No, he was handsome, especially tonight in his carefully chosen outfit. One meant to disarm. And it had, for a while. So had the *treats*. Seeing Tally so friendly, so open, so maddeningly attentive, Haru had almost forgotten the snake was why they would be stuck and miserable in Wisconsin.

The toast from their future father was the bucket of cold ice water they'd needed. The two of them were not destined matches, despite what the foolish uktena felt. Haru had been bought and sold, and if they screwed up, if Tally sent them back to the Akaikes? It hurt to think about it, an ache breaking their spirit into nothing but crumbs. Haru would be banished. Everything gone. Their world ripped away twice because some fool thought the two of them were mates.

The way Sam and Misaki were paraded in front of everyone stung too. They weren't commodities. None of them. Their children would never, ever be treated like such. But fear made them think the kids would be. Their heart and mind warred with what they felt and what they knew, which wasn't enough.

Haru couldn't let themself be left alone with Tally for fear their Xatiba would know, would somehow figure out that Haru did not want this match. The bastard paid too close attention to every little thing Haru said and did. It was alarming how much he *cared*.

When he'd tried to bring Haru into their suite? Gods, what would've happened? Haru still didn't have the stomach to lie together with someone who'd bought them. Not convincingly. When the time came, though, they'd have to be. Somehow.

Thank goodness Tally thought Haru was just trying to follow 'the rules'.

And what of our wedding night? What rules would Haru have to protect them then?

Yanking at his *koshi himo*, Haru managed to finagle it off before chucking his *nagajuban* off.

Out. Away. *Water*.

Haru needed to escape, just for a while. Each step brought them closer to their cage and jailer. The need to forage, swim — forget — battered at their heart. So they stopped trying to resist and ottered out. Let the Sahnkes flow over them. Fur pushed, claws formed — another nail job to be fixed — and while the world was much bigger, it was simpler too. The emotions drowning them muted as *water* and *play* became the focus.

Haru ran to the bathroom, the bend and stretch of their back teasing out the knots and tension, but when they got to the tub, all they saw was another cage. Small. Unnatural. A place they couldn't really be themself. They looked to the window, the stars outside.

There was *wet* outside. The lake. Haru bounded to the suite door, momentarily defeated by the handle but they managed to Sahnkes quickly, check the hall for interlopers, and escape, welcoming their otter back as quickly as they could. They stopped by Tally's door and listened. A hum of Tally's electric blanket came from the room, and the smell of *snake* filled their senses.

Haru ran, sliding down the stairs, ever on the watch for people. The house had hidey-holes, lots of them, allowing them to scurry past unnoticed, but going out the back seemed like a double-edged sword. Loud music played, alcohol flowed freely, and laughter and voices filled the night. Everyone happy — everyone but Haru. They rounded to the front door, making their escape that way, slipping into the night.

Earthy scents exploded the moment the night air hit Haru's nose. Dirt. Grass. Leaves. That tinge of decay fall had. Lovely yet sad. Haru bounced around the side of the house, loping toward where the *water* called to them. Waves lapped at the shore. Small, tiny ones, nothing anyone not an otter or water-going lijun would notice, but Haru did.

The water and they danced as they bounded along the shore, looking for a nice hidey spot. Somewhere they would be protected if someone snappy came along. An outcropping of rocks looked promising, and Haru climbed them, sniffing at the holes. Was anyone home?

Hmm. Yes. Someone made their home here. The scent too strong to be an abandoned dwelling. Something not warm. Not like Haru.

The next set of rocks carried no traces of animal smells. It wasn't as noisy either — only the sound of music drifted this far. Haru bounded around and over, double and triple checking before they clawed between a couple larger stones. The spot had den potential written all over it.

A 'pop' made Haru jump. They spun around and hissed at the noise.

Large yellow sparkles lit up the sky. *Ooh. Firies.*

More pops echoed over the water, and Haru slid in, watching the sky expectantly. As they floated on their back, new colors exploded across the sky then were reflected by the lake. Fun, bright circles were split by screamies, followed by small white flashes.

Then the water bounced the flashes back.

Music, loud and strong, beat in time with the sparkles until the sky filled with golds, reds and blues. The song of earth and sky filled Haru, the vibrations lapping against them with the water, surrounding them from all sides.

Then it was gone, a moment of silence, complete blackness leaving Haru breathless. Those had been for them. Them and Tally. The thought left them needing to swim, dive, take refuge away from the light under the water where it was calm, unlike the way their heart beat so wildly.

Haru's moment of panic, confusion was interrupted by a pure white flash filling the sky.

Silver-black dots danced in the air in front of their eyes. They ached, so Haru closed them and let themself drift away on the lake's surface. The music was gone, but murmurs—voices—flowed over the water. But then a distressed chirp caught Haru's attention. They rolled, listening for the noise again.

There! Over there. Haru dove under the surface, the refreshing water flowing over them as they swam. Oh, fishes. No, there was a sound. A familiar sound they had to check on. Haru came up for some air, to try to locate the chirping.

Otter. Otter. Their senses were going nuts. One of theirs needed help. It made sense others had wanted to watch from the lake, but this one was theirs to care for.

Then they found her, splashing offshore, pawing at her face.

The light!

Haru grabbed hold of Sam, eliciting a startled squeak. Nose. Kiss. Kiss. They wouldn't let anything happen to her. She settled, nosing Haru back. A sad chirp broke a piece of their heart. Yes, nose, nose. The light hurt. Haru would fix. With one of her paws in theirs, Haru brought them back to the den. Or where their den would be. They nudged her onto the rocks, over to the dry land.

Kiss. Kiss. Better to be here than drifting alone. But they couldn't take care of her like this.

Haru forced the Sahnkes. "Sam? Can you Sahnkes?"

Another squeak.

"Sammy, please. It should help. Just keep your eyes closed."

A moment later, all five foot nothing of Sam was in their lap, her eyes squeezed shut. Nose. Nose. Kiss. Kiss.

"Shhh. Shhh. It will be all right. Do not worry." Haru petted her hair, holding their friend close. "I am here."

A sniffle escaped Sam. "Haru."

"The flash? That bright one?"

She nodded.

"Just keep your eyes closed for a while. It will stop hurting in a bit. I promise."

"Cold." Her teeth chattered and she shivered in their arms.

"We will warm up together." Haru held her close, one hand over her back. "Do not worry."

"Sounds like a proposition," she chuckled, though it was tired.

"It was not, I mean…"

"What? I'm not to your liking?"

"You are lovely." Haru knew she was teasing, could tell by the light tone in her voice, and nosed her ear. "Beautiful." They squeezed her close. "And our pups will be gorgeous, just like you."

"I think they're going to look like you, Haru. Pretty sure your genes win." Her voice was lighter, not so pain-filled. She slid off their lap, but they missed her warmth, so they tucked their head onto her lap and buried their face in her abdomen. Sam's fingers began to comb through their hair, their otterness to preen and clean kicking in.

Haru kissed the flat expanse of her stomach. Their pups would grow here. Their family. Little ones they could love. If there was one good thing coming from their betrothal and marriage, the pups and Sammy were it.

Kiss. Kiss. They wanted the pups to know. The children weren't here yet, but pups would come from this woman, Haru's only friend in this new life of theirs.

"No matter who they look like, they will be loved. I promise, Sammy. I do. I will love these pups."

Chapter Six

A Death Served Cold

Tally woke to the distinct feeling of something being wrong. Still in serpent form, huddled in his blanket nest, he tried to wake up enough to sort through it. Vague hurt still from the rejection the night before, but he understood Haru's concerns, so it wasn't that.

No. He wasn't going to give in to unspecified anxieties and the whispered rumors of precognition still being in his bloodline. All nonsense. It was so easy to be anxious about a number of things, then point to it later to say *See? I knew something wasn't right.*

While it would've been nice to stay snaked and snuggled nice and warm in his room, Tally was now officially lord of the manor. Responsibilities didn't allow for wallowing in bed. A group of lijun teens were coming to help clean up the grounds after the party, since Tally had promised to pay them for their time. He still had to supervise and help with some of the heavier lifting as the responsible adult. With a reptile sneeze he regained his human form, threw on some old clothes and braided his hair back. No reason to shower yet if he was just going to go out and get dirty.

The young people had just started to pull up as Tally was gathering supplies out on the front porch. He smiled and raised a hand in greeting. The Eberhardt girls, all three of them, piled out of Mindy's rusty Jeep. Justin Tripp, who had probably only showed up because of his crush on Mindy, arrived with his friends Carrie Sommers and Tyler Hastings, Barry's oldest. Three more cars followed theirs. Peregrines, crows, boars, raccoons, kestrels—it warmed Tally's heart to see the kids willing to work together without regard to their lijun types or any of their parents' politics.

"Morning, everyone!" Tally called out as they approached. "Coffee and pastries in the kitchen if you want to grab some and I'll meet you out back. We'll start by the lake where all the cake and champagne was."

There were some groans and some good-natured grumbling about tipsy adults, but the kids trooped inside for the promised breakfast items. The bit of hurt from the previous evening evaporated as Tally breathed in the crisp morning air and allowed himself a moment's peace to gaze out over the mist-wreathed trees. It was a beautiful place. He was going to be married soon. He was a lucky, lucky man.

His good mood deflated a bit when he herded the youngsters out back.

"Man," Carrie breathed. "If we made a mess like this at a party, we'd be grounded for a month."

"Grownups do get a little carried away sometimes." Tally handed out garbage bags. "All right. Pick up any trash first. Anything that's glass or china, please take to the kitchen. Nature will take care of cake crumbs, of course, but any large dropped pieces, please include in the trash. Justin, Tyler, once we get the tables cleared, help me get them folded and out front for pickup. If everyone else could do the same with the chairs, please."

Cleanup went quickly with so many hands, the kids talking and teasing each other as they worked. Tally would've asked them to keep it down, but Hal and Che were sleeping in the closest bedrooms. On the outside chance the noise managed to wake their lazy butts up, Tally wasn't going to be heartbroken.

Once the main party venue had been picked up, Tally sent his helpers off to assigned areas to pick up any remaining trash while he rolled the rented punch fountain out front and took the lakeshore for himself. Not too bad, generally. A dropped napkin here. A piece of streamer there. He was humming to himself, enjoying the quiet, when he stopped at an odd sight past a stand of willows.

Ed Cohen's work truck was still parked, not too far from where the fireworks company had parked their trucks. Sure, Ed could've had too much to drink and decided to sleep it off there, but he was a widower with little ones. That wouldn't be like him at all. Come to think of it, Tally hadn't seen anything of Ed since the beginning of the party when he'd come to offer congratulations. That was also odd. He was a typical opossum lijun, a little awkward but sociable.

Something's not right. Disconcerted, Tally jogged closer to the silver-gray panel truck and checked the cab. Empty. He hurried past the *Cohen's Pest Control* logo on the side with its red expired termite. The back doors were open, a foot with a dress shoe visible just under the right-hand door.

"Ed? You all..." Tally's inquiry died away when he caught sight of Ed sprawled on the floor in the back. His suit jacket was rucked up under him. His eyes stared empty and sightless at the ceiling. "Oh Gods...Ed."

Footsteps crunched through the leaves and a young male voice called from behind him, "Urusar Bastille? The rental company's here for the table and stuff. Should we —"

The horrified gasp had Tally whirling around. Tyler Hastings stood not three feet away with his mouth hanging open and all the blood draining from his face. "Tyler, I need you to get the others to the house."

"Holy shit," Tyler whispered. His terrified gaze bounced between Tally and Ed's body. "Holy *shit!*"

"Tyler, wait!" Tally called out but the kid had already raced off, huffing and whimpering. He'd have to see to that later. Getting the police to the scene was the priority. He fumbled his phone from his jeans pocket and dialed with shaking fingers. "Damn it, what happened here? Hello? Yes. This is Tally Bastille. I need to report a death on my property."

Within ten minutes he heard the sirens, though it felt much longer standing in the peaceful grove with Ed's body. He was ushered back when the coroner and the first deputies arrived, trying to answer all the questions shouted at him. *Did you touch anything? Did you move anything? Is this how you found him? How long ago was that?* Of course he hadn't touched anything. He wasn't an idiot.

"Best get up to the house, Mr. Bastille." Sheriff Amick had arrived, his movements surprisingly careful for a man of his bulk as he took a cursory look at the scene. "Let us do our job here. I'll be up to talk to everyone."

Tally nodded and jogged up to the house, gathering his cleaning crew as he ran.

"Tyler's gone, Urusar Bastille," Carrie said, backing up as Tally approached. "He said you killed someone and he wasn't going to be next."

"For Gods' sakes, Carrie. Of course I didn't kill anyone. Into the house, please. I'm sure the police will want to know if you saw anything unusual this morning."

"But someone's dead?"

Tally stopped and turned to face the teenagers gathered in an anxious knot around him. "Yes. Ed Cohen died in the back of his truck. I don't know any more yet. Remember who's in the room when you talk to the police. This may be a human problem. It may be a lijun problem. No speculating, all right?"

Once he had nods from each of them, he dashed ahead to the house, leapt up the stairs and opened the doors to the bedrooms where Che, Hal and Lahi were staying. "Up. Up. Come on. I need someone to run to the cottage for Mom and Dad. The police are here. Stop hissing at me, Hal. Ed Cohen's dead. Move."

He waited until his siblings had thundered down the steps before he stepped over to Haru's suite and tapped on the door. "Haru?" he called softly. "I need you to come out. Something terrible's happened."

Several loud thuds, then there was some creative swearing—while it might not be English, but Tally knew swearing when he heard it, didn't matter the language—more thuds followed, and finally Haru appeared at the door, breathless, tangled hair flying about his bare shoulders and torso. Completely unkempt and exactly like Haru. His Haru. Open. Not concerned with what was proper.

"Sorry, it's urgent."

"What's wrong?" Haru stiffened, his eyes downcast. Did his cheeks darken?

"It'd be better if we—" Tally motioned to the room. "Please."

"Yes, okay." Haru stepped back, allowing him in.

Chaos. The room was in chaos. Tally couldn't believe all the clothes strewn about. The *furisode*, its underthings. The *obi* completely unraveled. Haru's cheeks darkened further, and he began to pick up, apologizing.

"Sorry, I, sorry. I ottered out."

"Haru, please, you don't have to—there are more important things to worry about."

An audible swallow escaped Haru, and when Tally looked closer, a visible tremor shook his chest as his breathing rabbited.

"I don't care about the room. It's fine. I'll help you pick up later." Tally took the clothes out of Haru's arms and tossed them on the chair. He pulled his otter close, petting his back. That's what they did when trying to comfort, didn't they? "I'm sorry. Really."

"You are not mad?"

"Never." Ooh, they were so close, and Haru wasn't pushing him away. The way Haru's hands dug into his back made Tally feel like the luckiest lijun there was. How to tell him there was a clan death?

Haru smelled of fireworks and lake. Someone had definitely ottered out last night. Tally understood. He'd needed his serpent after last night's dismissal. Was Haru as frustrated as he was?

"Listen, I have some bad news. I found one of our clan members by the lake during clean up. The police are here."

135

"Oh, oh no. Did they—were they?" The catch in Haru's throat made Tally's heart ache. "Did they drown?"

"I don't know what happened yet. Why don't you grab some clothes and meet me in my suite?"

Tally had just changed into a pair of clean jeans and a sweater when Haru peeked in, his instincts good enough that he didn't knock. He had brushed his hair and tied it back in some semblance of respectability, and was wearing the green corduroys with a cream button-down and an oversized black cardigan.

The outfit gave him a vulnerable, soft appearance and Tally just wanted to wrap him in blankets and hide him away from the ugliness downstairs. He took Haru's hand gently. "They're going to ask where everyone was last night. I just want to warn you ahead of time that the police will most likely be polite but they may not be friendly. I don't know much yet. Only that the victim is Ed, one of the opossum lijun who came for the party."

"Does he have a wife? Children?"

Tally's breath hitched on the answer. "Three little opossums. Their mother died two years ago. I have to find out who has them."

He took Haru by the hand and led him downstairs. Voices drifted out from the front room, Mom and Dad. When he turned the corner, he was surprised to find everyone there, all the local siblings along with the sheriff, human, and his senior deputy, cat lijun.

"Morning, Sheriff Amick, Melissa." Tally stopped just over the threshold, neither moving toward a chair not releasing Haru's hand. "Any idea what happened to Ed?"

"Mr. Bastille," the sheriff peered over top his glasses at Tally. "Nice of you and your, ah, boyfriend—"

"Fiancé."

Sheriff Amick neither acknowledged or apologized. "To join us. Need to ask you some questions if you don't mind. Deputy Kincaid, please clear the room."

"Now wait just a minute, Robert," Mom said as she set her coffee down with a definite clunk.

"No, Kara, I'm sorry. This is serious business. I need to talk to these two without interference, please."

"It's all right, Mom." Gods. Ed hadn't just died. This was a suspicious death. "We're happy to answer whatever questions might help."

The sheriff waited until Tally's and Haru's families had filed out before he pointed with his pen to the sofa opposite him. "Have a seat, gentlemen."

Tally took Haru's hand in both of his as they sat, maybe to reassure Haru, maybe for the warmth Tally felt seeping out of his own body. "Can you tell me what happened?"

"Understand there was quite the party here last night," Sheriff Amick began, not looking up from his notetaking.

So far, nothing outlandish. "Yes. It was our engagement party."

The sheriff glanced up over his glasses again. "You had pest issues at this party, Mr. Bastille?"

Okay, that went off the rails quickly. "Ah, no."

"Any idea why Ed Cohen was here with his truck, then?"

With his...? "Well, yes. I suppose. Ed was invited, of course. I think his work truck is his only vehicle right now."

"Hmm." The sheriff sat back to stare at him directly. "You in the habit of inviting the help to fancy parties out here?"

"Not sure I like that implication, Sheriff. I've known Ed since we were in grade school together."

"As you say. Witnesses state you left the party early, Mr. Bastille. Can you tell me where you were between nine and midnight?"

"In my room." But Haru wasn't in his. Oh Gods.

"Can anyone corroborate that?"

"I can," Haru replied, rather frostily, and slid his arm in Tally's. His normally bright eyes had cooled and narrowed. "It was *our* engagement party."

The sheriff's nose crinkled in obvious distaste. "So you..." He consulted his notes. "Mr. Tanaka, you were with Mr. Bastille the entire night?"

"Where else would I be?"

"Just answer the question, Mr. Tanaka," Melissa snapped out.

"I was with my loving fiancé, all night. Rather happily." Haru nuzzled Tally's neck, squinting over at the sheriff and Melissa.

Oooh. Otters and cats. Not the best of friends.

Sheriff Amick spoke without even glancing up. "Did either of you see a bright white flash over by the lake?

Tally shook his head. "I know there were fireworks, but I wasn't looking outside."

Haru stiffened, ever so subtly that only Tally would've noticed. "A flash? I could not say. We were *occupied*."

The lie protected both of them, in a way, but there wasn't any secret about where the suspicion fell here. Haru had lied for Tally, not prevaricated, but outright lied, not once but twice. He never wanted his love to do that for him but this once... His throat closed up a bit and he had to blink back tears.

"How well did you know Ed, Mr. Bastille?" Sheriff Amick had returned to scribbling.

"Fairly well." Tally shook his head. "We don't see as much of him since Jackie died."

"Anyone you can think of who might wish him harm? Someone he was having an argument with?"

The air turned to ice in Tally's lungs. "You think he was murdered."

"Too early and not enough information to speculate. In my professional opinion, it doesn't *look* like a natural death, but that's all I'm willing to say right now. The question?"

"Oh." Tally blinked, trying to get enough breath to speak. "No. I mean, not that I know of. Ed did his job, did it well, took care of his kids. I don't think he had time for much else."

Sheriff Amick gave his notepad one last tap with his pen before he heaved himself from his chair. "Thank you for your time, Mr. Bastille. Mr. Tanaka. If you think of anything, a noise you heard, something that didn't seem right, give us a call." He waved his hand at them in an almost dismissive gesture. "And congratulations on the...whatever this is."

While he strode out, Melissa stood, spearing Tally with narrowed eyes. "Cyanotic, Tally. I'm willing to wait for the coroner results, but you know how that looks, don't you?"

"I know. My family's all accounted for?"

"They are. Multiple witnesses put them at the party. You're the only one who wasn't in plain sight." Melissa fidgeted with her hat. "How am I supposed to handle this? A lijun death and I'm *supposed* to work with the Urusar."

"But your Urusar is a person of interest," Tally said as a cold ball settled in his stomach. "I didn't do this, Melissa, but I know you have to go by actual evidence. Keep me informed as much as you can. For the rest, you'll have to make reports to the senior-most council members. Clement's neutral enough that no one will worry about bias and Tyra's more likely to be fair than some others."

"All right." Melissa's lips pressed into a thin, unhappy line. "So long as you understand that I'm going to do what the job dictates. There's a reason uktena are scary."

Tally managed a curt nod before she stalked after her superior, and he finally released the breath he'd not quite been able to let go of the whole time. *Gods. Oh Gods. This is so so bad.*

"What did she mean?" Haru whispered.

"How much do you know about the uktena, really? Not the wild stories, the myths, but the actual biology?"

"None. Just the myths. Like the flash."

Tally puffed his cheeks out with a long breath. "Yes. The flash. There is a bright crest on our foreheads, it does...it *can* flash a blinding white under the right circumstances. One other thing you've probably heard is true. Uktena *are* poisonous. We don't have a fang delivery system like other venomous snakes, though. It's a, um, gaseous delivery system."

"Your breath is not that bad."

Somehow Haru managed a completely straight face after that remark. That was talent. "Ha. Well. We have specialized venom sacs right behind the jaws. A certain contracting of muscle, and thank goodness it's hard to do so it doesn't happen by accident, sends out poisonous vapors. The attacker, or victim I suppose, depending on the person, essentially dies of suffocation. Cyanosis, like Melissa said."

"I see. She suspects one of our family? You, specifically."

"Me, specifically. That's what I was getting, yes."

Haru closed his eyes, just for a moment, but when he opened them again—Tally saw the determination in them. "We will protect what is ours. This clan. This family. You."

"Thank you." Tally wrapped Haru in his arms and kissed the top of his head. "My fierce, brave otter. Let's hope it doesn't come to that."

* * * *

"Of course I defended him!" Haru huffed out. "I practically sat in his lap to defend him."

Otōusan and *Okaasan* both frowned, but it was Mother who spoke. "We *do* wish you had handled that differently. Did you have to imply you had relations before the wedding?"

"It was the best I could do." Under pressure. Sammy had understood Haru's need for discretion when he'd talked with her.

"Not good enough. You are Satislit. What if this gets back to Urusar Akaike?"

"I think he will understand there were more important things than my nonexistent virtue!"

"Haru, don't yell at your mother." His father's voice was hard, unyielding. Sounded very much like 'I will tell the Urusar if you don't behave' kind of tone. It had cowed Haru many a time. So many times. Some bruises did not heal so easily.

"*Gomen'nasai, Otōusan, Okaasan.*"

"Better. Remember your position here."

How can I forget?

"We don't want the Bastilles to think you're getting cold feet."

"What?" Oh, the hitch in their voice, it gave them away, but his parents couldn't be serious. Hiding their face was Haru's only option.

Mother sighed. The sound heavy, *serious*.

"It's one thing to defend him — the humans didn't seem so keen on the Bastilles — but are you saying you still want me to marry him?"

A long, drawn-out sigh, followed by Father's chair creaking, made Haru turn to face their parents. *Otōusan* was frowning, like usual, his hands clasped behind his back. He had *that* look on his face. The one where he thought Haru was being particularly dense. But they had hoped, honestly believed, there must be a spark of doubt within their parents since they wanted to talk. Talking meant concern. Haru wanted to think it had been concern for *them*, and that their parents had convinced Urusar Akaike to call off the contract.

"Tally is suspected of murder! Murder!" Haru's hands fisted at their sides. "It's one thing to defend him against a human, it's another to expect me to go through with the wedding. There has got to be some kind of get out of jail card."

"Haru—"

"Check the contract!" Haru pulled away from Father and started pacing. They needed to get away. How could their parents expect them to stay? "No marriage due to murder! It's got to be in there."

"We don't know anything. The police have not said the opossum lijun was murdered," *Okaasan* replied. Her words froze a piece of his heart. "Besides *you* were with him. You know he's innocent. We know he's innocent. It's the humans we have to convince."

Ouch. Oh fucking ouch. The chasm in their chest burned. But their parents really didn't know. Their mother's words hurt worse because Haru couldn't walk back on their claim without exposing themself or Tally. That would make matters more complicated, and Haru did not want questions as to where they'd spent the night last night, or what they'd been doing. Those would be uncomfortable to answer. The less others knew, the better. As long as everyone thought they had been together, the clan, Tally and Haru were safe.

"Have you considered *what* Tally and his family are?"

"Yes, when we signed the contract. Just because you're scared doesn't mean they are as ruthless as you think."

"Uktena are not otters. We are two different kind of lijun."

Otōusan shook his head. "We're still parts of the same. Besides, I am surprised to hear such talk out of you."

"You are not the one marrying him!"

"I told you before the Imsi Tamgradat not to screw this up." *Otōusan* grabbed Haru's arm. "He is a good match, Haru. We will never get a better one for you. The Kwebabaids, the land, the money, this is not a contract the clan can walk away from."

"Please, don't hold back, *Otōusan*." *Way to tell me how worthless I am. That my only worth is that of a* Satislit.

"This is your duty."

"I know! But—"

"Tally is kind. He has provided your every silly request. This house. The comfort you have been given. All because of his strength and position. The fact he believes you are Em'halafi, destined, means you will be treated fairly. This match gives you just as much as it does the clan."

"But—" *Not love.*

"You've already lain with him."

"I never said that," Haru snapped. Not with Tally, they hadn't.

Father scowled. "Then why did you say you did?"

"Because." The conversation was going in circles. "It was easy."

"Then you should have found a better lie. It isn't proper for a Satislit to make such implications."

"*Otōusan.* Aren't you a little bit concerned what kind of alliance the clan has made?"

"This argument is pointless," *Otōusan* replied. Father motioned to Mother and she stood, moving toward the suite doors. "The wedding is in two days. We need to pick up Urusar Akaike. Don't run your mouth when he gets here. Hopefully this match is salvageable if Urusar Bastille doubts you. You must be on your best behavior, Haru. You know what will happen if you fail your duties."

"I never said I wouldn't do them."

"Then start acting the part!"

"I have been!"

Otōusan snorted. "Barely. If he sends you back, you only have yourself to blame. Of course, you can't come back."

Haru flinched. They knew. They *did* know the stakes. How much their parents would loathe the shame of Haru failing—again. How angry they'd been with their 'childish rebellions'. Except this wasn't another Imsi they had tried to sabotage. This wager was much bigger than anything Haru had ever had to deal with before. A marriage. Haru's life. Hearing the cold-blooded way their parents sided with the Urusar, Haru thought they were better suited to be nure-onna like Misaki, not otters.

Banishment. All of them hung it over Haru like an executioner's blade. One wrong step and they'd be cut off. Ice, thick and poisonous, stilled their heart.

Mother cracked open the door. "We thought you were finally accepting your position here."

"I was — *am*."

"Good. Your sisters made decent matches. I don't understand why you've been so stubborn."

Father nodded. "I won't ask again, Haru. The clan needs this match. Do not dishonor the clan who raised you. Your training wasn't cheap."

"I won't, *Otōusan*." Haru swallowed back the scream building inside them.

"As long as you understand."

"I do." Perfectly.

"Now stay out of trouble while we pick Urusar Akaike-san up. You can do that, can't you?"

"Yes."

Otōusan and *Okaasan* swept out of the room, leaving it cooler rather than heated from the fight. The walls towered over Haru, looming over them, caging Haru in. Breathing hurt. The subarctic burn encased their heart and lungs, convincing them they'd shatter any moment. Wouldn't that be just perfect?

Death by heart failure.

Haru curled up on the wingback, desperately trying to hold themself together — literally and emotionally. Ottering out right now would only upset their parents. Their anger would only fuel Urusar Akaike's if any of them thought Haru was trying to shirk their duties.

Hope was a cruel thing to have.

There was a knock at the door, tentative. When it opened, Tally poked his head through. Haru almost threw a pillow at him, unable to face their Xatiba. Their jailer. It was a shame he was so good-looking, because Haru could at least appreciate his physicality. Though, the naiveté of someone so astute in his business dealings astounded Haru. How could someone from such a forward-thinking society actually believe in Em'halafi?

"Um, hi? Is it okay for me to come in?" Tally asked, still holding the door handle. "I heard…yelling."

"My apologies, Urusar Bastille." Haru automatically slid out of their chair and went into a *senrei*. How long had they kept Tally waiting? "My" —*heartless*— "parents had some concerns about the investigation. They could not quite keep up with all the questioning."

Tally's eyebrows had climbed his forehead. "I'm sorry about that. It must have worried them quite a bit." If Tally realized Haru was bullshitting, he was apparently opting for polite fiction instead of calling him on it. "Are you all right?"

"Yes, Ur—my Argaze. Thank you for your concern. It brings me pleasure."

Behave. Behave. Don't show how scared you are. Stop shaking. Haru had to be the Satislit their clan wanted. Had to. They couldn't afford to have Tally suspect how conflicted they felt. They had to keep the lies of last night going. Haru peeked up from their position on the floor, trying to gauge what the snake was thinking. Each beat of their heart hurt, cracks breaking deep, etching a web into their heart.

"Argaze?"

Haru's heart rabitted. "Have I done something to displease you? Would you rather me not call you

Argaze yet? We are not yet married. It was forward of me. My apologies." Their voice cracked a bit at the end. Opting for submission was probably better, so Haru turned their gaze on Tally's feet and shut up.

Tally's voice was soft, a shade husky when he spoke. "It's… I don't mind. Certainly a step up from Urusar. Haru, I wish… When it's just us, there's no need to be so formal. I know why, in front of your parents. In public. I *do* understand. But when it's just us, could you call me Tally?"

"As you please — *Tally*."

There might have been a sigh, just the slightest one. "I'd like it to be as *you* please."

"I am sorry? I do not understand."

The feet came closer, then Tally surprised Haru by taking a knee in front of them, one hand out. What had they done wrong to make his Xabita get on the floor with them? Haru struggled to understand what was wanted of them, but they had obviously missed something.

"Urusar Bastille?"

This time Haru heard the sigh. "Tally. Just Tally."

"Yes."

"How do I — Right." That wasn't a happy sound. *Right.* The word came out more like a swear. "Your gratitude pleases me. Now — " The hand came back. "How about making ourselves more comfortable?"

Haru let Tally pull him up and lead them to the sofa by the fireplace. There was wood in the stove, but it wasn't lit. Early days of October yet. Fall had just started. The Harvest Moon was two days away. Haru found this time of year to be some of their favorite weather, only second to winter. Snow slides were the best. The den would be a good spot for one—lots of fun for Haru and their pups.

"Mind if I light a fire?"

Oh, right, for Tally the room had to be freezing. "Yes, right away, if you let me—"

"I'm asking *you*, Haru. Is it okay if I light a fire in *your* room?"

Was this a trick question? Urusars did not ask permission. This kind of behavior from their Xabita outright confused Haru, and caused them to worry for the Bastille clan. Any American lijun, if they had to be honest.

One of those sighs came again. Haru was quickly associating it with frustration. It wasn't like the ones their parents gave, but it made Haru nervous just the same. They picked at the tassels on the woven blanket. They needed to give an answer that made Tally think Haru wanted it, whatever it was, and make sure the Urusar was being properly taken care of. Difficult bastard.

"Fires are nice."

Tally smiled, big and broad, like Haru had done something special.

After poking and prodding the fire until a warm orange glow filled the room, Tally stood close for a few minutes, not saying anything, and held his hands to the flames. The silence was actually nice. Tally wasn't trying to fill it with anything, make Haru say something which could potentially be disastrous, and they could just be.

When Tally finally turned, his gaze settled on Haru's, and the smile was back. Laugh lines were just starting around his mouth. The glow warmed their Xabita's hard lines and softened the expression on his face. He pointed to the sofa.

"May I join you?"

It was easier to nod than to reply. Haru had a feeling it would only upset Tally.

"Thank you."

The smile got bigger.

Tally settled close, but not too close. His hand could touch the back of Haru's neck if he wanted to, which apparently he did. His large palm rested right underneath Haru's hairline, just the solid feel of his hand against Haru's skin, the touch more erotic than what Haru expected. Being so exposed, in such a vulnerable position, made it hard to concentrate.

"This is nice," Tally murmured. "The fire."

Haru nodded again, unable to find the proper words to reply with. Silence was better. They couldn't stick their foot in their mouth if they didn't talk.

"Sitting here, with you."

This was something they needed to agree with. "Yes."

Tally's thumb pressed into Haru's neck, drawing circles, doing the same with his fingertips.

"Haru, I, uh… I want us to be happy. Me to be happy. You to be happy. I hope I am providing you with the support you need. I know I took you away from your home, your teaching position, for this marriage."

Haru waited, because they had a feeling that Tally was trying to say something important.

"It's unfair you had to give so much up for me. I mean, I know we're Em'halafi so we'll make it work, but I *am* sorry my position meant so much upheaval for you." Tally's thumb circled harder, his grip tighter. "Everything happened so fast, it had to be stressful, overwhelming. And Ed's death, that couldn't have made things easier. I know it's all different here. Not what you're used to."

What could they say? Anything Haru could think of would be accusatory. *Then why did you buy me?* That wouldn't go over well.

"So, what I'm trying to say is, if there is anything, anything at all I can do to make life here easier for you, then please say so. Just tell me."

It sounded sincere?

"If there are certain channels we can get here from Japan. We can get those." Tally's fingers thumped against Haru's neck. "Or books. Or talking. If talking helps. Or, or like the bath. Anything that would help your otter, we can change."

"My otter?"

"Yes, like how we have stoves in the suites because of our serpents. If your otter needs anything, I will make sure we get it. I just want you happy."

The look Tally gave Haru was so expectant, their mind went blank. The fact Tally was trying to fix *things* was generous, but Haru resented it, erroneous as it were. Money couldn't fix their problems. Tally couldn't buy Haru.

But he already did, didn't he?

"What can I do, Haru?"

"Rocks, for my den." Where did that come from?

"Your den?" Tally glanced over to the far door. "As in the bathroom?"

"No, I found a spot by the lake. It would be nice for me and the pups, but I need to build it out. Some rocks, wood, so I can make it properly."

"I'd be more than happy to get you some rocks. If you show me—"

"Could I not? I mean, not yet? It is nice, to have a space just for me, for right now. A place where I could just be? I do not mean to push you away." *Though I kind of do.* "I just need a place to otter and not worry."

The pinch around Tally's eyes lessened and his expression softened. "Of course, I understand. Everyone needs their own special spot. I have my own for the summers, when my serpent needs to sun."

"Thank you." Haru found they meant it, too.

"No need for thanks. It's what mates do."

Haru glanced over at Tally. Something in his tone felt *vulnerable.*

"I want what any Em'halafi have together. A life. A happy one. Shared together. I want to love and be loved."

The words, familiar, oddly familiar, struck Haru as hopeful. Wistful. Words saying what Haru desperately wanted for themself. When Tally pulled Haru close, settling one hand on their waist, they didn't have the energy to push Tally away. The humongous busybody who decided they should be wrapped in the blanket as well. They let their head fall against their Xabita's shoulder and focused on the red embers in the stove, glowing brightly against the chill in the air.

"Yes, do not we all?" Haru whispered as they settled in.

* * * *

"Cyanosis," Gun repeated, expression hard and flat. "I'd say it was an accident with the fumigation stuff that Ed carts around, but he was there for the party. In a suit. I mean, I talked to him. Shit."

With Gunther back in town for the wedding, they'd gone out, just the five of them. No significant others. Marnie joked that it was the closest Tally would get to having a bachelor party. It was a comfort thing, going out to 'their' restaurant, Happy Grazing, the elk-owned vegetarian brewpub they'd all agreed on when they were college-age. The predators had grumbled over eating bunny food, but even Marnie and Gunther found things to like.

"All a little weird," Pete said as he reached across for a big scoop of hummus. "I mean, if it was something medical, they'd say, right? And if it wasn't…"

"Who would m-murder Ed?" Lily whispered.

"Did the police question all of you, too?" Tally frowned and set his beer back down.

Marnie shot him a look. "They questioned *everyone* at the party, Tal. Everyone. Did we see anything, did we hear anything, was Ed having problems with anyone."

"And?"

"None of us have a clue." Pete shrugged.

"They asked me if he was having any problems with the Bastilles," Gun added with an angry snort.

Lily's eyes flew wide. "They d-didn't!"

"Sure as hell did." Gun pushed his falafel around his plate. "Didn't make any sense at the time. Now that you've told us what Melissa said, though? Now it makes sense."

"They can't think Tally did it. Or anyone in his family." Pete patted Tally's arm. "It had to have been some freak accident, Tal. There'll be tox reports and stuff."

"You sound like a police procedural show." Tally managed a little smile, a sip of beer, though his stomach was sour and wobbly. "Anyway, the kids are with Mrs.

Kaufmann for now. Poor baby opossums. But she's not as young as she was when she was *our* first-grade teacher, and three little kids are a handful. We'll have to figure out something permanent for them soon since they don't have grandparents or uncles and aunts."

"Sorry," Gun muttered. "We're supposed to be celebrating. Didn't mean to take us down dark roads there."

Marnie raised her glass. "To the Argaze!"

"To the Satislit!" Pete echoed. "To Tally going off the market, much to the sorrow of humans and lijun everywhere!"

Tally had to laugh at that, finally a lighter moment. "Thank you. I think."

After a good bit of snickering, Gun finally said, "I have to be honest, Tal. He's not what I pictured for you."

"Oh?"

Marnie poked his arm. "Kind of an odd duck, isn't he? And *not* what we expected after the dessert raid story."

"I guess we w-were expecting another S-Sam." Lily cocked her head at an inquisitive angle.

"He's—" Tally hesitated. He didn't want to justify Haru, to feel obliged to *explain* him to people. But these were his friends. They were only concerned. "Haru's family...they're very traditional in a lot of ways. Not like you see in some lijun families here where it's all about natural this and natural that. But very Japanese traditional. Proper behavior. Correct presentation. Honor attached to family. The Imsi Tamgradat was a little rocky—"

Gun nearly choked on a laugh. "Death wine."

Pete tried for a straight face, but the snicker still won. "Eels."

"Shh. Let Tally talk." Marnie rolled her eyes. "Boys."

Those moments had been mortifying then, but the horror and embarrassment had faded. "Yes. Right. That's exactly the point, though. Haru is trying extra hard to be the perfect Satislit in all things. I think...I *hope* he'll feel more able to be himself once the wedding's over and the family goes home."

"He's amazingly well put together," Marnie said. "Just so poised and composed. I think if I was marrying someone in another country, I'd be a wreck."

"Very traditional, as I said. Trained formally from a young age in all the things necessary for a Japanese Satislit." Tally took a bigger gulp of beer. *In all those things that make me want to get him alone and unwrap him.*

"I c-can't even imagine." Lily shook her head. "The only thing we got trained in was h-how to operate h-heavy equipment."

Gun raised a single black eyebrow. "Pete would make a terrible Satislit in Japan."

"Flower arranging by backhoe." Marnie clinked glasses with him. "Yeah. Don't see that happening."

Chapter Seven

One Wedding & an Inquest

Monthly lijun council meetings had never been Tally's favorite thing. This was the second one this month, since a death in the community necessitated an emergency meeting, but he knew the members well enough by now that they wouldn't limit discussion to Ed's death.

The venue moved depending on what was available, but his dad had tried to have them in town whenever possible. Tally had been tagging along since he was sixteen. For this one, he'd had an open slot in the Oak Room of the Bastille Arms in town, perfect for meetings, with its dark-paneled walls and well-insulated doors. The staff had a standing order for coffee and pastries whenever Tally scheduled one of his 'local business council' meetings and they never failed to come through. The cherry Danishes were the best reason to come.

All right, he had more vital reasons to attend these days. That evening, he really wanted to chicken out and ask Dad to come back, but that would've been so wrong. There were ten members of the council, picked by the community every seven years. With the Urusar and Uruma, that made twelve. Oddly, the same ten lijun had been on the council for as long as Tally could remember.

Barry Hastings, from an old boar family, always made sure he had the seat to the Urusar's left. He bustled in early, also as usual, snuffling as he pumped Tally's hand. "Congratulations, young man. Making a proper Urusar of you. Proper Satislit with Kwebabiads and all. Mind you, someone your own species would've been optimal, like your parents did. But you young people have your own ideas, I know."

"Thank you," Tally managed at his driest. Nothing he hadn't heard before. *Don't mix the species. Certain species were meant to lead.* Blah blah blah. "Barry, this is Haru Tanaka, about whom I'm sure you've heard by now. Haru, Barry Hastings. He owns several grocery stores in the county and other retail properties."

Barry extended his hand, perplexed when Haru had already bowed and didn't see it. "Oh, um, yes. Pleased to meet you."

"Hastings-san," Haru murmured. It seemed as much a greeting as a dismissal and Tally wasn't at all sad when Barry moved away.

He'd gone over the council members with Haru that afternoon, those dark eyes gleaming with a more lively intelligence than Tally had seen Haru allow himself to show in some time. These stand with us, he had said. Not in so many words, but he knew his Satislit understood. These stand against us in most things. These are the ones who are neither this nor that, the ones too frightened or too indifferent to take passionate sides.

They made the greeting rounds as council members arrived. Deer, elk, moose, fox, wolf, rabbit, peregrine, muskrat and mountain lion. Nostrils flared or noses twitched for each introduction, not something a human would necessarily notice, but normal among lijun as they identified type and wheels spun as to how the knowledge could be used. They all knew Haru was an otter. The scenting was simply an automatic habit of which many lijun were only half-aware.

Mom arrived last, with genial apologies, and even though he knew it was childish, relief swept over Tally in a heated wave to have her there.

"Hello, dear." Mom hurried over to kiss Tally's cheek. "I'm so sorry. Got caught on the phone with Aunt Emma and you know how she is." She turned and planted a quick kiss on Haru's cheek as well. "Thank you for coming, Haru. Not a happy place to start, but a vital one. You sit next to me."

She kidnapped Haru, tucking his hand into the crook of her elbow with a little pat and heading to her — *their* — spot at the long table. Seeing them together fueled that warm glowing globe inside Tally's chest even as he envied his mom her easy supremacy in a roomful of difficult personalities.

Gods. If he could only be like her, or like his father, who ruled every room he entered simply by existing in that space. But Tally's size made people wary, made them remember *what* he was, and his anxieties kept him from using that as a more ruthless man might have.

Not to mention, he simply couldn't pull off ruthless.

He let the council members settle naturally, all seasoned veterans. They knew how this worked and so far, no one had pulled any absurdly petty garbage like forcing Tally to call them to order just to see if he would.

So far. The power struggles might only begin when Mom ceded her place to Haru.

Tally took his place, hands laced atop the table. "Thank you, everyone, for coming out this evening. I wish we had a better reason to meet today."

"We all know it's about Ed," Dan O'Rourke broke in, brusque and dismissive of polite openers. Bull moose and banking executive together in one man were not a recipe for patience or tact. "Have the police said anything useful? All we've heard is it might be suspicious."

"Nothing more than that yet," Tally started to explain. "There will be an inquest, of cou—"

"He was killed on your property," Rose Howe cut him off in a trembling voice, fear and outrage in equal measures as only a rabbit could manage. "At a party full of your friends and family. How can you not *know*?"

Tally fought down the urge to lean forward and look her in the eyes. Intimidation. That's what it would be. "Because no one saw what happened, Rose. There were a lot of cars everywhere. Ed parked his truck out of the way, probably trying to be polite and give other people space for smaller vehicles. He...the death...was next to his truck. I don't really know anything else at this point."

He let his gaze fall on Haru's notepad, where his otter was writing in kanji. It could be poetry or pornography for all Tally knew. Haru was most likely taking diligent notes, but he could have been constructing unflattering nicknames for the council members, as Tally had done in his head when he was younger.

"Let's not beat around the bush here." Clement Black, the fox lijun who served as director at the hospital, leaned back in his chair, his casual air a bit too studied. "Rumor is they questioned every Bastille closely. The police, that is. That says to me that the death was unusual. Suspicious."

"And that flash! People are talking about the white flash!" Rose blurted out, though she stiffened and swallowed hard, nose twitching when Tally glanced her way.

"There was a flash." Mom leaned forward looking up and down the table. "It wasn't part of the fireworks and appears to have been in the vicinity of Ed's truck. But every Bastille has been accounted for that night, some by several witnesses."

"Well, I know it wasn't you, Kara," Tyra Pierce, the mountain lion software executive, purred. "You were playing tipsy bocce ball with me on the back lawn."

Mom reached over Haru and patted her hand. "We were. And you were losing. My family's been accounted for. We don't know any more than that yet."

An uncomfortable silence fell in which feet shuffled and throats cleared. Tally knew what they were thinking. The snakes protect their own. But without evidence, no one was going to make wild accusations. Not yet.

"Assets and orphans, then," Hakkon Eberhardt, their peregrine attorney, said with a sigh.

Tally nodded and glanced over. "Did you find anything, Hak?"

The rest of the council shifted restlessly, most likely confused, perhaps even more suspicious.

"I did. It was a few years ago, but I thought I remembered meeting with the Cohens in my office." Hakkon held up a document, one of those folded in such a way and backed by a blank piece of paper that screamed *legalese*. "I'm the executor. They didn't have anyone else nearby. There'll be some inventory to do. Perhaps a sale of the business. But mostly this will be a straightforward matter of holding the estate in trust for the little ones. The more urgent matter is getting them in a home before the human foster care system gets involved."

Opossum children who weren't even school age couldn't be placed with a human family. It didn't bear thinking about.

"Urusar Bastille?"

Tally's head whipped around at the unexpected sound of Haru's voice. "Yes, Haru?"

"Maybe we should take the children?" Haru's gaze never left his careful notes. "The house...has room."

"It certainly does," Tally said gently before he turned his gaze back to Hakkon. "After the wedding, we'll get that taken care of. When the household isn't in such an uproar. We'd be happy to take them."

He could have sworn someone muttered *of course you would be* but he couldn't be sure whom. The cynical part of him knew what that was about. Control the kids and control the assets. But what little Ed had left them wouldn't be a drop in the garden tub of Bastille money, what possible interest could they think he had? Or maybe, even worse, they thought he would eat them. Tally pressed his lips together hard and planted his palms on the table to keep them from shaking.

None of that mattered. He'd meant to talk to Haru about the kids, hoping he would agree to taking them in, but his Satislit had anticipated him. If that glowing globe in Tally's chest got any bigger, he might float off like a New Year's lantern.

"Debts," Dan said from the end of the table.

The rest of the meeting, short as it was, consisted of taking care of Ed's bank loans and mortgage. Tally waved off the dark frowns and concerns. He would take care of those if someone would compile a list, please.

"With all that settled," Barry spoke up almost before Hakkon and Dan had agreed to compiling outstanding debt information. "I'd like to discuss the Harris Street—"

"It's been a trying week, Barry," Mom cut him off, her tone clipped and sharp. One didn't have to be one of her kids to recognize that voice as the *this is not appropriate* one. "Any regular council business can wait until the next regularly scheduled meeting."

The council meeting broke up, slowly as members buttonholed each other to discuss other topics. Tally wandered over to where his mom and Haru stood by the coffee urn.

"Mom? Do you think we still have Duplo blocks down in one of the basement closets?"

She gave him a speculative look he couldn't quite read. "I suppose you'll just have to look, won't you?"

* * * *

"Sheriff, we have a wedding today." Dad stood in the doorway, obviously reluctant to let their visitor in.

"I know people think I'm a little slow sometimes, Achak." Sheriff Amick pushed his hat back. "But I don't think anyone could've missed that."

They both stepped aside to let boutonniere and corsage deliveries through and Dad relented, allowing him into the front hall.

Tally saw the exchange as he descended the stairs and hurried over. "Any news, Sheriff?"

"It'll take some time before Dr. Silva's done." Sheriff Amick got out his notepad, probably the only law enforcement officer Tally knew who still used paper and pen. "She's sending lab samples off, wants the whole coroner's inquest done."

"So what can we do for you today?" Tally tried to get the turquoise clip for his hair fastened for the hundredth time and finally held it out to his father. "Damn it. You'd think I never put my hair back."

"Being nervous on your wedding day is part of the package." Dad chuckled as he made short and adept work of the stubborn clip.

Sheriff Amick let out a muffled harrumph. "I'm sorry to interrupt preparations, but this won't take long. Just a couple of things I need to clarify. The night Ed died, Tally, did anyone see you and your, ah, fiancé go into your room together?"

That stopped Tally a moment. "Well…no. Everyone else was outside celebrating. They all knew to let us have some time alone."

"All right." Sheriff Amick nodded. "Thought it might be like that. And one other thing…" He pulled a plastic evidence bag out of his jacket pocket and held the object out to Tally. "You happen to recognize that?"

It was a glove. Men's. Extra-large. The cuff had been turned up to show the monogram inside—large 'T', two small 't's, large 'B'. Tally stared at it, brows furrowed. "That's mine. Undeniably. Mom gave me that pair a couple of years ago."

"Had you noticed one missing recently?" Sheriff Amick was writing again.

"No. I mean, I haven't looked for them yet this year. They're for colder weather." Tally strode to the front closet and opened the hanging bag where the family's cold weather items sat on little leather shelves. The glove's mate was also missing. "I don't understand. Where was this one?"

"On the ground behind Ed's truck."

"Just the one?" Tally asked, his voice distant in his ringing ears.

"Is there any reason you could think of that your glove would be there?"

Tally shook his head, trying to keep air moving in and out of his lungs. "No. I have no idea."

"All right, then." Sheriff Amick tucked the glove away again and fussed a bit more getting his notepad and pen back in their proper jacket pockets. "That's all for now. Don't leave town, Tally. None of your family should right now. I may have more questions later."

Tally waited until the door had closed behind him before he collapsed onto one of the hall chairs. "Dad? He really thinks I killed Ed, doesn't he?"

"He's only got evidence to go on, Tal. I can't say what the man thinks," Dad said with a pat to his shoulder, though his lips were set in a hard line. "It's our property. Your glove has every right to be on it."

"Right." Tally pulled in a deep, shuddering breath. "But *I* didn't put it there."

"It'll all come out right. You'll see. Let the police do their job and you do yours. Which, for today, means not fainting at your own damn wedding, hear me?"

Tally managed a weak chuckle. "Yes, sir."

* * * *

When they left for the resort, Dad drove. He'd said it wasn't going to become a new family tradition for the groom to wreck the car on his wedding day. At least they picked Gun up on the way, which helped Tally's nerves.

Gunther gave a low whistle. "Whoa. You look amazing in that, um, that kind of *hakama*."

"*Montsuki hakama*," Tally said in a stuffy, superior tone. "Is this one of those days where I need to use small words with you?"

"Jackass." Gun smacked him, but he was laughing. "You probably practiced saying that for days."

"A couple. Maybe. I just want everything perfect for Haru."

"Gods, you're so mushy over him, it's kinda gross."

Tally gave him a hard side-eye. "Just wait until you find the one. I'm looking forward to Gunther mush." He softened the teasing with a pat to Gun's knee. "The tux looks good on you."

"Trying to take short breaths." Gun tugged at the jacket. "These things don't leave much room."

"Thanks for being here, Gun. It means a lot to me."

Gun quirked a black eyebrow, his expression heralding another smart-ass remark. Then he shook his head, frowning at his shoes. "It's just good to see you so excited. So happy. I'm glad you found him, Tal."

Mom turned her head and called back, "I hope you two aren't going to be so serious and profound all day. You'll chase away the guests."

Tally grinned all the way to Sapphire Lake, riding on a euphoric wave until they reached the front lobby where staff raced for him the moment he set foot on the carpet. Laura, frighteningly fast on her high heels, reached him first.

"Mr. Bastille, I have Sarah Timms on the line. She's a little frantic because her van's broken down on her way here." Laura handed over the phone with a small grimace. "Her refrigerated van with your wedding cake."

"Do we know where she is?" Tally took the phone, holding his hand over to muffle his voice.

"Huntsman Road, she said. Just past the Meacham's place."

"Not too bad. Call down to catering. I know they're busy but they can spare a body for a few minutes and they don't need their vans today. Have them clear space for Sarah in the kitchen in case she needs to do touch-ups. And get..." Tally ran through his catering staff, trying to think of someone who would be cheerful and non-threatening. "Get Andy to drive."

"Got it." Laura walked away a few steps and took a phone from an assistant to get things moving.

Tally put the phone to his ear. "Sarah? It's Tally—"

The intake of breath on the other end of the line sounded perilously close to a sob. "Urusar Bastille! I'm so, so sorry!"

"It's going to be all right, Sarah. I promise. Deep breath. Good. One more." Tally gave Laura a thumbs-up when she signaled everything was set. "I'm sending a van for you. Andy Dignan's going to be driving."

Sarah sniffed and got out in a small voice, "Lily and Pete's cousin?"

"Yes, exactly. Hold tight. Rescue's on the way."

Another smaller sniff and Sarah sounded a bit more like herself. "Thank you, Urusar Bastille."

"That's what I'm here for. At least it's not August, right?"

Sarah managed a shaky laugh before she hung up and Tally turned to the next person waiting at his elbow. "Mr. Bastille, it's the chocolatiers convention…"

"How many are we overbooked?" Tally chuckled at the staffer's wide-eyed gape. "I do read my emails."

"Oh. Yes, sir. Looks like twelve, a possible thirteenth coming in this afternoon. I don't know how this happened."

"How and why for later. Guests now." It wasn't the busy summer season, so it wasn't a matter of space. It was a matter of promised room type. "Upgrade them on my authorization."

"*All* of them, sir?"

"Yes. Our mistake, we fix it. There should be plenty of suites and I don't think they'll complain about the lake view."

Gunther snorted as the staffer hustled away. "Can't even leave a man alone on his wedding day."

"That's what happens when you have your wedding on your own property. Besides, it's my job."

Mom slid her arm through Tally's. "He's handling it just right, Gun. Yes, this is Tally's day, but he's still Urusar. Showing people he's there for them even when he could by rights shoo them away? That's what the clan needs to see."

"Thanks, Mom." Tally would've said more but a rather flustered Harry Cosgrove was hurrying toward them. "Harry?"

"I'm so sorry, Urusar Bastille, but it was the angle of the sun. We have to make some changes in set up." Harry grimaced and took a breath. "And now Mr.

Voronoy says it doesn't match what you gave him and he won't proceed without your okay."

"Damn it, Fred," Tally muttered, then patted Harry on the shoulder as he started toward the back of the hotel. "Gun, see if the ushers are in place to direct folks. Mom, Dad, I'll be back. What a time for Fred to decide he wants to play temperamental florist."

Tally grumbled, but he wasn't really annoyed. This was what he did, what he was good at, and today a miniature sun burned bright in his chest that nothing could put out.

* * * *

Mother hadn't said anything since Haru had pulled their *shiromuku* out of the closet. None of the women had. Uruma Akaike's cluck of the tongue said more than the Awi's hushed tones as she talked with the women elders. It did fall within traditional Japanese *lijun* sensibilities. Most of it. Some of the design probably made *Okaasan* and the others think it was too much like an *irouchikake*. She couldn't argue that the fabric was the wrong color. It was the Bastille blue after all. Haru was taking on their Argaze's colors. The stitching and embroidery on *both* the *kakeshita* and *uchikake* on the other hand...

"Problem, *Okaasan*?"

"No."

"You sure— Ah!" The *koshi himo* tightened unexpectedly around Haru's abdomen. "Mother!"

"*Nani*?" *Okaasan's* head popped out by their right side.

"Isn't it a bit tight?"

"Of course not." Another *koshi himo* squeezed Haru, this time higher up on their chest. "We need to make sure the padding to shape the *shiromuku* stays in place under the *nagajuban*."

"More like prepping me to feed the beast," Haru muttered. Another belt tightened. "Ah!"

"What did you say?" Mother stepped in front of Haru, pulling the belts and adjusting fabric.

"Thank you for raising me."

"Hmmm."

The Awi asked after Mayu and Fuyumi.

Mother smiled, probably the first genuine one of the day. "The girls are good. Unfortunately, with the kids in school it was too hard on them to try to make the ceremony."

"Probably better to stay home," one of the elders murmured.

"Not something the kids needed to see," added another.

Haru opened their mouth. "A-omph!"

The belt just got tighter again.

The kimono was strangling Haru, from the inside out, and most of it wasn't even on them yet. Mother eyed the *kakeshita*. She sighed and grabbed a couple fabric clips to keep the material hanging to show the back of their neck properly. Uruma Akaike and women elders tugged the fabric, muttering as they adjusted the fall of the slit and the lines of the *kimono*. Then the evil *obasans* added even more *koshi himo* around his waist.

I am going to die of kimono strangulation.

It was probably mother's way of reminding Haru to stay on their best behavior. Though the rituals for the Japanese and Cherokee lijun weddings were similar to their human counterparts, the lijun had altered their traditions over time, to give them their own meanings. Haru was not to mess those up at any cost.

Several clucking tongues began waging when *Okaasan* pulled out their *obi*.

Too late.

The *obi* caused a stir among the women. Bright and bold. Not a shade of blue or white, but an iridescent rainbow of colors, much like the stitching and embroidery. Mother huffed, one of those long, drawn-out breaths letting everyone know her disapproval. All eyes went to Haru, so they did what any about-to-be-married Satislit would do. Ignored *Okaasan* and pulled out their *obiage* and *obijime*.

"At least those are respectable," Mother said.

"They are colors Tally likes." Haru smiled, not doing an initial dance when *Okaasan* gave them her back and fussed over the obi.

No way were they going to admit they didn't want the different parts of their kimono clashing, and the blues were the only colors that worked. She'd only yell. Haru checked their profile in the mirror. Despite the *shiromuku* being made to please Tally, little touches of Haru, and Haru only, were evident, their own personality shining through. And ultimately, Haru was happy with the *kimono*, as much as one could be in the situation.

The *uchikake* only loaded Haru down further, and they had to wonder if bridal *kimonos* were so complicated and heavy to keep them from bolting at the altar. The idea certainly had merit. Breathing wasn't easy, not with the multiple layers. Running was out of the question, *geta* or no *geta*.

"When is the *shinzen kekkon*?" the Awi asked.

Mother sighed. "They held purification rights in the traditional Cherokee way. They had the grounds blessed for the last week. Then they performed the *shinzen kekkon* this morning."

"Really?"

Another hush in the room. Haru was batting a thousand. The heavy weight of their gazes made them wish for a distraction.

"Where is the *wataboshi*?" Uruma Akaike asked.

Any kind of distraction but that one. "I don't have one."

Hell froze over, if there was one, considering how hard *Okaasan* grabbed onto Haru's arms.

"I'm wearing a veil, to honor the joining of the Akaike and Bastille clans."

It was a reasonable explanation, complete and utter bullshit, but one the women would swallow. Hopefully. Haru had no desire to look like a Q-tip, or to keep their face hidden. A perverse need for everyone to see them as the vows were exchanged to finish the sale echoed through their heart.

Uruma Akaike tugged on the *uchikake*, choking him. "Is that so?"

"Yes. Since the ceremony is combining the different traditions from the clans, the veil would please my Argaze, and not interfere with any other traditions."

"How would a *wataboshi* interfere with another tradition?" Uruma Akaike moved in front of Haru, adjusting their collar again, her eyes laser-focused on theirs.

"The ceremony involves a blanket being put over Tally and me. One the Cherokee use. Like their priest blessing the grounds for seven days before the wedding. The blanket *is* important."

"Hmph."

"It will happen, and it would pull the *wataboshi* off."

"As you say." She looked over his shoulder, probably at Mother. "This is why your hair isn't finished?"

"Yes, uh, I was going to add it after the final touches on my makeup." Though they no longer felt sure of *how* anymore. Would Haru be able to lift their arms higher than their shoulders?

"I see. Ladies. Urusar Akaike will be along to collect you."

They filed out of the borrowed suite at the resort, taking *Okaasan* with them. The air swooshed back into the room and Haru could breathe. Not really, but the unrelenting pressure that felt like drowning above ground was gone.

Haru added the jewels around their eyes that matched their nails, more gifts from Tally, to give their makeup a final bit of splash. Diamonds, sapphires, intricate jade carvings the size of a small pearl, and a beautiful turquoise stone. Haru didn't know what the stone was, but their otter liked it. A few minutes of preening in front of the mirror definitely happened.

The veil and the white jade hairpiece from Tally came out next. Haru eyed the last piece of their outfit with some skepticism. Did they just pull it over their head? Tally had given it to them yesterday night, awkwardly handing the box over. It irked Haru to cover up all the work they'd put into their bridal outfit. As Haru looked over the fabric, they realized the off-white veil had a scene woven in it. They took a closer look.

"Oh, oh, oh!" Haru's hands shook, and the veil dropped. A hunting scene. *Snakes* hunting. They grabbed their phone and nearly broke a nail punching Tally's name on the screen.

"Hey, love. What—"

"Is this your mother's veil?"

"Well, yes, I thought you might need something old."

"Old?"

"You know, something old, something new, something borrowed, something blue and a silver sixpence in her shoe?"

"*Shi'ne.*"

Silence.

Oh, Gods. It had just slipped out before Haru could stop it. "I mean, Argaze, would you do me the honor of helping place it."

Tally's throat cleared. "Aren't we supposed to wait to see each other?"

"Which tradition is that?"

"Uh, American?"

Haru dipped back to pick up the veil. "Then let us stick with two out of the three. It would please me greatly if you helped place your mother's veil on my head."

"I'll be right there."

The question of the minute became what about the rest of the silly rhyme Tally had spouted at Haru? Why hadn't anyone told them all the things expected to be fulfilled? If they had known, Haru would've made sure to find everything. They nearly ottered out, having to force back their dual spirit several times as they tried not to lose their mind. It'd work out. It had to. The wedding would happen. They wouldn't be banished.

A knock came at the suite door, and Haru bolted over to it. Or they tried. Instead they ended up on their knees, hands catching them before planting face-first on the floor.

"Come in!"

"Haru, is everything— Damn."

"What?"

"You don't have to bow."

Oh. That wasn't what he'd been doing, but Haru must fallen into *saikeirei* out of habit when Tally walked in.

"You have pleased me. Very much."

Didn't take Tally long to learn that one, though.

"Let me help you." Tally pulled Haru up, then swatted their arms and side, patting them almost. "It's beautiful."

Haru smiled, unsure of what to say.

"The embroidery reflects the light."

"It does. There is silver in the threading?"

"Oh, nice. You have your silver, too."

"I do not need a sixpence?"

Tally laughed, the corners around his eyes crinkling just a fraction. "No, most people just wear something silver these days. Wait, is that what worried you?"

"No?"

"Haru, please." Tally brought Haru over to the chair and helped them sit. "It's okay to let me hear your worries. We're in this together."

"I do not have something borrowed."

"Oh, Haru." Tally pulled him close and placed a kiss on his temple. "I'm sorry I said anything."

"I— It just needs to be perfect. My mother, the clan—" Their voice caught.

Tally leaned back, frowning at first, then a smile broke out over his face. "Wait a second. Oh, um. Just— wait here. Just, I'll be right back."

Haru was left on the chair, watching Tally's backside as he ran out the door. Shouts, a few expletives and heavy footfalls created havoc where there been quiet. What was that about? Tally had said to wait, so

Haru did, but what was so important that running was involved?

Though Haru had to admit the *montsuki hakama* looked good on Tally. Very good. Bone-worthy. The display called to something primal in Haru. Their otter certainly found it…amusing. Yes, Haru would admit to *amusing*. At least the groombrides were allowed the leverage to escape? The *geta* were no longer a problem for Tally as they had been at the betrothal dinner. When had the big guy found time to practice in them? He obviously had, since he could *run* in them now.

Maybe Tally would run right out of the resort. Save them both from their doomed fate. Haru sighed. No, Tally wouldn't run away. The bastard snake left wanting to help, of all things. What kind of special jerk did that?

The thunderous steps came back a few minutes or so later, accompanied by — *squealing*?

"Haru!" a familiar singsong voice squawked out. Soft, high. Not *male*. The door bounced open, hard enough it stayed connected to the wall. A crunch had been in there too. Haru flinched, thinking about the damage done.

"Oh, shoot, um, don't worry, staff will fix that right up," Tally said as he strode over to Haru. "Here. One second."

"Haru! Pretty!"

A cannonball lodged itself against Haru's legs. "Kaho-chan!"

"Miss you! Up!"

Haru swept the little tanuki up into their arms. *I am not going to cry. I am not going to cry.*

"Kiss. Kiss. Tears go away."

So I am crying. "You got her? They said yes?"

"You're holding her, aren't you?"

A horrible thought popped into Haru's head. "You cannot *borrow* people."

"What?"

"People. Lijun. You do not *borrow* people. Especially children."

Laughter, high and sweet, low and rumbly, filled the room. Kaho patted their cheek. Two strong arms surrounded them, and Haru found themself in a squishy hug. Confused and annoyed at their Argaze, Haru turned their glare on the 'responsible' adult. Tally kissed their forehead then winked.

"Kaho's parents are here as guests, but that's not what's important. Look at her hair."

"What?"

Kaho's little hand went to her perfectly done updo. "Flowers. We share flowers!"

Nope. Not crying. Those were not tears on their face. The flowers Fred had provided for the wedding were perfect for their little tanuki.

After a couple minutes filled with fixing the stones and reapplying their makeup, Tally then sat Kaho on Haru's lap.

"Hold her tight."

"Like I would let her fall."

A sneak attack—a quick kiss on Haru's lips—was followed by a hiss. "I know."

Tally looked entirely too proud of himself.

Then with careful hands, Tally picked out three flowers from Kaho's hair and put them in Haru's bun. No fuss. No muss. A silly grin was on his face when he attached the veil to Haru's hair using bobby pins and the white jade hairpiece. The fabric fell over Haru's shoulders and down the back on their kimono, falling just short of the ground.

"Perfect, everything's just perfect." Tally leaned into Haru, squeezing one shoulder. "I've never seen such beauty."

Kaho squealed, clapping and bouncing on Haru's lap. "Pretty Haru. Pretty snake!"

She did not!

"Pretty Kaho!"

She did. She really, really did.

A knock at the door quieted her down, and she swung out, holding on to Haru with one hand and watching Tally answer with her curious gaze.

"Urusar Bastille?" Akaike-san stepped in, his eyes cutting to Haru.

"Urusar Akaike." Tally bowed, though his voice had cooled, coming out hissy. "We ready to go?"

"Yes, of course. I was just collecting Haru before we got you."

"Now we can save you the trouble."

"Yes, yes." Akaike-san's gaze met Tally's for a second before narrowing back onto Haru. "Please, let us escort the happy couple to the grounds."

"Flowers!" Kaho yelled, nearly jumping out of Haru's hold. Hanging from one's feet never did much damage to any child, but Haru set her down gently. She rolled, hopping back to her feet and scooting out the door, leaving the adults watching after her.

Tally offered Haru his arm. "Shall we?"

"Of course."

Outside the door, Kaho was standing next to Tally's dad, a basket in her hand. One almost as big as her. Bastille-*otōusan* held the *wagasa* and a blanket. Haru was impressed, because a wedding *wagasa* wasn't exactly light. It was blue, like Tally's colors, but also deepened in color as it got closer to the outside. The symbolism was not lost on Haru. Their love would not grow deeper with time. Even though Tally seemed nice, he did not have Haru's heart.

No such things as Em'halafi existed.

"Thank you, Bastille-san." Akaike-san took the *wagasa*. He almost dropped it, needing both hands. "Urusar Bastille, please lead Satislit Tanaka."

A huff came out of Tally. Small, but it was there. "Thank you."

Kaho walked back out in front of them, her greedy little hands dipping into the basket and throwing petals high into the air. Haru wondered if the flowers would last to the altar. They eyed the basket.

"Why do you think it's so big?" Tally whispered.

"To slow her down?"

"Partly, but her hands are small, she can only grab so much."

Haru chuckled, getting a grunt from Akaike.

"I *have* seen what she's capable of doing to a cake three times bigger than herself after all." Tally smiled and patted Haru's arm.

Right. The night they'd met — according to Tally. The night that had changed Haru's life permanently.

Urusar Akaike and Tally's dad fell into step behind them. The umbrella protected them from evil spirits while the clan leaders guarded their back. While Bastille-*otōusan* was no longer head of the clan, he had been its leader for decades, and it wasn't like Tally could do it since he was the groombride. Knowing they were there didn't help settle Haru's nerves much. Their abdomen tightened, leaving them queasy.

The walk to the altar stretched in Haru's mind. People stopped and stared. Some pulled their cameras out and took pictures. Different lijun working at the resort paused in whatever tasks they were supposed to be doing and watched after them.

Outside was better, the pathway clear and open. No people or lijun to stop and stare. The beautiful rays of the sun cast a glow on everything. As they rounded the corner, chairs, many rows of chairs filled Haru's vision. So many. Their breath caught. Haru had known the numbers, but to see it up close and personal… Why did a powerful Urusar like Tally even think his was a destined match to someone like Haru?

A spray of flower petals obscured Haru's vision long enough to push the rising panic down.

Flutes played, a mixture of a serene downbeat with a joyful upbeat. Odd, but it worked. Haru had been unsure whether the two types of music would mix when Tally had suggested it. Now they felt glad for it. The notes cast an otherworldly spell over the event. Kaho's giggles and shrieks lightened the heaviness crushing Haru's chest.

Maybe that was what they needed to get through this awful day. Spells and giggles.

Before Haru could blink they had knelt at the altar, the blue blanket over both of them. Sake adorned the tables, all in old bottles, fine sake vintages from Haru and their clan to symbolize their contribution toward their new home and family. Food from the Bastille clan decorated the tables around the altar. All gifts to show Haru would be provided for. Fish. Venison. Bread. Salt. Oranges. They were supposed to symbolize the promise of a home. A new life.

A new prison.

The shackles clanged louder.

Bastille-*okaasan* was to the right of the altar while Tally's dad stood to the left with a white blanket. Sammy and Misaki flanked Haru's new in-laws while the Awi stood dead-center with Akaike.

So many smiling faces.

Words were spoken, ones praising the Gods, then Urusar Akaike poured into the first of the *sakazuki*. Their first sake of the *san-san-ku-do*. Three-three-nine. Three sips, three pours, all in increasing sake cup sizes. Shared joy. Shared sorrow. Shared fertility. Each drink hammered home there was no going back with every *sakazuki* handed to Haru. Each sip was like drinking their life away.

Numb. They became numb. No feeling left.

A white blanket replaced the blue one, with Tally and Haru standing together. Everyone was all smiles, including them. Haru wasn't sure how they could grin like some fool, but they knew it was there. The ache in their cheeks was enough to know.

The vows were spoken, thanking the Gods, their clans, giving proper respect to their parents. All of it grinding Haru to the bone.

When they turned to share in a drink with the clans, Haru caught the huge grin on Tally's face. The humongous snake was practically radiating enough of his own wattage to light up the resort.

The Awi called out, "To the happy couple."

The cheer from the guests hit Haru like a soundwave and echoed out over the lake.

Kaho ran up to them, handing Haru an evergreen branch bundled with berries and pinecones. She grabbed onto their legs, holding tight as they turned. Boom. Boom. Their heart kick-started again, but the pain cut deep. The ache a constant thrum. It hurt to have it beating so. Tally put his hand over Haru's and they placed the branch on the altar together.

Applause.

The guests were applauding.

"It's nice that we were able to create some new traditions," Tally whispered, taking hold of Haru's hand.

"What?" No. That—that hadn't been Haru's intent at all.

"Combining our traditions, making something new. It made today really special."

No, the wedding was supposed to be by the book. No breaking traditions. Haru was not supposed to make waves. They had been working so hard to stay in the lines. Something in their expression must've slipped, because Tally's bright demeanor dimmed.

"Today has been the best day of my life," he said, then leaned in for a kiss. Not a simple chaste one on the lips. One that pressed against Haru's mouth hard. "And it's only going to get better from here on out. I promise. New traditions are meant to happen."

Haru faced the crowd with Tally by one side, Kaho clinging to the other.

Somehow they'd get through the dinner party. Hopefully the caterers would break out the sake quickly.

Kaho tugged on Haru's sleeve.

"Yes?"

"Where is cake?"

Tally let out a muffled "Oh no", but Haru smiled at their little tanuki.

"I'll show you. Just hang on tight."

Okay, so the reception wouldn't be a total hardship.

* * * *

Water splashed over the edge of the tub. The warmth had been a refuge for the last twenty minutes, relaxing Haru, helping them pretend they hadn't arrived in the Honeymoon Suite overlooking Sapphire Lake with Tally. But they couldn't hide forever. Tally would be out there, waiting, until he thought Haru had ottered out then he'd probably come in.

Haru sighed.

Tonight had to be on Haru's own terms. They'd prepared properly. Hoped they had. Otters tended to be a bit aggressive in bed. The thought of the next morning turned Haru's stomach. Instead of psyching themself up for what was supposed to happen next, Haru had been daydreaming of playing in the lake. A swim would be nice.

No. No. Not the time.

Right. Fucking. Urusar Akaike expected their scents to be thoroughly mingled in the morning. For Haru to be *debauched*.

If Haru could separate how they felt about their position from Tally, it might make the next step easier.

It wasn't as if Tally were ugly, quite the opposite. Handsome. Gorgeous smile. Big. Maybe big everywhere? There could be fun to be had, being exposed to all that raw strength—if Haru kept it to fucking. Pleasing their new Argaze didn't have to be a hardship. Hopefully Tally was a considerate lover. That would make servicing him easier.

Now or never. Out of the tub.

Water dripped from Haru as they wrapped the towel around themself. Obviously they'd missed a spot, but they felt too nervous to recheck. They nearly walked into the door because they didn't turn the knob, and they stopped short when they re-entered the suite.

"What is *all* this?"

"You like it?"

Candles lit the room. Warm, orange glows softening even the hard edge of the giant snake. Flowers covered almost every available surface *but* the bed. Haru was almost disappointed there weren't rose petals on the comforter.

"Too much?" Was Tally nervous? He kept shifting on the bed, making it creak.

"No, it is...sweet."

A nice gesture. Tally was trying. He didn't have to create a mood. Haru should appreciate that.

"And unexpected." Also true.

"Good, good. I didn't want it to be too, um, eager."

Tally stood and joined Haru, enveloping them in an embrace. Strong. Warm. Most people would enjoy such a feeling. Haru could enjoy the physicality — being close to someone. Tally's nose pressed against Haru's temple, a breath went out and in, and maybe even a little tongue-flick. Haru shuddered, unable to keep the small bit of fear away.

The embrace tightened for a second. Great, strangled on their wedding night. Haru laughed, and was quickly joined by Tally, who took a step back. His hands didn't leave Haru, though, still caging them in.

"We really haven't had this kind of time alone, have we?"

"No."

Tally smiled. "Argaze and Satislit, alone at last. It's been so frustrating not being able to spend time with you."

Fireworks & Stolen Kisses

Haru dipped their head, hoping they wouldn't be made to answer.

"Come on. I've got something for you." Tally tugged Haru over to the bed. "You disappeared into the bath so quick... I thought this might help."

Thud. Thud. Now or never.

Beside the bed was a tray. Champagne and prawns. All different kinds of prawns prepared in different ways.

Grilled jumbo prawns with — *oooh* — coriander and chilies. *Mmm. Yums.*

Grilled buttered prawns.

Baked coconut prawns.

Were those scallops? *Yes, yummy treats.*

One of the jumbo prawns had a bit too much chili and it went the wrong way. Haru started coughing, and was surprised by a champagne flute pushed in front of them as a hand pounded on their back.

"Try this."

After several large gulps, Haru was able to breathe properly again. Mostly. It was Tally's hand stroking up and down their back that made their heart knock in an allegro. The motion was meant to soothe Haru, intellectually they understood. Unfortunately, the touch did anything but.

"It's nice," Tally said.

"What is?"

"Seeing you happy and enjoying yourself."

Bastard had to be all nice about it too.

"These glimpses of you are what I've been feasting on during the engagement." Tally sighed then pulled Haru onto his lap, still petting them. "Everything had to be so proper all the time. It was driving me nuts."

"Oh."

"But when you're happy, like with Kaho today, it makes you light up. Your smile and laughter is infectious. I hope" — Tally swallowed — "now that all the formality of before is out of the way, we can focus on the happy."

"As you please."

The sigh was heavy, and the hand on their back stopped petting them.

"Argaze?"

"Tally. We settled on Tally, remember?"

Haru dipped their head. "We did."

"Nervous?"

"Yes." That much was the truth.

"I wish they had let us spend more time together before the wedding. Just us, you know?"

Like Haru's parents were dumb enough to let that happen. The times they'd been alone had been pure luck on Tally's part, and Haru had been smart enough not to say anything. But now? Now Haru had no barriers to hold their Urusar back. Tally could take whatever he wanted, as was his right.

Tally cupped Haru's jaw, running his thumb along the edge. "You were beautiful today."

"Thank you."

"I thought my heart would stop, seeing you in your wedding kimono. Absolutely devastating, my Em'halafi, my destined."

Those were wooing words. "And you looked...powerful...in your *montsuki hakama*."

"You thought so?"

"Very alluring." Haru rubbed their cheek against Tally's chest.

"I wish you would've let me undress you. I bet we could've had some fun."

"It is not that sexy. Anime lies." Oh shit. *That really popped out, didn't it?* "I mean, there were a lot of layers involved with the *shiromuku*."

Tally's chest rumbled against Haru's ear.

"Maybe you can undress me the next time I wear a kimono."

"I'd like that. Find out for myself." A kiss pressed against Haru's head. Then another. The hand was on their back again, making small circles — soft, light touches that built up into firm, harder ones. The kisses didn't stop either. There was a bit of adjusting and Haru found themself straddled over Tally's thick thighs, drowning in deep kisses.

Kiss. Kiss. Tongue — hot and firm. Kisses were nice. Gentle and insistent. Haru opened for Tally, letting him take what he wanted. Hands cradled their head, then moved down Haru's back. Between the onslaught on their mouth and the roaming hands, Haru missed when Tally hooked his fingers under the towel. A tug pulled it against them tighter momentarily, then the last sliver of fabric covering Haru was gone, leaving them exposed to Tally's eyes. They shivered, but didn't try covering themself.

"Oooh." Tally nuzzled Haru's neck, leaving more licks and kisses behind.

"Happy with what you see?" Haru asked.

Tally pulled back, a smile, warm and inviting on his swollen lips. A groan was Haru's answer.

The hard bulge under Tally's flannel sleep pants made for another good indicator. Haru leaned back, hoping to give their Argaze more of a view while letting them get some much-needed air. They burned from the contact. Too close. Much too close. They'd get pulled under, never able to resurface, if they let the touches continue.

Tally attacked their chest, kissing, nipping, licking. Featherlight touches, hard, wet ones, and the wicked fast flick of Tally's tongue against their nipples. Haru moaned, the sound startling them.

Yes, Tally knew what he was doing. Most definitely. At least pleasuring him wouldn't be as daunting as Haru had worried. They pressed a hand against Tally's shoulder, who caught on after a minute and scooted against the bed frame. He hooked his fingers under the waist of his flannels and lifted his ass. The pants went flying. Right into Haru's face.

"Oops. Sorry, uh, sorry."

Haru dislodged them and tossed them on the floor.

"Little excited."

"So I see." Because they could, too. Tally was all in, whereas Haru's cock was only at half-mast. They gave it a couple of tugs, hoping to convince the rest of them fucking would be fun.

"Come here." Tally waved Haru closer, but their heart struck a vivace. They did what was easier.

Starting at Tally's feet, Haru placed kisses. Chaste, quick kisses. The lack of hair up his leg was not unsurprising, but different. *Snake.* Though the skin was warmer than Haru expected from a reptile lijun. Beautiful, deep russet-color skin with warm copper and golden undertones. Strong calves supported powerful thighs. They massaged the tension out of the muscles as they laved their way up. Haru was only about four inches shorter, but their sizes were entirely different things. Muscle. Mass. Tally's build was so different from Haru's own svelte swimmer's body.

Those meaty thighs were definitely made by the Gods. Haru gave a nibble. Just a taste. One wouldn't hurt.

Groans, harsh and needy, fell over them. Hands tightened and loosened their grip on Haru's shoulders the closer they got to Tally's girth. A deep, musky scent filled Haru's nose. They edged closer, their tongue slipping out, caressing the skin at their Argaze's hip.

"*Haru.*"

Tally's cock brushed Haru's cheek. Throb. Throb. Hot. Hard. The girth a bit intimidating. Heavy and solid. Tally settled more, pumping his hips and spreading his legs. He gathered up Haru's hair and moved it to one side, exposing their face.

"Lovely," Tally hummed.

Haru smiled then licked up their Argaze's thick pecker. Flavorful, heady. Each throb of the dusky meat a little more insistent and harder than the last. Haru tongued around the tip of Tally's cock, the head almost completely out of the foreskin. Haru sucked, and an ardent moan, deep and cavernous, filled the room. Tally cupped the left side of Haru's head. Raspy breaths wheezed in and out.

"Gods, Haru."

With their mouth on the prize, Haru added their free hand at the base, finding a rhythm. Down with up. Bunch and stretch. Tally added little thrusts, hunching his hips, rocking. The hefty weight stretched and filled their mouth, a pleasant ache Haru enjoyed when they gave head. The hold Tally had on Haru never wavered. Saliva built up, dripping down Haru's chin and Tally's dick to his balls.

"Finger me."

Haru glanced up, unsure if they heard right. Tally held lube in his hand.

"Do it, please."

Confusion must've shown on their face.

"I love ass play." Tally tapped the lube against Haru's palm, and there was a chuckle, though it didn't sound *happy*. "Both ways are good for me, too."

That had Haru off Tally's cock. "Both?"

"You expected to only be on the receiving end, didn't you?"

"Yes, I am Satislit." It was their place.

Tally shook his head, making his hair cascade down his muscular chest. "We please each other, okay? I like both, and I love ass play. We figure out what works for us."

As Haru took the lube, they nodded—confused, but a happy confused. Sex definitely wouldn't be a problem. It might even be fun. Good? That had to be good? They pressed around Tally's rim, teasing, getting closer, listening to Tally's breath hitch, and watched as his hips wiggled as Haru finally pressed their lubed finger into Tally's ass. The pleased grunt, the spreading of Tally's knees as he pulled them up, excited Haru. A steady pulse of need hummed through them.

"Oh, yes, good." Tally hunched his hips, his thick bone tapping at Haru's lips. They captured it, sucking the tip hard.

"Ah!"

Heat filled Haru's mouth and surrounded their finger. Losing themself in the act, pushing all the ugliness away, was easy. Fucking was about release— whether happy, sad, angry or even if all those emotions were swirling inside, entangled—one could find release. Haru tapped against the one place they hoped would set Tally on fire and was not disappointed.

Pure sex like this was easy. Only the end game mattered. Getting off. Feeling good. Physically they would get there. Haru added a finger and twisted their hand. Rub. Rub. Feel the sparks. Find that edge and make their Argaze teeter on it.

"Gods. Ah! Haru."

Wet, obscene sounds joined the gasps and moans. Yes, wonderfully erotic noises as Haru brought about Tally's pleasure. They loved those noises. Whether eating someone out or sucking dick—those sounds made their knob hard, ready and impatient. The sizzle from before was now a burning fire, roaring in their ears to finish. The moans were just what they needed to really get going, desire enough to chase after their own release. The needy push into their mouth, how Tally tensed around their fingers every time they tapped their Argaze's prostate, all of it switched Haru on— *now*.

Tally's thighs trembled against Haru's ribcage. Close. Too close. They pulled off and out. A disappointed *nooo* came out of Tally with a hiss.

"Do not worry. A minute. Just a—ah!" A quick check between their cheeks, and yes, the party was still a go. A little extra lube wouldn't hurt. Not with the meaty snake Tally had. "Close your legs."

"What are you—? What are we?" The questions came out breathy, Tally's eyes glazed over. A sheen covered his chest. Strands of his black hair stuck to it.

Haru scooted up, grabbed Tally's thick pecker, and sank down.

"Ah! Wai-wait! Haru!"

"Good. This is good," they breathed out.

Now wasn't the time to slow down. Both of them cranked. It wouldn't take much. Haru didn't want easy. Gentle, slow would give the chance for Haru's brain to catch up, to think. They only wanted their body reacting.

"Ahn—mmm. Thick." Filling. Just the right amount of pain. Haru rode through it, one hand on Tally's shoulder, the other on their cock. They jerked hard. "Gonna help?"

"Ah! Ah! Gods." Tally grabbed on and pumped his hips. "But—"

"Mmm, harder."

Tally gave them exactly what they asked for. Grunts, groans, sweaty skin—pure sex. Nothing but fucking. Hardness split Haru apart and left everything else behind. They squeezed their glutes and ass. Much better. The battle between in and out.

"Haru, my Em'halafi, my heart. Going to— I can't. Ah!"

Warmth flooded Haru's ass, spurt by spurt. They twisted their hand over the tip of their own cock, then pumped hard. Tally crushed them together, wrapped his arms around Haru—hips still humping—and sucked on a nipple.

"Yes!" Haru jerked, tensing up, drawing another pained moan from Tally. Cum spilt between them, covering their abs. "Like that. Exactly like that."

They rocked, breaths raspy, hard.

By the time they stopped, aches in their body were already voicing themselves, but another feeling was making itself known—the one listening to Tally, hearing his words of devotion, of love, to his Em'halafi—to Haru—and feeling the kisses Tally was showering on them.

Instead of the euphoria of orgasming, the realization that Haru had trapped Tally just as much as them hit. Guilt. Anger. Shame.

Banishment would've been a blessing.

Shouldn't have been such a coward. Shouldn't have tied someone to them who honestly, reverently believed they were destined mates. But the greater shame was knowing they would stay a coward and say nothing.

Chapter Eight

An Ugly Truth & a Death Warmed Over

The bed was too small. No, actually, it was more than big enough to hold two people the size of Tally and Haru — if those people respected personal boundaries. Tally was most definitely not. He had wrapped around Haru like a...a *snake.* A cold serpent ready to constrict around them and suffocate Haru to death. Tally's deep, sleep-laden breaths tickled the back of their neck.

Escape. Haru needed a way to escape this death trap. They couldn't sleep like this. Too many different feels were churning in their chest, falling asleep was impossible. Pride wouldn't keep them from admitting that seeing Tally sleep scared them.

Old wives' tales were old wives' tales...but Ed's murder hung like a bright spot in Haru's mind. They'd seen the flash. A flash only an uktena could make. While they didn't want to think someone as naive as Tally could kill someone, the seed had planted itself nonetheless. If Tally could make the poison, then what else could he really do?

The rational side of Haru knew their mind was just winding them up, giving them reasons to worry. But they couldn't shut them off, especially since Tally held them hostage in the bed.

"Just a little—" Haru wriggled to the side. "And— yeah. Ah!"

Haru rolled right off the bed and onto the floor, landing with a whump. They popped up, checking Tally's breathing. Not even a deep beat missed. Man certainly slept hard. The clock read three in the morning. Haru scooted into the bathroom, finally able to breathe with some relief.

More than anything, they wanted to scrub all the scents of Tally off them. They felt…dirty. There was a throb, a stark reminder of the sex from earlier. They should probably check, because their asshole felt raw— except then they would try to clean up. Something Haru could not afford to do. Urusar Akaike wanted to smell them, make sure they'd mated. The Awi would want to examine them. Could anything else be more humiliating? Haru would have to settle for washing their face.

Cool, clear water always helped them solve their problems. Maybe if they just ottered out, they could stop thinking. Stop feeling all these unwanted emotions. That would make too much noise at this hour, though. Haru tied up their hair so they could get a little less sticky. They ran the sink tap, and gave their face a few good splashes. There was an urge to put their face under the tap but they managed to push it down. As they patted down, a knock came at the door.

"Haru?"

Shit!

"Are you okay?" Tally popped his head in. "Are you hurt?"

"Hurt?" Fear made their heart rabbit out an allegro.

"We were, uh, *enthusiastic* during our mating."

Had Tally actually called their fuck a mating?

"Not that I didn't like mating with you. I hope to have many more chances to mate with such *enthusiasm*. But not all of them have to be so, uh, vigorous, if you don't want. To be loved like that — it's a gift."

He is killing me. "Yes — ah, yes, we were. I am fine."

"Good. I was worried, love." Tally wrapped his arms around Haru, pressing a kiss against their temple. "Wouldn't want to break my Em'halafi the first night out. It would be like breaking my own heart."

"There are no such things as Em'halafi."

Both of them tensed. Tally's robust russet paled to a tawny brown.

That came out — out loud — of Haru's mouth. Not that they'd meant to say it, but the denial had come out of nowhere. Lack of sleep. Had to be. The pinched brows and the frown Tally wore said he'd heard them too.

"Apologies, I—" Haru gulped, twisting, turning desperate to get out of Tally's hold. Next thing they knew, Haru fell right on their ass. "Ow. Ow."

"Sorry, let me— Okay, yeah. Sorry. Didn't mean to drop you."

The throb in their ass hurt, but Haru's panic was crushing their heart.

"Haru? No, don't bow, please — just, let's get out of the bathroom." Tally tugged Haru after him, plopping the two of them on the bed, pulling a blanket around their shoulders.

"Apologies, Argaze. I spoke out of turn."

"Tally, just Tally."

"Of course." Haru refused to look up, though they could tell by how Tally held their jaw that their Argaze wanted them to.

"Did you mean that?"

"What?" Haru's breath stuttered.

"That you don't believe in Em'halafis?" Tally's voice came out rough, raspy. "Please answer."

"I would rather not."

"Gods." Tally sank down in front of Haru and took hold of their hands. They tried to get on the floor too, but Tally wouldn't let them down. "If...if you don't believe in Em'halafis, why did you agree to marry me?"

The words sank hard and deep like a red-hot poker into Haru's gut.

"Why, Haru?"

"Was I given a choice?" Haru looked beyond Tally, at the suite doors. Maybe Tally wouldn't be trapped like them. Maybe neither of them would be. It came with a cost, though. "Did you ask me if I believed? Did you even try to date me?"

"No... But your clan—"

"Yes, my clan. I know my duty. What I am to them. I am Satislit, and you offered to buy me. You got what you wanted."

The pain-filled gasp didn't cut as deep as those naive questions.

"My Urusar promised to banish me if I refused." Haru swallowed, but pushed on. It really was better if they did. "You bought me, Tally."

"But—no, I was just trying to bring us together. We're destined. We belong together."

This time Haru's resolve set in. "And so we will be together."

"I don't... Haru, I don't understand why—"

"You bought me, Tally. I will be the perfect Satislit for you. I will stand by you, protect the clan, our family, raise the children, serve you—"

"Wait, no, that's not what I want."

"Then why did you buy me?"

Tally's breath hitched. "Your clan. They're traditional. I just... I wanted my Em'halafi. I thought you wanted me too. I thought they agreed because... That moment...that you..."

"The fucking is not bad. I will not say 'no' when you ask me to service you."

Another one of those pained gasps came out. "We can figure this out, Haru. I promise. We are—"

"Not destined," they interrupted, the fury white-hot, raging in their chest. How could an Urusar be so gullible? "Bought. You bought me, thinking I am your destined match, and it is your right as the big and powerful uktena Urusar from Wisconsin. I will never contradict you. I will do my duty. I will be the perfect Satislit for you."

"But you don't love me?"

Haru did look at Tally now. "That is the one thing I cannot do."

"What about last night? That meant..." Tally swallowed hard. "It meant nothing to you?"

Haru held back a scream. "It was a good fuck."

"Then you can go back." Tally stood and walked away from Haru, then began pacing back and forth as he waited for Haru to respond. But it wasn't so easy.

Talk about a surprise. "You are willing to let me go? Just like that?"

"No— I mean, yes. Until we figure this out. I will fix this, Haru. I believe we can make this work?"

"With your money?"

Tally's voice trembled. "I— Damn it. I… You *are* my Em'halafi. I won't make you unhappy. I can't live with this if you… If you don't…"

"You do remember what happens if you return me, right?"

"I pay a Satislit fine—" Tally cringed. His 's's came out long and exaggerated. "For used goods. Help place you with another clan. Is that what you want?"

"Do not bother. It is… If you could give me a reference to find a job somewhere in the US."

"Whatever clan—"

"No clans."

"What?" Tally stopped his pacing. "Why no clans? Otters need family more than other lijun."

Haru focused on the bathroom door.

"Haru? What happens if you return?"

Because it was the easy thing to do, Haru shut up.

"Can't answer or won't?"

No, they could not dig themself in further.

"What happens if you get sent back?" Tally sounded much closer. So light on his feet for such a humongous guy. "Haru, will Urusar Akaike still banish you?"

"If you could give me some references—"

"That *bastard*!"

Haru panicked, grabbing Tally. "Do not! Do not dare confront him. All of us will lose face on that deal. Especially with the Cohen murder hanging over you."

"But—"

"The Bastilles, the Akaike, my family, me—we all lose if you call Urusar Akaike out. Besides, no one would blame him. I can do alone."

"You can stay here. For as long as you need. Forget Urusar Akaike. Forget your parents. We can figure out us."

"Us?" Haru asked then shrugged. "You bought me. You can do whatever you want to me. I get no say, remember?"

"With me you do. With me you always have."

"Okay, how do you want to settle the Cohen children in tomorrow? Should we also pencil in when you want your cock sucked?"

"No, not— Damn it. I'll never touch you unless you sssay. Never asssk you," Tally hissed out. "It was all going so well. It wasn't sssupposed to be like this. Not...like this. Why didn't you ever *ssssay* anything? You could've come to me at any time."

"You bought me, what else did you expect?"

"To be loved by my Em'halafi. The one who asssked to be loved by the pool." The broken, trembling words were followed by a thud.

No more big hulking figure, just a huge—snake! "Snake! Fucking snake!"

Haru jumped on the bed, hissing.

A pointed head rose from the ground. The snake stared at Haru for a minute, its large forked tongue flicking. A low hiss came out as he lowered to the ground, and Haru watched as he slithered over to the couch, sliding up and over until he coiled himself in a blanket.

Haru sat back, achy in even more places. "Do not eat me. *Please*."

The snake just curled tighter, making itself into an impossibly small, neat coil, and hid his head in the folds of the blanket.

* * * *

Haru didn't love him. Of course he didn't. Even a relationship with one's Em'halafi didn't work if it was forced. And, oh Gods, had this ever been forced. Tally should've seen it, should've picked it up from the harsh words, the angry undercurrents from Haru's family and Urusar, from Haru's own actions. The snake wine, the eels — every small act out of place had been screams of defiance. Screams for help.

And Tally hadn't heard.

He'd wanted what he'd wanted and he hadn't *listened,* even if Haru hadn't felt comfortable enough or desperate enough to say the words. Oh Gods, what had he done? Haru hadn't even wanted... Tally's shudder rippled along his scales. It was too close to being nonconsensual, far too close. *Just sex*, Haru had said, as if he'd been some hookup from a bar. Except it wasn't just sex. It was Haru fulfilling what he felt was his obligation.

Snakes didn't cry or throw up when they were upset. Tally had to stay snaked until he got both of those urges under control. *Gods... Haru...*

You bought me.

Everything he'd done, oh so cleverly, to bring them together, everything he'd done since out of love, out of the overwhelming need to make certain Haru was comfortable and happy? Haru saw it as oppression. Another show of wealth and power.

He couldn't do this. Couldn't lie here with Haru's scent so close, with his words echoing in the air. The ache around his heart had become so painful he thought he might be dying. Was this how a snake heart attack felt? Not only did Haru not love him, the anger and contempt underlying so much of what he'd said... Gods. How could he conceivably fix this?

How could he have been so *stupid*?

A flash fire roared through his brain. He couldn't think through the excruciating pain, his thoughts reduced to *How could this happen? How could this happen?*

He couldn't stay here. Haru saw him as threatening. Dangerous. He couldn't... Tally lifted his head from his blanket nest. Haru's back was to him, ribcage rising and falling evenly under the blankets. Either he'd fallen into an exhausted sleep or he was pretending. Didn't matter.

Tally returned to human form and snagged the Sapphire Lake notepad and pen from the nightstand. Naked, shivering, sitting cross-legged on the floor, he wrote.

Haru —

I'm so terribly sorry. For everything. I wish you had told me, but I should have asked. You are safe. Still loved. And I won't say a word to your clan. We'll talk about what works for you when we can both —

Tally stopped to swipe the tears from his eyes so he could see. Crossed out *we can both* and replaced it with —

when we're both calmer. I'll be back at the house before the Cohen children arrive. I don't shirk my responsibilities.
~ Tally

He was hiccupping now and sniffling, trying to keep from sobbing and waking Haru.

PS – I don't know what I've done to make you think I could possibly murder anyone.

Which wasn't a denial, and Haru might misinterpret.

PPS – I didn't murder Ed. And I don't eat meat.

There. That was the best he could do with tears falling on the paper and a broken brain. *Should've known better. Should've known better. Oh Gods help me, it hurts so much.* More chunks of Tally's heart broke off with each passing second. He had to go. Carefully, he opened one of the windows in the front room of the suite, snaked out and slithered over the casement onto the tree growing against the building.

The night air shivered against his scales. He had to hurry or he might not make it to his destination. The last thing he needed was to be caught out in the open in uktena form, too cold to move any farther, too exhausted to care. At least it wasn't far and uktena could move fast through the undergrowth.

Subtle shades of gray painted the eastern sky when Tally spotted the house through the trees — two stories, cozy, with a round turret on top. He didn't know where else to go. Not feeling like this. He crawled up onto the front porch, lifted the front third of his body off the boards and pounded on the door.

Lights came on inside. A deep voice growled, "I'm coming, damn it. Hold your ponies. It's too damn early for this." The door jerked open and Tally barely kept his balance. Gunther jumped back a step. "Whoa! Tal? Oh, yeah. I'd know the shape of that seven-spot anywhere. Get in here, you idiot. It's freezing out there."

Tally dropped back to the boards and slithered in, going right for the space heater in Gunther's front room, flicking his tongue as he went. The house tasted/smelled musty. Not shocking, since it had been empty for a while. Someone from the family came to check on things every week. Someone kept the weeds in check. But no one had been inside. A hollow house. Like Tally's insides. He curled up by the heater and tucked his head into his coils.

"Oookay then." Gun's heavy footfalls moved away, then returned as he tucked a fleece blanket around Tally. "You're supposed to be in your honeymoon suite, chucklehead, curled up around your lovely Satislit. Not curled up on my floor. What the hell happened, Tal?"

He couldn't answer yet. Couldn't return to human form. Too cold. Too miserable. Gun's footsteps moved away again, little earthquakes vibrating through the hardwood. His voice came from the back of the house, rumbling to someone on the phone, perhaps. Tally couldn't make out the words with his head tucked away, though.

It could have been five minutes later or an hour when a human knock sounded on the front door. Voices. Marnie. Lily. Pete. More footsteps. Tally peeked out, already knowing he was surrounded.

Marnie crouched down beside him, stroking his head scales. "You want to maybe de-snake and tell us what's going on?"

Tally heaved a snake sigh and changed to human, pulling the blanket close around him. "I screwed everything up. Everything. It's all wrong."

"If this is some kind of thing where you couldn't perform, Tal, maybe you shouldn't be talking to us," Pete said, though he didn't sound serious.

"I… Haru…" The tears were starting again. How was he even supposed to explain if he was going to break down every two words? Deep breath. "He doesn't believe in Em'halafi. He… Gods…"

"T-take your time." Lily sat on the floor beside him. "H-h-however long you need."

He managed a sorrowful chuckle at that since it was what they had always said to Lily when words frustrated her. "He doesn't think it's real. He…he said I *bought* him from his clan. Bought and paid for. They *forced* him into the match."

"What do you mean forced? How could they force an adult?" Gun crouched beside Lily, his eyes telegraphing worry.

"Marry the big, scary uktena, or be banished from the clan." Tally buried his head in his hands and burst into tears. Damn it, he *hated* being like this. Warm arms wrapped around him. Several sets. Of course, the hugs only made him cry harder. "He didn't…didn't even want to be with me tonight. To…to have sex. He said it was his duty to *service* me. Oh Gods…it was practically rape, wasn't it?"

"Okay, hold on there, Mr. Urusar." Marnie stroked his hair. "First off, you were doing this for love, the negotiations, because you *do* believe. So let's get that straight. His family sold him. You actually wanted just *him*. No, it wasn't the usual way of courting someone. I get that. Maybe you were too eager. You rushed too much. But Haru's not a child. He could've told you, at any point. And he sure as hell could've told you no tonight *before* anything happened. I know you, Tal. You would've asked if stuff was okay. If it was what he wanted. Right?"

Tally managed a nod through his snuffling. All the arms holding him were making a collective effort to get him off the floor. Gun brought sweats, too short, and an old, stretched-out shirt, likewise, but it worked well enough. Coffee all round, extra blankets and slippers later, they'd gathered around Gun's kitchen table, all trying to convince Tally he wasn't a horrible person.

Except he was. He should've seen.

"You're not gonna fix everything right this second, Tal." Gunther patted his arm. "And sure as hell not the way you're feeling now. How about breakfast?"

"I'm not very hungry," Tally whispered.

"Well, I am." Marnie gave him a quick hug. "Let's get you to eat something and then we'll take you home. Get you looking respectable for opossum littles, right?"

Tally nodded, swallowing against the several lumps in his throat. *Right. Responsibilities.* His personal life was nothing compared to orphaned lijun kids.

* * * *

The house had been silent when Tally returned. He'd waved goodbye to his friends, all stuffed into Marnie's little hatchback, and tiptoed inside. No way to know if Haru was home yet, since a car service would drop him off when he was ready, but there were still guests in the house who might also still have been sleeping. The kids weren't due until ten. He had some time to collect himself.

A quick half-hour nap, a shower and more coffee helped him at least look human again. Not much he could do about the baggage under his eyes, but at least he could pull on his own jeans and a good sweater so he wasn't so chilled. Screw the person who said there was no bad weather, only bad clothing. Anything under fifty was getting iffy if one was a snake.

Calm, responsible, that was the face he needed now. His worry stone would've helped but he wasn't about to take it back from Haru's tub rock collection, especially not now. No more things were going to happen to make Haru feel powerless. Ever.

Tally gulped down his fifth—sixth?—cup of coffee and slogged down the basement stairs to look through the closets for old toys. He'd make sure the kids had their own stuff from the house and new toys, of course. This was just for today since he hadn't had a chance to get them anything. Most of the toys still in the closets were from the youngest Bastille kids. Hal's and Che's cars and action figures were mostly wrecked. They'd never been careful with their play. Nan's kitchen set, which she'd inherited from Tally, was in good shape, though. Might be something to carry up later. *Ah. There.* Shoved toward the back of the last closet were the buckets of Duplo blocks. *Several.*

It took shoving his head and shoulders into the corner of the closet, which was a painfully tight fit, and some grunting and swearing, but he got them out without disarranging too much in the overstuffed closet. There. One thing accomplished for the day.

By the time he'd stomped back up the stairs with two buckets in each hand, the old grandfather clock in the front hall read quarter after ten. *Oh. Oh, no.* He poked his head out the front door. No car in the drive. Mrs. Kauffman hadn't come with the kids yet? Wait, no. Little suitcases sat by the stairs, one with Hello Kitty, one with Batgirl and one with yellow flowers. Those didn't belong to the tanuki family or either of the visiting elderly aunts.

Someone had been here to greet the kids and it hadn't been Tally. Hooray for failing once again. But where had they gone? He stood in the front hall, flicking his tongue into the air. Opossum joeys. Yes. Here at the door and... They'd gone upstairs. All right, he supposed that made sense. Maybe Addy had been here and was getting them settled. Tally huffed at yet another set of steps and clomped up, Duplo buckets still clutched tight.

Huh. They weren't in either of the unoccupied guest rooms and no Addy. Flick-flick. Oh, of course. Haru had been the one to greet the kids. Great. So Tally hadn't managed to do the right thing in Haru's eyes again and now he would somehow have to face his new spouse. He wasn't ready for this. He didn't have the luxury of not being ready for this. With a heavy sigh, he straightened his shoulders and turned the corner toward Haru's suite.

The door was ajar, so at least Tally didn't have to knock. Though when he shoved the door open with one shoulder, he had to stop and try to process what he was seeing. At first, the room appeared filled with fur-bearing critters, but as his brain adjusted, he realized there were only six — two otters, three baby opossums and a young tanuki.

One of the smaller opossums clung to the back of the larger otter with all her might, mussing glossy black fur. The second smaller opossum was trying to climb up with many desperate chirps and nudges from the otter's nose. The tanuki teetered on her hind paws with the larger baby opossum in her forepaws as she tried to place him on the smaller otter's back.

Despite his broken heart, Tally believed he might die of cute.

He set the buckets of blocks down and cleared his throat, which turned out to be a mistake since both otters jumped and squeaked, and the little tanuki fell on her cute little raccoon-dog butt. Slowly, carefully, he knelt on the edge of the carpet and set the Duplo buckets in front of him.

"Hello, little ones. I'm glad you're here."

While he would've said more, he found his arms full of tanuki as Kaho launched at him and licked his face. The joeys trundled over, sniffing and pawing at the buckets until Tally put one on its side for them, one of the building sets. Much excited squeaking followed as Amelia and Olivia began to shove all the blocks with eyes on them into a pile, and Jackson carefully gathered specific blocks for...something. The little girl joeys nipped at Tally's fingers until he helped them place their eye blocks together into some sort of mythical cherub monster while Jackson worked with claws and teeth to make his architectural masterpiece on his own.

Tally caught himself smiling, taken out of his own heartache in the little ones' determined play. He might have even found a laugh hiding in his jigsawed chest if the doorbell hadn't rung.

"Be good for Haru and Sam," Tally said as he started to get up carefully. Kaho yipped angrily. "And be good for Kaho. Especially. I have to answer the door."

Sam galumphed up and stood on her hind legs to give Tally an otter kiss before he could clamber to his feet. "Thanks, Sam," Tally murmured, risking a quick glance at Haru. He had to do a quick second take, squinting. Sure enough, the glint of Tally's red and gray worry stone caught the light when Haru moved his head, the stone clamped tight in his mouth.

Wonder what that's about? He promised himself to ask later as he hurried down the stairs to the front door. Gun, Marnie, Mom, he expected any number of visitors but not...

"Sheriff?"

"Mr. Bastille. Good. You're home. Mind if I come in?"

"Um, of course. Please." Tally stepped aside, waving Sheriff Amick into the front hallway. "How can I help you?"

"Just a few quick questions." Sheriff Amick pushed his hat back and got out his ever-present notepad and pen. "Were you here all last night?"

"I...no. Yesterday was the wedding. Haru and I spent the night in the honeymoon suite at Sapphire Lake."

The sheriff nodded, writing. "When did you arrive back home?"

Tally had to think about that. It had still been relatively early. "Around seven, I think. Haru may have come back a little later."

"Oh?" Sheriff Amick's eyebrows climbed. "You didn't come back to the house together?"

"No, we, ah." Tally huffed out a breath. "There was business to take care of. I went to a friend's house for a couple of hours."

The sheriff rubbed at his hatline. "Now, I want you to think before you answer. When exactly did you leave the hotel?"

Where is this going? Tally did his best not to panic. *Think. Think.* The clock on the nightstand had read 5:13 when he'd collapsed on the floor to write his note. "Quarter after five, as close as I can estimate."

"And your husband, spouse, whatever you're calling it these days, he can verify that?"

"No," Tally got out in a strained murmur. "He was asleep."

"I see. What's the latest he *could* vouch for you?"

"We last spoke…" Tally drew in a long, shaky breath, trying his best not to hear echoes of that conversation. "A little after three. I left the hotel, probably got to Gun's house twenty minutes later."

"Anyone see you or talk to you between the hours of, oh, let's say three in the morning and five-thirty, then?"

"No," Tally managed to get out though ice had filled his lungs. "Sheriff, what's this all about?"

Sheriff Amick pursed his lips, staring at the entryway floor tiles. "The ME sent samples from Ed's body to the state lab. Someone broke in early this morning and killed the tech on night shift. Far as we can tell, only the samples from Ed's autopsy were missing. Sure there's nothing you want to tell me, Mr. Bastille?"

Tally shook his head, trying to find his voice. "No. No, I wasn't anywhere near the lab."

"All right. Your, ah, spouse around? I'd like to speak to him too, please."

"He's…" *An otter right now. Looking after toddler opossums and a small tanuki.* "I think he went back to sleep for a bit."

"Big day yesterday." Sheriff Amick snapped his notebook shut with a nod. "He can come down to the office to make a statement, if he likes. That's all for now, Mr. Bastille. Don't —"

"I know, Sheriff. Don't leave town. I've no intention of doing so."

With a last quick glance around, Sheriff Amick stepped out and shut the door behind him. Tally collapsed on the bottom stair with his head in his hands. He wanted to say the day couldn't possibly get any worse, but he knew better than to think such dangerous things.

The sounds from upstairs were happy ones, so Tally decided to pull himself together and get some work done. Yes, he was officially on vacation and managers had instructions to contact him only in dire emergencies, but emails still needed sorting, international contacts dealt with, questions from the clan seen to.

After clearing the essential issues, he wandered down the backstairs from his office to the kitchen. Coffee, then he would go see how the kids were doing. It would be lunchtime soon. He hoped they had things small opossum kids liked for lunch. Every kid liked peanut butter, right? Thoughts of what to feed toddlers had him so preoccupied that he nearly missed the fact that someone was in the kitchen.

"Oh." He drew up short at Haru's wary glance from where he was pouring juice into sippy cups. The kids must've brought their own since Tally didn't think there were any in the cabinets. He kept his voice soft and polite. "Good morning, Haru."

Haru turned and offered a bow. "Good morning, Argaze."

"Tally." His response was automatic by now, but Haru's formal address was no more than he deserved. Well, best to get things out in the open now. "If you have a moment, I have some things I need to go over."

"Rules of the house." Haru gave a sharp nod. "As you wish, Argaze."

The sigh escaped before Tally could stop it and he leaned back against the wall nearest the pantry, as far away from Haru as he could be and still stand in the same room. "Not rules. But information and my promises to you. Those first."

Haru's gaze was guarded, but at least he'd put the bottle of juice down and was listening.

"Your suite is inviolate. Unless I hear obvious sounds of distress or danger, or if you call for me, I won't step foot in it. If I need you, I *will* knock, and you aren't under any obligation to let me in. Second, unless you come to me of your own volition, enthusiastically and because you *want* to, I don't want to be *ssserviced*." He took a deep breath to stop the hissing. No getting upset. No scaring Haru again. "Please, please don't. I'm stunned to find that you think I'm the sort of person who would want that."

Haru flinched then huffed out a breath. Tally held up a hand before he could say anything.

"Let me finish. Please. These things are important. All for different reasons, but all important. Next, if you want to rush off elsewhere, I will give you top-notch references to wherever you feel you'd be comfortable. But I ask that you stay and consider your choices. You're welcome to stay here forever if you choose. I won't insist, but it would be better if you had a plan first if you feel you must leave. I will finance anything you need. Educational, business startup, living expenses until you're settled."

Oh *Gods*, those words hurt to say. He had to say them even as they ripped ragged threads off his unraveling heart. Haru stared at the floor, so Tally went on.

"While you are here, you are still Uruma, as my mother was, as my grandmother was, a role I hope you're still willing to fill, for now at least."

He got a short nod for that, but still no answer. Tally ran both hands over his face, fighting back the urge to fling himself, weeping, to his knees. *Almost done for now. You can do this.*

Little tremors chased his words as he finished. "All right. Finally, household items. The tablet on the stand there is for the household accounts. I've left the password on the sticky note for you. Grocery order comes every Friday. If there's anything you want or need, for you, or if you think I've forgotten something for the kids, please add it. If you need something the store doesn't have, please order it. The Amazon account is always signed on for the household."

"What would I need?" Just the slightest hint of snark colored the polite words. "You provide everything, Argaze."

"Mrs. Kauffman said the kids like spiced crickets, for instance," Tally managed, though his breath hitched. "And they need kid-sized beds for their room—"

Haru drew himself up. "I want the children to sleep in my room."

"But they—" *Opossum children. Who sleep in piles. And don't like to be far from their parents. Yes, all right.* "They'll still need beds."

"They will sleep with me. If it pleases you."

Tally covered his eyes with one hand, unable to look at this cold, distant version of Haru any longer. "You are Uruma, Haru. Your decisions are as important as mine in this house, and for the clan. If you feel that's best, then it's best."

There were plenty of references about how to recognize your Em'halafi. The joy that came in finding them. No one ever talked about what to do if your one destined match hated you.

Chapter Nine

What's an Uruma to Do?

Haru trundled down the stairs, joeys along for the ride. It took some getting used to, having babies hitchhiking along all the time, though the company made the living situation bearable. Concern that the Cohens hadn't humaned much since moving into the house gnawed at Haru, but it had only been a couple days. Sometimes the animal side of things made life easier to deal with, so they really couldn't blame the pups. Haru certainly hadn't humaned much either.

Otterring out made avoiding more uncomfortable conversations easier too. Haru wasn't going to admit that they had gone actively into denial about life, but yes, they most definitely had. He didn't even bother to human when their Urusar and parents came to say goodbye. The morning of the wedding had been humiliating enough, and Haru never wanted to relive another examination. They'd been just a tool for the clan.

Served them right, getting ignored. The red-faced glare Akaike-san had bestowed upon them had been worth it. He couldn't discipline Haru anymore. There had been a moment when it had looked like Akaike-san was going to strike them anyway. Not being able to be punished by their former clan felt *nice*. The snub hadn't been missed by Tally either, who had dismissed the group rather promptly.

That had earned their Argaze some rocks in his shoes. Though that had ended up in swearing, but Haru *had* meant it as a thanks.

The rock was what they could do, confused and bewildered about...*everything*.

A sneeze made Haru stop their descent. The tiny, barely audible sound was cute, but the noise was also how joeys got their parents' attention. They turned on the stair to get level, then glanced back. Amelia sneezed again, wriggling from her sideways, half-fallen position onto a better spot on Haru's back.

Nose. Nose. *Sorry, little girl.* Haru never imagined they'd have pups riding them around on land — in the water was one thing — but here they stood, married with pups already and completely clueless. They needed to do better.

Amelia made an unusual noise. It almost sounded like a chirp, something Haru used when calling them. They chirped back. Were the joeys adapting? A spark of parental pride warmed their chest — their pups were trying to communicate — Oh, oh, dear. They had already started thinking of the joeys as *theirs*.

But the precious pups weren't, not yet.

Tally had said there was a *process*. Explained it. Adoption in America felt like a nightmare.

Too bad. Haru's otter didn't agree with the process.

Being so young and tiny, how well would the joeys remember their parents? An ache filled Haru's chest. The girls and Jackson had obviously been loved, considering how trusting they were. Not like Haru. Not unlike Tally. Their parents didn't deserve to be forgotten. Hopefully there were some albums or something they could find. That meant talking to Tally, though.

Tomorrow. They'd ask tomorrow.

Haru had just rounded into the kitchen when an excited chitter filled the room followed by a thunk. Claws clicked along the wood floor and Kaho came into view, her stubby legs wheeling as she slid into them.

The joeys scattered, sneezing and squeaking as they tumbled around the floor. Haru kept an eye on the balls of fur while moving toward the fridge. All of them needed fuel for the day's activities. They stood on their back paws and wedged their fore claws behind the handle. The door popped open, all available contents on display.

Oooh, someone had moved around the drawer contents so the yummies were on the bottom.

Snails and crayfish — the freshwater cousin not as yummy as prawns, but still good. Haru pulled the bags out with their teeth. Nice and easy. The bags fell open, drawing the attention of Kaho and the joeys. The kids tumbled over, squeaking and chittering. Little paws immediately began tearing the yummies apart as Haru watched. The scrape of claws against the snail shells occupied the gaps between satisfied chirps. The pups would need something more, though. Omnivores could not abide by fishy foods alone. Something green for the joeys and Kaho.

Frilly greens that tasted okay, and little carrots, were in the crisper. Haru dumped the icky tasting bags out. Carrots rolled, sending the pups chasing after them. Food scattered everywhere. The joeys didn't know which way to go. Kaho batted several carrots toward the twins, helping them gather treats. Jackson added to the pile. Sneezes and chirps filled the room as they shared the food, the pups and Kaho snuggling close.

"What happened in here?"

Haru turned, putting themself between the voice and their pups. Amelia, Olivia and Jackson pressed against their bum, but Kaho leapt over them before they could stop her. She landed squarely against Tally's chest, his arms curled protectively around her, supporting her.

"Oh, um." Tally stopped, then actually took a step back. "I heard noises."

The damage to the kitchen floor was quite extensive, yes. Bits and pieces of the yummies and veggies were, frankly, everywhere. Haru peeked up at Tally. He didn't look mad. In fact, he seemed to be content petting Kaho and surveying the damage with no mad feels.

"Are you guys done?"

Several sneezes came from the joeys. Kaho patted Tally's chest and he loosened his grip to let her down. The pups started gathering up the food. Kaho held open a bag for them to drop foodstuffs into. Haru joined them, using his nimble claws to pick up the smaller pieces.

"I can do that," Tally said. "You guys don't need to clean up."

But they had made the mess. Haru snuck a piece of crayfish into their mouth.

"Go, play, do whatever. I'm not mad."

"*Hah!*"

"I take it that's your 'I don't believe you' sound?" Tally sighed, wiped his face, and sighed again. "Really, you and the kids can go play. I'll clean up."

"*Chep!*" Haru chirped then skittered toward their pups. The joeys jumped on while Kaho waddled up next to them with the bag in her forepaws. Nose. Nose. Treats for later. Smart girl. "*Chep!*"

As they scooted around Tally, Haru heard a whispered, "I wouldn't hurt any of you, especially not your pups."

So Tally saw it too. What the joeys meant to them. Would he use it against Haru? Would the family? Everyone acted like everything was fine between them and Tally. Bastille-*okaasan* smiled every time she saw Haru running around with the Cohen children clinging to their back. Lahi had come every night with her guitar to sing the joeys to sleep, and while a part of Haru itched to play for them on their own biwa, that would mean they'd have to human. If they did that then they'd have to talk to the Bastilles —

Did they not *know*? Had Tally told *no one*?

Broken. That was what the two of them were. Irrevocably broken.

Kaho's excited chittering broke Haru out of his humdrum bluesies. Their ragtag group had managed to make it outside without Haru noticing. The smells of the lake, of fresh air, the woods — all invigorated them. The joeys tried to match the noises Kaho made, more sneezing, less che-sound, but they sounded adorable.

Haru scurried along the bank — running resulted in flying joeys. Also something Haru would rather not experience a second time. Scared the crap out of everyone. Literally, for Jackson.

Their holt came into view, earning several excited chirps. The pups had been helping every day at the den, clearing out the dirt, packing it down, fixing the rocks. Today would be the finishing touches, really. Just stuff for the nest inside. Really just Haru futzing because Kaho would be leaving soon — too soon for them.

When she left, that meant Haru was on their own, and the idea of being ready to face...anything, by themself, caused a pang of panic to well up inside them.

Olivia jumped off their back, followed by Amelia. The twins ran toward the high grass. Haru gave a bark, but the girls were already gathering so they headed down the entrance with Jackson. The two rooms in the burrow were still dry. Good. Good. Don't want wet pups if they decided to nap.

Kaho dumped out the treats, which in turn had Jackson tumbling off Haru with excited sneezes. Those two could chow down while Haru checked on the girls and got some gathering done. The grass would be best, but twigs and bark weren't bad either.

"Chep!"

Amelia's head popped up, dried grass between her teeth. Her sister wasn't far behind. The brown coloring meant their nest would feel nice underneath them, but they'd need more of it. Haru nosed the girls toward the entrance, preferring them inside than out.

Out meant danger. Predators. Pups should eat treats so Haru wouldn't worry.

But as soon as the twins were down the holt, Kaho and Jackson were out of the den.

Four against one sucked sour grapes.

So they made a line. Haru gathered the grass and twigs, passed to Kaho who ran on her hind legs to give the bundle to Jackson, who gave it to one of the twins. It worked well until a pixie showed up, bent on havoc.

The evil little bastard.

Amelia chittered and tugged on the rock Jasper had 'borrowed', except borrowed meant taking. The girls took issue with the theft and chased, leaving them in their current tug-o-war crisis. Olivia hissed and batted at his feet. Jasper hovered just beyond reach, laughing and taunting the two young joeys. That was until Kaho stood on her hindpaws, plucked him out of the air and stuck him in her mouth.

Haru had never humaned so fast. "We do not eat pixies!"

Kaho snuffed.

"Spit him out right now! Jasper is not a bug."

Kaho gnashed her teeth together. Muffled cries emanated from her mouth, and Jasper's legs pedaled wildly.

"No. Eating. Pixies." Haru held out their hand. "Spit him out. Now."

One sopping wet and sobbing, most likely traumatized pixie ended up spat onto the hard October ground. His wings were crinkled and heavy with spit. There didn't seem to be any blood, not that Haru got a good look — besides Jasper's backside as he ran into the brush. Despite his hasty retreat, Haru had a feeling they'd be seeing their pixie friend again.

Haru frowned down at their chortling tanuki. "That was not nice, Kaho-chan." Effective, but not nice. "Even if he is making a pest of himself."

All they got was a raspberry in return.

"Quite. Let us get the den finished up."

Haru ottered back out and went back to helping gather grass. Their little conga line of lijun were so involved with packing the holt the first screech didn't register. But the second did.

Loud, ominous, the second screech sent the joeys down the burrow in no time.

Kaho's frightened chirps scared Haru more than anything. Their little tanuki was exposed.

They ran, bouncing over the land toward her as the large bird dove. They barked, hoping to scare the stupid bird going after their tanuki. Haru slid to a stop in front of Kaho. They hissed as the bird's wings stretched open and his claws came down.

Sharp talons never dug into them, though.

A whoosh of air hit Haru, then there was a thud.

Gunther.

Looming over Haru was Tally's friend, not a bird but—duh, Gunther was golden eagle lijun. Still, it hadn't been necessary to frighten Haru and the pups half to death.

"Whoa! Whoa! Can you cool it with the hissing? You sound like an uktena."

That shut Haru up. Never did they want to be compared with those bastards.

"Tally needs you at the house. A clan dispute has come up and they're asking for Judgment from the Uruma."

Was Gunther joking?

"I'll watch the pups, you need to hurry up."

Apparently not. Haru went from a floor-level point-of-view to seeing eye-to-eye on two feet. He pitched forward only to be caught by Gunther.

"Do not touch me!" Haru pushed back so hard they went flying in the other direction, landing squarely on their ass. "Oof!" *Ow. Ow.* Not that Haru would show how embarrassed they felt. They slapped away

Gunther's hand. "I do not need your groin in my face. Thank you."

Gunther stepped back, hands up. A frown pulled at his mouth, lines accentuating the blunt beak of a nose. A frosty breeze wrapped around them, causing Gunther's hair to sweep his black curls around his deep sepia skin with its golden glow. *The face of a disapproving Inuit god, that is what it is.* Elegant and foreboding.

Unlike Haru's own long tresses which whipped and cracked. A warning. A hiss in the wind.

Gunther sighed and took another couple steps back. "Look."

Haru raised their head, cocking it to one side.

"What you did to Tally was a shit move."

What I did?

"He doesn't need your fucked-up baggage on him. He's a good guy. So, if you're going to stick around, the least you can do is pretend you care about your position as Uruma so the council doesn't have ammunition to rub in his face."

The words were a physical blow. Sharp, fast, straight to Haru's heart. They almost collapsed beneath the harsh accusations. But they hadn't softened just because they had a new clan. No, Haru knew better, and they knew these types of words well. Haru understood duty. And apparently Tally had told someone about their brokenness, or perhaps a few someones?

"As you say, Curley-san." Haru offered an *eshaku*. A noise made Haru glance at the holt, heart frantic. Kaho chittered, but hustled back down the entrance when they waved her off.

"Your pups and Kaho will be safe with me, for fuck's sake. We're not going to hurt you. We're clan."

"How could I possibly know how safe I am with a bunch of strangers? How safe my pups are? But, I am perfectly aware of my duty. It is what I was bought for after all. I do not get a say."

Gunther reared back, one hand over his chest.

Instead of facing more cutting remarks, they ottered out. Would the pups be okay? Haru's heart seized. Maybe the joeys would just hole up in the den until they came back. They barked a warning at Gunther then ran, bounding along the banks, the rocks and dead grass a blur. The huge Bastille abode — manor, truly — loomed over the lake and into sharp contrast the closer they got.

The scents surrounding the house startled Haru. So many smells.

Haru scuttled through the cat door installed in the back, the sheer number of voices setting them on high alert. Exactly how many lujin were here? Had another death occurred?

The front room was bursting at the doors. Angry voices. Shouts. Tally's deep voice rumbled, but the voices were mad. Haru's name got thrown into the pot. More voices, younger ones, defiant, scared, rose to meet the racket. The heavy musk of moose and boar stank up the place. Their owners were some of the loudest voices too. The scent of rabbit and fox also lingered.

How many of the council members were here?

The feet made the room an obstacle course of stomps and thumps. Haru made for the snake by the fireplace. Tally had his back to the wall — literally. Cornered. A weak position. He was rigid, shoulders back. Coiled. Their Argaze was coiled, ready to strike. His eyes narrowed at something Councilman Black said.

"*Hah!*" Haru barked out.

"Shit!"

"What!"

"*Hah!*" Haru jumped Tally, scaling him to reach the mantelpiece. "*Hah!*"

The room fell into silence, all gazes focused front and center right on them.

"Everyone, you remember my Satislit, Haru?"

Haru ran up Tally's arm, nosed his cheek then sat on his shoulder. One paw had a firm hold on Tally's hair while the other fumbled against his jaw. Not the most graceful of displays, but it got the point across.

Councilman Hastings barreled to the front and crossed his arms. "And where was Uruma Bastille while we have a clan crisis to deal with?"

"With our children," Tally answered coolly. "Or have you forgotten we now have the Cohen joeys?"

Hastings-san looked only slightly mollified. Councilman O'Rourke, who stood next to him, frowned. Haru tugged on Tally, who reached up and put them on the floor. Falling in front of the aggrieved council members, Haru offered the best *senrei* they could under the circumstances.

Both councilmen cocked their heads, big, fluffy brows drawn together. Hastings-san rudely pointed at Haru. "What is your Satislit doing?"

O'Rourke-san grabbed Hastings-san's hand and pulled it down. "I believe Uruma Bastille is offering his apologies. Thank you, Satislit. Good to see someone remembers their manners."

Haru pushed up, clapped their paws together then wriggled. He repeated the performance a couple times before Hastings-san's eyes lit with an awareness. It shook Haru bone-deep. His former Urusar had those eyes. The Bastille Clan was not as progressive as Tally led Haru to believe.

"Yes, please Sahnkes. We will wait for you."

Finally, the room wasn't awash in musk and ragey hormones. Haru tugged on Tally's pant cuffs, and their Urusar was intelligent enough to follow.

"Why the kitchen?"

Haru chirped, patted the refrigerator door and looked at their floundering Argaze.

"Right, food. You Sahnkes and get dressed. I'll stall with food. I called Sammy to help with the pups."

"*Chep!*" Haru turned and grabbed Tally's leg. They patted it a couple times then was off and running.

A mumbled, "Was he comforting me?" was all that followed Haru out of the kitchen.

In the suite, Haru allowed a moment of panic when they looked in the mirror. Yeah, they'd definitely had better days. Their hair. Gods. Haru hopped in the shower, scrubbed fast and determined, then managed to get a brush through their hair without losing too much of it. To make it look better they put it up in a bun with Tally's white jade hairpiece.

With a towel wrapped around their waist, Haru hurried into the room.

There was no time for a proper *yukata*, but... Tally *needed* Haru to be Uruma.

Bold, bright colors with flattering basic makeup. The falling leaves kimono would do. It was traditional enough to appease the council members, flashy enough to say who ran the roost.

A knock sounded at their door, followed by Sammy popping her head through the door. "Need help?"

"Oh, yes!"

Sammy smiled. "Thought you might."

"Thank you." Nose. Nose. Kiss. Kiss. Haru's nerves settled as their one and only friend hugged them.

"What was that dance you did earlier?" she asked as she helped them with the *nagajuban*.

"You were down there?"

"Yes, though there were so many smells, I'm not surprised you didn't see me. The dance?"

Haru shook their head. "It was not a dance."

"Then what was it?"

"Asking permission to leave and get dressed. They are the council members after all. I was not in proper attire to great them. It was just a formality."

Silence followed.

"Can you grab me another *koshi himo*?"

"Yeah." Sammy wrapped her arms around Haru, giving them a hug. She nosed their chest and quietly asked, "Exactly what kind of clan did you grow up in?"

Haru patted her back rather than answering. It was easier not to. And Haru didn't want her upset on their behalf. They had enough anger for the both of them. To light a star, really. One small nuclear explosion packed in an otter-sized lijun.

Thirty minutes later, Haru was back down the stairs in proper attire, their *geta* making more noise than they would've liked. Didn't want people to think they had gotten nervous. Haru slowed purposefully. *Our guests have waited this long*. No one had come bursting into their room. Tally was obviously surviving whatever havoc had rocked up on the Bastille doorstep.

Murmurs instead of shouts met them as they entered the front room.

"Welcome to the Bastille home," Haru said over the buzz and bowed. "Sorry to have made you wait."

The noise level went down to nothing.

There was a "Wait!" from Tally followed by sneezes. So, the pups hadn't waited in the holt. Momentary panic kicked in, but Haru pushed it back with a smile. One they'd given Urusar Akaike many times. People parted as the Cohen joeys and Kaho ran up to him. Haru immediately bent at the knees and welcomed the children.

After several noses and kisses, Haru smiled as they scratched behind Olivia's ear. "Sammy has the Duplo blocks out upstairs. Why not go and see what she has made?"

Excited squeaks went up, noses twitching. Kaho led the charge out of the room. Loud thumps on the stairs followed. Hopefully that meant the pups were going up and not falling down. Haru turned to listen for a minute. No cries of pain.

Haru faced the room, wished they hadn't, then straightened. "Apologies, Councilmen Hastings-san, O'Rourke-san. The pups are still settling in. They have been through so much recently, I am sure you can understand the need to comfort them?"

Black-san nodded. "It's what an Uma is for."

Hastings-san agreed.

"It's good to see such a dedicated Uma," Councilmen O'Rourke agreed. "Just what young lijun need. Leaves me in high hopes."

A reply of *high hopes for what?* seemed inappropriate so they bowed. "Thank you."

"Now, the reason we're here," O'Rourke-san said.

"I was informed you are asking for Judgment?"

"We are."

"May I say hello first?" Haru wasn't about to let the council members control the conversation. They didn't know enough of the clan yet.

"Of course, Uruma Bastille."

Haru wove through the crowd, saying hello, offering *eshaku* to their new clan. It was a mixture of adults and teens. There was a divide between families, several positioning close to the council while the others had clustered near the drinks and snacks. Haru never gave the council members their back, and they didn't dawdle among the families, but they refused to be rushed too. The adults were the ones who were angry. Seven families. Two against five. Mixture of lijuns. The kids were giving each other furtive glances, no matter which side of the room they had gotten corralled to.

The teens were friends. Close friends. Upset by the divide.

Adults sucked.

Whatever the council members and the families were about to hit Haru with was going to hit hard. Be uncomfortable.

It was a test.

Tally seemed to know it too. The way he stood so carefully, apart.

Well, as far as Haru was concerned, the clan needed to know who was in charge. They made their way over to their Argaze. Tally offered an arm, and Haru linked them together as they faced the crowd together.

"So, what mischief have the children gotten into?"

Councilman Black chuckled, while Howe-san shook her head.

But it was O'Rourke-san who spoke. "The *children* have been sneaking out of the Redtails' or Blue Hollys' house during the weekends and playing tag."

"Tag?"

"An inappropriate version of tag. Late at night."

The teens all scowled in unison, crossing their arms. It was almost funny. Almost. Except the poor kids were obviously hurting.

Because *adults*.

"We are not discussing normal teenage hijinks, are we?"

"No, unfortunately not, Uruma Bastille." Hastings-san let out a long, dramatic sigh.

Haru tipped their head back. They knew upbraiding gestures all too well.

"The youngsters are sneaking out well past curfew and hunting each other, sometimes the local wildlife too." Hastings-san frowned, huffing as he looked at the two ostracized families. "Not only are the Redtails and Blue Hollys setting a bad example for the teenagers, they're endangering us, possibly exposing us to the humans."

"By letting the children take part in traditional Evade and Hunt games?"

"Yes, by — what?"

"Do your mentors normally chaperone these?" Haru asked. "Is that the problem? These teens are obviously older lijun. Do they not start playing without supervision once they reach age?"

All that met Haru's question were blank stares, though a few of the kids had perked up.

"The traditional Evade and Hunt games? To help teach the prey and predator lijun evasion from hunters and how to hunt? My former clan tends to do them only a couple of times a month, but we are smaller. How often does the Bastille clan have them?"

The families looked at each other in confusion, as did the council members. Haru glanced up at Tally who seemed to be trying not to move his mouth. His lips twitched. However, their Argaze seemed to be catching on.

Tally cleared his throat. "I don't remember the last time there have been any Evade and Hunt games. I remember some from when I was in high school, but since then…"

Haru turned to the crowd. "Really? But how do you teach survival skills and control? There are too many hormones disrupting growth. What do the clan mentors say?"

"Mentoring usually happens within the families these days."

The lijun in the room might have flinched a little when Haru turned their disapproval on the adults.

Councilwoman Howe spoke up. "With the developments in technology, the council felt it was better."

"To deny youth proper outlets for their spirit-halves? Children surprise and play with each other. They don't pick the *right* moments. It is why those of age should play alone — they get sneaky. The games are the lessons to protect us *all*."

That got more flinching.

"The games have been around since the Gods blessed lijun with their spirit-halves. Why would you deny your youth the instinct to learn and protect themselves?"

"Uruma Bastille, with camera phones and digital recorders, the risk of — " began Councilman Hastings.

"That is what planning is for. Guidelines and rules. It is the job of the adults to adapt the games to the new circumstances and teach their children." Haru frowned, then glanced over at Tally. "What are the rates of accidental change because of surprises and the like? What kind of lessons were set up to replace the games?"

Councilman Black shook his head. "The rates have gone up. It's left to the individual family to teach the children. As it should."

"Connecting to our spirit-halves, acknowledging our dual-nature, being able to control the *Sahnkes*, is the clan's duty to all children." Haru turned to Tally, giving the room their back. "We need to implement procedures for Evade and Hunt games. We cannot endanger the children further."

"The next council meeting is soon. We can put it on the docket." Tally smiled and reached for Haru.

When their hands connected, Tally seemed to remember his promise and tried to pull away. Haru stepped into the hold and turned toward the room. Too many people were here. Last thing the others needed to see was a broken front. The children would be the ones to pay the price. Haru held Tally's hand firmly against their hip.

"Mr. and Mrs. Redtail, Mr. and Mrs. Blue Holly, thank you for wanting to make sure the children were able to control themselves. Puberty is an especially difficult time for lijun." Haru gave them a *saikeirei*. "I am sorry we have gotten so far away from our roots. We will do better. Do you think you could be on the committee to help plan the Evade and Hunt games? Though, maybe we should get some mentors for these kids for now so they are not floundering until then?"

No one spoke. It was quiet. Too quiet.

Haru peeked up through their lashes.

Tally stared down at them. The council members stared. The families stared. Staring all around.

Laughter startled all of them. Councilman O'Rourke's deep, low bellows were loud against the interrupted silence. Hastings-san, Black-san and Howe-san glanced over at him then each other. The fidgeting Howe-san sidestepped away then back. If she had rabbited out, her ears would have been twitching — actually, they still were even humaned.

"Uruma Bastille has passed Judgment," O'Rourke-san said. He sounded too happy. "And it's on the adults."

Oh dear. Haru faced the councilman who dipped his head, a smile firmly in place.

"You have every right to chastise us. Such a passionate Uruma." O'Rourke-san motioned toward the doorway. "We will abide by Judgment since it was what the council asked for. I will personally make sure to have a list of mentors for you, Satislit Haru. Until the council meeting, Urusar Bastille.

"Oh, before I go. May I congratulate you on your marriage, Urusar Bastille?" Councilman O'Rourke approached Tally and shook his hand. He bowed to Haru. "Urusar Akaike informed us your wedding night was indeed a passionate one. Congratulations. But that is expected of Em'halafi, isn't it, Satislit Haru?"

"But, of course, Councilman O'Rourke," they answered, though the moose's words had been a punch to the gut. Tally went tense beside Haru.

"Then we are most fortunate. The Gods blessing our Urusar with his Em'halafi. We thought Tally would never settle down. May the clan have your guidance for years to come."

"Thank you, it is my hope as well."

Trap. Trap. The words were closing the cage all around Haru.

The families and council members filtered out of the front room, leaving Haru behind with Tally and Gunther. The latter surprised Haru. Had Gunther been there the whole time? Though he would've been the one to bring Kaho and the Cohens back.

The front door banged shut, dropping the house into silence.

Gunther was on the couch, arms crossed, gaze pinned on Haru.

It was not a happy expression. Probably had some more words for Haru if his frown was anything to go by.

A squeeze on Haru's side made them remember Tally. That their Argaze had Haru firmly against his side and in his hold. Haru stiffened, straightening almost painfully upright. Their heartbeat kicked up a notch, all the adrenaline breaking loose at once.

Tally had focused in on Haru, his gaze open and questioning. Many questions flashed across his face. More than what Haru knew what to do with, so they turned away. Only that meant they had to face their Argaze's best friend.

Not the happy expression one hoped for when facing a supposed ally.

Gunther's eyes narrowed. "You wear two faces, Haru. And I'm not sure I like either one."

"Gun!"

Right. Right. What Gunther had said by the den came back to Haru, resonated down to the marrow. The confrontation with the council all but solidified where their place was. The joeys meant they'd be going nowhere. Might as well accept their fate. Do their duty. Haru pressed a hand against Tally's chest, then placed a kiss against their mouth. Stopped the big guy cold.

"If it pleases you, Argaze, I would like to check on the children."

"Of course, Haru, but—"

"Thank you." Haru fled the room as fast as they possibly could, leaving behind all hopes and dreams. It'd hurt less that way.

Chapter Ten

Missing Parts

Something had gone terribly wrong during the Judgment. There were also things that had gone right. Tally hated seeing the friends being wedged into a pissing match between adults. It wasn't fair to them. Haru had seen it too, then fixed it.

Then the end went sideways.

The comment from Dan O'Rourke about Urusar Akaike meant something. It felt wrong, dirty somehow. Tally had his suspicions, and they were nothing good. The way Haru had paled made Tally's stomach twist up in knots.

What Gun had said didn't help either. He loved his best friend, but his comments only made things worse.

That kiss. What was that, even?

Watching his Em'halafi flee from the room, from *him*, made it hard to breathe.

"Tally, look, I'm sorry." Gunther stood and joined him by the fire. "But I don't like seeing how that manipulative bastard hurts you every time he pretends like he actually cares."

"But he does care, Gun. Haru does *care*."

"About being Uruma, maybe. How he looks —"

"Sss-stop!" Tally hissed out.

"Whoa, whoa. No need to snake out on me." Gunther pulled Tally into a hug before pushing him back and holding on to his shoulders. "I'm sorry. I am. I just... He hurt you, Tally. Now he's... I don't know what he's doing. But I know he's hurting you."

"I don't think he does. Know what he's doing, that is." Tally shook Gunther off and sighed. "I think...he's frightened. In public, he falls back on his Satislit training, like an armor. The way he handled that Judgment?"

"Was pretty fantastic."

"They were testing him." Tally sighed.

"Though he messed up a bit, didn't he? Haru played right into Hastings' and O'Rourke's hands."

Gunther and Tally both winced and shared a look. That had been hard to not step into. Watching Haru so frantically try to figure out the situation with the bare minimum of information. He had known who were friendly, not so friendly, but the realization of how he'd played into the hands of the people against him had come too late.

"He was protecting the kids. I think that was his first instinct." Tally saw how keenly Haru had picked up the teens' distress. "To protect them."

"True." Gunther shook his head. "Can we agree this is all kinds of fucked up?"

"Yes. I... I can't do this ssss-sober."

"Drinks on me then."

"Pretty sure it's my houssse." Tally didn't even try to smile. His heart wasn't up for it. Hadn't been for days.

"Then they're on you. How about a movie?"

They raided the kitchen for some wine and cheese, pilfering two bottles and an assortment of Cheddars and soft cheeses, then retreated to the entertainment room. Gun was good enough not to ask what movie to watch, putting on an old *Thin Man* without question. They settled in, Tally glad for the company. He'd been out-to-sea for the last few days. Unsure of his next steps. Not something Tally was used to. Being lost. Haru wanted — needed — space, and escaping with the Cohens gave him that out.

He wanted to explain Haru's situation to Gun better than he had on his wedding night — the parts about being forced into a match by his clan, the parts where Haru felt trapped and bought. Even if Haru hated him, he didn't want Haru and Gun to hate each other, too. But he didn't think Gun was ready to hear it. All he saw was Tally's shattered heart, and that was their Gun. Had this been a medieval European court, Gunther would've been his champion, set to take all comers who rode against Tally. The best Tally could hope for was that Gun would see through Haru's actions that the otter was doing the best he could.

By the time Tally was on his second glass of the pinot, an ache filled his chest. Instead of dulling the pain, it had only gotten worse, mainly because the comments from O'Rourke kept repeating in his head.

"I think I'm going to call it a night." Tally stood and stretched. Thinking was too hard right now.

"You sure?"

"Yeah."

"I'll clean up," Gunther offered.

"Thanks."

"Hey, Tal?"

"Hmm?"

Gunther played with a cheese rind before saying, "I hope things get better."

"Me too, Gun. Me too. Oh, um…"

"What is it?"

Tally hemmed and hawed for a minute, considering. "Would you mind staying for a while? I mean, I know your mom's clan needed the help, but I could use a friend around."

"I'll see what I can do," Gun replied and scratched his chin. "I'll give Mom a call and let her know."

"Thanks, Gun. I mean it. Should we be discussing the Urusar Pike situation? It's your mom's clan but are — "

Gun held up his glass of wine. "Later, Tally. Don't worry about it right now."

"If you're sure?" Tally hedged, hoping he could just go upstairs and pass out.

"Yup."

"Okay, thanks again," Tally said, and headed upstairs.

"Any time, Tal. Any time," Gun answered quietly.

Tally almost turned back—Gun sounded off—but exhaustion moved him forward. They could hash it out later. Momentum kept him moving. Not that his legs didn't protest every step.

So many stairs. Why did the house have to be so big? Nights like this one made Tally seriously consider getting an elevator put in. *Too many damn stairs,* the only consistent thought in his muddled brain. Why hadn't his parents put something in? Surely they could've seen its uses? The question was which rooms could go to get one installed?

Tally meant to go to his room, but his feet brought him in front of Haru's door. He knocked, though he wasn't sure why.

"Come in."

"Hey." Tally left the door open, standing just inside the suite.

The joeys were sleeping together in a human pile. Haru was sitting on the bed, wearing a plain *yukata*, watching them sleep.

"Oh, they humaned."

"I humaned so they thought it was a good idea." Haru brushed a piece of hair out of Jackson's face then shrugged.

"Yeah."

"Is there something you need, Argaze?"

"Um." Tally hadn't actually come with something in mind. "What did O'Rourke mean? About Urusar Akaike?"

"Yes, that." Haru winced. He tucked the blankets around the children tighter then stood. "I would rather not discuss that in front of the children."

"Of course."

Haru stood. The *yukata* split open to give Tally a peek at the wondrous expanse of Haru's skin. He might've groaned, just a tiny bit, out of appreciation. Despite his standoffish nature, Haru was beautiful. He was still Tally's Em'halafi. He couldn't just stop feeling. All Tally wanted to do was bundle Haru up and protect him from the world, but his destined had been through enough.

"Your room," Haru said as he slipped past Tally.

"Um, sure?"

Tally left his door open, giving Haru an escape route, but Haru closed it. He was torn as to whether to open it again or leave it be.

The choice was decided for him when Haru said, "I would rather the pups not hear this."

"All right." Tally moved to the far side of the room with the bed between them, though it killed him to do it. Didn't matter. Haru was never going to be frightened of him again. *Never.*

"Urusar Akaike informed your council that we had mated properly."

"I…wasn't informed of this. I'm not even sure… What does that mean?"

"In the contract…" Haru frowned. "There is a section that allows the Urusar and the Awi Tamgradat to verify consummation of the mating."

"No."

Haru crossed his arms and leaned against the door. "Why do you think the Awi was here?"

"Because she helped arranged the marriage?" Tally was trying his hardest to keep breathing. The Awi had come because it was polite to invite them. Wasn't that…? Oh Gods…

"They also have the duty to verify the Satislit has been accepted by their Argaze. Otters are known for their…*rigorous*? *Enthusiastic*?…matings. It's easy to verify visually." Haru's shoulders curled forward as he hugged his abdomen harder. "I think the phrasing on the contract is 'The Awi Tamgradat shall ensure fulfillment of mating contract.'"

Tally's hands curled into fists despite his best intentions. His initial reaction was wanting to fly to Japan to pummel a certain Akaike into the ground. How dare they? How could they? And even sneaking around it while he wasn't there to object. He stood staring at the floor so his anger wasn't directed at Haru, breathing slowly, carefully. *Gods, Haru must think I'm a huge, bumbling idiot not to have known these things.*

A worse thought crept through his anger. He had to whisper to keep the snarl out of his voice "What about…our Kwebabiads? Are they going to come and *ensure fulfillment* of that too?"

"Did Misaki write the contracts?"

Tally blinked and dared to raise his head. "She did."

"Then they will be fine." Haru smiled, a genuine one. "Misaki is good at what she does, and, despite our upbringing, she has her own way of doing things. It helps most traditional clans in Japan actually prefer the modern method of fertilization. Cuts out complications."

"Thank Gods for that at least." Tally sank onto the bed, rubbing at his chest. "Saying I'm sorry won't fix it. But I am so sorry I wasn't there. That I didn't know. Too fucking *much* I didn't know. I only wanted all the best things for you. And I've brought you nothing but pain and humiliation."

"If it had not been you, someone else would have been matched with me." Haru shrugged it off, but his eyes were drawn tight and he was looking at the wall, not Tally. "Akaike-san was determined to get rid of me at the conference. Too much trouble. The clans were talking. At least you are attractive."

Tally shook his head. "That's not something you have to worry about with me. What I look like." His chest hurt so badly, he wanted to curl over his knees and rock. He was heading into an anxiety attack with no worry stone and no right to have an attack. "I want it clear that with me you have choices. I'll never touch you again if that's what you want. I'll never come near you. Never snake out and frighten you where you can see. You are your own person and in this household, as long as you choose to stay, *you* say what you will and won't do."

There was silence in the room. A vacuum between them. Haru was frowning, watching Tally, and not saying anything. He pushed off the door and walked toward Tally and not away, like he'd expected.

"You believe that? What you say?"

"Of *course* I believe it." Tally's voice hitched and cracked. *Damn it. Hold it together. Just a little longer.* "I wouldn't say it if I didn't."

"Power has a strong hold. The relationships of power, the inequity of it, can determine a lot between people. Especially between lijun. Choices can be taken away whether or not *you* believe. Because you already have the power." Haru turned, still tightly wound up, shoulders tense. "You need to start looking at the world for what it is, not what you want it to be."

Tally dropped his gaze back to the carpet. As if he hadn't heard such things all his life. "And be like Barry Hastings? I can't live like that. And I make mistakes trying to make things better, just like anybody. But I can't change who I am."

Haru had one hand on the door. "No, not like Hastings-san. That man...no. He is not our friend, not even close, is he? But maybe, if you could acknowledge the world does not work the way you want it to, someone like me wouldn't be in the crossfire. To make changes, you have to acknowledge the faults."

With that one final little blow, Haru escaped the room like rabid dogs were on his heels.

Tally would never have told him so, but he was glad of it. His limbs shook, his temperature dropping. *I do acknowledge them. I'm just not a cynic like you.* Though Tally would never say that to Haru. He turned up the thermostat in his room and snaked, unable to stay human one instant longer. Curled up by the air vent, with the heat flowing over his scales, he tried to put himself back together again.

* * * *

By the next council meeting, Tally had recovered his outward calm. If he thought about things too much, he still felt like falling apart, but the solution to that was a simple one. He had too many things other than his own stupid feelings to worry about. At least he had a new worry stone in his pocket. One of the river stones Haru had left in his shoe had been a good candidate, a smooth ovoid shape of red with gray lines running through it. The Shafa had been happy to spell it for him when he'd explained why he needed a new one.

Otherwise, he'd been all business at home, going to work as he always did, taking the kids to give Haru a break when he got home. When Kaho had left, there had been a little retreating into their shells, but every day got a little better. The joeys at least trusted him and ran to him when he came through the door. They were even all right with his snake form and happily rode on his back as he slithered around their play space. Haru would probably have been horrified to see it, so Tally was careful about when he offered snakeback rides.

The Blue Holly and Redtail parents were in attendance along with the council members and Tally hoped their presence would keep the snarking and snapping to a minimum.

"First order of business." Tally tapped his pile of papers straight on the wooden conference table to get everyone's attention. "Uruma Bastille has drawn up a proposal for the new Evade and Hunt sessions. I did send these out to everyone, but the physical copies are for reference."

And in case some of you ignored my email, which I'm pretty sure you did. Tally passed the documents to the left and right.

"You'll notice that the children are divided by age group rather than lijun type —"

Clement Black wasted no time raising his hand. "Tally, I'm not sure that's the best idea."

"Predators and prey together?" Rose Howe's hands shook as she put the document down. "I'm not at all comfortable with that."

Tally cleared his throat. "That's the nature of traditional Evade and Hunt exercises. We need the children to be able to evade the most dangerous predators, the humans. So we practice with our own. Rose, I'm sorry. That part's non-negotiable. Otherwise, it doesn't make sense."

"If you're dictating terms," Dan O'Rourke said with a snort that was all bull moose, "I don't see why you're running it past council at all."

So much for behaving in front of guests. "You came to the Uruma for Judgment." Tally fell back on tradition, as much to throw it in certain lijuns' faces as to make a point. "Are you now deciding to pick apart and gainsay that Judgment?"

There were mutters, certain council members leaning heads together to whisper in each other's ears. Tally let it wind down, meeting Haru's raised eyebrow with a quick, tight smile, but that line of objection ceased.

There were niggling, quick disputes here and there as they went through the document point by point. The sessions would be held on private land — whose private land caused some bickering, but in the end they established a rotation. Twice a month even received some grumbling from Barry Hastings, who thought once a month was plenty. Adult supervision turned into who could be trusted to be vigilant and effective with the children so Tally tabled that point for committee discussion. And so on. Gods, they were exhausting sometimes. Half of the council members would object if he said the sun rose in the east.

He kept his temper and the meeting moving forward as planned until there was a knock on the conference room door. Hakkon Eberhardt was closest and all conversation ceased as he rose to check who it was. He let the visitor in, so it had to be a community member, always welcome at council meetings, but no one ever attended since they were often so deadly boring.

Tally's head jerked up from his notes when he caught sight of who it was. "Deputy Kincaid? How can we help you?"

In uniform, expression closed and bland, Melissa radiated official business. "Urusar Bastille, Uruma Bastille, council members, sorry to interrupt. I thought this was something that couldn't wait, though."

"Someone else has been murdered, haven't they?" Rose whispered, her eyes far too wide. Clement patted her arm, probably trying to keep her from hysterics.

"No, it's not that at least." Melissa took her hat in her hands. "But it's obviously related. Ed Cohen's body's missing from the morgue."

"How did the coroner manage to *lose* his body?" Barry was half out of his chair.

"Not a matter of lost, Mr. Hastings. There are clear signs of forced entry. The body's been stolen." Melissa pulled herself up straight, chin raised. "Mr. Bastille, I'm going to need a few words, please."

"Can it wait until after the meeting?" Tyra tried, casting quick glances between Tally and Melissa.

"I'd rather not, Ms. Pierce. Mr. Bastille? If you would, please? There's an empty conference room next door." She held up her hand when Haru rose as well. "Just Mr. Bastille, please."

"I am Mr. Bastille," Haru replied, raising his eyebrows.

Melissa made a frustrated sound. "Just *Tally* this time. I'll have questions for you next, Uruma Bastille."

"Sorry, everyone. Haru, if you could keep going with that next bullet point of yours, the taking suggestions of which adults to approach for supervision duty, that would be wonderful." Tally rose, straightening his jacket and trying not to loom. "I hope I won't be long."

Melissa waved him out of the room and marched beside him to the empty conference room where she leaned on the table and Tally propped himself against the wall. Another deputy stood outside the door, but Melissa closed it, so she still trusted Tally that far.

"I've never been anywhere near the coroner's office, but I guess you knew I'd say that," Tally began in as dry a tone as his hammering heart could manage.

"Don't really need the sarcasm right now." Melissa scrubbed a hand over her face. "Where were you last night, Tal?"

"At home. All night."

"Anyone verify the all night part?"

Tally's brows furrowed. "I had the kids with me until about eight. Well, closer to nine. They were a little wound up and didn't want to get ready for bed."

"And after that?"

"I cleaned up the bathroom and went to bed to read for a bit."

Melissa's dark eyebrows crept toward her hairline. "Haru was with you then?"

The urge to lie was huge, but Tally hadn't *done* anything and was done with lies. "Haru's been sleeping with the kids. They get scared at night sometimes. So, no."

She huffed a sigh and tossed something on the table between them. Tally leaned forward and frowned as he recognized one of his business cards.

"That was found at the scene."

"Okay. A lot of people have my cards." Tally leaned back again. "I didn't kill anyone and I didn't engage in body snatching, Melissa. You know me better than that."

"I want to believe you." She pocketed the card again. "Believe me, I'm the last person who wants to destabilize the community by arresting you. But you're making it freaking hard, Tally. You just don't know."

"Have you told Tyra and Clement about this find yet?"

She shook her head with a grimace. "No. I thought I'd give you the courtesy. The theft of the body happened at the same time the lab tech was murdered and the samples stolen. Someone *may* have broken in again last night—maybe whoever it was thought they missed something—but we can't be a hundred percent since the damn lab hasn't replaced the door. The scratches from the original break-in are still there. A couple broken beakers alerted the lab folks to a possible intruder, though. It's hard to be unbiased, Tally. I don't *want* it to be you, but right now, everything's pointing right at you."

"Why didn't you tell me Ed's body was gone, too?"

"Sheriff wanted to keep certain details back. It's not something I'd share with the press, but I couldn't keep it from the clan anymore. Damn it, Tally, if there's something going on you need to *tell* me. Your damn card under the broken glass."

"Then why aren't you arresting me?"

"Not enough yet. But it's looking bad and I'm gonna have a hell of a time explaining this to the humans if this turns out to be an uktena killing." She pointed a finger at him, practically spitting her words. "You think about *that*, Mr. Urusar, while you're thinking about maybe having to turn yourself in."

Tally stayed where he was, completely stunned, as Melissa stormed out. All the evidence pointed to him, which meant Melissa was certain it was an uktena killing. She *seemed* certain. There were no uktena in the area aside from Tally's family and all of them had been accounted for. He shivered on a terrible thought.

Could I have done it? Could I be so unstable that I've gone Xus? He didn't feel as if it were possible, but lijun often didn't when their animal nature sickened and twisted. All his anxiety issues? Was it possible they were worse than he or his parents thought? If he was going rogue in uktena form, he wouldn't remember it. Lijun who went Xus never did.

Problem was, he really didn't have anyone who could say for certain where he was during any of the incidents around Ed's death. No one who could say to him, *No, Tally, you were right here with me.*

Even worse? During all of them, he'd been snaked out. He reached for the new worry stone in his pocket, forcing a calm façade on himself before he left the room to return to the meeting. But inside he was shaken to the core.

* * * *

The meeting hadn't lasted much longer after Melissa took a couple of minutes to question Haru on his own. Tally hoped he'd told the truth as well, but he hadn't asked yet. As it was, they had to hurry home and get the kids from Tally's parents, who'd frankly been much happier babysitting than going to a council meeting.

Tonight was the annual Harvest Festival and they'd promised the joeys they would go. Not unlike a county fair, though a little smaller, there were performances, food stalls, games and rides for the kids, a bit of contra dancing for the grownups, and of course fall favorites like caramel apples and fresh hot cider. Tully McPherson always brought out the old wooden cider press with its ancient chugging engine. This was their first stop, as Jackson tugged them over to watch in fascination as the apples tumbled onto the conveyor and into the huge barrel where the screw press came down and squished all the cider goodness out.

Tally had Olivia riding on his right arm so she could see, Jackson hanging onto his left hand while Haru lifted Amelia up. She munched from a bag of kettle corn from a nearby stall where they stirred the popping corn in a huge copper kettle all three joeys could've crawled into together.

Olivia put her tiny arm around Tally's neck and snuggled closer and something in his tightly wound insides relaxed. This felt...right. As if they were an actual family. Maybe it wasn't really true, but Tally was going to enjoy the evening as if it were. He almost managed to forget the disaster of his marriage, the council members, the fact that he might be periodically losing his mind, and the fact that the police thought he was a murderer. Almost.

The warm fuzzies only lasted until their little family grouping stopped to watch a particularly talented fiddler up on the festival stage. The whispers started behind Tally. He tried to ignore them.

...but what if he did?

Killed Ed. I hear there were bite marks.

Contract dispute, that's what I heard. He's taken over and now we'll see the real Tally Bastille, the one who flattened my kid when they were in school.

Forced his dad into retirement...

"Tally?" Olivia asked in her soft, tiny voice. "Are you mad at the man playing?"

"No, Livy. Of course not."

She ran a finger down the crease between his eyebrows, the one that appeared when he frowned. "You have a mad line."

"Sorry. Just thinking too hard."

A closer voice didn't even bother to whisper. "He'll end up eating those kids. Mark my words."

Tally leaned over, not bothering to look around. "Haru, I think we should move on."

"Absolutely not."

Haru quirked an eyebrow at him, though he didn't turn away from the stage. If Tally had been by himself, he probably would have confronted the speaker, quietly, gently, but with the kids, maybe walking away was better.

Another voice answered, "That Jap otter's gonna be dinner too. Should've married a snake like he was supposed to."

When Haru's eyes narrowed ever so slightly, Tally almost missed the flash of defiance in them. It was the expression Haru had worn the night they met. Then his head cocked to the side, gaze assessing, just like he'd looked at Tally when he'd interrupted the raid.

"My Em'halafi?"

"Uh?"

Haru snuggled in close and placed a kiss against Tally's jaw. "Mind giving Amelia a ride too? You know how much the kids *love* your piggyback rides. Plus I think you have a better view of the stage."

Amelia immediately began pulling, asking for "uppies," and Haru obliged her by moving her onto Tally's shoulder with a serene smile, leaving all three children perched on him like a coat tree. There was a startling realization that Haru must've seen the snakeback rides, or was taking a huge leap of faith. No. That wasn't quite it.

What is my contrary mate doing?

That was when it hit Tally. *Contrary.* Haru loathed unfairness and being told what to do, but he was also a traditionally trained Satislit. He was a knot of contradictions and rules.

Haru turned and burrowed close, holding Tally. Kiss. Kiss. "I am getting us some of those delicious hot dogs. You want a veggie one or something else?"

"Um." Tally tried his best not to look stunned. He knew…part of him figured out that Haru's actions were for onlookers, not for him, but it was tough to tell certain parts of his anatomy that. He managed to smile. "Veggie's good."

The smile slipped a little when Haru snuggled closer and slipped a hand into Tally's front pocket. *Don't swallow your tongue. Gah.*

Haru's fingers slid deeper, slowly brushing along Tally's cock as he worked his hand into Tally's close-fitting jeans. Tally had children on him or he would've been cussing up a storm. Haru, damn him, shot him a look that was positively smug as he fished Tally's wallet out. Then he leaned over to plant a solid, unambiguous kiss on Tally's lips.

"Kissy faces," Olivia crowed happily.

Tally stood trapped as a child shelf while Haru turned and strolled away. His fear that his Satislit might confront the bigots never materialized. Oh, there might have been a pointed glare, but Haru didn't say a word as he walked off with Tally's wallet.

Come to think of it, *Haru walking off with my wallet* should've made him nervous—at least a little anxious. Tally shrugged internally and turned back to watch the musicians. Maybe he wasn't Haru's favorite person in the world, but Tally trusted him far more than he would his own brothers.

Which, perhaps, wasn't saying much.

The voices behind Tally didn't return, so he had to assume his detractors had moved on. One of the voices had been Mrs. Hasting's. She'd made no attempt to disguise the fact. Better that he weather the current crisis with a smile and do the best job he could. If he wasn't really falling apart, of course.

When Haru came back, he helped Tally get the kids down and gave everyone their designated hot dog from the cardboard tray he carried. Livy dove right in, noshing away while Melia watched on in a rather scrutinous fashion. Jackson tucked between Haru's legs and wrapped one arm around his knees as he began sniffing and biting his hot dog. The whole scene felt rather domestic. If Tally wasn't careful he'd get carried away, thinking it wasn't just an act for the clan and other onlookers.

"Dragon!" Jackson shouted, pointing toward the stage.

Haru's eyebrows shot up, most certainly taking the declaration the wrong way if the shock his face betrayed was anything to go by.

"Dragon!" the girls sang out, mimicking their brother.

This time Haru squinted as he looked at the stage.

"It's a ride, behind the stage. They can see the tail each time it passes," Tally finally explained, covering his laughter with an attempt at clearing his throat. If he wasn't careful he'd choke.

"Ah, thank goodness. I was going to say..." Haru's head cocked to the side the way it did when he was thinking. "I am not sure going on rides after eating is such a good idea."

"Dragon!" the pups shouted en masse in one combined coordinated attack.

"You just ate."

"Dragon!"

Tally chuckled, but stopped the second he was shot a dirty look. His poor otter. Haru was fighting a losing battle. Their little family had lined up for the miniature roller coaster with the kids still singing its praises and Haru arguing against it when comments started again.

An Uma should know better...

Those joeys are going to fly right out of the car...

No respect. Kids these days. Who can blame them with an Uma like that?

What are two men doing with those babies?

There is no way a tart like that could make white babies. Should we call the police?

The last question knocked Tally for a loop, but he was more worried about Haru and the way he sucked in a breath. His beautiful dark brown eyes went wide for a moment, his coiffed eyebrows shooting up. For one horrific second, Tally thought he'd have to explain an otter attack to the council, but the air vibrations stopped when the pups whimpered. Haru knelt beside the children and gave them a hug, giving them nose rubs. They swarmed him, holding on tight.

"Now, now. Your..." Haru frowned as he glanced up at Tally. "*Usar* needs some loves too."

For a fraction of a second the air and noises all around them disappeared. The joeys stood stock still, wide-eyed in front of Haru, their little sniffles all dried up. Then their bright little eyes turned on Tally, and he took a step back without even thinking. Retreating seemed to be a signal to small children. The Cohens attacked at once, using Tally for a tree yet again.

"Oh, no! No! I'm being swarmed! Aahhh!"

Giggles and squeals erupted as Tally swayed back and forth, the joeys clinging to him instinctively.

"Again!" Melia cried. "Usar again!"

Usar. Gods. How much more could his heart swell hearing that word for him? Jackson squealed as Tally spun them, the girls laughing in fits.

"Again! Again!" was called out to Tally until he was too dizzy to keep going. They collapsed in a puddle of giggles, squeaks and sneezes. Tally checked to make sure he wasn't crushing anyone. Nope. All alive and accounted for, using his chest for a pillow. Several deep breaths later Haru appeared overhead, a half-smile twitching one side of his mouth.

"We lost our place in line," he said, pulling Tally up and plucking Amelia away from him. Jackson and Olivia settled on either shoulder. "How about we try again?"

This time they made it through the line with no interruptions, but when they got to the loading deck, Haru frowned. The dragon roller coaster pulled in, clunking and clicking as the gears locked it onto the track.

"Are you going to fit?" Haru asked, eyeing the cars then eyeing Tally again. "I think you'll break it."

Tally surveyed the small kiddie cars too.

All of them turned to the ride attendant.

The young girl was backed against the controllers, hair up in a cap and ponytail. A frown twisted her pretty face into fear. His uktena spirit. Tally sighed and tried to pull back, as much as he could. She relaxed, then swallowed.

"I think you exceed our max capacity," the attendant managed.

"Oh, hmm."

Jackson pulled on his pant leg. "We go with Haru?"

"Can they?" Tally asked.

"I don't see why not. As long as the girls sit with him, the boy can sit in his own seat." The attendant smiled. "He's big enough to do it on his own."

A high-pitched, eardrum-splitting squeal pierced the air. Jackson was off like a shot, buckling himself — or trying to — into the car. Haru handed over the backpack of kid supplies and abandoned Tally to the attendant. They both nodded to each other and she sighed, then moved toward the cars.

Once Haru and the girls were settled, the ride attendant had Tally back up. "Everyone ready?"

"Yes!" the pups yelled together.

Laughter burbled up from the cars as the dragon went around the loop. Every time Jackson went by the loading station he screamed "Look at me! Usar! Look!" waving his little arms and smiling. Tally managed to get a couple discreet shots and a video on his phone to send to Mom and Dad in the family group chat.

Che: It's finally happened. Tally's a middle-aged dad >.<

Hal: Ten bucks says the girls throw up on Haru, who's in the $$$

Nan: They're adorable… Gross Hal.

Addy and Lahi: We're over by the music if you want to say hi.

Lahi: I put $20 on the girls.

Meli: Sooooo cute! I wish I was there. Don't encourage them, Lahi.

Che: You'd only get stuck on the ride, Meli

Hal: LOL

Meli: Shut up dorks. The joeys are happy screaming!

Mom: Did you really go to the Festival without us? You better not take my grandkids trick-or-treating without your dad and me.

Che, Hal, Nan, Addy, Lahi and Meli: Oooooooooooooooooh. Tally's in trouble.

How did they even manage to type the same thing all at once?

Dad: There is nothing wrong with being a middle-aged dad.

Hal: Late as always, Pop!

Dad: I know where you sleep.

Tally closed down the chat as the cars slowed, but the last message he saw as he exited the chaotic conversation was Mom's. *Good to see Haru so happy.* Yeah, it was.

"Where to next?" Tally asked as Jackson flew into his arms. He swung him around and propped him on his shoulders, two strong little arms wrapping around his forehead.

"Cotton candy!"

The look on Haru's face said it all as he lifted Livy up with one arm and plopped her on his hip. *It's your head he throws up on.* Several humans and lijun from the line guffawed. Melia took Haru's free hand and pulled.

"Candy!" she parroted her brother's calls.

"Let's see what else the food stands have," Tally responded as their troop followed him down the stairs.

The food stalls had so many scents intermingling. Livy's and Melia's noses vibrated trying to keep up. Tally could only picture what Jackson's looked like, but the hums of pleasure meant business.

"They just ate," he sighed.

"And they are children," Haru responded with a wistful tone. "It is a noisy festival with lights and rides, games and people and food. Their stomachs are black holes until they are not."

"Chocolate!" Melia tugged on Haru's hand. No wonder those two were peas in a pod. She led them over to a stall full of — Oh, no.

"Urusar Bastille!" Alan jumped back a foot. "Uruma. How-how good of you to stop by."

"Jones-san." Haru smiled, mouth wide with a head dip. It was his formal nod, used when he felt uncomfortable.

Delight that Tally now knew the difference between Haru's polite greeting and his happy one warred with guilt knowing how uncomfortable his otter was.

"Are those chocolate chip cookies?"

"Why yes," Jean answered with a smile. "I bake all the cookies Best Bakery produces. Would you like a sample?"

"Thank you." Haru took a careful nibble, then visibly relaxed. Guess the talent was in the cookies and not the cakes. That would explain why the bakery kept afloat. Tally hadn't been interested in cookies for the resorts since they were so easy to make in-house. "Could we get one of your dozen baggies to go?"

"Of course, Uruma."

Alan had moved over to the side of the stall and was motioning to Tally. "Urusar, if I could have a moment."

"Oh, um… I'm not sure if now —"

"It'll only take a minute. It's about the proposed extension of the bakery?"

Yes, Tally thought so. The emails had started coming daily since the wedding. "I have seen the proposal, Alan, but I'm afraid it'll have to wait until the next council meeting."

"But, Urusar Bastille, it would only take a minute," Alan continued until Jean shushed him.

"Careful, honey. There are ears around."

"Oh, right."

Tally kept a sigh back. "O'Rourke and Howe do have interest, Alan, but we need to discuss funding and space."

"Thank you, Mr. Bastille. For your business, as always," Alan said, slowly backing away.

No, please don't look terrified of the big bad serpent. Tally huffed.

"Here," Jean said. "A few extra for the joeys."

Haru brightened, as did the girls. "Thank you, Jones-san. They will be appreciated."

"Oh, you," Jean said, blushing as she waved them off.

They wandered off, the awkward confrontation with Alan quickly forgotten by the pups. There was still a little tension in Haru's shoulders, though. He snagged the backpack, pulling out some hand wipes—when had they gotten those?—and cleaning off the girls as they tried to wriggle away from him.

"Play fishies," Amelia said as she managed to pop out of Haru's hold. She went straight for the games.

Rows upon rows of games, and Amelia was darting through them impossibly fast. Haru and Tally chased after her, both yelling and dragging Livy and Jackson with them. Except she was small and they were big—er, bigger—with a load.

"Melia! Wait for us!"

"Little girl! Slow down!"

"Melia!"

A happy—not frightened, Tally had to remind himself—squeal rang in Tally's ears as they broke through a mass of humans all pressed together in uncomfortable ways.

"Weeee!" Amelia screeched happily as she went up into the air and came back down.

"Melia!" Haru yelped as he dove forward.

"Again!" she squealed.

Mindy tickled Amelia's stomach then blew a raspberry on her cheek. "I think you have two someones who'd like some kisses."

"Usar!"

"Thanks, Mindy," Tally said, catching Amelia as she barreled into him.

"Any time, Tally."

"Melia!" Haru knelt down next to her, checking her over, then pulled her close for a hug and kiss. "Please, please do not run off like that."

Kiss. Kiss. Amelia snuggled close, petting Haru's hair. "Is okay, Haru. Is okay. Mindy played."

"You have your hands full, Urusar," Mindy said with a laugh, standing. Her sisters and several friends shuffled behind her, including the evasive Tyler. The insubordinate lijun still avoided his calls about the incident at the lake with Ed.

"We do."

"Mom and Dad always said it got harder after they had Mason. She turned the odds on them."

"Mindy!" Mason stuck out her tongue.

Tally fought back a smile. "We wouldn't know what only one kid is like."

"True." Mindy nodded when a calculated expression entered her eyes. One Tally had seen often in Hakkon. "If you need a babysitter sometime, just call." She handed over a business card. Tally took it out of sheer reflex. "Me, Morgan or Mason would be happy to watch them."

"Thanks."

"If you really wanted to thank me, you could catch me one of those fish."

Haru glanced over at the bowls. "To keep or to eat?"

They shared a look. A gleeful one filled with the waggle of eyebrows and smiles. A look only predators would get on a hunt.

"Guys," Tally moaned.

"You just say that because you can't stand anything bloody or yummy meat treats," Haru chided.

"Eww. Just no."

Justin glanced between them. "Tally doesn't eat meat?"

"Cannot stand the stuff. Poor bastard. Means more for me." Haru grinned, his tongue snaking out. "Fish are nice."

Mindy nodded seriously. "So you can really catch some?"

Carnivores.

"Easy-peasy, as you Americans say."

The vendor was down fifteen fish by the time Haru was done. A record with one string. The man was red-faced and flustered handing the bags of fish over to Mindy and her sisters. It didn't help when Haru and Mindy both licked their lips at the same time and smiled.

"Yummies," he said.

"Definitely yummies," Morgan agreed.

"Really, Haru, guys. Humans," Tally pleaded.

"Your Satislit giving you grief, Tally?" Hakkon asked, interrupting the shenanigans.

"Dad, look what Haru caught me!" Mindy said, holding up her bundle of bags.

The same gleeful expression the Eberhardt girls wore blossomed on Hakkon's face.

"Ooh, yum. I mean"—Hakkon cleared his throat— "they could do with some growing. The pond in the backyard, perhaps?"

"Yes, Daddy," the girls called back, but they were moving on with their friends.

Justin called out, "Thanks, Haru, Mr. Bastille."

Hakkon chuckled and shook his head. "I doubt one fish will make it back to the pond."

"Maybe. Hunting practice would be good, though. It is good to see you, Eberhardt-san."

"Let me text them." Hakkon punched out a few words. "That might do it."

"You just want some for yourself, Hak," Tally said.

"True. Well, enjoy yourselves!" Hakkon thumped Tally on the shoulder a few times. He held up a stuffed unicorn. "I have a wife to catch."

"Good luck!"

"I'll need it in this crowd."

A tug brought Tally's attention down. Jackson and Livy leaned against him, their eyelids drooping. A big yawn went from one pup to the other. Sleepy joeys needed bed.

Olivia lifted her arms. "Uppie, Usar."

"Me too," Jackson yawned. "Me too, Usar."

They climbed up, Livy pressing hard against Tally's chest as she settled.

A laugh had Tally glancing over to Haru, who had the backpack on and Amelia snuggled close. Had that been Haru? It had sounded like it. But all he got was a sly smile from his otter.

"Bed time," Haru said.

"It's been an exciting night."

Haru glanced around, eyes assessing. He leaned in and planted a kiss right on Tally. Solid, warm, making his insides do all kinds of dances. When Haru pulled back, Tally followed his mouth until a hand pressed his chest. It didn't matter it was for show. It felt good, nice. Like Tally actually mattered.

"Thank you, my Argaze. We could not have asked for a better night."

"Me too," Tally whispered. "Me too."

By the time they walked back to the car, Jackson clung to Tally's back while Olivia slumbered in his arms. All the pups were wiped. Amelia cracked huge yawns against Haru's shoulder.

"I wish Daddy was here," Amelia whispered.

Haru kissed the top of her head and whispered back, "I know, Melia. I know."

It tore at Tally's heart to see Haru so attached to the children. Yes, he was good for them and, in their way, he knew they comforted some part of Haru. Except, one more obligation to tie him down... Not that he *wanted* Haru to go away, but he wished Haru would choose to stay on his own terms.

They drove home in silence, letting the kids snooze in their car seats, then wordlessly crept up the stairs at the big house to put the little ones to bed. With a few nods and gestures, they agreed that PJs and baths could wait for another day, settling for wiping off sticky hands and removing shoes. The minimal disturbance barely woke them and the joeys were soon in a kid pile, fast asleep in the middle of Haru's bed.

Tally squeezed Haru's shoulder as a good night as he left the room, shocked when Haru followed him out and eased the door shut.

"I need some water after all the sugar," Haru whispered with a grimace.

"No one ever finishes those cotton candy things," Tally whispered back as they made their way to the stairs. "I did warn you."

Haru's snort might have been half snicker. The peace between them became awkward again as they faced each other across the kitchen, each with his own glass of ice water.

"Thank you for coming," Tally managed after a few sips and his fingers finding his worry stone in his pocket. "I know it's not anything much, but the festival's tradition. Couldn't have handled the kids on my own."

"You could have." Haru's regard was steady and unreadable. "But it was good to see them smile."

Tally nodded. They both returned to sipping water, looking everywhere but at each other.

"Haru... Could I ask you something?"

One black eyebrow quirked, now Haru's gaze zeroed in on him, wary and chill.

"Do you think a lijun can go Xus?" At Haru's snort, Tally waved a hand in negation. "I don't mean the old meaning. Not possessed. But in the more psychological sense. A loss of human self, human feelings, episodes of missing memory during *Sahnkes*?" Tally put his water down and buried his face in his hands. "That is, I know it *happens*. I just..."

"You want to know if I think you could have." Haru's voice was suddenly closer and Tally glanced up, shocked to find him leaning against the center island, in arm's reach. "That is what you are really asking?"

Tally nodded, unable to speak past his constricting throat.

"Do you think you could have?"

"I'm not sure what to think anymore." Tally wrapped his arms tight around himself. "Evidencssss."

Haru gave a sharp nod. "Yes. Though not what I asked."

"I was alone during both murders. During the theft of Ed's body. I was...upset for at least two of those and feeling off balance the other. I *was* uktena'd each time."

Another step brought Haru beside him, though he stared out the window. "You have your faults, Tal-tsu'tsa Bastille. But no, I do not see the signs of anger and malice there should be for something like that."

Haru leaned his head against Tally's arm. "You cannot even eat a steak."

Tally let go the breath he was holding, then took another shaking one. "I guess that's good to hear. Thank you for the, ah, united front this evening."

"Horrible people." Haru snorted.

"Every clan has horrible people." Tally shrugged, in no mood to defend them. "Bastille clan has a small pervasive faction of *traditionalists* who never seem to quite go away. They use tradition to justify everything from bigotry to bullying to greed." He managed a bitter chuckle. "Lucky Urusar me."

In another unexpected move, Haru wrapped an arm around Tally's waist and gave him a quick squeeze. "Better you than O'Rourke-san, or that Hastings-san person. You do try, my Argaze."

With that, Haru picked up his water and left the kitchen, leaving Tally to gape after him. *Will I ever find my balance with him?* Tally's skin still tingled where Haru had touched him. *More importantly, do I really want to?*

Chapter Eleven

Waves

Who knew joeys could swim? Or, at least, swim so well. Opossum fur was different from otter fur, though, so chances to let the pups swim out in the lake with them and Sammy would dwindle as the weather cooled further. Until then, they would all swim every chance they got.

Melia's and Livy's little noses and ear twitches helped settle Haru's confused emotions as they watched the joeys paddle in the shallow end of the lake near their den. Jackson, however, seemed to be ready to create trouble. He ran from the edge of the rocks and splashed into the water, a small spray of droplets covering his sisters. The girls sneezed at their brother before scrambling to the banks.

Deep satisfaction weaved through them as Amelia jumped off the outcropping of rocks and bobbed right back up, *chirping* at Haru. Her tiny paws kicked furiously underneath the water.

Haru glided over to their girl. Nose. Nose. *Good job, little girl.* They twisted and turned through the water, though Melia never went under. None of the joeys wanted to. They liked jumps and paddles. Mainly jumps off Haru, though. Good thing they had core strength.

Another chirp came from their left. Olivia and Jackson cut a line straight toward their way, little heads lifted out of the water. Sammy was right behind them, nosing Livy when she turned the wrong way. Haru turned over, chirping at their pups. They pulled a couple of claws through their fur, cleaning. They should be fine for a ride.

Up the joeys came, all three of them tussling each other for the best spot—which was apparently right in Haru's face. Not surprisingly, Amelia won out. She tucked her nose right under Haru's chin. Sammy floated nearby, watching, humming at the pups as they floated across the lake. It was a good day for floats. Livy dove off Haru and climbed up on Sammy's back, giving one of those sneeze-chirps the joeys did. It sounded triumphant.

Jackson sneezed, repositioning on Haru. Suspecting their son would dive off after his sister, Haru wrapped a paw around Amelia. Their brother could send Haru or Sammy spinning off in various directions with his jumps. Physics was his friend and their enemy, especially when the odds were three to two.

The jump sent Haru spiraling toward the shore. Rocks and some cottontails slowed their progress. Haru let out a bark of surprise, but quickly grabbed one of the stiff stalks to steady themself and Melia. She sneezed and slid off them into the water. Her little nose worked a mile a minute as she sniffed the new

Fireworks & Stolen Kisses

surroundings with a curiosity only a pup could have. Amelia bit several stalks, sneezing and spitting little chunks each time.

By the shore, the cottontails thickened so Haru herded Melia away, toward deeper water and less dense vegetation. Except she had to be contrary, like most pups, and paddled off to something arching in and out of the water instead. She bit into it, but instead of spitting it right back out, she kept chewing. *Why must they bite everything?* It sounded *squishy.*

What is in her mouth? It didn't look...*natural.* Didn't sound natural either.

Haru shot over to her and pulled the black squishy out of her mouth. They pawed at her. She sneezed then moved away, giving Haru a better look. The coil of black connected to something shiny. Amelia climbed up onto their back, little claws pulling their fur, then started hacking. The distressed coughing struck fear into Haru, their heart hammering away. Thoughts whirled into pictures of horrific imagery. They called for Sammy.

"*Hah! Hah!*"

Several barks echoed over the lake, followed up by a series of sneeze-chirps.

The shiny was a metal can, about the same size as Haru. One with dead bugs on it.

Dead bugs? As in *exterminated* bugs? What would that type of canister be doing in the lake? In fact, the smell around its silver tube was off.

Poison.

The more human thought jarred Haru so hard he almost humaned. Instead he whipped around and paddled away from the cottontails—into the open water. Haru barked at Sammy and the pups, and she

267

turned, pulling the joeys with her. Melia's distressed coughs began to get wheezy.

Sammy nosed their side. Pat. Pat. Haru took her assurance then shot toward the south side of the lake. Water split in front of them as they swam toward the house. Determined, Haru barely broke stride as they surfaced by the patio. They pulled Amelia off and humaned, then cradled their little girl as they sprinted into the house.

The mudroom and kitchen flashed in and out of existence as Haru plowed their way to where Tally's scent was the strongest.

"Tally! Tally! Argaze!" Haru bellowed as they cradled their daughter. "A Tabib! Now!"

"What's wrong?"

"Poison!" they hissed out. "The lake! We need a Tabib! Now!"

"What?" Two hands grabbed their shoulders. "What poisssson?"

"Yes, Mr. Bastille. What poison?"

The strange voice made Haru startle and their daughter go limp. "No!"

"Is your husband all right, Tally?" Sheriff Amick stood in their front room with the deputy cat Kincaid flanking him.

"Perfectly, Sssheriff." Tally tried pulling Haru close. "Haru, sssshe's just playing opossum."

"Then why is he running around naked with a rat?"

"She is not a rat!" Haru snapped, turning on the sheriff. They winced as the implications of the sheriff being there sank in. So Haru did what they did best, an offensive defense. They stood, perfectly posed and displayed for viewing. "Why are you in my house?

How I dress in the privacy of my own home is none of your business."

"Mom! Robe! Towels!" Tally yelled out the front room doorway. "Lahi, call the Blue Hollys. Ask them to send Ted if they can!"

"Mr. Bastille. I think we have more important matters at hand than a drowned rat," the sheriff continued.

"She is not a rat!" Haru snapped again.

"Sir, I think if we let the Bastilles take care of the opossum first, we might be able to get better answers once they're done," Deputy Kincaid said. Her lips were turned down, looking on with squint.

"Fine."

"Tally? Haru?" Bastille-*okaasan* said as she swept into the room. "What is the—oh! Oh! The poor girl!" She tossed the robe at Haru and plucked Amelia out of his arms. "Lahi! Call the Blue Hollys!"

"There is some kind of extermination canister in the lake," Haru explained after her. "She mouthed the hose!"

"You take care of that, Sheriff!" Bastille-*okaasan* shot back. "I got her."

"You are certainly passionate about your animals, Mr. Bastille," the sheriff said from behind Haru.

"Of course, all living beings are to be respected," they answered as they tugged on the robe and tied it up.

"May I ask why you were swimming naked in the lake with an opossum? Get your rocks off that way?"

The conceit in the sheriff's voice was too much. The man was an eyesore and causing complications every which way. Too bad he was human. Haru turned on Sheriff Amick, ready to eviscerate him. Slowly. Painfully. Tally and Deputy Kincaid stiffened, the deputy edging closer to her boss.

"Cold swims are good for the health. We— I enjoy the refreshing feeling of a brisk swim. Have you not a Polar Bear Club here in Wadiswan?"

"We do," the sheriff answered. His caterpillar-like eyebrows quivered for a few seconds.

Haru straightened their shoulders and pushed them back. "I found the opossum while swimming. Well, then, why are *you* here, Sheriff Amick?"

"We would like to bring Tally in for some more questioning."

"Why?"

The sheriff looked confused, eyebrows vibrating. Maybe they would fly off? Insta-metamorphose into moths?

"Why are you bringing my husband in for questioning?"

"The evidence—"

"Is circumstantial."

"We have a witness—"

"Someone was in our bedroom during our engagement party?" Haru pushed on, stalking closer to the Sheriff.

"Mr. Bastille, would you please restrain your husband?" Sheriff Amick asked as he recoiled.

"My husband needs no restraints."

"I meant you."

Haru smiled, crossed their arms, and leaned in. "I think the more important matter here is that someone is trying to poison my family, Sheriff Amick."

Deputy Kincaid pulled on her boss's arm. "You said something about a canister, Mr. Bastille?"

"One of those large silver extermination canisters is sunk in our lake, leaking its poison everywhere. Do you know how harmful that is to people and wildlife?"

"Was there any kind of markings on the canister?" Kincaid-san asked, her voice rumbly and rough. "Like a red termite on its back?"

"I...do not know. I was rather flustered."

Tally hugged Haru close, burying them against his side. He kissed Haru's temple. "You think it's one of Ed's?"

The deputy shrugged, but the comment made Haru glance over at their husband.

"His truck was here the night of the flash. Parked over on the west side with the crew who set up our fireworks." Tally frowned. "Those pesticides have all kinds of nasty chemicals."

Deputy Kincaid nodded. "Why don't you show us where this was?"

"But—" Their girl. Haru needed to check on her in the worst way.

"I'm sure Tally can show us, Mr. Bastille. Check on your opossum," Deputy Kincaid said as she passed him, her chest rumbling in warning. Someone was being a hissy cat. "Sir, should we get a crew out here to collect the canister?"

"It's possible evidence," Sheriff Amick answered, but he went for his phone. "That's been compromised by rats and—"

"Finish that ssssentence, Ssssheriff," Tally hissed out. One hand went into his suit pocket and came out with a stone. It weaved through his fingers with a practiced ease. It was one of the ones Haru had presented him. "Please, so I can file a complaint with the county."

The stocky sheriff growled out, "Show us the way, Mr. Bastille."

Tally gathered up Haru in his arms and pressed their foreheads together. "Little girl is fine. Mom's got her.

I'll call you when they need to retrieve the canister if we can't see it."

"Okay."

There was a quick press of lips against Haru's, heat and comfort, before Tally stepped away. "Sounds like a car's coming up the drive. Best let the Blue Hollys in, though it's probably just Ted."

"Sure."

"This way, Sheriff, Deputy."

Haru stood in the front room, momentarily at a loss, the havoc of the afternoon catching up with them. A solid knock on the front door snapped them out of their stupor, though, and they threw the door open.

"Uruma Bastille?"

The second eldest Blue Holly child was staring at them with a disturbing intensity, so Haru looked down. The robe clung indecently, their chest exposed, completely soaked. Not the best way to present themself to the Blue Hollys. These were extenuating circumstances, however.

"Excuse me." They pulled on the robe's lapels. "This way, please." Haru swung around and headed to the back of the house, scenting for Lahi and Bastille-*okaasan*. They found the family huddled over a towel in Tally's office. "It is Amelia."

"She playing opossum?"

Haru did not laugh, but their mouth went rigid.

"Right, so what happened?" Ted knelt down next to her and opened his bag. He pulled out a stethoscope and several bottles, listening with one ear to Haru's explanation while assessing Amelia with his hands. "You know opossums are immune to most venoms and poisons, right?"

"No."

"Well, they are. It's why Ed was in the extermination business. They aren't completely invulnerable. Our human side. Enough poison could kill them too, it'd just take a lot more. Most likely our little Amelia here has a bit of the tubing stuck. Luckily it's not blocking anything too bad."

"Should she human?"

"No, don't know what'll happen during the Sahnkes."

"Ah."

Ted picked Melia up with one of his huge paws, rumbling a soft tune as he did so. "Let's get you on the desk so I can get a better look at you."

With extreme care, Ted put her on the desk, then pulled out a pen light. Amelia was alert now and holding as still as she could. Her coughs made it hard, because her tiny body shook violently with each one. Ted pet over her head and scratched behind her ears. She sneezed then coughed again. Haru's heart squeezed hard as they stood next to her, one hand over her rump in comfort.

"Poor little opossum," Ted crooned as he petted her. "Doesn't feel good, does it?"

Amelia's head wobbled.

"Can you open up?"

Soon her tiny, pointed teeth were on full display.

"Good, now you're going to feel some pressure when I place the tongue depressor down. I need you to try and hold still."

Amelia's little back rose and fell rapidly, but she held her head still.

"There. I think I can tweezer it." Ted held his hand open and tweezers plopped down into it.

Bastille-*okaasan* nodded. "Won't be the first or last time a young lijun nibbled on something they shouldn't."

"Got it!" Ted crowed as Amelia coughed hard enough her bottom slammed back into Haru's hand. "Oh, yes, go to Uma."

Amelia clawed at the cuff of their robe, and Haru immediately cuddled her close. "You scared me."

Opossum kisses showered their face as she nosed them.

"Never going to leave you, little girl. Never."

Several chirps followed their declaration and she pressed up against their face.

"Love you, little girl."

Ted coughed, interrupting Haru's finicking over Melia. He held up a glass bottle. Golden liquid sloshed about as he shook it.

"I've got a honey mix that should feel good on her throat. Fred does a good job with growing our supplies and helping with the tonics. Should I leave it here or the kitchen?"

"Why don't you— Oh, now what?" Bastille-*okaasan* said as the phone rang. "Bastille residence. Oh, yes, Sheriff. Of course." She hit the mute. "Sheriff wants you, Haru, dear. Now, don't you frown at me. Lahi and I will warm your girl up and shower her with cuddles. Sammy already has the others down in the entertainment room. They're probably wanting to know how their sister is. Poor pups. But you might want some pants if you're going back outside."

"Or swimming trunks," Lahi added with a smile. "What? The sheriff can't swim if his life depends on it."

"You too, Ted. Let's make sure everyone is okay."

Not only did Lahi and Bastille-*okaasan* vacate the room in under five seconds flat, Ted wasn't far behind them, even with having to clean up his supplies. Haru stared after Bastille-*okaasan*. Woman just stole their pup. No qualms about it or anything. The phone rang again, jolting Haru into action and getting dressed. They did consider going back out in their robe, but that would make Tally look bad. Last thing they wanted was to give the hateful sheriff more ammunition to use against the clan. By the time they got down by the shore, there was a crew of people swarming the property — gloves and all.

"There you are!" Tally pulled Haru into him again. "Everyone okay?"

"Yes, please, do tell us if the rat's all right."

Tally's arms tightened around Haru. "Don't."

"But —"

"He's the sheriff."

"She is not a rat."

Tally petted Haru's back and placed a kiss against their temple. "*I know.*"

"The opossum is fine. Your mother and Lahi are with her."

"Good." Tally turned toward the lake. "Think you can pick out the spot you found the canister?"

"Yes." From the lake it'd be easier. Not like they could otter out in front of present company, unfortunately. "This way."

Haru led the sheriff and his department up the shore, doing their best to sniff discreetly. Now that they knew the smell, they could try to scent it. Tally caught it first, though, cringing and hissing as he shook his head.

"Problems, Mr. Bastille?" one of the other deputies asked.

"No. No. Just…wish Ed was still here."

"Yes," Haru agreed but had to fight against the urge to say 'no'. If Ed were here, the pups would still have their dad and Haru wouldn't have their responsibility to the kids. Now the Cohens were *theirs*. What kind of asshole did that make them?

Deputy Kincaid's head went back a fraction and her nostrils flared. "It is a loss to everyone."

"Here." Haru pointed out over the lake.

Everyone lined up on the shore, overlooking the still blue waters. Sheriff Amick shouldered his way up next to Haru and Tally, those caterpillar eyebrows of his working hard to lift off. The urge to pull on one of those huge strands had to be squashed down as Haru pointed out the canister.

Some young kid who had to be older than he looked got sent out to fight the cottontails to retrieve the canister. Low man on the pay scale. He swore, tripped and face-planted in the mud a couple times, before pulling on a pair of latex gloves and finally wrangling the canister out of the water. Two of the other deputies exchanged a look and some money.

Poor kid.

A bright red logo was emblazoned on the silver canister — a dead termite.

Deputy Kincaid growled. "That's Ed's all right. We should get some soil and water samples. Just in case."

"What does that mean?" Haru asked.

When she looked at Haru, her eyes had slitted. "It means your husband isn't getting pulled in just yet."

Suddenly everything went wobbly, Haru's chest no longer heavy, an impossible weight no longer crushing them.

"But don't go anywhere, okay, Tally?"

"For Gods' sakes, Melissa, you guys need to stop saying that." Tally huffed in ill-contained frustration. "My family, my life, my responsibilities are here. Where the *hell* would I go?"

"Simmer down, Mr. Bastille," Sheriff Amick cut in. "We need to process this and I'd like you to come down for a full set of prints, just in case."

"Of course. I'll be in this afternoon."

And just like that, the boulder was bearing down on Haru again. Weird how they didn't want Tally to be the murderer. They never had, really, but the desire for Tally to be innocent meant a lot more to Haru than they wanted to admit, even to themself.

* * * *

The family was snuggled together, in human form, on the couch. All of them. The joeys, Haru and Tally. Movie on the television, fire in the fireplace, lights off. The kids had wanted both of them for cuddles as they watched their latest obsession — *Totoro*. Haru wasn't about to deny them. It had been a trying couple days. Strange too. A familiar movie should've settled their nerves. But the close proximity to Tally, in human form yet again, also made Haru acutely aware of him.

Unlike Haru who radiated heat like a furnace, Tally was cool to the touch. Not cold, like when someone suffered hypothermia, but cool like the hands of someone lacking good circulation. They wondered if Tally understood whose hands were holding whose. Haru glanced over Jackson's head and saw Tally watching them, not the movie.

So he was aware.

There was a squeeze before Tally let go, moving to ruffle Jackson's hair. Their boy glanced at Tally long enough to smile before focusing back on *Totoro* and roaring as Mei roared. They might have watched the movie a lot recently. Good thing Haru had a soft spot for it. They could understand why the joeys identified with the girls from *Totoro* so much.

Amelia leaned into Haru's side, nuzzling.

"How is your throat feeling, little girl?"

"M'kay."

"Any soreness?"

"No, Uma." She paused then tilted her head back to lock eyes with them. "You *my* Uma now, yes?"

The words and question thrown at Haru in her soft, quiet whisper made their voice disappear.

Amelia pressed hard against them, trembling ever so slightly.

Tally spoke for him. "Yes, Haru's your Uma. He loves all of you very much."

"Do you love us, Usar?" Jackson asked, tearing his gaze away from the screen. His little fingers dug into Tally's thigh, betraying how much the answer mattered to him. "Do you want us?"

Tally hugged Jackson close, tucking his head just under his chin. "I love you, to Pluto and back. I hope we stay a family for a long, long time."

"Me too." Jackson rubbed noses with Tally then slid back down to his spot between them on the couch. Life problems solved in two seconds flat, their boy content to watch the movie again.

When was life ever so easy? Problems didn't just disappear because one said so. Was it really as simple as saying 'Don't worry, you will be loved'? To the children it seemed to be enough. The pups accepted

Tally at his word. Could they? If Haru trusted Tally's promises, would their heart be held ever so gently too?

The pups made it look so easy. But they were young. Complications had been thrown at them. First their mother, then their father, but those years with their parents had shaped them. They'd had years filled with love.

Sammy had told Haru the Bastille household was a good one. They knew it was offered as reassurance, because of the chaos in the household. She had known how they felt in a holt with snakes. The right words had come out of her mouth, though Haru had questioned them. That all the kids were loved and would give love in return.

Had Tally been like Jackson as a child? Boundless with energy. Inquisitive. Loving unconditionally. Accepting of life.

Then why did his Argaze carry a worry stone? In some ways, being the Sardu had to have its own kind of complications, restrictions just as a Satislit did.

Haru cast their gaze across the children to Tally, who was watching the screen along with the pups. A large, warm smile curved his lips and turned his fierce but handsome features soft and welcoming. Haru could almost see the little boy buried beneath the humongous body. Their heart jumped, catching Haru's breath and stealing it. Such an unfair thought to have, wedging sympathy into their heart. It infuriated Haru in a way. Softening against the man who'd bought them.

A motion caught Haru's attention, pulling them away from their morose wallowing. Tally was turning something in his hand — the one stretched away from them, settled on the arm of the couch. It took a moment for Haru to place the movements. The motions were Tally's fingers weaving the worry stone between them.

Here the two of them were, sitting in front of a Tally-size flat-screen, snuggled with the pups, and he was worried? What did he have to worry about right now? Even Tally couldn't let the troubles and the problems Ed's death had started bother him all the time, could he?

"Something wrong?"

"Hmm?" Haru answered, caught off guard when Tally looked over. "Ah, thinking maybe the mudroom should have a space for robes. In case of any future unexpected guests."

"Yes, that was…different."

"Quite. Glad that nasty business is over and done with." For now. They'd know more when the fingerprints came back. Haru had a moment of panic when they considered the prints might be Tally's, then pushed it away. The idea of the murderer being Tally no longer made sense to them. Not after the way Tally had been with the pups and them. Unfortunately that meant someone else was going around killing people.

That scared Haru more. How would they protect the joeys properly? The lake was already out of bounds until it got treated properly, leaving Haru without a refuge. How much did that suck? Not being able to otter probably.

Haru sighed.

"Are you sure you're okay?" Tally's fingertips slid over Haru's hand in the barest of touches. "Tired?"

"Only a little."

"The pups certainly seemed tuckered out."

"Mmm. Yes." Amelia and Olivia had cuddled up, holding each other. Jackson snored away against Tally, little fingers clinging to his shirt. The great debate was if they should move the pups upstairs or not.

"Let them sleep a little longer. We'll see if they wake up when the movie ends."

Nodding, Haru yawned then agreed. "Sounds like a plan."

Resettling next to the joeys, Haru found the warmth and snuggles relaxing, and made them more than a little sleepy themself. In fact, it was hard to keep from yawning or keep their eyes open. Haru stopped trying to fight the motions and let them happen, their eyes watering. The screen blurred as they listened to the breathing of their pups and Tally.

But then those sweet noises were gone.

Haru blinked, then rubbed their eyes. The title menu for the movie was on the screen. Music played softly in the background. There was a slight chill in the air, the pups and Tally gone. It took a confused minute for Haru's brain to catch up and realize that their Argaze had probably taken the children up to bed.

It was too warm to move. The fire crackled, the wood's red coals glowing brightly in the darkened room. Though they supposed they should get up to bed. Who knew when the joeys would wake up?

After a nice long stretch, Haru pushed the blanket — when had that gotten there? — off. They folded it carefully before settling it over the arm of the couch. It looked to be handmade. Something Nan had knitted, perhaps? She always had a bag with yarn, and needles or a hook, with her.

Haru shut off the entertainment system, temporarily throwing themself into darkness. As soon as their eyes adjusted enough, Haru followed the wall around to the stairs. When their hand touched one of the door jambs, though, they stopped. Haru hadn't exactly spent a lot of time exploring the house. Probably because they spent most of their time avoiding it. But they had snuck peeks when Tally and the kids were down here...*because*.

Whenever they disappeared into this room, Haru couldn't hear what their pups were doing.

Time to find out what the secret hideout was.

As soon as the door swung open, Haru reached for the lights.

"No way." Talk about ridiculousness. A recording studio? "Is there anything this house doesn't have?"

"Elevators."

Haru jumped, hitting one of the drums and nearly knocking it over.

"But I'm seriously considering having that remedied."

"Tally!"

"Sorry, didn't mean to scare you."

"No, I—I was not scared. Just surprised." There had been lots of surprises since moving in—the way Tally was with the pups, the space he'd given Haru. The Harvest Festival had certainly put their Argaze in a new light for them too. Haru just didn't know what to do with the feelings. That was the trouble.

After a few hesitant steps, Tally joined Haru in the studio. "I was on my way back for you."

"Going to carry me up to bed like a prince?"

"Heh. Something like that."

"I didn't think you played," Haru replied, motioning to the room instead of the flirting. Was it flirting?

"I don't." Tally shrugged. "But Lahi can learn to play any instrument she gets her hand on."

"That is a lucky talent to have."

Tally nodded, fiddling with the tuners on one of her guitars. There were a lot of guitars. Not to mention drums, basses, horns, a piano. Haru should've been playing his *biwa* down here instead of their room. Dear Gods. Haru *knew* the Bastilles were rich, but every once in a while it struck them dumb. The family was always so down to earth that they'd forget.

"You realize this kind of money is obscene, yes?" Haru asked as they glanced around Lahi's studio again.

"A little, yeah."

"What some people would give to live in this kind of opulence."

"Also true. Greed has darkened many spirits. Wilted them," Tally said as he picked up one of the guitars then put it back down. Fidgeting. "Our holdings have created conflict, but they've also brought opportunities to the clan. Helped create jobs. Helped keep lijun safe. The clan safe. Not that everyone's good with people like us Bastilles having that much influence."

"Because you are uktena?"

"That too, but here in the US it's also because of the color of my skin. Who I am."

"Ah."

Tally sat on a stool, dwarfing it. "It is what it is. We do the best we can. Help where we can. Make connections to strengthen the integrity of the system."

"Is that why you were in *Nippon*?" Haru asked. They pressed their face against the glass and checked out the engineering station. The recording equipment looked professional grade, not that they would know, but it was certainly better than what their school had provided for the music club. "To expand?"

"Yes," Tally said with a bit of a smile. "The resorts here in Wadiswan are home base. We have more—

Central America, Brazil, a few places in Europe, Australia. Different family members and staff help with the operation. I've been wanting to expand into Africa and Asia for a while, but the timing has never been quite right until the last year or so."

"Is Antarctica next?"

"No, too cold for snakes."

Haru laugh-snorted at the seriousness at which Tally answered, but their Argaze's gaze was shining with amusement, the laugh lines around his eyes deep and crinkled. "Not too cold for otters, I think."

"Hmm. Maybe I should look into it. Why let the scientists have all the fun?"

"Very true."

Silence lulled between them. The awkwardness from before gone. Something different in between them now. Haru wasn't sure what it was, wasn't sure they wanted to name it. The feeling felt akin to friendship. But the idea of liking their jailer scared Haru. How could they take such a leap of faith? Hope had only crushed and bloodied their spirit before.

To keep from nervously sharing more information than they felt comfortable with, Haru began studying the instruments littering the studio. Lahi had really made herself an extravagant setup down here. For all this work to have been done...she had to be recorded? In fact, were those records on the wall hers? Haru moved around the different guitars and drums to get a closer look.

"Haru, how about we— Shit."

A *biwa* sat on display, it's pear-shaped body quite out in the open and hard to ignore. Haru had been too focused on the rest of the room to notice before. The deep red color was a sharp contrast to the inlay across the widest part of the body. And the inlay. That must've cost Tally a fortune.

Not to mention the *chû*. What those frets cost—Haru was unable to control themself. They picked up the *biwa*, cradling it, staring at this beautiful piece of art. Why had no one told them it was here? He turned to Tally, questioning, needing answers. Confused.

"Is…is this for me?"

Tally stood, his cheeks darkened with rosy undertones, his shoulders hunching. "It is."

"Then why haven't you given it to me?"

"I—uh, it was supposed to be your wedding present from me, but…*things* happened."

Many things.

"Then I thought maybe you might not like to play…so it just stayed down here until I had the time to figure out what to do with it." Tally backed against the glass. He looked away and shrugged. "They made you, right? Play, I mean."

"Yes."

"So, I figured it was better not to give it to you."

Haru dropped down to the floor, holding the *biwa*, frowning at it. The familiar weight helped calm the storm of emotions crashing through their chest.

"You were forced," Tally said quietly. "I don't want you to feel like you have to do anything you hate."

"Hate?" Haru asked.

"You do hate playing, don't you? I mean…you play for the joeys, but your clan forced you to learn." Tally's gaze was steadfast on the wall and not Haru, his body had coiled in on itself. It felt like there were two conversations going on, but Haru didn't know what the other half of it was.

"I do not hate the *biwa*," they answered, still trying to figure out why Tally was so upset all of a sudden.

"How can you not?"

"It is a part of me. The music speaks to me."

"Even though you were forced?"

Haru frowned, unsure of what Tally was asking. "I cannot separate it from me. Just as I cannot separate being Satislit, or how I was raised. Playing the *biwa* soothes me. Gives me peace. I do not know… I do not know *how* to hate the *biwa*. It has always been a part of me. It would be hating myself?"

"Even though you were never given a choice?" Tally's chest jerked as he hiccupped.

"I…" The answer felt important. Haru held the *biwa* close to them and looked at it, trying to see the instrument through Tally's eyes. An instrument forced upon them. "I — I do not think I will ever know if I love playing the *biwa* because I chose it to play over the other instruments or if it was because I had no choice. I have always played. We will never know if it is because of how I was raised, or because I fell in love with it despite being forced. It is a conundrum with no answer. We will never know because I was not raised with a choice."

"Oh."

The barely audible gasp sounded painful. Haru frowned again. Apparently the answer had been wrong.

"I apologize, Argaze." Should they bow?

"No, please don't. Don't say you're sorry."

"I have upset you, after such a nice evening too." Haru did not like the guilt weighing against their heart. "We are talking about the *biwa*, yes?"

"Yeah, kinda." Tally slumped, sliding down the wall.

"Kinda? What does this mean?"

"It's nothing, Haru. Don't worry about it."

The dismal hurt stung their heart in a way Haru feared. "You said we would discuss what happens. That I would have say. You are asking me something I do not understand. I would like to know what you are asking me."

A broken, shuddering breath escaped Tally and he closed his eyes. He let his head fall back against the wall, wincing.

"Argaze?"

"You're not going to leave, are you? Not with the joeys here. You're stuck. Trapped. Again."

The words were a splash of cold water in the face. Harsh and unforgiving. Haru held the *biwa* just a little bit tighter.

"I do not know. Maybe. I could leave."

"Haru, please. We both know what otters are like. Be honest."

"No. I won't leave the pups." An ache, deep and wide, cracked their chest open as they admitted the truth.

"Because you're you. You don't know how to be anything but you," Tally said with a sigh. "I've trapped you just as much as your clan did."

"No—"

But the cutting expression Tally gave them silenced Haru's denial. The stern way his face closed up and sharpened—the snake coiling.

"You did not cause Cohen-san's death." Haru wasn't sure what else to say.

"You believe that?"

"Mostly."

Tally nodded, his gaze unfocused. "Thank you, for admitting the truth."

"You are welcome." Though it felt weird to say so.

The next question tilted Haru's world sideways. "Where does that leave us?"

Haru shook their head, their chest tight. Those words they dreaded. *Us.*

"I think Gun and Marnie got it wrong. Maybe I was a little wrong too."

"What *wrong*?"

Another one of those big, heavy sighs escaped Tally. "It doesn't matter that we're adults. Or that I thought you had a choice."

"I am not following."

"Our wedding night." Lines grooved into Tally's face around his mouth. "What happened between us, that was never consensual."

"I—" The pain in Haru's chest got hotter, burned harder.

"Listen, please." Tally fiddled with his worry stone. The one Haru's otter had been eager to give him. "You had to prove we mated, right?"

Haru gave a sharp nod. The memory of submitting to the Awi and Akaike-san was still too bright in their mind. They loathed the memory. Wished it would disappear altogether.

"Then there was never a choice. Even if I didn't know, the ssssituation was not one of consent. What happened was never consssentual. I think... I think we're both going to have to come to termssss with what happened that night. Of how that night was not what either of us wanted it to be."

"I..." Haru gulped. Their emotions raged together in a storm, making them unsure, unable to respond. It took a few moments to gather themself. "You are not a rapist. Those men we see on all the news. Those are terrible men. You are…*nice*."

"No… I'm not like them…but men like that are easy to vilify. It's easy to see what they've done wrong and bring them to justice. It's these gray areas, like us, that are harder to understand. To work through." Tally took a shaky breath in. "Those muddy areas of whether people are really listening, of whether they really understand how the other person feels, how we are making them feel. Whether we notice we're putting them in a bad situation. I should've waited, the night we got married, really seen the timing wasn't right. The culture we live in can make those gray areas hard to navigate. To understand when you've crossed a line because we haven't been talking about them."

Haru stared at the *biwa* because it was easier than acknowledging the rock weighing down their chest.

"You don't think I've noticed how much you don't human? How much you've ottered since that night? How much you play in the clean, cold water *away* from me? The house?" Tally's voice wobbled and pressed his lips together. "How upset you got when the water was dirtied by the poisssson?"

"Please, I…do not want to hear this." Drops fell onto the *biwa*. Wet, large drops. Was it possible for it to rain inside?

"I am sorry, Haru." Tally's voice shook harder. "I *really* am."

The rock in their chest cracked, pain slicing Haru's heart in two. How were they supposed to feel? The apology… Tally had said it before, but this time *felt* different from the others.

"So if you're going to stay, be Uruma, where does that leave *us*? Because if you don't know how to separate it, like you don't know how to separate how you were raised from playing the *biwa*, how will I ever be able to know how you feel? Will we ever be able to move past our beginning?"

"I do not know."

"Yeah. That's what…" But Tally didn't continue.

Haru glanced up to find their Argaze wasn't in much better shape than them—eyes red-rimmed and heavy. Those black eyelashes lush and wet.

"It's okay," Tally said, nodding, mouth tight, one hand over his heart. "It's okay."

What was okay?

"Thissss, this isn't something we have to figure out tonight."

"Yes, Argaze."

Tally's brows came together, then he directed a forced smile toward Haru. "Come on, it's late and I think we both could use some shut-eye."

"You go ahead."

"Sure thing, Haru." Tally used the wall as leverage to get up. "Take as much time as you need. I'll stay with the kids. If you want to spend time playing down here, anytime, just let Lahi know so she can give you some space."

The cryptic comments hung in the air, the comfortable space between them gone. Haru watched as Tally walked out of the room with his too-stiff shoulders and rigid back, confused and unsure exactly what just happened. All they knew was they didn't like how defeated Tally looked as he left. And didn't that leave a knot of jitters whirling in their chest.

Haru glanced at the door then over to the stand where the *biwa* had been waiting. They picked up the *bachi*, positioned themself with the *biwa*, and began plucking the strings. The melodic, familiar sound curled around Haru — protecting them, buffering Haru from the noise in their heart, letting them breathe, even if only for a song.

Chapter Twelve

The Death Knock

Tally stared out his kitchen window, watching the mist curling around the dormant flowerbeds in the gray of first light. The house was silent except for the soft hum of the refrigerator and the occasional ticks in the ducts when the heat kicked on. He wished he could do that, simply lie dormant in the garden like a crocus bud waiting for spring. Waiting for everything to be all right again.

Nothing was ever going to be all right again. He had to face that head-on. Be the adult in the room, because maybe Haru's family had done some cruddy things, but the current situation wasn't anyone's fault but his own. He wiped at the tears sneaking down his cheeks again and wished at least that he could stop crying. Yes, his heart was broken. Didn't matter. He had a community to look after, a business to run, a family to see to and, damn it, he needed to try to make Haru as happy as he could since he'd chosen to stay. Maybe not entirely *chosen*…

A beep came from near his right elbow. The world might have become a gray, difficult place, but at least there was coffee.

The kids would be up soon. Breakfast. Getting them dressed. Jackson would be going to kindergarten next fall. That was something they should talk about. Refuge in normal things. Small things. It was possible. He would make it possible.

Tally was just reaching for the big mixing bowl to start pancakes when his phone rang. He frowned at the name on the screen. "Melissa? Everything all right?"

"Good morning, Tally." Melissa's voice was brisk and clipped. Professional. "The handprint on Ed's canister wasn't yours, but you knew that. And it wasn't Ed's."

Tally sagged against the counter in relief. Finally, a physical piece of evidence that led to someone *other* than him. "That's good to hear. Thank you. I understand if you can't tell me any more yet."

"Tally." Melissa's voice had gone soft, sharp as razors. "It's clan."

"Oh, no." Tally pulled a stool out from the center island so he could sit. "Whose is it?"

"It's Alan Jones'."

"Alan?" Tally nearly dropped his phone, little scenelets playing through his mind. Alan's reaction to his presence at the cake tasting. The increasingly desperate pleas to the council for his proposed expansion. The...wait. "How do you know it's Alan's? He's never been arrested that I know of."

"We have his prints on file from a DUI a few years back. I didn't bother you with it since it was a first offense and just a fine in the end." Melissa hesitated. "How do you want to handle this, Urusar Bastille?"

"Let's keep it clan for now. All we know is that his handprint is on a canister. Ed could've been doing work for him, I suppose. There could be an everyday explanation."

"All right. I'm in the car headed to Best Bakery now. They don't usually have much of a morning rush, so probably a good time to catch him. I'll keep you informed."

"Thank you, Melissa. I appreciate the heads-up and your forbearance during this investigation."

"Forbearance. Good word there. I'll talk to you in a bit."

Tally hung up, tapping his phone against his thigh. Why Ed, of all people? What possible argument between him and Alan could have become so heated that Alan had *killed* him? Or was that first murder an accident? Even so, the lab tech certainly wasn't. What if Alan...?

"Oh Gods. Holy *shit.*"

Tally jerked up and snatched his keys from the hook, stomped into boots and raced for the garage. Early morning the bakery would be empty or nearly so, the street likewise. It was clan business, so Melissa would be going alone. Gods. *Melissa.*

He hit the return call as he reached his car, but she didn't pick up. *Damn it, damn it, damn it.* She'd probably been calling en route to the bakery. Still, Tally had to try, juggling the phone between ear and shoulder as he started the engine and backed out into the driveway.

"Melissa, *wait* for me. Please. Do not go in there alone with that deer. Alan... I don't think he's... I think he's desperate. Wait for me."

At the first stop sign at the end of the drive, he texted a similar message. Then at the first stoplight in town, he called Haru. He didn't pick up either, but that wasn't shocking. Tally hadn't heard him come up the steps until two in the morning.

"Haru, I'm on my way to Best Bakery, the place Alan Jones owns. I need someone to know that, just in case. It was Alan's handprint on the pesticide canister. Melissa's gone to confront him and I'm worried that she's done it alone, on clan business. I'll call you when I know more."

The streets were empty enough that Tally ignored the next two red lights, guilt gnawing at him all the way, vying for prominence with his worry. When he pulled up across the street from the bakery, he spotted the squad car out front. The empty squad car.

Damn it, Melissa.

He slammed the car door and hurried across the street, nearly taking himself out since he'd neglected to tie his bootlaces. There was someone in the store, thank Gods. Tally could make out the shape of one of the delivery drivers by the uniform. His relief evaporated the moment he opened the door to the bakery.

Melissa lay crumpled by the pastry case in an ever-widening pool of blood. The delivery driver from Midwest Flour stood several feet away, frozen in horror. His head snapped up when the bell jangled.

"He shot her," the young man whispered, though Tally wasn't sure he actually saw him. "He just shot her dead."

"Did you call the police?" Tally asked, trying his best to keep his voice gentle while he wanted to scream. Tally didn't have to check. He could smell death from across the room. *Too late, oh Gods, Melissa. I'm so sorry.*

The driver nodded. "They're coming."

"Who shot her…?" Tally squinted to read the driver's name tag. "Toby. Who was it?"

"Mr. Jones. I just… I can't…"

"Toby." Tally let his voice sharpen before Toby could drift into shock again. "Where is he now? Mr. Jones?"

"He… He…" Toby swallowed hard and leaned against the counter where the register sat. "He ran out the back. I saw…his car… He drove like he was on fire down Harris Street."

Running away? Trying to hide? Alan had killed and killed and killed again. His grievance with Ed didn't make sense, but everything after was done to cover his tracks. Melissa had come in, he must have known she'd figured it out and that she'd come on clan business…

"No. Oh…no." Tally gripped the doorframe for balance as a terrible thought hit him. "Toby, tell the police there's a good chance Alan's headed for the Bastille place. His problem is really with me, I think. I have to go."

Because Alan was coming after *him*. Because he wasn't there and Haru and the kids were. *No. Fuck, no.* That rabid deer was *not* going to hurt his family.

The drive back home was a blur. Tally disregarded every traffic rule and pushed the Bentley hard in his frantic bid to reach the house in time. How far ahead of him was Alan? Why hadn't he seen him and his rusty blue Cadillac yet? As a guilty afterthought, he hoped Alan's wife Jean was all right. Why hadn't she been at the bakery that morning?

There. Up ahead, just turning onto the long drive to the house, Tally spotted a flash of powder blue. He accelerated to an insanely unsafe speed on the country road and took the second drive entrance to cut Alan off from the house. He knew the terrain and his car was considerably more powerful. This would work to get him between his family and the horror coming toward them.

Barely. Alan was coming up the hill when Tally skidded around the last corner and heaved the wheel around to put his car across the drive. Alan screeched to a stop and stared at him while Tally got out of the car. The paralysis only lasted a moment before Alan reached for something on the seat beside him and calmly got out of the car.

"You just won't go down, will you, Urusar Bastille?" The smallest tremor shook Alan's hand as he leveled a pistol at Tally. "This really shouldn't have been so hard, and you should be in jail for murder."

"Whatever your issue with me, I won't let you hurt my family." Tally realized how stupid that was when he said it. If Alan shot him, he couldn't defend them anymore, could he? "Leave them out of it."

"Whatever my issue?" Alan snorted, one foot pawing at the ground like a buck getting ready to charge. "You're not stupid. Not that stupid. You cancel contracts, take business away, won't let me expand like I need to. Your favoritism for your predator friends and your cronies and the *humans* needs to end, Bastille. We're going to end it today."

"If you shoot me, the police will know who did it. Someone saw you shoot Melissa, you know."

"More loose ends. Not that it's that important anymore. I could always say Melissa threatened me and I panicked. Even if I go to jail, I'll have done my duty to the community and removed the bullying snakes who've been in power too long." Alan waved the gun at him. "And I'm not going to shoot you. We're getting in your car and you're going to put it in the garage."

"What...why?"

"Just do it. If you want to save your foreign husband."

Tally did as he said, sliding carefully back into his Bentley with Alan in the seat behind him with the gun to Tally's head. The police might be on their way. If he did things slowly enough, he might survive.

"Drive to the garage. If I even get a hint that you're going uktena, I'll blow your brains out and leave you here for your Jap otter to find."

The reasonable way Alan spoke chilled Tally to the core. He swallowed hard as he started the car and drove toward the garage. It was still too early for the kids to be up. He hoped. His best chance was to keep following instructions because Haru might not love him, but the thought of anyone finding him with his head blown apart? Anyone would be traumatized and at least Haru might be...a little attached to him by now, in some respects.

If only the house was smaller or the garage door opener wasn't so quiet and efficient. Not that Tally wanted anyone to come out here while Alan had a loaded gun. But at least it would be some indication of where he was when the police arrived. Alan instructed him to close the garage door and get out of the car. *Ah. That makes sense. He'll shoot me in here and it will be a while before anyone finds me.*

Part of Tally was horrified that he could think through this sanely, the part that wasn't screaming in frustrated fear. What Alan did next puzzled him, though. He put a notepad and pen on the workbench at the house side of the garage and slid them toward Tally.

"You're going to write a little note. Keep it short and simple. You're sorry about killing Ed and the lab tech and you can't live with the guilt anymore. Then you're going to sign it."

"I..." Tally stared at him. "I'm not going to shoot myself for you. And forensics can tell that I didn't."

Alan gave him a tight, humorless smile. "Don't worry about that part, Bastille. Write."

If he'd been within reach, Tally might have tackled him. Alan stayed well back, though, gun trained on Tally every moment. *Time. Right. I'm buying time.*

So he wrote a note that Haru wouldn't believe he'd written willingly.

My dearest Tislit —

I regret to inform you that I was the one who murdered Ed and the lab tech. I'm unable to live with the crushing guilt of killing by uktena poisoning. It's so easy, though, and I was so angry. I will miss our long mornings in bed together.

All regrets —
Tally

Alan motioned for the notepad and Tally slid it over, hoping the deer's attention would waver for a second. It didn't. He managed reading while keeping his aim and an eye on Tally quite well. Alan nodded and slid the notepad back.

"Now tear off the page and put it in your pocket."

Tally bent over the notepad to do as he'd been instructed. There was a shuffle behind him and his heart jackhammered as he turned just in time to see Alan there and a tire iron coming at his head. He tried to get an arm up to block it. Too late. The metal connected with Tally's head just as he heard something that worried him more.

"Get away from my husband."

"Walk away, otter."

Haru frowned at Jones-san. Something had obviously gone very wrong at the bakery. Tally hadn't gotten back up after the blow, and that worried them more. A pool of blood grew around his head.

The gun *looked* real. Too real. The gun pointed at them made them want to otter out. To defend their territory. But the human in Haru knew better, even if they'd never encountered a man bent on murder before.

Could anyone just buy a gun here? Just walk in and buy it?

"You should've stayed in the house." Jones-san kept the muzzle on Haru. He sounded so calm.

"I wondered why my husband had not come inside for breakfast."

"I see. The good little Satislit looking after their Argaze."

"Yes," Haru answered flatly. They wanted to check on Tally, but movement meant danger. Where was Melissa?

"If you had stayed inside, this would've been much easier."

"I doubt it."

Jones-san sighed. "Hmm. Possibly. But I've done my duty."

"By trying to kill your Urusar?" Haru huffed, then checked their nails to portray a calm they did not feel. Though it would suck to break one in a tussle—they'd just had them done.

"Certain lijun should never be in power. You of all people should understand."

Haru held their head higher. "You are talking about my Argaze, Jones-san."

"Quite right. Your *Em'halafi*. You sure about that? Problem is—" Jones-san coughed, his breath ragged.

The air was definitely getting foul in the garage. Were there vents? The last thing they needed was it getting into the house.

"Predators like *them* don't care about the rest of the clan. It's bad enough the Bastilles gave humans jobs and contracts, those greedy uktena kept the lands and the businesses to themselves."

"Tally shares his wealth." Which was true.

"Then he should've approved the bakery expansion!"

"Your business is struggling, Jones-san. The proposal sloppy. You have not bothered to ask why your sales are slumping."

"Sloppy? An Uruma has no business looking at financial proposals. Did you just call me sloppy, you pansy?"

Luckily it was not the first time that particular word had been thrown at Haru, otherwise it could've knocked them for a loop. Instead, they used the hot coal of anger it invoked inside them to center their rage on the one person who deserved it.

"You are forgetting something, Jones-san."

"What?"

"I am a predator too." Haru hit the garage opener. The protests were immediate, but no shots fired because Jones-san was looking at the garage door with worry. He really should've taken the warning to heart and paid better attention.

It was like hitting a wall. Hard, unforgiving, until momentum carried the two of them forward. Together they rolled in a writhing mass of shouts and hits. The gun went off. Another punch hit Haru, harder than the last. Rocks dug into their back as they hit the drive, the crunch of gravel deafening against the roar of pain. Heavy weight crushed them into the drive. Breathing hurt. The gun was now angled over their shoulder, Haru's hand firmly on Jones-san's wrist, desperately holding onto it.

One wrong move and that gun would have a permanent effect on their life.

Haru bit down on Jones-san's wrist, sinking their teeth in and ignoring the blood as it spilled into their mouth. The screams, the angry vile words thrown at them were almost harder to ignore.

"Stupid Jap! Messing up everything."

No.

"Don't you know your place, Satislit? Or are you defective, you little cunt? That's what you are, aren't you. Bastille's little hole to fuck? How much did he pay for you? Rumor says quite a bit."

No.

"That money should've gone toward the growth fund for the clan. Not some little otter with no teeth. Urusar Bastille deserves everything coming to him."

A growl escaped Haru.

"Oh, don't like your match being disrespected? Whoever saw such a fucked-up family? Just wait until we toss those pups of yours— Ahhhh!"

Haru shook their head, hit Jones-san's elbow and brought up their knee. More screams, threats, but Jones-san's hand opened. The gun fell, the soft crunch almost a relief. But they couldn't stop. Vigilance always. Haru kicked again, threw an elbow in, getting an "Ooophf" from the stupid deer.

Vomit went everywhere. All over Haru. Guess they got a good hit in?

A push sent Jones-san back, stumbling. Haru rolled up and threw another punch.

The snap as his head went back was so loud it echoed through the garage. Blood spurted from Jones-san's nose in a great torrent. He alternated between wheezing and gagging. Haru growled again, then got a solid kick in the bastard's stomach. It sent him to the ground, Jones-san's moans almost satisfactory. Jerk shouldn't have scared Haru so fucking much.

Or threatened what was theirs.

Aches made themselves known through a tidal wave of pain erupting all over. Haru swayed as they went over to the gun. What were they supposed to do with it?

The answer came in the sound of sirens breaking through the fog in Haru's head. It hurt too much to move. Something wasn't right. They'd taken plenty of punches in their days. They didn't burn like this. Didn't feel so heavy. Haru glanced down. There was something in all the vomit.

Two cars fishtailed to a halt on the drive, spewing gravel everywhere, nearly scaring Haru to death. Deputies jumped out of their cars with guns drawn.

"On the ground!"

"We said on the ground!"

Haru dropped—a little too hard—they hadn't gotten their hands under themself like they should've. The fuzz in their head buzzed, but the officers were still shouting. They flattened themself as much as possible. Guns. Why had they come out with guns?

"Hands on your head! On your head!"

Haru did as asked. Pain shot through their left side. Jones-san groaned but complied as well. Tally's breathing changed, meaning he was now awake and had some kind of level of alertness.

"Identify yourself!"

Really? Weren't these the same men and women who were with them at the lake? The officers should know them. Shouldn't Deputy Kincaid be here?

"I am." Huff. English was not working quite right for them. "Haru Bastille."

"And who is with you?"

"Alan Jones." Huff. "The man who attacked us." This time Haru didn't bother to keep from rolling their eyes. "And Tally Bastille."

"Keep your hands where we can see them," one of the men ordered, then said, "Check for weapons."

Squawking sounded over the radio. The deputy in charge squinted, tilting his head to the side as he listened. The deputies frowned at Haru and Tally simultaneously. Never a good sign. Their stances stiffened and they both leveled their guns with more urgency than before. The squawks weren't making sense, though. The deputies frowned in unison.

Creepy.

"Please. Let me." Huff. Huff. "Check on my Ar-Ha-husband."

Deputy Frowning flicked his gun once then holstered it, the rest following suit.

"I can get up?" Haru eyed the policeman warily.

"Yes," the deputy said with a grumble.

Don't sound so disappointed.

The second deputy approached Jones-san, talking and saying things. The deer shouted back, but the officer kept his gun out. The one watching Haru motioned for them to get up, though his attention was more on Jones-san.

Haru stood, but everything wobbled. "His gun."

The deputy squinted at Haru. "Sir — "

"Jones-san's gun." Haru pointed.

"Oh!" The deputy motioned for Haru to back away, which they did readily. "Sir, you sure you're all right?"

"My husband, he's bleeding."

"I think you are too. Dispatch, we need two ambulances. I repeat. Two ambulances."

"What?" Haru shook their head and went over to Tally. His eyes were open — wide and wet. "You with us again?"

"Haru. W-what did you do?"

"Do not worry, Argaze. The deputies have Jones-san. We are safe. The children are safe."

The hot flare went through Haru's chest again. Sitting might be easier. They slid down next to Tally and moved his head to their lap, listening to him breathe. The sirens from the cops were replaced by another set, this time by those of an ambulance pulling up.

"Is there anyone else on the premises?" the deputy asked as he waved the paramedics toward them.

"Our children, and a few of the Bastille siblings." Haru bet Lahi had the kids and were holed up somewhere. The others? Who knew. They came and went. One more thing Haru needed to get a handle on.

"Ginny, Tom, check in with the family."

"Yes, sir."

The two young deputies went to the front door, knocking, just as the paramedics came around to Tally and Haru.

"Mr. Bastille, can you tell us what happened?"

Haru did the best they could, saying Tally was surprised by Alan and had been hit. Haru finding their husband because of the noise as they'd opened the garage door. Only a little fudging, but it was the closest they could get to the truth considering. As the pretty young brunette was listening to Tally's chest, she looked at Haru with a frown.

"Melissa." Huff. Huff. "Deputy Kincaid. Where?"

"Oh, sir." The girl faltered.

"What happened?" Haru pushed, holding Tally's head a little tighter.

"She was declared dead at the scene."

"No." That was...was...too much. Alan deserved a fate worse than death.

"Shhhh, my Satislit. Don't cry. It'll be okay," Tally crooned softly, lazily petting Haru's hand.

A wet snort escaped them. "The injured should look after themselves, not others."

"We should get him in the ambulance," the paramedic said.

"It's not for me, my Em'halafi. You need to let this young woman take a look at you, Haru." Tally shook his head, or tried to, groaning and stopping. "No, no ambulance for me. Lahi, have Lahi call the Blue Hollys."

"Sir—"

"No ambulance," Tally hissed out.

It took a moment for the young woman to recover, but she did. The paramedic reached for her bag, but Tally grabbed her hand.

"No, Haru. It's my husband's blood. Not Alan's. Haru's blood."

Chapter Thirteen

All Hallows' Eve

Hospitals suck. Tally sat beside Haru's bed, holding his hand while his otter slept, and wondered if anyone in the universe didn't feel that way about hospitals. Maybe if a person worked in one... Though that didn't count. He was sure even nurses and doctors didn't enjoy being patients or sitting beside a loved one's bed.

Haru had saved him. Most likely out of a sense of responsibility and a need to protect the children, but there it was. His fierce otter had taken down a man with a gun. Tally swiped at his eyes, torn between being grateful and wanting to shake Haru for not barricading himself in the house and calling the police.

Not that he could judge the situation. He hadn't been awake for the confrontation and Alan had probably left him little choice. They'd struggled. The gun had fired. Even shot, Haru must have kept fighting, since Alan had been a mess.

"The doctor said it's not serious," Tally murmured, speaking to his sleeping husband as an excuse not to talk to himself. "Silly thing to say. You were shot. Of course it's serious. But not life-threatening. Didn't hit any of the important bits. Alan's even an incompetent shot. Not complaining about that, of course..."

A knock on the door had Tally straightening and Haru muttering as he woke. *Damn it.* Tally frowned, tensing as the visitor came around the partially drawn curtain. "Sheriff."

"Mr. Bastille." Sheriff Amick pulled up one of the plastic visitor's chairs and sat with a huff, putting his hat on the remaining chair. The lines on his face seemed deeper that afternoon, the shadows under his eyes more pronounced. "I know you talked to the deputies, but take me through what happened that morning."

Tally gave an abbreviated account, leaving out the part where Melissa had called him. He'd been concerned about certain things Alan had said recently about his stalled expansion project. He'd gone downtown to talk to him and discovered Melissa dead and Alan gone. His fear that Alan was coming after him and his family had been realized when he'd gotten home.

"Most of the rest Haru will have to tell you." Tally spread his hands. "I don't know what happened until the ambulances got there."

The bed's motor hummed as Haru raised his head to join the conversation, or maybe just to hear better, his eyes glittering and cold as he regarded the sheriff. "You know what happened after that, Sheriff." Haru's voice was a spare whisper. "But Alan's animosity toward my husband does not explain Ed Cohen. He did commit those murders?"

Sheriff Amick twitched and nodded. "It's all connected, when it comes right down to it. Alan's confessed. Guess he figured there wasn't a point pretending anymore."

"So what was it, Sheriff?" Tally leaned forward, arms on his knees. "I know Alan was struggling, has *been* struggling for years now. It's only got really bad this year, though, when he was having trouble getting credit at the bank and when investors started to walk away."

"Sure. Seems like things snowballed on him." Sheriff Amick ran a hand back through his short-cropped hair and Tally realized what made him look so reduced and lost. He didn't have his notebook in his hands, the damn, ever-present notebook. "What set him off was an infestation of roaches and moth larvae, though. In the flour and the sugar. If you've ever had those damn moths, they're hard to get rid of. Mary brought them in with the birdseed one winter. In all the cabinets..."

"Bob. Look at me," Tally said softly. "I know losing Melissa was hard. She was in my class at school. I know. But you're losing focus here."

With a heavy sigh, Sheriff Amick sat back, nodding again, staring at the ceiling a moment before he could continue. "Alan called Ed Cohen in for an estimate. It was more than he was willing to pay. Maybe more than he could pay, but it would've been a big job, not just a one-visit thing. Ed told him that if he didn't have the work done, he'd have to report Alan to the health department, that they could work out a payment schedule. Apparently wasn't good enough for Alan."

"He *murdered* Cohen-san for that?" Haru's scratchy voice conveyed all the horror Tally felt.

"Claims he didn't set out to. He and Ed had it out at your party when Ed got there. He had the back of the truck open, probably to make sure things were secure.

The argument turned into a fight. Alan reached for a screwdriver and, in their tussling, managed to knock the valve loose on one of the pesticide tanks as they're rolling around on the floor of the truck. Confined space, pesticide escaping under pressure, Alan panicked and the damn fool shut the doors with Ed inside, which surely killed him."

Tally reached for Haru's hand, surprised when he took it. "Ed's murder was an accident, then?"

"Maybe." Sheriff Amick shrugged. "I'm not convinced. He was angry enough that night that it might've been ruled second degree. But Alan didn't want to take that chance, I'd guess. Instead of reporting the incident, he decides to cover it up and blame you Bastilles. So he drags Ed out of the truck and leaves him on the ground, disposes of the tank in the lake and sneaks into the house for one of your gloves."

"What about the white flash that night? The one that was too close to the house to be part of the fireworks?"

Sheriff Amick picked up his hat, turning it in both hands. "Don't know what he was trying to do with that. He says it was a distraction. That he got one of the white charges from the fireworks contractor and set it off to look like a small explosion. I don't really know what he was thinking there. Could've blown his fool arm off."

I know what he was thinking. And it worked, making every lijun in the county think it was an uktena flash. Tally exchanged a glance with Haru and, though his husband had his stony face on, there was the slightest twitch at the corner of his eye. Haru understood.

"The lab tech, stealing Ed's body—all that was to cover his tracks of course." The sheriff slumped in his seat. "And poor Melissa. He knew it was over when she went to question him about the handprint."

"I'm sorry I didn't get there sooner." Tally swallowed hard against the lump in his throat, grateful when Haru gave his hand a squeeze.

"We might've ended up with two dead on scene then." Sheriff Amick heaved himself up with a nod for each of them. "Come down for a statement when you can, Mr. Bastille. And... Mr. Bastille. I assume you want to press charges."

"Too damn right. We'll talk soon, Bob. Again, I'm so sorry about Melissa."

Watching the sheriff walk out, shoulders hunched, hair streaked with white, Tally ached for the man. He'd aged since Melissa was killed. Tally had too. When was the last time something as awful as serial murder had happened in Wadiswan? Not any time in recent memory.

"I cannot stay here, my Argaze," Haru said.

Tally noticed the frown. "The Blue Hollys have doctors here. We do have workarounds in the system."

The tension around Haru's eyes eased a fraction. "I would heal better with my pups, not getting interrupted by nurses every few hours. We are more resilient than the humans."

"Certainly scared me, though," Tally responded.

"My apologies, Argaze."

There was a hand squeeze, making Tally really look at Haru.

"I was afraid...he had killed you. You did not deserve such a death. I never want to see you bleeding like that again."

"I—"

"Please, Argaze. Let me go home." Haru's gaze was so big, so sad. Tally heard the ache in his voice. And Haru had called the house 'home'. It might be home because of the pups, but Tally had some hope that wasn't the only reason now.

"I'll see what I can do about the paperwork."

Haru sighed and settled back on the bed. "Thank you."

Tally leaned over Haru and placed a kiss against his forehead. "I'm not the only one who wants you home."

The doctors protested the minute Tally asked for Haru to be released, but he'd already been out of surgery for twenty-four hours. That was the big cutoff. Haru had exceeded their expectations in that part of the recovery. They did not know his otter like Tally did. The Blue Hollys on shift helped get the paperwork moving and a little over thirty hours after the worst possible moment in Tally's life, he was carrying Haru into the house.

"I can walk."

"The doctor said no exertion. Stairs are exertion."

"You need an elevator."

"I really do," Tally agreed. He shifted Haru's weight again. The princess hold was harder than it looked while climbing stairs. But Haru hadn't protested when Tally had frowned between the car and the door and offered to pick him up.

"I thought you meant to settle me in one of the front rooms," Haru continued, but his hold tightened. "Where are the pups?"

"Lahi's got them in the playroom downstairs. We wanted to get you settled first."

"Ah, makes sense. Has she moved back in?"

"Basically. Says it's about the studio, but I think she wanted to even out the odds with the joeys. *And—*" Tally hip-checked the door open to Haru's suite. "Here we are."

After settling Haru in bed, propped against pillows, Tally retrieved the girls and Jackson. Melia's legs wouldn't stop pedaling, but Tally wouldn't put her down. She was the one most likely to jump Haru. None of them needed those consequences.

"Uma! Uma!" she squeaked out.

"Oomph!" One of her feet connected to Tally's stomach.

"Sorry, Usar."

"It's okay, little girl. Almost there."

Haru's voice carried out into the hall. "You giving Usar a hard time, Melia?"

"No, Uma!"

The sight of Haru, gray, weakened, propped against the bed, startled Tally every time he saw it. The shot might not have hit anything vital, but the blood loss. It had been close. The smile, though, Haru's real smile, blew Tally's worry away.

Amelia's squeaks went up a decibel.

"Patience," Tally reminded her. "Remember, Uma needs special care."

"Yes, Usar." Amelia flopped, going completely relaxed against his abdomen.

The children settled around Haru. Livy and Melia cuddled close on his left, Jackson resting his head against Haru's thigh, stroking it absently. Melia recounted their sleepover with Lahi and Sammy. Caramel popcorn was involved. *Sneaks.*

"Sammy smells yummy," Jackson added. "Sweet."

"Yeah," Amelia agreed and rocked forward. "She misses you too."

"We will get a visit in when I am feeling better. I miss her too." Haru yawned, eyes tearing up. "But I think a nap is in order."

Three identical yawns mimicked Haru's. Tally yawned too. *Make that four.* He'd been running on adrenaline since the confrontation with Alan. That needed to be addressed, but later. Definitely later. Tally helped Haru scooch down and tucked the joeys in. Livy had a death grip on Tally's fingers while a smile went between Tally and Haru as Amelia nuzzled close. Livy, Amelia and Jackson all dropped off within minutes.

Deciding sleep was a good idea, Tally turned to leave, only to be stopped by a hand. Haru had hold of him. Right by the end of his shirt. Several images, ones Haru would've frowned upon, went through Tally's head before he got himself under control.

"Stay."

"What?" The word had barely been audible. Tally had to be mistaken.

"Stay, please. I need... I need to know everyone is all right."

For a moment, Tally thought he was still hearing things, but the pink tint on Haru's ears said otherwise. His otter had just taken a huge step out of his comfort zone.

"Yeah, okay, Haru."

Tally slipped under the covers, surprised but happy. When Haru's fingers slithered between the pillows and kids to touch his shoulder, Tally thought his heart would break. The touch was more than he could ask, and not only was it wanted, the gentle touch helped lull him to sleep too.

* * * *

"Usar, now?" Amelia tugged at Tally's sleeve.

"Is it time *now*?" Jackson echoed.

Tally nearly burst a blood vessel trying not to laugh at their impatience. "Dinner first. Then costumes. You don't want to get spaghetti sauce on them, do you?"

The question of costumes had been a bit of an issue. The kids had all wanted to be otters, then they'd all wanted to be snakes. Both Tally and Haru had encouraged them to try to pick different things and the choices had ranged from mythical beasts — mostly Olivia — to inanimate objects, like rocks — mostly Jackson — to the conceptual, like sunshine — mostly Amelia.

Jackson had finally settled on being a bat. He liked bats. Amelia and Olivia had decided to be Totoro of different colors. All a little last minute, but Tally's own tailor was a talented designer as well and had managed to fit costumes in for all of them. All except Haru, who declined politely. He would take care of his on his own.

Life hadn't exactly settled, but there was routine and comfort in the small everyday necessities of being parents. Getting the joeys cleaned up and dressed, making certain all of them felt loved first thing in the morning. Sometimes they still slept in Haru's room, though sometimes they slept in Tally's and Haru would join them. It wasn't quite sleeping with his husband, but Tally found he didn't mind with the joeys safe between them. They always had breakfasts together and, unless Tally had an evening meeting, they always had dinner together as well, and when Lahi was home, she'd join them.

Haru lifted the twins into their booster seats while Jackson climbed into his own since, as he put it most emphatically, he wasn't a *little* kid like his sisters. Lahi got the kids their sippy cups of milk while Tally brought the plates to the table. Spaghetti was one of the few things Haru and Lahi let him cook, which he wasn't *bad* at. Just not good enough for some people, apparently.

"You must have *real* food before trick-or-treats," Haru said with a little sniff. He didn't approve, but he had done his best to go along with yet another odd American custom.

"But, Uma! We're not hungry!" Amelia spoke for all of them as she often did.

"Uma is right." Tally waved a serving spoon as he took his seat. "No dinner, no costumes. That's the deal."

Amelia gave him a hard stare, then nodded. A deal was a deal.

"You guys going in costume with the joeys?" Lahi asked as she cut spaghetti up for Olivia.

"That's a joke, right?" Tally gave Jackson two of the seitan not-meatballs and passed them on. "I can't drive in that thing."

Lahi rolled her eyes. "Well, since you haven't let anyone see your costume, Tal, there's no way I'd know that."

"Tally and I will be changing at the resort." Haru picked seitan balls off the plate with his sticks for Amelia. "All the necessary items are there."

"Have you seen Tally's costume?"

Haru's eyes twinkled with a hint of mischief. "No. And he has not seen mine."

"Oho. This should be interesting." Lahi flashed Tally her *you're in so much trouble* grin. "I'm getting popcorn."

A few minutes of serious eating followed, with the kids getting some nutrition in before the bargaining started.

"Can I be done, Uma?" Olivia's plea was plaintive enough to melt a stone.

Haru was unmoved. "Not yet."

"How many more bites?"

Tally leaned over to consider her plate. "Three more dinosaur bites."

"Triceratops bites?"

"No, at least allosaurus bites."

Olivia groaned but soldiered on through the nearly identical bargaining tactics of her siblings. All things considered, Tally was proud of them for managing as much as they had on excited stomachs.

A wild flurry of activity followed dinner, and soon Tally had one bat, two Totoro, one husband and one sister-dressed-as-a-purple-fairy in the family van headed to his parents' cottage for the first stop. He absolutely didn't snicker when Lahi decided to take her wings off until they got to the party. When the door opened, a dahlia and a tree greeted them. At least, Tally thought his dad was a tree. Maybe he was a shrub...

"Dad? Are you a..."

"Tree. Don't start with me." Dad-tree crouched down and opened his arm-branches as the joeys ran up the steps. "What amazing visitors we have!"

"Abay! Abago!" the kids called out as they assaulted their new grandparents.

"Wait." Jackson stepped back. "We're supposed to say trick or treat."

Serious about the proper order of things, Jackson herded his sisters back down the steps so they could approach the cottage properly with a resounding, almost coordinated, "Trick or treat!"

Mom-dahlia laughed and tipped way too many chocolates into each joey's plastic pumpkin basket.

"They won't have room for anyone else's, Mom," Lahi said in exasperation.

"That's why I'm bringing pillowcases," Mom said with a wink.

Haru's expression was just short of scandalized and Tally's stomach hurt from holding in a laugh. "I hope that's the extent of the spoiling. We have to get moving."

Everyone piled back in the van for the drive into town. They had one stop to make there before they swung out in an arc to hit a few more important houses, then on to the resort. The kids bounced with excitement as Tally pulled into the drive of a neat white house set behind a pair of black oaks.

Mrs. Kaufmann came out onto the front porch to wave and to hug the joeys when they raced up the walk to her. Tally stood back to let her exclaim over the costumes and the excited chatter of small people but when they had their candy and had raced back to the car, Mrs. Kauffman came to pat Tally's arm.

"I knew it wasn't you, Tal. Every sensible lijun knew it wasn't you." She peered up into his face and Tally was shocked, as he was whenever he saw her now, at how small and old she appeared. Part of his brain would never see her as anything other than the imposing figure of his childhood. "You've done so well with the little Cohens, too. Are you adopting?"

"We've started the process, yes, ma'am."

"You know that makes Jackson your oldest son, don't you?" Her eyes glittered with humor and calculation, her own opossum half-peeking through.

"We'll see if he wants it when he's older, Mrs. Kaufmann. But I don't think an opossum Urusar would be a bad thing, do you?"

She laughed and gave him a quick hug. "Keep surprising them, Tally. Don't let the ones who fear you wear you down."

Tally got back in the van feeling taller than he had in a while. Good thing he wasn't, or he wouldn't have fit in the van. Haru gave him an arched eyebrow look but didn't ask. At Lily and Pete's house, where they lived with their elderly mother, Uma Dignan let the joeys pick from an assortment of tiny stuffed animals. They picked dragons since the basket didn't contain otters or snakes. At Marnie's house, they squealed over the insect lollipops she had set aside special, just for them. Olivia and Jason took crickets while Amelia took a scorpion and stared at it in rapt fascination all the way to Gun's house.

"I do?" Olivia said in a whisper that could've woken mammoth fossils.

Jackson and Amelia stepped back to let Olivia ring the doorbell. The joeys managed their "Trick or treat!" in unison this time since they'd had some practice, but then fell silent when the door was flung open by a dashing Musketeer.

"*Bonsoir, mademoiselles et monsieur!*" The Musketeer, probably Athos knowing Gun, swept off his feathered hat to give the joeys a bow. When they kept staring, he straightened with a laugh. "Hey, kids. You look great. Go ahead and grab candy from the bowl on the table. I just need to grab my keys and we'll go."

Gun was lucky to keep his feet as the joeys stampeded past, but they didn't take long to add to their hoards.

Amelia took Gun's hand as they came back to the van. "Uncle Gun, is that a real sword?"

"No, sweetie. I have a couple of real ones, but Urusar Bastille forbids real weapons at the costume party."

"Oh." Amelia considered that a moment before she turned a serious expression up to Gun. "Usar is smart, I think."

Gun greeted everyone and climbed into the farthest back seat to chat with Lahi. If his greeting to Haru was a little chilly, at least it wasn't hostile anymore. Tally swallowed a sigh. They'd probably never be friends.

At the resort, Tally sent the kids off with his parents and Gun — quite the escort for three little opossums — while Haru took his arm and ambled with him back to the offices. Tally took the zippered garment bag with Haru's costume off the back of the door and handed it to his husband, then gaped in surprise as Haru started to leave Tally's office.

"I'd gladly help. Or stand outside if you want me to."

"No need." Haru scurried out the door. "Lahi has offered to assist me."

"Oh, well, I'll see you at the party then!" Tally called after his fleeing husband, shaking his head in bemusement.

He closed the door and took his own costume out of its bag before he stripped to his underwear. It would've been nice to have some help climbing into the damn thing since it was skintight and all one piece, but he managed, careful to tuck himself in securely before pulling the zipper up all the way.

It was something of a work of art. The pearlescent material had been stitched to imitate scales. The long tail trailing behind him managed to look elegant rather than clumsy. The shaped hood, which Tally could pull down to wear as a half-mask or push up more like a hat, had a long lean snout with gleaming teeth and a rainbow-feathered crest. Something between an Asian dragon and a quetzalcoatl, Tally was absurdly pleased with the overall effect.

He strode out of his office with the tail draped over his arm, waving good-naturedly at the whistles and calls from the front desk as he whisked by. He didn't feel too self-conscious since there were plenty of other costumed people in the lobby, until someone whispered, "God I would *die* for that ass," as he walked by.

The mask probably hid his blush. Most of it.

Murmurs reached him long before he entered the ballroom, a soft ocean of sound interrupted here and there by spiking fountains of laughter. The attendant at the door, lijun of course, smiled and waved him in and Tally rounded the corner into a wonderland of fable, history and fantasy. The riot of colors alone would have stopped him but the variety of shapes and textures pulled the eye in every direction, from sleek leather and vinyl to feather plumes to bell-shaped dresses to something in the corner with edges and planes that looked like Picasso and Miro had tried to make a sculpture together.

If he hadn't been so distracted by the beauty before him, he might have noticed Barry Hastings and Dan O'Rourke lurking just inside the doors. Barry, dressed as a vampire cliché, stepped in front of him. The council members were all smiles, but the approach had the feeling of an ambush.

"Outshining the room, Urusar," Barry said in a jovial tone that held a tiger trap worth of spikes beneath it.

"Made by an artist. I just stand back and watch the magic happen." Tally nodded to them both, willing to keep the pretense of sociability as long as the councilmen were. "Dan, excellent owl costume."

"Thank you, Urusar." Dan gave him a polite nod, then bulled on in his typical blunt way. "Heard you spoke to the human city council about Harris Street."

Tally didn't let his smile slip. Not yet, even though this was neither the time nor the place to discuss sensitive business. "I have. Nothing formal, of course, but I've met with some of the council members for dinner here and there."

"So you've decided to back the project?" Barry stepped closer, an unholy glee lighting his eyes.

"To a certain degree," Tally allowed cautiously. "Harris Street is in dire need of revitalization, but I remain unconvinced that the destruction of a historic theater and a purge of human-owned businesses is in anyone's best interests." *Not to mention my selling the section of the street I own to your development consortium.*

"You're backing human interests?" Dan's growl rose to indiscreet levels.

"We'll go through everything at the next council meeting. This isn't the place and we're attracting attention." Still cordial and polite, he nodded to each in turn. "Barry, Dan, good to see you. Enjoy the party."

Tally greeted people as he strolled a circuit of the grand ballroom, the people he could recognize at any rate, trying not to let the encounter ruin his good mood. It helped that Olivia spotted him from across the room where she stood with Tally's parents. She raced over to take his hand and walk with him.

"Dragon," she announced with obvious pride as she grinned up at him.

Tally nodded. "Have you seen Uma yet?"

She shook her head, perhaps just a little concerned, and Tally felt bad for mentioning it.

"Stand still or I'll never catch up!" Sammy called to them a few steps farther on. Her rather impractical mermaid costume explained the strange request as Sammy shuffled toward them with tiny steps, hampered by her narrow, curve-hugging tail. With a little *oof*, she glomped onto Tally, who was uncertain whether he was being hugged or used as a steadying pillar.

Misaki, in the guise of mourning cloak butterfly, followed close behind, her tightly pressed lips betraying her amusement. "Sammy also has brought pants that shimmer, though she says these are for later."

"Sammy fish!" Olivia called out and thumped against Sammy's legs.

"Good thing your Usar is so strong and can hold us both up." Sammy bent at the waist as best she could to get a better look. "I love your costume, Livy. Does Melia have the same one?"

Olivia shook her head with a frown. "No. Melia's is gray."

"Of course." Sammy nodded, just as serious. "Where's Haru?"

"He's with Lahi getting changed. I should probably worry that his costume needs two people and that he's taking so long, shouldn't I?"

"As your siblings would say, Bastille-san, I believe you are in trouble," Misaki said with a small hissing laugh.

"Have you found an apartment you like?" Tally changed the subject in an unsubtle bid to keep everyone within hearing from chiming in about how much trouble he was in.

Misaki had accepted his job offer after careful evaluation and confirmation that it was a position the business truly needed filled, but she'd refused the offer to live at the house. "I see one tomorrow that appears promising. Much more space than I am accustomed to for the price and for one person. It is near my office in the Bastille Arms, though. I think it will suit."

"Good. Please let me know if you need anything at all."

"I am long used to seeing to my own needs, Bastille-san. Your heart wishes to give too much sometimes, I think, but thank you."

Only a moment later, Lily and Pete arrived to help keep Sammy upright as she and Misaki continued their rounds. The twins were wearing salt-and-pepper-shaker costumes for whatever strange Lily-and-Pete reason there might have been for the choice.

Gun spotted Tally when he'd made it about halfway around the room and charged over, making a motion as if he were throwing something.

"That's it, flag on the field." He stopped in front of Tally, hands on his hips as he gave the dragon costume a furious looking over. "Not fair, Tal."

"What's not fair, Gun?" Tally tried for serious and snickered anyway.

"It's bad enough that you take up so much space. But now you have to be this mountain of shining scales." Gun threw up his hands. "No one's going to look at anything but you."

"You mean you want all the attention."

"Well, yeah. Duh."

"I apologize for being so shiny." Tally continued his circuit, Musketeer and Totoro by his side, until he reached the spot where Marnie and Hakkon were talking with his parents. Here Olivia abandoned him for her siblings and Gun was pulled away to dance with an Imperial Stormtrooper.

"Well, that's quite the costume, Tally," Mom said with pursed lips. "Doesn't leave much to the imagination."

"Leave the boy alone, Kara. It's gorgeous." Hakkon, dressed as a pirate, clapped him on the arm. "We were just talking about Jean. Any idea how she's taking all of this with Alan?"

Tally pushed his dragon mask up onto his head so they could see his face. "I have spoken with her, both in person and on the phone. She's shocked and furious. I get the feeling from some things she said that the marriage was already on rocky ground, but as she told me, she didn't realize she was married to a monster."

"Is she staying with him through the trial?"

"No." Tally accepted a glass of punch from Marnie with a nod. "She's already filed for divorce. She intends to keep some of the business, if she can. We'll see if he fights her on it. But for now, she's concentrating on cookies and small pastries and she's traded in some of the equipment she feels she doesn't need for good coffee machines."

"Ah, more of a café setting. That's a smart idea." Dad nodded in approval.

"I'll be checking in with her. I know Alan had some sporadic support in a certain faction of the council. I hope they extend the courtesy to Jean, though I have my doubts." Tally sipped, turning to watch revelers enter the ballroom. "I don't like the rumblings, Dad. It's not like I can read minds, but things just feel *off* in council meetings, and Barry and Dan even tried to buttonhole me *here*."

"Watch your back, Tal," Dad said with a pat of sympathy. "Hastings' little cabal can be vicious."

Tally searched his father's face intently as he asked, "Dad? Am I doing the wrong thing? Not always putting lijun interests before human?"

"There's a thing Barry and his cronies have never gotten a grip on." Dad gave him a sad smile and shook his head. "They think, like they do with most things, that it's an either/or choice. Either lijun prosper or humans do. It's not one or the other, Tal. It's always been both for us, way back from your great-great-grandfather's time. Not a choice. Just a bigger table."

"Thanks, Dad," Tally managed softly. "I think I just need to hear it sometimes."

The kids had scurried over to say hi to the Eberhardt girls, where there was much excited jumping up and down and chattering. It was good to see them more sociable again, if selectively, and nice to see that they'd taken a shine to Hakkon's daughters. Tally was about to make his way over there to talk to Mindy about her babysitting offer when movement at the doors arrested him and nearly stopped his heart.

There was Lahi, grinning like she'd swallowed the proverbial canary, and on her arm was a being of divine beauty. Part of his brain knew this deity who glided so effortlessly across the floor was Haru, but the rest of his brain had leaked out his ears at such a gorgeous sight. He wasn't the only one. Half the party stared in frank admiration, a little too frank in some cases.

The kimono was bright blue with a white and gold crane design, though the sleeves were wider than Tally had seen in any of Haru's previous kimonos, and the collar was more open to show his long graceful neck. The obi was in a box shape at the back, the pink *obijime* a bright contrast to its golden color. Haru had gone with traditional geisha makeup, white with red lipstick along with the gems beside Haru's dark eyes, and his hair was up in a more formal, stiff style than Haru usually favored. The white jade comb Tally had given him had pride of place near the top along with several jewels and an ornate ribbon.

Tally took as deep a breath as his tight dragon skin allowed and started across the floor to them, irrationally fearful that someone would try to claim geisha-Haru before him.

"Uh-oh." Lahi leaned in, stage whispering to Haru. "A fierce and mighty dragon approaches. Do you think he'll eat us?"

"Not half so fierce as he appears," Haru said, altogether too serious.

"You look amazing," Tally blurted out when he reached them. "I mean, you both do…"

Lahi laughed. "Your *face*, Tal. I don't expect to compete with your beautiful husband. Ah, there's Mom and Dad. I need to say hello."

With that, one of Tally's best allies among his siblings abandoned him abruptly, leaving him feeling exposed and awkward. Silly, of course, but there were moments when it felt like he was meeting Haru for the first time again, moments when his tongue still made a tangle of itself.

"Uruma Bastille, you look to be in fine condition tonight," Black said from one side. "No flowers for your hair? Long flashy sleeves?"

"Those are for *maiko*, Black-san. Apprentices."

"I see. Are we being treated to a song?" Black motioned down, and for the first time Tally noticed the *biwa*.

"Of course. What kind of Uruma — *geisha* — would I be if I did not give tribute to the Gods for such a feast on All Hallows' Eve?"

"I look forward to it."

"As you should," Haru replied with a smile.

The stage was cleared easy enough. Lahi was already overseeing the setup. Her smile said she knew what his husband was up to, but she shook her head when Tally looked at her. When Haru took the microphone the crowd hushed.

"Evening, everyone. It is wonderful to see so many here to celebrate All Hallows' Eve with the Bastilles."

There was a light smattering of applause.

"I wanted to thank everyone who has made my transition to Uruma so seamless."

The smile screamed *liar*, but Tally caught himself. This was his otter playing the game. Calculating. Mischievous. Up to something. So Tally waited and watched to see how it played out.

"It is daunting to come to a new place where the customs can seem so foreign and strange, but the welcome I received from *Fred* and his flowers, *Sarah's* beautiful cake for the wedding — even if it ended up slightly tanukied" — the crowd chuckled. The chocolate hadn't gotten *everywhere* — "made Wadiswan feel like home."

This time the applause sounded sincere. Haru really had them eating up his little speech.

"It is also the similarities we carry, because of the traditions we have in this room, made my welcome all the better. The fact Councilmen Hastings-san and O'Rourke-san trusted me with a Judgment so readily also made me feel trusted by our clan. I have prepared a song for them and the Gods in thanks."

Oh, Gods. Haru's smile was sharp enough to cut the stones he wore. His otter had just thrown a gauntlet. When the music started, the hush continued. Just the sound of Haru's voice with his *biwa* settling out over the crowd. By the time he ended, the silence was like a bubble, ready to burst at any moment.

Then the applause and shouts came, the clan's energy broke in a tidal wave. The musicians hurried on stage, Lahi prodding them along. Haru waved with a smile, arching one eyebrow when his eyes met Tally's.

Those moments of rediscovery, of *this is my Em'halafi*, still stabbed at him, but he no longer went down despairing tunnels of *why doesn't Haru feel it too*. He knew why now, understood Haru's desperate wish for independence denied, understood that any feelings Haru might have had were buried under the oppressive weight of responsibilities and winnowed away in a famine of choices.

Not what either of them wanted. Though perhaps there would be little paths and trails that would get them both through.

Tally offered his husband a formal, Western bow and kept a respectful distance. "Would you do me the honor of a dance, beautiful otter?"

A little twitch at the corner of Haru's mouth was the hint of a smile Tally had wanted, those tiny smiles that were really for him and not for show. "I think I can spare a dance for a handsome dragon."

Their costumes made it clumsy to dance close, so Tally held Haru as he would for a waltz and managed a two-step to the slow song playing. Everything else melted away around them, the rest of the partygoers fuzzy blurs in Tally's vision as he moved them across the floor. Haru kept up with amazing agility in his *geta*, never fumbling a step.

"I've been thinking," Tally began as he gazed into the depths of Haru's dark eyes.

"Dangerous, my Argaze." Haru tipped that little smile at him again.

Tally gave him a nod for that. "I feel like I've done everything wrong where you and I are concerned."

"Not...everything." Haru's brows had drawn together in concern.

"Enough that a lot has been backward. I know we can't start over, really." Tally halted them so he could take both of Haru's hands. "But I'd like..." Tally ducked his head, suddenly uncertain, knowing he was flushing under the dragon jauntily perched atop his head.

"You would like?"

"I'd like the opportunity to court you properly, if you'd allow it."

Haru gave him one of those stares he couldn't quite read before he gave Tally's hands a quick squeeze. "I am curious what that would be."

"So...yes?"

"It is a maybe."

A sudden clinking of utensils on glassware nearly drowned out Haru's answer and Tally looked around in shock to find most of the room watching them.

"Tally?" Haru whispered. "What is this?"

"Ah." Tally cleared his throat and glanced back at Haru apologetically. "They want us to kiss. Like at the engagement party and wedding."

"I see."

The clinking grew louder and the joeys pushed around the adults, jumping up and down and calling out, "Kissies! Uma and Usar, kiss!"

Tally's brothers and sisters looked too smug not to have something to do with their predicament.

Haru arched a perfectly shaped brow at Tally, pulled his fan's loop over his wrist and brought his hand up to the side of Tally's face. With that tiny smile-hint playing at his mouth again, he leaned in and placed a soft, lingering kiss on Tally's lips. It didn't feel like a kiss for show and Tally almost let surprise ruin the moment. He recovered in time to cover Haru's hand with his own and return the kiss with gentle fire.

When they broke apart, the room erupted in applause and kid squeals, but Tally held Haru's gaze as he ran a thumb across Tally's bottom lip to clean up the lipstick smudge.

"Strange Americans," Haru said, with a head tilt toward the partygoers. His expression turned thoughtful as he stroked Tally's arm. "I... They are not so bad. The kisses."

"Good. It's nice to hear." Tally offered a soft smile, not invading Haru's space further, but not backing away. They would be small steps forward. He knew that, but he also knew those small steps were possible now and they had their entire lives for the journey.

Haru gazed up at him as they turned slowly across the floor and Tally swore he could hear the gears turning. Finally, he cocked his head. "This courting. What would it include?"

"Polite conversation in the front parlor with my parents as chaperones, mostly. Maybe a carriage ride around the park on Sundays." Tally chuckled at Haru's wry, skeptical expression. "Joking. Anything we can agree on, really. We get a babysitter or three once or twice a week and we could go out to dinner, to the movies, off to a big city for the weekend."

"Amusement parks?"

Tally tipped his head in a nod. "Of course. When it's warmer."

"Rowing out on the lake? For me to otter and swim?"

"Certainly. Ice skating when the lake freezes over."

"Concerts?"

"Any kind you like."

"Shopping?"

"Not my favorite pastime but I'll be happy to play beast of burden for you."

"Dessert sieges?"

Tally did his best to look terribly serious. "I'm going to have to draw the line there. Dessert sieges are hell on clothes. And swimming pools."

The little smile Haru granted him was well and truly Haru, half-mischievous, half-pleased, the polite mask no longer in place despite the geisha makeup. "All right. I accept your offer of courtship. Though…"

"Yes?"

"I would enjoy tea with your parents, but if you include it in courting, I will cancel the arrangement."

"Fair enough."

Tally stole another quick kiss and his heart, so long chilled and contracted with anxiety, warmed under his breastbone, feeling as if it were trying to expand beyond his ribs. He laughed for no other reason than the joy of it and swung his Haru across the floor.

They would have time, yes, and space to breathe around each other. He still believed. How could he not? It might be slower than a lightning glance across a crowded room, but he and his Em'halafi would find their way to each other now.

Someday it would all come 'round right.

Glossary of Terms

Abay/Abago: grandmother/grandfather

Akka: daughter

Argaze: husband

Atigislit: dowry

Awi Tamgradat: matchmaker (literally: brings together before the wedding)

Em'halafi: destined match

Idinen: spirit

Imsi Tamgradat: matchmaking dinner

Kwebabiad: birther/carrier — person who carries child of same-sex couple ("egg carrier")

Lijun: dual-natured (a being who has both a human and an animal spirit)

Ruh: ghost

Sa: son

Sa-awi Tamgradat: matchmaking

Sahnkes: shift (to change, to swap)

Sardu: heir to the Urusar (gender neutral)

Satislit ("the bride-son"): son raised to be "bride"
Shafa: witch
Tabib: medicine man
Tamgrakwal: betrothal contract
T-ɑsnɑ: clan
Tislit: wife (also betrothed)
Uma: mother
Urusar: village father
Uruma: village mother
Usar: father
Xatiba: betrothed/fiancé (male)
Xus or Tarir: possessed spirit (male and female)

Organization: GLA—Global Lijun Alliance

Japanese terms

Arigatou: thank you
Bachi: straight, wooden sticks used to play Japanese *taiko* drums, or the plectrum for stringed instruments such as the *shamisen* and *biwa*
Biwa: a Japanese short-necked fretted lute
Dogeza: kneeling directly on the ground and bowing to prostrate oneself while touching one's head to the floor
Dōitashimashite: you're welcome
Eshaku: a brief courtesy bow between acquaintances or equals
Furisode: the most formal style of *kimono* worn by unmarried women, brightly colored with long, hanging sleeves
Futsurei: a more formal bow offered out of respect to an elder or someone of higher social standing

Geisha: one who is trained as an entertainer, with specifically training in music, dance, and the art of conversation

Geta: a wooden-soled, elevated sandal with a thong that passes between the big toe and the second toe

Gomen'nasai: I'm sorry

Hakama: loose, pleated trousers with many pleats in the front — part of Japanese formal dress for men

Irouchikake: a brightly colored bridal *kimono*, often worn untied and over the *kakeshita*

Itadakimasu: a phrase said before eating, meaning "I humbly receive," or in less literal terms, "thank you for the food"

Kakeshita: a bridal *kimono* worn under the *uchikake*, usually tied with an *obi*

Kawauso: a river otter (can also refer to otters of folklore)

Kimono: a long, loose robe with wide sleeves often tied with a sash

Koropokkuru: the little people of Ainu folklore

Koshi himo: a thin belt used to hold kimono or *yukata* material in place before the *obi* is tied over it

Maiko: an apprentice geisha

Montsuki hakama: the most formal *hakama*, worn by bridegrooms

Nagajuban: a simple *kimono*-shaped under-robe worn under the *kimono*

Obi: a broad sash worn around the waist of a *kimono*

Obiage: a smaller sash worn between the top of the *obi* and the *kimono*

Obijime: a thin decorative cord worn around the center of the *obi*

Okaasan: mother

Otōusan: father

Saikeirei: a reverent bow, deeper than the *futsurei*

Sakazuki: a ritual exchange of *sake* cups

San-san-ku-do: three-three-nine times, the wedding drink from ever larger *sake* cups binding the bride and groom

Seiza: an upright kneeling position sitting back on one's feet

Shi'ne: a Japanese curse, meaning, literally, "die"

Shinzen kekkon: a Shinto purification ritual

Shiromuku: a white wedding *kimono,* sometimes worn under a more colorful one

Suminasen: excuse me, or I'm sorry

Uchikake: (see *irouchikake)*

Wagasa: a traditional bamboo and paper parasol — ones used to escort the bride in weddings are often larger

Wataboshi: a traditional bridal *kimono* hood

Yukata: a casual, light summer *kimono*

Want to see more from Angel Martinez? Here's a taster for you to enjoy!

Endangered Fae

Finn

Angel Martinez

Excerpt

The figure crouched on the bridge shocked Diego so thoroughly he drove a hundred yards before he realized what he had seen.

A man squatted on his heels on the rail, one hand on a cable, the other clutching a ragged blanket at his throat. Threadbare cloth flapped around bare ankles. The persistent wind yanked it this way and that to show flashes of naked legs.

"Holy shit," Diego muttered, as he wrestled his ancient Toyota into the nearest side street to park. This was none of his business. Didn't he have enough problems? Even as he argued with himself, he ran, dodging traffic and ignoring angry epithets as he pelted back up the bridge against traffic. The inevitable gaper delay had slowed the flow at least, making his precarious journey easier.

People stared from the safety of their vehicles as they inched along but no one stopped to help.

Diego ignored them. His primary concern was to not startle the man into falling. He slowed his approach, ready to offer soothing words, but the man heard his footsteps. Long black hair whipped and snaked in the wind, hiding his face, though Diego caught a glimpse of bared teeth.

"Did you come after me?" the jumper snarled. "I won't go back."

"Go back where?" Diego seized the opportunity to start the man talking.

The jumper shook his head to clear the hair from his eyes and peered at Diego. Black eyes, not dark brown, but black, set in deeply shadowed sockets. "No, I suppose you don't look like one of those," he said in a softly accented, weary voice.

"One of who?" Diego edged closer to stand next to him.

"The ones who shut me in the iron cage. I changed. I escaped." His words seemed to stick in his throat and even above the traffic, Diego heard him swallow hard. "But now I'm too tired. I can't...and the river is so filthy. I think it might kill me."

At least he doesn't sound like he wants to die. "Look, if you don't want the police catching up to you, or the hospital staff, or whoever it is, this is about the worst thing you could do. You're upsetting all these people and attracting a lot of attention. They'll be here any minute." Diego reached out a hand, palm up. "Please come down. Let's get you safe and out of the wind. Then we'll see about straightening all this out."

The man regarded him through the shifting curtain of hair for a long moment. "What are you called?"

Depends who you talk to. "My name is Diego. Diego Sandoval." He lurched forward when the man swayed, his stomach plummeting to his feet, but the jumper retained his place on the rail.

The man repeated his name a few times as if trying it out, then nodded. "It's a good name. Pleasurable to say."

"And you?"

"I am called Fionnachd."

Diego tried to repeat it and won a hint of a smile from the man when he mangled the pronunciation. "Could I call you Finn?"

That got a shrug. The blanket fell back from his shoulder to reveal all too prominent bones. "You could. Some have. I don't mind."

"Climb down, Finn," Diego urged again. "I'll help you. Let's get you somewhere quiet where you can rest."

Finn took his fingers in a light grip and Diego caught a whiff of rotten orange rinds as he slid from the rail.

What the hell am I doing? He could have hepatitis or HIV or tuberculosis, or worse. He's probably crazy. Maybe even dangerous.

The intense plea in those black-on-black eyes silenced his practical objections. Lost and alone, he needed someone. Diego had never been good at walking away.

He slipped out of his trench coat, placed it around Finn's shoulders, followed it with his arm and led him away. His 'latest project', Mitch would have sneered. Not that he should care anymore what Mitch thought.

They reached the car without incident, but here, Finn balked. "They put me in one of those before."

One of...*the car?* "Well, I doubt it was as beat up as this one," Diego tried to joke, but Finn backed up a step.

Diego patted the car's roof. "No lights. Not a police car. Or an ambulance."

Finn lifted his chin and sniffed the air. "You do smell kind and trustworthy. But some of the others did, too."

"They probably wanted to help you and didn't know what would upset you. Why did they arrest you? Did they say?"

Finn rubbed a hand over the side of his head, further snarling the mess of hair over the top half of his face. "Indecent exposure. I don't know what's indecent about standing on the dock watching the boats, though."

Irish. Diego was certain he'd placed the accent. "It's usually because someone's stark naked, not because they're watching boats."

"Oh."

He had no idea how much of this was a put-on. No one could be that naïve. Though someone could be that deluded. Time enough to sort it all out later. Right now, he had to get Finn off the street before he crumpled to the pavement.

"Look, this goes both ways. I don't know if I can trust you either," Diego said, as he opened the passenger door.

A Cheshire-Cat grin bloomed under the flying mass of hair. "Well said. You may be the first sensible person I've met since I woke."

Finn took the two steps to the car and let Diego help him in. He gingerly avoided touching the doorframe but finally settled back with an exhausted sigh.

Diego drove away just as sirens began to sound on the bridge.

* * * *

The ordeal of the shower seemed cruel, but Finn was filthy and smelled like a dumpster during a garbage strike. Diego placed one of his plastic kitchen chairs in the middle of the shower and installed Finn there, but he slumped against the chair back, eyes closed, face turned into the spray.

Too exhausted to even flinch.

Diego fought down the little shiver of revulsion at the stench, stripped to his boxers and stepped into the stall with him. He attacked the tangled mass of hair first, positioning Finn so his head hung back over the chair. No lice—a good sign. He might have been homeless, but he couldn't have been living on the streets too long. The nest of midnight snarls unwound under the caress of water and shampoo. If Finn stood, his hair would reach at least to the top curve of his butt. A strange blue-black iridescence shone in it, his natural coloring, as far as Diego could tell, rather than bottled special effects.

The rest Diego washed with a loofah, shoving away modesty out of a need to get Finn to bed. An ache lodged around his heart to see how malnutrition had ravaged what probably had been a lean-muscled frame. An athlete, perhaps, before he went off the deep end, an impression reinforced by the absence of almost all body hair. Waxed or electrolysis-denuded—only Finn's crotch sported a black thatch of soft hair. Swimmer, perhaps. The Olympic competitors often shaved it all off for every small gain in streamlining.

He turned off the water and tugged at Finn's arm. "Come on. Let's get you settled. You can't sleep in the shower."

Finn staggered to his feet and Diego all but carried him to Mitch's room. *The spare room*, he corrected himself. He usually kept the door closed so the stark, unfurnished space wasn't glaring at him.

He sat Finn down against the wall, brought him a pair of flannel pajamas, soft with age, then went out to the front closet to retrieve the air mattress and vacuum. Six boxes lay stacked against the wall — all that remained of Mitch's things. Diego ran a hand over one then shook his head against the temptation to open the top and look at its contents. When he returned, Finn hadn't moved from where he sat, naked and dozing in a patch of sunlight.

"You might want to put those on." Diego toed the pajamas closer as he dragged the air mattress into place. When Finn's only response was a long sigh, he added, "We need to get you warm. I don't want to have to take you to the hospital."

With a puzzled frown, Finn unfolded the material and managed, after looking back and forth between the pajamas and Diego's jeans a few times, to pull the bottoms on. His efforts with the top, though, were sabotaged when the vacuum roared to life. He startled and scuttled sideways, wide-eyed and panting.

Diego hurried to switch it off. "Sorry. Should have warned you."

"Is it some sort of small dragon?"

For a moment, Diego stared in blank surprise before he caught himself. At least the nature of Finn's delusion was becoming clearer. He might even share his history later when he had the energy, perhaps some tragic story of an exiled prince. For now, Diego thought it best to play along.

"Not a dragon. Just a machine. It blows out and sucks in air with great force."

"Ah." Finn seemed disappointed, but waved a hand for him to continue.

Mattress inflated, Finn dressed and installed in bed, Diego thought he should get something in him before he drifted off. He tried tap water first but Finn jerked his head away, the color draining from his face.

"Tainted," he gasped. "Great Dagda, it reeks."

Diego sniffed above the glass, puzzled. New York City water, piped in from the mountains, was cleaner than most but it was treated. Chlorine. Fluoride. Maybe Finn had an allergy to one or the other.

Bottled water produced a less violent reaction. Finn smelled it, nose crinkled, but he downed half the bottle in desperate gulps before Diego could take it back from him. Hydration, at least, wouldn't be an issue.

The hurdle of food remained. Starvation often did terrible things to the body's ability to accept nourishment. Not the best time to offer a hamburger and fries. Diego decided he should start with the foods one was supposed to give sick kids — bananas, rice, applesauce and toast, minus the applesauce, since he didn't have any.

Finn wouldn't touch the boiled-in-tap-water rice. He nibbled a corner of the toast and set it aside with murmured apologies. The banana completely stumped him. He turned it over and over in his hands and finally tried to bite through the skin.

"You eat these?" He handed it back to Diego with a grimace.

All right, so his reality doesn't include New World fruit. Diego peeled the banana for him and handed it back. "You don't eat the skin. Try the inside."

Finn took a careful bite and his eyes widened. "That's not bad."

Diego could only watch anxiously, praying his guest wouldn't choke, as the rest disappeared in three bites. With a contented sigh, Finn handed the peel back, gathered the covers into a circle in the center of the mattress and curled into a tight ball inside his nest. By the time Diego brought an extra comforter to cover him, Finn was fast asleep.

Clean and at rest, his face had a childlike quality, with his hair tucked behind one finely curved ear. Diego wasn't certain it was a handsome face, almost unearthly in its delicacy, and though Finn stood six inches taller, he had the odd feeling he could scoop that long frame up in his arms without much effort.

He backed out and closed the door as quietly as he could, confident Finn wouldn't die on him. Tomorrow he would see about finding the right agency to take his guest, preferably one that wouldn't hand him right over to immigration.

A few hours of peace while Finn slept should let him at least get through the current chapter he was writing.

The moment he sat ready at his desk, fingers poised over the keys, the phone rang.

About the Authors

Angel Martinez

The unlikely black sheep of an ivory tower intellectual family, Angel Martinez has managed to make her way through life reasonably unscathed. Despite a wildly misspent youth, she snagged a degree in English Lit, married once and did it right the first time, (same husband for almost twenty-four years) gave birth to one amazing son, (now in college) and realized at some point that she could get paid for writing.

Published since 2006, Angel's cynical heart cloaks a desperate romantic. You'll find drama and humor given equal weight in her writing and don't expect sad endings. Life is sad enough. She currently lives in Delaware in a drinking town with a college problem and writes Science Fiction and Fantasy centered around gay heroes.

Freddy MacKay

Freddy is a bisexual, biromantic, genderfluid nerd and geek who grew up in the Midwest playing soccer, diving, swimming and doing gymnastics, along with running around outside as much as possible—preferably spending that time in swamps and hiking through forests. The haphazard escapades have not changed, except some of them have been replaced with a healthy geocaching addiction and a love for Science Fiction and Fantasy. This love of SFF developed into a writing passion and has led to several awards in the gay science fiction and fantasy categories. Freddy likes worms, dancing and being outside... and toll passes, but you'll have to ask on that one. (They/Them/Their pronouns.)

Angel and Freddy love to hear from readers. You can find their contact information, website details and author profile page at http://www.pride-publishing.com.

PUBLISHING